FOR

Seeing Jerrold's anguished expression, hearing the hopelessness in his voice, Zoë responded without thinking. She put her hand on his arm, saying, "You're not to blame for Philip's kidnapping. And God won't punish you for loving your own son. God won't punish you for being the best father in the world."

For a moment Jerrold stood frozen, staring down at Zoë. Then he reached out gropingly to fold her in his arms and bent his head to her mouth. At first there was no passion in the kiss. It was almost as if he was simply seeking warmth and comfort from physical contact with another human being. She made no attempt to draw away, even when his breathing quickened and the pressure of his lips on hers became harder and more demanding. She felt a stab of a familiar fiery, enticing sensation in her loins.

Releasing her mouth, Jerrold buried his face in her hair, murmuring huskily, "Zoë, darling, on this terrible night I need you so much. For just a few hours, can't we put the past behind us? For those few hours let me imagine you don't hate me, that you love me as much as I love you. For those few hours let me love you. Please, Zoë . . ."

Hesitating for only a moment, she slowly slipped her arm around Jerrold's neck and relaxed against him . . .

A Reluctant Heart

Lois Stewart

ZEBRA BOOKS
KENSINGTON PUBLISHING CORP.

ZEBRA BOOKS are published by

Kensington Publishing Corp.
850 Third Avenue
New York, NY 10022

Zebra and the Z logo Reg. U.S. Pat. & TM Off.

First Printing: September, 1994

Printed in the United States of America

Chapter One

Gretna Green, Scotland, 1807

Zoë awoke, shivering. Instinctively she pulled the coverlets up around her shoulders, only then realizing with a dazed dismay that she was naked, and that she was in an unfamiliar bed in an unfamiliar room. And there was a strange man lying in the bed beside her.

In a moment her mind cleared, and she remembered the wild dash across the little River Sark to the tollhouse on the Scottish border at Gretna Green and the brief, hurried marriage ceremony performed by the itinerant preacher in the town.

Clutching the coverlets more securely around her shoulders, Zoë leaned forward slightly to gaze at the sleeping features of her new husband. The Honorable Jerrold Layton. She was now the Honorable Mrs. Jerrold Layton. His handsome chiseled features, topped by a mane of tousled black curls, looked deceptively young and innocent now with the wickedly dancing dark blue eyes closed and veiled by absurdly long black lashes. The bed coverings had slipped off his upper torso during the night, revealing in the early morn-

ing light the sloping broad shoulders and the powerful
chest.

One of his arms lay outside the coverlets, and as she
glanced at it, Zoë's cheeks flamed with a sudden painful
warmth as she remembered how those long slender fingers had caressed the most secret, private parts of her
body. She caught her breath at the thought of the delir-
ium of ecstasy that had followed.

She put her hands to her face. Had she really married
this man she'd known for only a few short hours? Could
she explain, even to herself, how it had happened?

"You look lovely, my dear," said Mrs. Randolph as
Zoë entered the drawing room and pirouetted in front
of her hostess.

"Thank you," Zoë murmured. She looked down at
her square-necked frock of sheer white figured muslin
over a green satin slip and felt a glow of pleasure. She
did look well, and it didn't disturb her sixteen-year-old
heart that this, her very first evening gown, really belonged to her bosom friend, Charlotte Randolph.

"It was so kind of you to take me under your wing tonight," she said with real gratitude to plump, motherly
Mrs. Randolph. "I was so afraid I wouldn't be able to
go to the ball. Papa considered I was too young to attend such a grand event."

"Well, my dear, since Lord Rosedale extended a general invitation to the neighborhood to attend a ball in
honor of his heir and his heir's new bride, I thought it
would be a great shame for you to miss the affair for
lack of one birthday. After all, I'm allowing Charlotte to
attend the ball. Granted, she's a year older than you,
but then the pair of you graduated from Miss Drayton's

Academy at the same time." Mrs. Randolph's eyes twinkled. "As for your papa, we're both aware that, though he's a saintly man, he's also very unworldly and knows *nothing* about balls!"

Zoë nodded ruefully. She dearly loved her father, the Reverend Damien Bennett, but her upbringing in his household had been different from that of most girls of her station. Zoë's mother had died many years before, and though not deliberately neglectful, her gentle, scholarly father had been so engrossed in parish concerns that he had had little time or expertise to devote to the rearing of his only daughter. Mrs. Randolph, whose family belonged to the church, had often acted as a surrogate mother, as had, later, Miss Drayton, the headmistress of the academy, but to a large extent Zoë had reared herself, taking charge of the rectory household from an early age. Her brother Edmund, five years older, had been away at school for most of her growing-up years, first at Eton, then at Oxford, where he was now a candidate for Holy Orders.

Zoë smiled at Charlotte, a rather plain-featured girl whose vivaciousness made up for her lack of beauty. "My thanks to you, too, for allowing me to wear your gown."

"Nonsense. There wasn't time for you to have a dress made. And I couldn't wear two gowns at once, could I?" Charlotte hugged her friend. "I'm so glad your papa gave his permission for you to spend the night at our house."

"Yes, indeed, how fortunate," said Mrs. Randolph in amusement. "When you two return from the ball, you can spend the rest of the night until dawn discussing every detail of the evening." She looked up as her husband entered the room. "The carriage is ready, John? Then come along, girls. Let's be off."

The Randolphs' prosperous estate was on the outskirts of the village of Heathfield, which in turn was located a few miles north of Carlisle on the Solway Plain of Cumberland, not far from the Scottish border. As the Randolph carriage rolled through the High Street of Heathfield, Zoë glanced at the rectory, next to the Church of St. Bride, and noted that the house was dark save for the inevitable light in her father's study.

"Papa's working again tonight," Zoë fretted. "He should rest more. He's still recovering from a dreadful cold in his chest. Perhaps I shouldn't have left him tonight."

"Your papa can survive without you very well for one night," said Mrs. Randolph firmly. "And I'm sure he wouldn't wish you to spoil your evening by worrying about him."

And indeed, Zoë's slight guilt feelings faded and her excitement began to rise as the carriage swung into the driveway of Merefield Park, the seat of the Earl of Rosedale, the principal landowner in the area. Swaying lanterns in the trees lining the winding drive illuminated the roadway like fairy lamps, and the portico of the vast Tudor pile, when they rolled up in front of the entrance, was brilliantly lighted also.

The former Great Hall of the mansion had been transformed into a large ballroom, lit by a myriad of blazing candles. Musicians comprising a full orchestra sat in the old musicians' gallery, tuning their instruments. Already the room was crowded. The earl's neighbors from near and far in the county had gathered to welcome his heir, Viscount Stratton, and his bride back from their honeymoon.

Sitting with Mrs. Randolph and Charlotte at the side of the room, Zoë watched rather nervously as the dancers began to form for the minuet that would open the ball. She knew how to dance, of course. The gifted dancing master at Miss Drayton's academy had seen to that. And she had danced at several small and very informal gatherings in Mrs. Randolph's drawing room. But this was her first formal ball, and a hard knot was beginning to form in her stomach. Would anyone ask her to dance? And if someone did ask her, would she step on her partner's feet, or trip on the hem of her gown and fall ignominiously on her face on the ballroom floor?

She soon discovered her fears had been groundless. Mrs. Randolph was acquainted with everyone, and a line of young men formed in front of her chair, begging for introductions to her daughter and her guest.

An hour later, a breathless Zoë dropped into a chair beside Mrs. Randolph after a strenuous country dance, saying laughingly, "I can't quite believe everything that's happening. I've danced every dance. But I'm beginning to feel like Cinderella at the ball. At any moment I expect midnight to strike and then I'll be forced to leave here in a pumpkin!"

Mrs. Randolph smiled. "Oh, I don't think you need worry about being a Cinderella. You're a great success tonight, my dear. I daresay you'll go on dancing every dance until the small hours of the morning."

The earl's daughter-in-law, the new Lady Stratton, had been circling the ballroom, making the acquaintance of the guests and thanking them for welcoming her to her new home. She sat down with Mrs. Randolph and Charlotte and Zoë, introducing herself.

She was a pretty girl with dark hair and sparkling brown eyes and a smile of great sweetness.

"What a charming gown," she remarked to Zoë, who, though she suspected that Lady Stratton had probably made the same remark to every female she'd greeted that evening, still felt flattered.

Lady Stratton went on to say, in what Zoë suspected also was the same set piece she'd employed to all the earl's guests, but which still sounded fresh and gracious, "I'm so sorry I won't be able to become better acquainted with you and all the wonderful people I've met this evening, not for some years at least. My husband has accepted a post in the diplomatic service. We'll be leaving for Vienna shortly."

"Well, Melicent, before you leave for Vienna, will you be kind enough to introduce me to the young lady?" said a laughing voice.

Zoë looked up into the intensely blue eyes of the handsomest young man she had ever seen, tall, slender, but broad-shouldered, with a mop of black curls styled in the fashionable Brutus and just the hint of a dimple in one cheek.

Lady Stratton said with an amused smile, "Miss Zoë Bennett, may I introduce you to my cousin, Mr. Jerrold Layton?" She shook her head. "I love him dearly, but I must warn you that he's a sad fribble of a fellow!"

"Lawks, Melicent. I'd have expected you to give me more cousinly support than *that*," said Mr. Layton in mock indignation. He looked directly at Zoë. "Will you dance a quadrille with me, Miss Bennett?"

"Yes." Zoë was irretrievably lost in the depths of those dark blue eyes. She had tumbled into the first love of her life in the flash of a second. If Jerrold Layton had asked her to walk on burning coals, she would unhesitatingly have set her bare feet on the red-hot embers. He extended his hand to her, and she rose and walked, mesmerized, into the set with him.

Two dances later, when Jerrold Layton returned Zoë to Mrs. Randolph's side with a murmured, "Don't forget, you promised me the next dance," the older woman leaned close to Zoë and spoke to her in a low voice.

"My dear, believe me, I don't enjoy playing the squinty-eyed chaperon, but I must tell you that it simply won't do for you to dance three dances in a row with the same gentleman. You won't wish to appear fast."

Zoë's face fell. "Oh, Mrs. Randolph, I don't think I could refuse Mr. Layton's invitation to dance. He—he might not ask me again."

Mrs. Randolph's gaze sharpened. Her voice sounded urgent as she said, "Zoë, listen to me. Lady Stratton was funning, of course, when she warned you about Mr. Layton, but she was half serious, too. It happens that I know something about that young man. He's the younger son of the Earl of Woodforde, he'll come into an independent fortune when he reaches twenty-one—or perhaps when he's twenty-five, I don't remember—*and* he has the reputation of being a dreadful rake. I'd advise you not to dance with the young man anymore tonight. No unmarried female can be too careful about her reputation. And besides, I suspect that Mr. Layton is more than a little foxed. I think he's been sampling the earl's wine supply between every dance. No telling what he might decide to say to you while he's half seas over . . ."

She broke off as the music started again and Jerrold Layton strolled up to them, extending his hand to Zoë with a beguiling smile. "My dance, I believe, Miss Bennett?"

Like a person in a dream, Zoë rose and took Layton's arm. One tiny corner of her brain registered a stab of remorse for disregarding Mrs. Randolph's kindly meant words of warning. Mrs. Randolph would undoubtedly be either offended or hurt. But all Zoë could think of now was Jerrold Layton.

She looked up at him in surprise when, instead of moving toward the set that was forming, he said, "You don't really wish to dance anymore, do you?"

"Why . . ."

"I thought we might go somewhere where we could talk privately," he said persuasively. "It's very hard to become better acquainted with someone on the dance floor, don't you agree? We might go to the conservatory."

Socially inexperienced though she was, Zoë knew quite well how negatively Mrs. Randolph would react to Jerrold Layton's suggestion of a *tête-à-tête* in the conservatory, but she found herself saying weakly, "Well, perhaps for a little while . . ."

"Splendid." The dimple was definitely showing now. He tucked her hand under his arm and walked her out of the ballroom and down a long corridor. On the way they met a footman whom Layton intercepted, saying, "Bring a bottle of champagne—no, make that two bottles—and some glasses to the conservatory, there's a good fellow." He slipped the man a coin.

The conservatory was a large building with a high glass roof, through which Zoë could see the emergent stars beginning to twinkle. Dimly burning lanterns hung from the ceiling, producing enough illumination to create the effect of a verdant moonlit landscape, and the air was fragrant with the scent of growing things.

"Here we are," said Layton. They had reached a table and several chairs set beneath an arbor of vines. "My cousin, the earl, likes to come sit out here and watch his grapes grow." Layton drew out a chair for Zoë. As he leaned over her, she caught the scent of crisp, freshly laundered linen, and the stronger odor of wine.

The footman appeared with a tray containing several bottles and some glasses and set it down on the table. Nodding a dismissal to the footman, Layton uncorked one of the bottles and poured two glasses of champagne. He handed one to Zoë. Lifting his own glass, he smiled, saying, "Here's to a much better acquaintance, Miss Zoë Bennett."

As Zoë took her first sip of wine, she noted that Jerrold Layton's eyes were unusually bright and that his voice was slightly slurred. However, since she had very little experience of gentlemen in their cups, she paid scant attention to the signs indicating, as Mrs. Randolph had warned her, that he was inebriated.

"Well, now, first things first," he said. "How did you chance to be called Zoë, Miss Bennett? It's a very pretty name, but rather out of the ordinary."

Zoë smiled. "That was my father's doing. Papa is a clergyman and a classical scholar. Zoë is from the Greek, you know. It means 'life.' "

"The name and its meaning suit you." Layton added teasingly, "Lord knows *I'm* no classical scholar, but I seem to remember that Zoë was also the name of a famous Byzantine empress."

Laughing, Zoë said, "I don't think Papa likes to dwell very much on the Empress Zoë. From what I've read, she wasn't a very—a very reputable person."

"No, indeed. Hardly a lady to be emulated by a clergyman's daughter!" Layton leaned across the table and took Zoë's hand. "May I call you Zoë? Somehow, it doesn't feel right, calling you Miss Bennett."

"I . . . yes." Confused by his nearness and the pressure of his fingers Zoë hastily swallowed half a glass of wine to hide her discomfiture.

"Thank you." Layton released her hand and poured two more glasses of champagne. "I'm Jerrold, of course."

"Jerrold." Still feeling confused and out of her element, Zoë took another sip of wine and cast about for a more comfortable topic of conversation. "Your cousin has a lovely name," she said.

"Melicent? Oh, yes, it *is* a lovely name. But then, everything about Melicent is lovely." He added, in a tone obviously meant to be jocular but which instead sounded rather strained. "When I was a callow youth, I actually fancied myself in love with Melicent. Of course, with her usual good sense, she chose Stratton and put me out of my misery."

He paused, his lips tightening, as if he regretted saying what he had. Then the beguiling smile appeared again, and he began deftly questioning Zoë about herself. Before she quite knew what she was about, she found herself telling Jerrold about her daily activities at the rectory, about her brother Edmund's divinity studies at Oxford and even about her attendance at Miss Drayton's academy.

"I daresay you're a most accomplished young lady," Jerrold observed.

"Oh, no. I've no skills at all at embroidery, or netting, and my French accent is atrocious. And I play the pianoforte very badly. I *can* draw and paint, though. Sometimes I wish . . ." Zoë's voice trailed away.

"What do you wish?" Jerrold had been sitting back in his chair, the fingers of his right hand hooked around the stem of his wineglass, watching Zoë closely while an amused little smile played about his lips.

"Oh . . . I expect I'm being very silly, but I often wish I could be a professional painter. It's not completely unheard of for females, you know. There's Angelica Kauffman, and Madame Vigée-Lebrun in France, the lady who painted the poor queen and her family before they were murdered."

Jerrold's smile widened. "I see no reason why you shouldn't become a professional painter. In fact, as of this moment I'm volunteering to be your first sitter!"

Zoë didn't return his smile. She was suddenly aware that she'd been chattering inconsequentially about subjects that couldn't possible interest a man of the world like Jerrold Layton. She picked up her glass and gulped down several swallows of champagne. "Now it's your turn to talk about yourself," she said rather breathlessly.

Shaking his head, Jerrold laughed. "I'm really a dull sort of fellow. I'm a second son, you know, so I have no estate responsibilities. I spend most of my time in London, engaged in activities I'm sure your revered papa wouldn't approve of." He dexterously removed the cork from the second bottle of champagne, poured Zoë another glass, and refilled his own.

"Such activities as?" Zoë said, cocking her head at him as she took another sip of wine.

He laughed again. "Are you really interested? Well, let me think about what I might do on a typical day . . . box a round or two at Gentleman Jackson's Saloon, cup a wafer at Manton's Shooting Galleries, drive with the Four-in-Hand Club, go to the races at New Market . . ."

"And gamble at White's," said Zoë daringly.

"That, too."

"Do you win?"

He lifted an amused eyebrow. "A good deal of the time, yes."

"My brother Edmund was taken to White's as a guest last year when he visited London. He says the club keeps a Betting Book in which some very strange bets are recorded."

"Lord, yes. The strangest bet of all, I think, was when two members wagered a hundred guineas that one raindrop would run down a window faster than another raindrop." Jerrold rose, coming around the table to pull Zoë to her feet. "I believe we've wasted enough time talking about my very mundane activities, don't you?"

Zoë gasped. Her head was swimming. She wasn't accustomed to drinking wine. Papa's idea of liquid refreshment suitable for females was a very mild, and very occasional, ratafia punch, with perhaps an occasional rare glass of claret.

Jerrold's hands cupped her face. "You have such beautiful eyes," he said softly, "the exact shade of my mother's emeralds." Zoë felt a tremor of a strange new emotion as Jerrold brushed her closed eyelids with his lips. A moment later his fingers touched the clustered curls on the crown of her head. "Did you know your hair is the color of beaten honey?" he inquired huskily. "And it feels like silk." Zoë could only stare up at him, transfixed, as his arms slid around her waist, and he pulled her closely to him. Slowly he bent his head and his lips pressed against hers. Her body felt afire. She had never been kissed before.

"Zoë, my beautiful one, I want to love you," Jerrold murmured against her mouth. His kiss deepened and grew more insatiable.

Zoë didn't notice that his speech had become even more slurred, and that he was having some difficulty holding himself upright. She was only aware that Jerrold had mentioned the magic word, "love." She twisted away from him slightly, looking up at him with widened eyes. "You mean you want to marry me?"

For a moment he appeared completely startled. Then a smile spread across his face. "What a capital notion! We could be married in little more than an hour. I believe we're less than ten miles from the tollhouse at Gretna Green. Let's do it, beautiful Zoë. Let's do it now!"

"Get married tonight? Elope to a Scottish tollhouse? Oh, no, I couldn't. What would people say? What would Papa say?"

Jerrold put his hands on her shoulders. "Do you really care? Zoë, my lovely one, what really matters is this: do you love me?"

Zoë looked up at him with her heart in her eyes. "Yes. Oh, yes."

"Well, then?"

Before Zoë quite knew how it came about, she had written a note to Mrs Randolph, explaining that she had taken ill and Mr. Layton had kindly offered to take her home to the rectory, so as not to inconvenience the Randolph household. Then she was seated in Jerrold's curricle, riding pell-mell for the River Sark and the Scottish border . . .

As Zoë lay propped on her elbow, looking down at this man she had so suddenly and inexplicably married, Jerrold Layton's eyes slowly opened. At first his expression was blank and unfocused. Gradually his eyes cleared and he smiled. "What a pleasant surprise, my lovely one."

"Surprise?" said Zoë uncertainly.

"Well, I hope you won't take this amiss, but I haven't the faintest recollection of how we chanced to meet last night. I must have been more completely foxed than I realized. So yes, it's a most pleasant surprise to find that I had the great luck to tumble into bed with a beautiful creature like you." The blue eyes kindled, and he reached out his hand to pull Zoë down to him.

Her heart turning to ice, she jerked away, pulling the coverlets tight around her chin. "Don't touch me," she gasped.

"What the devil . . ." He started to sit up and sank back to the pillows with a groan of pain, closing his eyes. "Oh, God, my head—it feels as if a thousand devils with red-hot hammers were pounding away inside it. You're quite right, my dear. I'm in no condition to perform."

Scrambling to her feet, Zoë looked around her frantically, discovering her discarded clothes thrown carelessly over a chair. She dressed hurriedly, keeping a wary eye on Jerrold Layton. But he had buried his head beneath the bed clothes and didn't stir.

Zoë reached into her reticule for a comb to smooth her disheveled hair, and froze. There was nothing in the reticule except the comb and a handkerchief. Steeling herself, she approached the bed and said in a trembling voice, "I must go home, and I have no money."

"Oh, God, didn't I pay you last night?" came a muffled reply from underneath the bed covers. "Look in my purse. Take what you want."

Zoë located Jerrold's coat on the floor where he'd tossed it the previous night. She took the purse out of a pocket and removed a bank note from it. She took something else, too: the marriage lines that the preacher had delivered to Jerrold Layton after receiving his fee for performing the ceremony. Without a backward look, Zoë walked out of the bedchamber and slammed the door behind her.

Chapter Two

London, 1814

"Must you really leave so soon?"

As he buttoned his waistcoat, Jerrold Layton glanced at the speaker. "I have a full evening, Dorothea."

Placing another pillow behind her back, Dorothea, Lady Harlow, sat up in bed, allowing the sheet to slip down to her waist, fulling revealing her creamy shoulders and opulent breasts. With her dark red hair, violet eyes and small, even features, she was one of the handsomest women of Jerrold's acquaintance. She had been his mistress for almost five years.

"I never see you anymore," she said, pouting. "I begin to think you're growing tired of me. You come to me and use me as if I were one of your Cyprians from Covent Garden, and then you leave."

Sitting down in one of the gilded chairs that crowded the ornately furnished bedchamber, Jerrold said curtly as he started to pull on his boots, "You must know you're talking fustian, Dorothea."

"Prove it. Come sit with me for a bit. I want to talk to you." Dorothea patted the bed invitingly.

Hesitating only briefly, Jerrold walked toward the bed, easing his arms into his coat as he went. He sat down on the edge of the bed. "Now, then, what's this Cheltenham tragedy you're enacting?" he asked with a rather forced smile. "You must know you bear as little resemblance to a Covent Garden Cyprian as the queen does to one of her scullery maids."

Dorothea smiled. She drew his head down for a lingering kiss. "Oh, I know I was being difficult. It's just that I want to see more of you. What engagements do you have tonight, for example, that will keep you away from me?"

"First I go to the House, and afterwards I dine with my brother at White's."

"Oh, the House! I've never been able to understand your fascination for being a member of the House of Commons. It takes so much of your time. Why don't you leave all that to one of the petty squires or townsmen in your brother's borough?"

Jerrold's lips tightened, but his tone remained light as he said, "I happen to enjoy being a member of the House, and I like to think that my service is of some use. And at the moment we're in an anxious time. The Allies may have signed the Treaty of Chaumont, pledging to fight on for twenty years if need be, until Napoleon is defeated, but the Emperor of the French was still strong enough to capture the city of Rheims a few days ago."

"And you really think your participation in the debate tonight will make a difference in the fate of the kingdom?"

Stiffening at the jibing remark, Jerrold waited a moment before replying in a level tone, "My participation may not make a difference, but it will at least show support for the government."

Dorothea's pouting expression faded. She put up her hand to stroke Jerrold's face, saying, "Darling, forgive me. I didn't mean to tease you, truly I didn't." She changed the subject. "Such exciting news in *The Times* this morning. Your brother is engaged to be married."

Relaxing slightly, Jerrold nodded. "High time, too. Trevor is more than two years older than I am, nearing thirty. He needs an heir. He couldn't have chosen a more suitable bride than Lady Susan Allingham."

"Oh, indeed. Lady Susan will be a perfect Countess of Woodforde—a duke's daughter, beautiful, accomplished, well dowered." Dorothea paused. After a moment she said, "Have you given any thought of late to marrying yourself?"

His gaze sharpening, Jerrold replied, "You're funning, naturally. You know I have no intention of marrying."

"Oh . . . I thought you might have changed your mind. I never intended to marry either, as you know. One bad marriage was enough for me. I wanted to enjoy my freedom. But Jerrold—it's been five years. Don't you think we should make our relationship legal? Don't you have an urge to be respectable? Aren't you weary of subterfuge, of having a hackney cab drop you off in Grafton Street and walking to my house, to avoid admitting to the world that you're visiting me? Actually, everyone in the *ton* knows about us, but we're accepted because we've followed the rules and been discreet."

"When we began our affair, we agreed that marriage was out of the cards," Jerrold reminded her, his voice cold. "We both wanted a physical relationship only. That was your choice, even more than mine. If you've now changed your mind, I'm sorry. I don't wish to be married." Rising, he reached into the waistband of his breeches for his watch. "I'm late, Dorothea. I must be off. I'll see you on Wednesday—that is, if you still wish to see me."

He bent down to kiss her. She turned her head slightly so that he brushed her cheek, not her lips. Shrugging, he left the bed and walked to the door, pausing only to pick up his hat and stick. "Goodbye, Dorothea."

Leaving the small but fashionable house in Albemarle Street, Jerrold walked a short distance to Piccadilly, where he hailed a hackney cab. As he rode along toward Westminster, he thought about his confrontation with Dorothea. He realized with a flicker of surprise that they had been growing apart for some time. Sex between them was still hotly satisfying, but these days they had very little else in common.

Five years ago it had been different. Then he was a brash twenty-two-year-old, a penniless younger son with little ambition in life except to plant a facer on Gentleman Jackson, emulate or outdo Beau Brummel's tailoring, and break the faro bank at White's. Dorothea came into his life as the most exciting woman he had ever met. She was then a new widow in her late twenties, heartily glad to be rid of the dull, elderly husband her family had foisted on her, living in comfortable financial circumstances on a substantial jointure, eager to enjoy London society without a heavy husbandly hand to guide her. However, she was also a sensual woman, and she had responded wholeheartedly to Jerrold's advances. It had suited both of them to engage in a passionate physical relationship without ties or obligations of any kind.

Until now. He was twenty-seven years old now, Jerrold mused as he rode in the hackney cab to the House of Commons, and his life had changed. His father had died, and his brother, the new Earl of

Woodforde, had persuaded him to enter public life and take up the family seat in the House. Rather to his surprise, he found that he enjoyed politics. At the age of twenty-five, too, he'd inherited a handsome fortune from a bachelor uncle, a director of the East India Company.

Jerrold shifted uncomfortably in his seat. Was it time to break off his affair with Dorothea? Well-to-do, with a satisfying career, he no longer felt so strongly the lure of the purely physical. Now, in addition to sexual attraction, he admired brains and ability in a woman. Lady Melbourne, for example. One of the great political hostesses of the age, she fascinated him, though she was many years older and belonged to a different political party.

Several hours later, after the sitting in the House, Jerrold descended from another hackney cab in St. James's Street and walked into White's Club. At the door of the dining room he nodded to the attendant, saying, "Evening, Davis. Is my brother here yet?"

"Yes, indeed, Mr. Layton. His lordship's over there, at the table in the corner."

"Well, Jerry, how goes the campaign of France?" inquired Lord Woodforde with a smile as his brother sat down at the table.

"Not so well at the moment. Schwarzenberg's still retreating. His troops are all scattered between Sens and the Aube. Not to worry, though. We'll come around. Napoleon is finished."

Trevor Layton, seventh Earl of Woodforde, chuckled. "I wish you could hear yourself talk, Jerry. Five years ago you couldn't have located the Aube River on the map, and what's more, you wouldn't have cared. Now you sound like an insider in the Cabinet."

"That's your doing, Trev," Jerrold retorted with a grin. "You pushed me onto the hustings. But for you, I'd have been satisfied to continue trying to become a Nonpareil among the Dandies."

Jerrold gazed affectionately at his brother. The pair, with their dark hair and blue eyes and classically severe features, strongly resembled each other, although Jerrold would have been the first to admit that Trevor had always been the more serious and conscientious of the two. Despite the differences in their personalities, the brothers were very close.

Trevor replied, laughing, "Well, someone had to make you realize your potential. I ran into Uncle Rupert the other day. He told me you're being considered for an undersecretaryship."

"Uncle Rupert's being premature," growled Jerrold, trying not to look pleased. He was referring to their father's younger brother, a power behind the scenes in the Tory party.

After the waiter had taken their order, Jerrold poured himself a glass of wine and raised it to his brother. "Although you didn't see fit to tell me your news beforehand, allow me to wish you happy."

"Susan wanted the announcement to be a surprise to everyone," Trevor replied with a mixture of pleasure and embarrassment.

"No need to apologize. Your engagement is your own affair. You've chosen wisely, Trev. I not only wish you happy. I *know* you'll be happy."

"Thank you." Trevor reached over to clap his brother on the shoulder. "Now it's your turn. When can we expect an announcement of your betrothal? You're not getting any younger, Jerry. You can't stay a bachelor forever."

A muscle twitched in Jerrold's cheek. His tone, however, was light as he replied, "Who says I can't? I have every intention of doing so. I've decided I'm not the marrying kind."

Taken aback, Trevor said, "But—what about the family?"

"Providing an heir for the title, you mean? Good God, Trev, that's your responsibility. You and Susan are bound to have at least one son. That will ensure that Oliver is kept out of the succession."

A tall man stopped beside the table. "Did I hear my name? I trust you weren't taking it in vain."

"Evening, Oliver," said Trevor. Jerrold merely nodded.

"May we join you?" Oliver Layton motioned to his companion.

"Please do." There was a noticeable lack of cordiality in Trevor's voice.

Oliver Layton and his friend sat down on opposite sides of the table. "You know Percy Davenant, of course," said Oliver.

Glancing at the slender, fair-haired man with the deeply lined face and the curiously repellent eyes with their whitish irises, Trevor murmured, "Oh, yes, I'm acquainted with Captain Davenant."

Jerrold eyed both men coldly, saying nothing, not volunteering a greeting. From their boyhood, he had made it a point to avoid his cousin Oliver's company as much as possible. He was sorry that Trevor's customary amiability had made it necessary for him to sit at the same table with his cousin.

Oliver was his Uncle Rupert's son. He and Oliver were the same age, and they even shared a certain dark-haired, blue-eyed family resemblance. But since their school days at Eton, Jerrold had despised Oliver, a mean-spirited, dishonest bully whose disposition hadn't improved as he grew older. As a man about town he eked out a precarious existence, borrowing from his friends, cadging as much money as he could from his father, in and out of the hands of the cent-per-centers, suspected by many of fuzzing the cards in the clubs. Most of his friends were from the disreputable fringes of society, like Percival Davenant, a one-time Guards officer who had the reputation of being a Captain Sharp.

Holding up his hand to a waiter, Oliver ordered a bottle of champagne. He smiled at Trevor, a smile that didn't quite meet his eyes. "We must drink a toast to you, coz, in honor of your engagement."

"Thank you," Trevor murmured. He shot Jerrold a resigned glance. Oliver was clearly already half drunk.

When the wine came, Oliver poured out four glasses. Lifting his own glass he said, "To Trevor, who has just had the great good fortune to become engaged to marry Lady Susan Allingham."

"Thank you," Trevor murmured again.

Oliver drained his glass, poured himself another, and drank it down in a gulp. Glaring at Trevor, he said truculently, "I hope you're suitably grateful, my dear cousin, for your title and your fortune. You must be aware that Lady Susan wouldn't have accepted you without them."

Trevor's normally good-natured face turned cold. "I'm sure you'd like to reconsider that statement, Oliver."

"Why? It's true. Lady Susan wouldn't have looked at you twice if you weren't a belted earl, and a wealthy one, to boot. Oh, the lady passed out her smiles and her little favors to all the poor souls who made up her court—myself included, I admit that!—but when it came to feathering her nest she chose you, because you could make her a countess and support her in the style to which she'd become accustomed."

Clenching his hands so tightly that his knuckles showed white, Trevor said in a strangled voice, "I've borne with your boorish selfishness for more years than I care to count, Oliver, for your father's sake, but enough is enough. Please leave my table. I never want to see you again."

A sneer distorting his features, Oliver lurched to his feet and stumbled off. His friend, the ex-captain Davenant, also rose, but he remained standing beside the table.

Trevor looked up, saying impatiently, "Well, sir?"

Davenant stared down at him. "Perhaps my friend Oliver is too deep in his cups to resent the insult you just tendered him, Lord Woodforde. Or it may be that he has too much family feeling to strike back at you. I, however, have no such compunctions." Davenant raised his hand and struck Trevor across the face.

The captain's loud, angry voice had begun to attract attention. Now the occupants of the dining room became still, watching as Trevor slowly rose to his feet, his eyes blazing. "I don't allow any man to slap my face, Davenant." He looked at his brother. "You'll act for me, Jerry?" When Jerrold, his face set, nodded, Trevor turned back to Davenant. "What's your direction? My second will wait on you."

"Certainly, my lord. I have rooms at Stephen's Hotel in Bond Street." Davenant bowed and swaggered off.

With a strained smile, Trevor said to his brother, "I apologize for the interruption to our dinner plans." He beckoned to a waiter. "Shall we order? They tell me the venison is particularly good tonight."

As soon as the waiter had moved away, Jerrold said

under his breath, "For God's sake, Trev, I said I'd act for you, but you can't really intend to fight Davenant. He's a crack marksman. Boasts about being able to split the edge of a playing card."

Trevor poured himself a glass of wine and took a sip. "Oh, come now, I'm not so very bad a shot myself. Besides, I challenged Davenant. I can't cry off now."

His voice growing urgent, Jerrold said, "Listen to me. Davenant pushed that quarrel on you, for no reason at all. What does it matter to him if you gave a tongue-lashing to Oliver? I tell you, the man's by way of being a professional duelist. He enjoys his reputation. He likes to intimidate his victims, to injure them. A few years back he killed his man. He had to leave England for a spell. No one would blame you if you changed your mind about fighting him. You were the injured party, after all."

"Perhaps no one else would blame me, but I'd blame myself," said Trevor quietly. "I issued the challenge. I'll abide by it. Go to Stephen's Hotel tomorrow and arrange the details. I'd like the meeting to take place as soon as possible."

Jerrold gazed into his brother's eyes and shrugged. It was useless to say any more. Good-natured and obliging Trevor might be. Beyond a certain point you could never move him.

Two mornings later, as dawn was breaking, Jerrold stood at the gate of the Piccadilly entrance to the Albany, where he had his lodgings. A fine, cold drizzle was falling, and he shivered slightly in the dank early-morning April air. Under his arm he carried a wooden case.

A closed, unmarked carriage drew up beside him. A footman leaped down to open the door of the vehicle and he climbed in.

"You're in good time," he remarked to his brother as he sat down, holding the wooden case on his knees. The footman let up the steps and the carriage moved off.

Trevor shrugged. "I saw no point in being late." Dressed in a black coat and pantaloons, he seemed somewhat subdued, but otherwise he was much as usual. He motioned to the wooden case. "Thank you for loaning me your pistols. The doctor is meeting us in Westbourne?"

Jerrold nodded. "I'm glad you followed my suggestions about your clothes and the carriage."

A faint smile appeared on Trevor's lips. "I know. In a black coat, buttoned to the chin, I'll be a far less visible target. And in case the worse happens, my town carriage with the Woodforde crest won't be observed lingering at the scene of the catastrophe." He paused. Then he reached into an inner pocket of his coat and handed Jerrold a letter. "That's for Susan, if need be. And I wanted you to know that I reinstated my old will yesterday, leaving you all my personal property. I'd made a new will, of course, looking forward to my marriage, but under the circumstances . . ." His voice trailed away.

In an angry burst, Jerrold exclaimed, "That was totally unnecessary. You'll only have to go back to your solicitor tomorrow, you know, to change your will again, leaving your personal property to the eldest son of your issue by Susan."

Trevor leaned over to clasp his younger brother's shoulder in silent sympathy.

After a moment Jerrold sighed, saying, "I haven't told

you something, Trev. Something you must know before we get to Westbourne Green. I've been so filled with disgust that I couldn't bring myself to talk about it."

"What is it?"

"It's Oliver. He's acting as Davenant's second."

"My God!" Trevor's tone was a mixture of horror and astonishment.

"Yes. I could hardly restrain myself when I went to Stephen's Hotel yesterday and Davenant introduced Oliver as his second and left us to the details. I asked Oliver why he agreed to act for Davenant. He said he couldn't bring himself to refuse a friend. Can you believe it? For the sake of a hell-kite like Davenant he's prepared to abandon all family feeling."

Drawing a long breath, Trevor said, "Don't let it concern you so much. We've both known for many years what a havey-cavey creature Oliver is." He was silent for a moment. "I'd rather Uncle Rupert didn't know. He's a decent sort. He wouldn't approve of Oliver's actions."

"No, he wouldn't."

For the remainder of their journey to Paddington the brothers spoke desultorily. They didn't mention the coming duel. The carriage stopped at the side of a road bordering a sparsely wooded field in the hamlet of Westbourne Green. Several other vehicles were already waiting.

As Trevor and Jerrold got out of their carriage, a man carrying a black case came up to them. He nodded to Jerrold and said, "Good morning, Lord Woodforde. I'm Doctor Grey. I trust my services won't be needed this morning."

"I hope so, Doctor," replied Trevor gravely.

Oliver Layton hurried over to them. Percival Davenant, dressed in black, stood off to the side.

"Good morning, Trev, Jerry." Oliver sounded nervous, and he avoided Trevor's eyes. "Shall we have a look at the pistols?" To the doctor Oliver explained, "We're only allowing the one shot. Don't require more than one pair of pistols."

Jerrold reached into the carriage and brought out the wooden box. "A very nice pair," said Oliver as he examined the finely balanced pistols with their ten-inch barrels and steel sights. "Manton's, I presume? Well, let's load 'em up, Jerry. Davenant wants to finish this affair as soon as possible."

"Oh, by all means, let's not keep Captain Davenant waiting," observed Trevor dryly.

Oliver flushed. "I hope you understand my position, Trev. I daresay you think it a mite odd that I'm acting as Percy's second, but I say, what's a friend for if you can't count on him?"

"Never fear, Oliver. I understand you perfectly. I always have."

Oliver shot Trevor an uncertain glance, but chose not to continue the conversation. Turning toward Davenant, he called, "I believe we're ready, Percy."

Davenant, who had not uttered a word, nodded, and the party moved to the center of the field, where they paused beneath a pair of spreading oaks. Jerrold opened the wooden box. Oliver handed one half-cocked pistol to Davenant, Jerrold gave the other to Trevor. The opponents saluted each other briefly and then moved off to face each other at twelve yards. It was still raining, and a sharp wind had arisen. Moisture dripped from the oak leaves.

"Steady on," Jerrold murmured as he stood at

Trevor's elbow. "I don't like this wind. Keep to your concentration. And remember to come up quick to the mark. Shoot as soon as Oliver drops the handkerchief."

Trevor shot Jerrold a crooked grin. "I hear you, brother-mine. Any further advice?"

Jerrold grinned back. "No. Just good luck." He clapped Trevor on the back and moved off to stand beside the doctor.

The duel was over in a second. As soon as Oliver dropped the handkerchief, both men fired and Trevor dropped to the ground. Davenant remained motionless in place, the hand holding the pistol hanging by his side.

After kneeling beside Trevor in the briefest of examinations, Doctor Grey rose to his feet, shaking his head. Jerrold didn't need to hear the doctor's verdict. He could see the blood oozing from Trevor's mouth. He dropped to his knees next to his brother. Trevor's eyes opened. "Sorry to land you with the strawberry leaves and the coronet, Jerry," he said in a strangled whisper. "I know you never wanted to be a belted earl." Then he died.

Jerrold stood beside the open grave, gazing down at the polished wooden coffin. A steady, fine drizzle was already turning to mud the handfuls of earth deposited on the coffin by the mourners before they departed from the cemetery of St. Michael's and All Angels Church in the Herefordshire village of Stonebridge.

"Jerrold? Are you coming?"

Turning, Jerrold watched his uncle as the older man walked toward him down the path from the church gate.

"Are you all right, my boy?"

"Yes, Uncle Rupert. I was just saying a private goodbye to Trev."

Rupert Layton eyed his nephew sympathetically. Rupert was a tall, impressive-looking man of fifty, with the Layton dark hair, now streaked with gray, and blue eyes. A power in the Tory party, he spent most of his time in London, where he occupied a permanent sinecure post in the Treasury. His government salary, together with a family allowance and his wife's income—she was the daughter of a prosperous landowner in Derbyshire—enabled him to live comfortably. He and his nephews had always been on cordial terms.

"Such a tragedy," Rupert sighed, looking down at the grave. "A young man not yet thirty, titled and wealthy, newly engaged to be married, universally liked . . ." He hesitated, biting his lip. "I've been waiting for a private moment to talk to you about Oliver. I was devastated to hear that he'd acted as second to Trevor's killer. I hope you won't judge Oliver too harshly. He's young—well, I know he's not that young, he's your age, actually—but sometimes he doesn't use good judgment. And perhaps he's overly loyal to his friends."

Jerrold's face hardened. "He should have been more loyal to his family than to that blackguard, Davenant. I'll be frank with you, Uncle Rupert. What Oliver did was damnable, unforgivable. If it weren't for the affection I have for you, I'd never willingly see or talk to him again. The very sight of him at the funeral sickened me."

"Jerry . . . aren't you being very harsh?" Rupert looked stricken.

"I don't think so. For the sake of family peace, just use your best influence to keep Oliver away from me in future. I won't cut him if we do meet, but more assurance than that I can't give you. Shall we go?"

Jerrold fell into step with his uncle as they walked toward the gate. Rupert still appeared shaken at Jerrold's condemnation of Oliver's behavior. Jerrold knew that Rupert had a blind spot as far as his only child was concerned. He and his wife had spoiled and coddled Oliver from babyhood, never acknowledging any of his faults.

Rupert broke a rather awkward silence. "I hear Percival Davenant has left the country," he observed.

"What?" Jerrold stopped in his tracks, staring angrily at his uncle. "He must have read my mind. As soon as the funeral was over, I was going to do everything in my power to put him on trial for murder. He *is* a murderer. He challenged Trevor to a duel and killed him simply to add to his reputation as a deadly marksman."

"I know, my boy. However, I don't think you'd have had much success in bringing Davenant to trial. During the last fifty years there must have been close to a hundred fatal duels in Britain. I can only remember hearing about one or two executions of convicted duelists."

Jerrold nodded. "I'm aware of the statistics," he said grimly. "But I tell you this, Uncle Rupert: if or when I hear that Davenant has returned to England, I'll use every bit of power and influence that I possess to put him on trial for murder. He won't escape the consequences of this killing, I promise you." He stopped short, his face a mask of pain. After a moment he said, "Will you go on ahead to Malvern Hall, Uncle Rupert? Tell our guests I'll be along shortly."

"Yes, of course." Rupert looked somewhat taken aback, but asked no questions. He walked to the gate and climbed into his waiting carriage.

Emerging from the churchyard, Jerrold ordered his own coachman to wait for him and went down the village street to a large "black and white" timbered house. A flustered maidservant ushered him into a parlor.

An elderly man walked hurriedly into the room.

"Jerrold, my boy, this is a surprise. Do sit down. May I offer you a glass of wine?" He paused in confusion. "I'm sorry. I should have said 'my lord.' "

"That's all right, Dr. Gates. I haven't quite taken in the fact that I'm the new Earl of Woodforde. Thank you for coming to the funeral."

"The whole village attended, naturally. And in my case, how could I not come? I brought your brother into the world. You, too."

"Yes, and you tended to all our scrapes and bruises over the years." Jerrold fell silent. After a long pause he said. "Doctor, I didn't come here for small talk, or for medical treatment. I do need your expert opinion. Do you remember that time, five years—no, six years ago—when I came down with the mumps?"

"Indeed I do." The doctor laughed. "Oh, how humiliated you felt, bedded by a childhood disease when you were a grown-up young man—let's see—twenty, twenty-one years of age."

Jerrold smiled faintly. "I recall you told me that childhood diseases incurred in adulthood sometimes had serious medical consequences. Fortunately, I didn't suffer any lasting physical ill effects. However . . ." Jerrold hesitated. "You also told me you'd observed several cases during the course of your practice in which an adult male had contracted mumps and later became sterile."

His gaze sharpening, the doctor said, "Yes, I remember telling you that. Understand, I don't know that all my fellow doctors would agree with me, but I'm inclined to believe that sterility as a result of adult mumps is more common than many doctors realize. But Jerrold—my lord—why are you concerned about this problem now?" He stopped short, looking embarrassed. "Oh, of course. You're thinking of the succession."

Nodding, Jerrold said, "My possible sterility was of no consequence as long as my brother was alive. I fully expected that Trevor would have a large family and keep the succession in the direct line. Now . . ." He shrugged.

"I see." Dr. Gates looked thoughtful. "Obviously, you wouldn't be here discussing this matter if you were aware that you'd fathered any children since you had the mumps."

"That's right. Actually, since I came down with the mumps I've had a more or less permanent physical relationship with a certain lady. For several years now we've taken no precautions. I simply assumed there was no danger of a pregnancy. There's been none."

Leaning back in his chair, Dr. Gates looked at Jerrold compassionately. "You've come to me to ask if it's likely that your situation will change in the future." He shook his head. "I'm sorry. If, in five years of continuous sexual relationship with a young and healthy woman you haven't produced a child, I doubt very much that you ever will."

Rising, Jerrold extended his hand. "Thank you, Doctor. I suspected what your answer would be, but I wanted to be sure."

Jerrold walked slowly down the village street to his waiting carriage. His mind was seething. He felt helpless, trapped. In the normal course of events he would survive Uncle Rupert, who was now the heir presumptive to the family estate. He couldn't be at all sure he would survive Oliver. His vicious cousin, who was at least indirectly responsible for Trevor's murder, might well succeed him as Earl of Woodforde, and there wasn't a damned thing he could do about it.

Chapter Three

"But Mama, there must be *some* reason why that lamb is black when all the other sheep are white."

Zoë eyed her six-year-old son with affection mingled with a touch of exasperation. This was the third time since Philip had spotted the black lamb in the field during their afternoon walk that he had questioned her remark that nobody really knew why some sheep were born with black fleece. Philip had an inquiring mind, and when he came upon a puzzling concept he was loath to relinquish it, worrying over it like a dog with a bone.

"I have it," Zoë said suddenly. "I think your Uncle Edmund would tell you that the lamb was born black because it was God's will."

"Oh." Philip considered the matter gravely. "Well, I expect Uncle Edmund is right. He usually is."

Zoë gave a sigh of relief, thinking, as she so often did, how fortunate she was that her brother Edmund had stepped in to fill the void in Philip's fatherless life. When her father died, some five years ago, Edmund had taken his place as rector of St. Bride's, and Zoë and her infant son had come to live with him. Edmund liked children,

though he was unmarried and had none of his own. He
and Philip were almost like father and son.

Drawing a deep breath, Zoë drank in the sweet air of
this brilliantly beautiful late April day. She stooped to
bury her nose in a clump of sweet violets in the hedgerow. This was her favorite time of year, when the fragile
wild flowers of spring began to bloom in profusion in
the hedgerows and ditches and fields. Already this afternoon she'd pointed out to Philip the scarlet flowers of
the vetchling, the butter-yellow of primroses, the deep
blue of forget-me-nots and bluebells, and the first tiny
white blossoms of the wild strawberry.

"It won't be very long before we can pick our first
batch of berries," she'd told Philip.

"And then Cook will make us some tarts. I can't
wait!"

As they walked along, Zoë reflected that this was her
favorite time of the day, too. Every afternoon, no matter
at what stage of her work she might be, and no matter
what the weather, she and Philip took a leisurely
walk along the roads leading in and out of Heathfield.
Some in the village had expressed surprise that she
didn't leave Philip's nursemaid in charge of his outdoor
exercise, as most mothers in her social position would
have done, but she treasured these private moments
alone with her son. He was the single most important
thing in her life, and all too soon he would be going off
to school.

As they neared the outskirts of the village, Philip remarked in a faintly dissatisfied tone, "I do wonder
though, Mama, why God willed the lamb to be black.
The poor thing must feel so different from all his brothers and sisters and his friends."

Zoë laughed. Philip was irrepressible. Doubtless all his life long he would never accept the easy explanation.

"I'll race you to the rectory, Mama."

Zoë laughed again. "Wretch. You know it won't be very long before you outrun me, even though I'm so much older than you are!" She gathered up her skirts and began to run. Philip sprinted ahead of her, only to fall heavily a short distance down the road.

"Philip, what is it? Are you hurt?"

Sitting up, Philip grimaced in pain. "I think I turned my ankle. My foot struck a stone in the road."

"Here, let me help you up. Can you put any weight on the foot?"

Clinging to his mother, Philip shook his head. "It hurts a lot, Mama."

"Can I be of any assistance, ma'am?"

Startled, Zoë half-turned to look at the tall man who had just dismounted from his horse and was striding toward them. As he came nearer, her eyes narrowed and her heart slowly began to turn to stone. "No, thank you," she said stiffly. "My son has turned his ankle slightly. We're very close to home, fortunately. We can manage."

"Are you sure? Where do you live?" The newcomer's dark blue eyes beneath the fashionable beaver hat seemed genuinely concerned.

"At the rectory," Philip volunteered before Zoë could answer.

"Oh, I know where that is." Dropping to one knee beside Philip, the man gently touched the boy's injured ankle. "I don't think you have a broken bone," he told Philip. "It's probably just a sprain." As he spoke, the man glanced up into the child's face, and his expression of kindly concern altered to one of intent scrutiny. He drew a sudden sharp breath. A moment later he straightened up, saying cheerfully to Philip, "You certainly can't walk home on that ankle. Would you like to ride my horse?" At Philip's quick, pleased smile, the stranger deftly scooped up the boy and deposited him in the saddle. "Hold on to the pommel, lad. We'll have you home before the cat has time to lick behind his ears."

Gazing at Philip's face, flushed with excitement to be taking his first ride on a horse, Zoë forced herself to be silent and followed along behind as the strange gentleman led the animal past the church and paused in front of the gate of the rectory. After opening the gate, the man lifted Philip from the saddle and carried him up the path leading to the door. Zoë hurried ahead to open the door.

As the gentleman walked into the foyer, carrying Philip, an agitated maidservant raced down the stairway from the floor above. "Philip, my lamb, are ye hurt bad? I saw ye from the window, being carried into the house by the gentleman."

Zoë said soothingly to the nursemaid, "No, Sarah, Philip's not seriously injured, but you should take him to his bedchamber and start soaking his ankle in hot water."

"The Lord be praised the child's all right." The nursemaid plucked Philip from the stranger's arms and started up the stairs, turning her head to call behind her, "I'll do jist what ye said about soaking the ankle, Mrs. Manning."

Emerging from his study into the foyer, the Reverend Edmund Bennett said, frowning slightly, "I heard raised voices out here. Is something amiss, Zoë?" He was a tall slender man who in coloring and features greatly resembled his sister. He flicked an inquiring glance at the stranger.

Zoë replied quickly, "Nothing's amiss, Edmund. Philip turned his ankle while we were out walking, and this—this gentleman kindly came to our aid. He brought Philip home on his horse."

"I see." Edmund glanced from Zoë to the stranger, as if he was expecting his sister to make an introduction. When she didn't do so he turned to the stranger. "You've been very kind, sir. Might I inquire your name? I'm Edmund Bennett, the rector of St. Bride's. This is my sister, Mrs. Manning."

The stranger bowed. "How do you do, Reverend Bennett, Mrs. Manning. I was glad to be able to render some slight assistance. I'm Jerrold Layton." He stopped short, his lips tightening. "Actually, as the result of the recent death of my brother, I'm the Earl of Woodforde. I'm staying with my cousin, Lady Rosedale, at Merefield Park."

Edmund's eyes lighted up. "Indeed. Here in Heathfield we're so happy to have Lady Rosedale in residence at last. What a tragedy, losing her husband, and almost losing her son, so far away from England."

"Yes, Dickie caught the fever that killed his father in Vienna and nearly died of it himself. He had a long convalescence in Austria. My cousin is very glad to be safely at home at Merefield Park." The earl smiled. "It's been a great pleasure to meet both of you. Now I'd best be off. My cousin is expecting me for tea."

Walking to the door with his guest, Edmund said, "Thank you again for coming to the rescue of my nephew, Lord Woodforde. I hope to see you again during your visit to Lady Rosedale."

After the door had closed behind the earl, Edmund

remarked. "So that's the Earl of Woodforde. I'd heard he was some connection of the Rosedales . . ." He broke off, staring, as his sister, her face a frozen mask, brushed past him and headed for the staircase. "Zoë! Is something wrong?"

As she mounted the stairs, Zoë called back in a voice that sounded close to breaking, "Good heavens, Edmund, what could possibly be wrong? I'm just going up to see to Philip."

Jerrold walked into the morning room at Merefield Park, where his hostess sat in a comfortable chair, reading a book. She looked up with a smile as he entered the room.

"Sorry I'm late, Melicent. As you see, I didn't even stop to change from my riding clothes. I didn't want to keep you waiting."

"Jerry, you goose, there's no need to apologize. It isn't as if I had a host of calls on my time. I lead a very quiet life these days. Ring the bell for tea, won't you?" After Jerrold had pulled the bellrope, she asked. "Did you enjoy your ride?"

He sat down in a chair near her. "Very much. It's a lovely day and I rode for miles, trying to reacquaint myself with the countryside. I haven't visited Merefield Park for a very long time."

Melicent nodded. "I've had to become familiar with the area all over again, too. As you probably know, during our marriage Tom and I came home to England very infrequently."

A footman arrived with the tea tray just then, and while his cousin busied herself with pouring the tea, Jerrold studied her closely. With her dark hair and eyes and charming smile, she was as attractive as ever, but these days she looked a little fine-boned and fragile. He had arrived at Merefield late yesterday, and he and Melicent had had little opportunity for an intimate talk as yet. He said compassionately, "You've had a bad year, my dear."

"Yes," she admitted with a rueful smile. "It hasn't been easy. First my father-in-law died, and Tom had to start making plans to return to England and take up his new duties. Poor Tom. How he hated to leave Vienna and the diplomatic service, and at this time, too, with Napoleon on the run. Then he fell sick with that wasting fever. Each time I thought he was recovering, he would have a relapse. Soon after he died, Dickie came down with the fever. I was sure he would die, too, but he survived, only he had such an agonizingly slow convalescence. For months I was afraid to run the risk of subjecting him to that long drive across the Continent. And yet Dickie belonged at Merefield Park. He *is* the new Earl of Rosedale."

Leaning forward, Jerrold reached across the space between them to clasp Melicent's hand. "I wish I could have helped."

"Oh, but you're helping now," she said warmly. "It's so good of you to come, Jerry, so soon after poor Trevor died."

"I felt a great need to be with family. You're almost my only family now, Melicent."

Melicent looked a little surprised. "Except for Uncle Rupert and Aunt Beryl, of course."

"Yes, well . . . you know that Oliver acted as second to the court card who killed Trevor?"

A shadow fell over her face. "Yes. I wonder that you can even speak to him."

"I was tempted to cut off all contact with him, in effect to read him out of the family, but that would have meant punishing Uncle Rupert, too, and I'm fond of the old boy. So I've settled for keeping out of Oliver's way as much as possible. Which creates a certain awkwardness with his parents."

"I can see that. Well, I'm so glad you're here, my dear. We can help each other heal."

Jerrold looked at his cousin with a rush of affection. Once, all those years ago, he'd fancied himself romantically in love with her. He realized now that what he felt had been the throes of calf-love, but Melicent remained one of the warmest and sweetest influences in his life.

A maidservant entered the morning room, leading by the hand a small boy in a low-necked frock with cotton trousers showing beneath.

"There you are, Dickie," said Melicent. "Come give Mama a kiss." She nodded a dismissal to the nursemaid. "Did you have a good supper?" she asked her son with an adoring smile. "Good. I want you to meet a new relation, Dickie. This is your Cousin Jerrold."

"How do you do, Dickie," said Jerrold gravely. He extended his hand, which the child took with a shy smile. "Do you have a hobby horse? You do? Well, never mind. I've brought you a new one, a superior model that will make you feel you're riding a real horse. And do you have a bull roarer? No? Now you do. I'll bring it up to the nursery tomorrow."

"Jerry, how could you?" protested Melicent. "Dickie will drive his nursemaid queer in the attic with the noise."

"Every English child should have a bull roarer," retorted Jerrold. "It's part of his heritage." He continued to talk to Dickie, drawing him out, making him laugh with droll stories about Jerrold's childhood pets, until the nursemaid arrived to take the little boy away to prepare him for bed.

"I always have Dickie brought down to spend some extra time with me at this hour," Melicent observed. "Some people say I'm spoiling him, paying too much attention to him, but he's so important to me. He's all I have left." She lifted an eyebrow. "You were very good with Dickie. I didn't know you liked children."

"I didn't know it either," replied Jerrold in some surprise. "I've never had any dealings with children. But it would be difficult not to like your Dickie." He fell silent, thinking of the child he'd assisted that afternoon. He'd felt such a strong feeling of familiarity with the boy, and yet he could swear he'd never before met the child or his mother. He said to Melicent with a smile, "This seems to be my day to associate with children. I met a little boy today while I was out riding. Matter of fact, that's why I was late for tea. The boy fell and sprained his ankle, and I brought him home on my horse. He was your rector's nephew, as it turned out."

"Oh, yes, little Philip Manning. A delightful child. I met him when I called at the rectory. His uncle is much respected as our new rector, I'm told. He's the son of our previous rector." Melicent began to laugh. "Actually, you and Philip Manning's mother are old acquaintances."

Jerrold looked blank. "I met Mrs. Manning today for the first time, as far as I'm aware."

"No, no. Don't you recall the ball my father-in-law gave for Tom and me when we returned from our wedding trip? I introduced you to Mrs. Manning—she was Zoë Bennett then, of course, the daughter of the rector of St. Bride's. You seemed to take quite a fancy to her. You certainly danced often enough with her!"

Shaking his head, Jerrold said, "I haven't the faintest memory of meeting the young lady. To tell the truth, I was pretty badly foxed that night. I can't remember much of anything about the ball. Well, then, so I met Mrs. Manning all those years ago. How is it that she still lives in Heathfield? Is she a widow?"

"Yes. She married an American, an officer on a merchant ship, I believe. He was lost at sea shortly after they were married. When her father died a few years ago, she came back to Heathfield with her son to live with her brother, whom my father-in-law had appointed to the living to succeed his father. Apparently the arrangement has been very successful. The Reverend Bennett, who is unmarried, dotes on his nephew, and Mrs. Manning is free to devote her time to her work."

"Her work?"

"She's a portrait painter. She specializes in painting pictures of young mothers with their children. I consider her very talented. On one of my visits to the rectory she showed me a nearly finished portrait of the Marchioness of Overdean and her daughter. Quite exquisite. I'm thinking of asking her to do a portrait of me and Dickie similar to the painting that hangs in the drawing room of Woodforde House in London. You know, the picture of you and Trevor with your mother, painted when you two boys were only a little older than Dickie."

Jerrold experienced a kind of electric shock as he gazed in his mind's eye at the portrait hanging in Woodforde House. Of course. Now he understood the nagging sense of familiarity he'd felt when he'd looked into the face of little Philip Manning this afternoon. The child was the image of himself at about the same age.

The resemblance was purely coincidental, obviously. Philip was the son of an American naval officer and the highly respected sister of the rector of Heathfield. And yet ... Melicent had said that he'd met and danced with the young Zoë Bennett at that long-ago ball at Merefield Park on the one night of his life that was a complete blank to him. He'd drunk so much wine at the ball that he could remember nothing he'd said or done until he woke up in the inn at Gretna Green the following morning. Even then his mind was still so befogged with liquor, and his head ached so badly, that he had only the vaguest memory of the young woman who had shared his bed.

"Jerry? Is something wrong?"

Jerrold blinked. "I'm sorry, Melicent. I was wool-gathering. What did you say?"

"I suggested that you might like to call on Mrs. Manning and see her work."

"That's a splendid idea," said Jerrold promptly. Too promptly? he asked himself. He added rather lamely, "In any case, I should stop at the rectory to inquire about young Philip's ankle."

As he spoke, Jerrold reproached himself mentally for his vulgar curiosity about Mrs. Manning and her son. It was insane—it was, in fact, an insult to the lady—to allow himself to speculate that he might be her son's father. He knew the thought would never have occurred to him before Trevor's death. Until then his childlessness had meant nothing to him. Now that he was the Earl of Woodforde his sterility, and the strong possibility that Oliver would succeed him, had been preying on his mind. He was simply being unduly sensitive to the subject of children.

But Jerrold found he couldn't control his unruly

thoughts. He couldn't dismiss the fact that little Philip Manning was the spitting image of himself at the same age, and that he'd known the child's mother at approximately the correct time. Supposing he had managed to seduce the virtuous daughter of the rector of Heathfield in a drunken stupor, Philip could be his son, the only child he would ever have. Even so, Jerrold jibed at himself, the boy would then be illegitimate and couldn't affect the succession to the Woodforde estates. But still . . . Jerrold acknowledged ironically that his fatherly instincts seemed to be struggling to come to the surface. If there was the slightest chance that this child might be his, he realized suddenly he wanted to know the boy, to contribute to his support, to have some say in his upbringing.

"We might call at the rectory tomorrow," he said to Melicent with an air of calm disinterest. Time would tell. Doubtless, he told himself firmly, after a meeting or two with the prim and proper Mrs. Manning, he could banish the foolish notion that he'd fathered a child with her.

Zoë made a last brush stroke and looked up from her palette, saying to her sitter, "You can relax now, Mrs. Randolph. I think we've done enough work for today."

Mrs. Randolph flexed her shoulders and leaned back against her chair. "Thank you, my dear. I was beginning to feel a mite stiff. How is the picture coming along?"

"Come see. I'm nearly finished."

Mrs. Randolph left her chair and came to stand beside Zoë at the easel. After a long look she said accusingly, "You're flattering me, you know."

Zoë gazed with affection at the older woman. Mrs. Randolph was plumper and grayer than she'd been seven years ago, but otherwise she was much the same. "Nonsense," said Zoë lightly. "I took away a few gray hairs, that's all."

Shaking her head, Mrs. Randolph said, "La, my dear, you can stop flattering me. Unfortunately, I know quite well what I look like!" She turned thoughtful. "Lord, sometimes I find it hard to believe that you've become a famous painter. It seems like yesterday that you and Charlotte were schoolgirls together. I'm so happy for you. You never actually told me about your circumstances, but I've always assumed that your husband didn't leave you very well provided for."

"No, not very. However, my painting fees enable me to provide very comfortably for me and Philip, so that I'm not a burden to Edmund. And I owe it all to you."

"To me? Oh, no."

"Oh, yes. You praised my painting to the skies to your cousin in Harrowgate, and she commissioned me to do a portrait of her and her children. That was my first sale, and your cousin recommended me to a friend, and that friend to another, and so it went."

"Yes, and now you're painting duchesses and marchionesses," said Mrs. Randolph, laughing. "Well, I must be off. I don't wish to keep you from your work." As she put on her bonnet and pelisse, she looked closely at Zoë and said, hesitating, "Not to pry, my dear, but you've seemed a little blue-deviled this afternoon. Is something wrong?"

"Not at all," said Zoë brightly. She kissed her old friend. "Goodbye. Don't forget to come back for your last sitting on Wednesday."

After Mrs. Randolph had gone, Zoë began slowly to

clean her brushes. She ought to put the final touches on the new commission for Lady Althorp, but she lacked the heart to do any more painting today. Glancing around the large sunny bedchamber that had been converted into a studio for her on the second floor of the rectory, she felt trapped. The room no longer seemed like the haven of refuge it had been for so many years. She felt a renewal of the panic she'd experienced yesterday when she encountered Jerrold Layton. Obviously he hadn't remembered her. Just as obviously, though, he'd recognized something familiar in Philip, as well he might. The two faces, the boy's and the man's, were mirror images of each other.

What would happen now? Would Jerrold Layton's momentary flash of recognition prove to be ephemeral, unimportant to him? Or was her flimsily constructed house of cards about to collapse around her?

A knock sounded softly at the door. "Come."

A maidservant poked her head around the door, saying apologetically, "I know ye don't like to be disturbed while ye're painting, ma'am, but Master says as how Lady Rosedale and Lord Woodforde have called and are asking to see ye."

Swallowing a hard knot in her throat, Zoë said, "Present my compliments to Lady Rosedale and Lord Woodforde and ask them to excuse me. Tell them I can't leave my work."

"Yes, ma'am."

After the door closed, Zoë sank into a chair and stared numbly at the floor. She was still in the same position half an hour later when, following a perfunctory knock, Edmund strode into the studio.

"You're not working, Zoë," he said in a carefully controlled voice.

"No," she replied dully.

"I thought as much. I knew Mrs. Randolph had left some time before Lady Rosedale arrived." He cleared his throat. "Zoë, why didn't you come down to greet our guests? Lady Rosedale has become my patroness, so to speak, on the death of her father-in-law, and she's been most gracious to both of us. I fear you may have offended her. Lord Woodforde, too. He called to inquire about Philip. He also seemed very interested in your painting. Matter of fact, he said he would call at the rectory tomorrow, at which time he hoped you would show him your studio."

Involuntarily Zoë snapped, "I won't see him, Edmund."

"Zoë!" Edmund looked and sounded outraged.

Drawing a deep breath, Zoë said, "I must tell you something, Edmund. I've been living a lie, and now it's caught up with me." She paused, collecting her thoughts, recalling the difficult memories she'd tried so hard, and for so long, to suppress.

Slowly she began to talk. "Edmund, seven years ago, while you were still a student at Oxford, I went to a ball at Merefield Park, where I met a man named Jerrold Layton."

"The present Lord Woodforde," Edmund said in surprise. "Yesterday neither of you mentioned you'd met before."

"His lordship didn't remember that first meeting," Zoë said acidly. "He and I eloped to Gretna Green that night and were married. He doesn't remember that, either."

"My God!" Edmund stared at her in shock.

Zoë went on talking, describing how, on the morning after the ball, she had walked into the hallway of the rectory just as her father was descending the stairs. He said with a kindly smile, "Well, well, my dear, Mrs. Randolph certainly brought you home at an early hour. I expected that you and Charlotte would sleep until noon, after dancing the night away."

"No, Papa," Zoë had replied. "I wanted to get home early. I have so many things to do today."

Zoë looked at her brother with a bitter little smile. "I didn't tell Papa that I'd been dropped off at the outskirts of the village, not by Mrs. Randolph's coachman, but by a farmer's hired man to whom I'd given a few coins to transport me in his cart from Gretna Green. You know how absentminded Papa was, Edmund. He never discovered the deception, nor did Mrs. Randolph ever learn that I left the ball at Merefield Park to elope to Gretna Green rather than to return, ill, as I wrote her in a note, to the rectory. I thought I'd covered my tracks rather well."

Zoë fell silent. She couldn't talk to Edmund about her bouts of guilt and shame in the dark reaches of the night, when she realized the enormity of what she'd done, eloping to Scotland with a man she barely knew, a man so drunk he didn't remember he'd married her. However, she'd comforted herself with the thought that at least no one would ever know about the experience. The comforting feeling had lasted only a few weeks.

"I found out I was carrying Jerrold Layton's child," she told Edmund. "I didn't tell anyone. I couldn't bear to disgrace Papa. What would his congregation, what would the world say, when they learned his daughter was having an illegitimate child? I couldn't bring myself to tell Mrs. Randolph, either. She'd always been so kind to me."

Edmund was beginning to recover his composure. "But Zoë, you and Jerrold Layton were legally married according to the laws of Scotland," he said slowly. "Your child wouldn't be illegitimate."

"I wasn't thinking clearly. I was utterly confused. Since Jerrold Layton didn't even remember the ceremony, I somehow reasoned that no marriage had taken place. I panicked. My only thought was to go away somewhere and hide. So I went to visit Cousin Augusta in Bristol."

"I remember. Papa wrote me that you were planning to spend several months with Cousin Augusta."

Zoë's thoughts turned with gratitude to the gentle, elderly spinster, the daughter of a Bristol shipowner, who was a distant relation of her father. "Cousin Augusta was shocked by my predicament, of course, but she was so kind and understanding. She was the one who thought of the solution to my problem: I was to marry David Manning."

A frown spreading over his face, Edmund said sharply, "Zoë, in heaven's name, how could you consider that a solution? You were already married to Jerrold Layton. You committed bigamy."

"Edmund, you don't understand. There never was a David Manning. Cousin Augusta made him up. Bristol is a very busy port. It swarms with seafaring men from all over the world. Cousin Augusta suggested I 'marry' an imaginary American sea captain named David Manning who would unfortunately go down with his ship during a storm in the Atlantic, leaving me a widow. A widow who was expecting a child. Cousin Augusta's friends were so sympathetic."

Drawing a deep breath, Edmund said, "You were playing a dangerous game, you know. In the ordinary course of events you would have been expected to have some communication with your husband's family—to notify them of your son's birth, if nothing else. Papa might have thought it odd that you didn't receive any letters from your American relatives. But then . . ."

"But then politics, or world events, or whatever you care to call it, played into my hands. Shortly after I was 'married,' the American government passed something called an 'Embargo Act,' which closed American ports to foreign trade, and some time after that the Americans passed a law called the 'Non-intercourse Act.' The net result of these acts by the American government was that practically no American ships have docked in British ports for many years. And now, of course, England is at war with the United States. So I've had a perfectly good reason for not being able to communicate with my new American relations."

The look of animation slowly faded from Zoë's face. Sighing, she said, "I'm sorry I had to lie to you, Edmund, and to everyone, all these years. I felt I had to protect Philip. Now the lies are unraveling. I think Jerrold Layton—Lord Woodforde—has spotted a family resemblance in Philip."

"Zoë, for God's sake, you still haven't faced your most important problem," Edmund burst out. "You're legally married to Lord Woodforde. You say he was too drunk to realize he'd been married. It's beside the point. No matter how humiliated you felt, you should have informed him about the marriage. The time to correct the situation was then. Annulment. Divorce. I don't know what."

Edmund paused, his face twisted in distaste. He went on, saying, "What if Lord Woodforde had contracted another marriage in the intervening years? He would have been guilty of bigamy. Any children born of such a marriage would be illegitimate. No, Zoë. You must meet now with Lord Woodforde and make some arrangement in regard to Philip. As I see it, my nephew is Lord Woodforde's eldest son—to date his *only* son—and the heir to his estates."

Zoë's heart began to pound. "No," she choked. "I refuse to have anything to do with Jerrold Layton. I won't allow him to have any connection with my son." She broke off. Not even to Edmund could she reveal how much she hated the Earl of Woodforde. He'd stripped her of her human dignity, he'd seduced her into thinking he loved her, and then he'd accused her of being a loose woman, a creature he could hire for a night. Never, if she could help it, would he ever be in a position to hurt her again, or to claim Philip as his son.

Chapter Four

Leaving his horse tied to the gate, Jerrold walked up the path to the rectory and knocked vigorously at the door. To the housemaid who answered his knock, he said, "I'm back with my usual request. Please ask Mrs. Manning if she will see me."

Looking flustered, the servant said, "Mrs. Manning isn't at home, sir—my lord. She went away early this morning."

"I see. Then I should like to speak to Mr. Bennett."

Moving aside to allow Jerrold to enter the foyer, the housemaid said, "I'll tell the Reverend." She returned a minute later. "The Reverend will see you now."

Edmund Bennett waved Jerrold to a chair in his study and sat down behind his desk. "What a great pleasure to see you again, Lord Woodforde. And how is Lady Rosedale?"

The words were warm, but to Jerrold the rector of St. Bride's appeared ill at ease. He failed to meet his guest's eyes.

"Lady Rosedale is in good health, thank you." Jerrold moved quickly to the attack. "Mr. Bennett, are you aware that I've called at the rectory every day for the past four days, asking to see Mrs. Manning?"

"Er—yes. I was aware."

"Then perhaps you can tell me why she has refused to receive me."

Edmund Bennett looked away. "As I'm sure the servants told you, my sister is a very busy woman. She's becoming more and more in demand as a painter, and she has many commissions to complete. I assure you that she had no intention of offending you."

"If Mrs. Manning is so very busy, I marvel that she could tear herself away from her work to go off on a journey. Your servant told me she went away this morning."

More ill at ease than ever, the rector said, "Actually, she *is* working. She went to London. She goes there several times a year, where she schedules appointments for sittings. These trips to London make for more convenience, both for her and for her clients."

"Indeed. Mr. Bennett, I'll be returning to London myself shortly. Perhaps I could visit Mrs. Manning there. Can you give me her direction?"

His lips compressed, Edmund Bennett stared at Jerrold for a long moment. At last he said with an obvious reluctance, "Usually she stays at the Pulteney Hotel in Piccadilly."

"Thank you. I won't keep you any longer."

As Jerrold mounted his horse at the rectory gate and set off down the village street, he had already made up his mind to leave Heathfield and Merefield Park the following day for London. His hunting instincts were on the alert. A few days ago he had been more than half prepared to admit that his suspicion that he might be little Philip Manning's father was a figment of his fevered imagination. A friendly chat with the boy's mother, perhaps another close look at the child, and he would be free of his delusion.

But he'd never had that friendly chat with Zoë Manning, nor had he seen Philip. Each time he'd called at the rectory, he'd been turned away with the curt message that Mrs. Manning wasn't at home to visitors. Though Jerrold had never been particularly high in the instep and didn't demand that people kowtow to him because of his rank, he considered that Zoë Manning's behavior had verged on open rudeness. He was, after all, a close relative of her brother's patroness. One would have expected her to treat him with at least a nominal courtesy for her brother's sake. So she must have a powerful personal reason for so brusquely refusing to see him.

As Jerrold turned his horse into the driveway of Merefield Park, he made a vow to himself. He wouldn't rest until he'd discovered why Zoë was avoiding him.

When Jerrold arrived in London several days later, he paid a duty call at his uncle's house in Bruton Street. Seated in the well-furnished drawing room, he almost immediately regretted paying the call, despite the cordiality of his welcome by Rupert Layton and his wife, Beryl, a thin, colorless woman whose only interests in life were her husband and her son.

Unfortunately, Oliver was present too, and, even though he had promised Rupert to behave civilly to Oliver, Jerrold could hardly bring himself to speak to his cousin. Oliver hadn't pulled the trigger of the gun that killed Trevor, but Jerrold still held him as responsible for Trevor's death as his malevolent friend, Percival

Davenant, and the thought that one day this dissolute weakling might become Earl of Woodforde remained a festering sore in Jerrold's heart.

"I say, Jerry, I hear you've been visiting Cousin Melicent in Cumberland," said Oliver with a show of warm interest. "Is she as pretty as ever?"

"Oh, yes."

"Will she be coming to London for the Season?"

"I doubt it. She's still mourning for Tom."

"Now, wait," said Rupert. "Melicent's husband has been dead for almost a year. No one would look askance if she were to open her London house and take her place, in a quiet way, in society."

"Yes," said Beryl Layton thoughtfully. "Melicent is almost certain to wish to marry again at some point in the future. She's a young woman, very comfortably off. I believe she has a handsome jointure and a tidy fortune, besides, from her mother's family. She really ought to begin easing herself into the social scene."

As Beryl finished speaking, she glanced from her husband to her son, and the look of perfect understanding that passed among them made Jerrold's blood run cold. Could Oliver and his parents be considering the possibility of a match between Oliver and Melicent? Obviously, the marriage would solve Oliver's money problems and establish him in society. But no. Melicent wouldn't consider such a marriage for an instant, Jerrold assured himself. She knew what Oliver was like, and she'd despised him from their childhood. No amount of wooing by Oliver would make her change her mind about him.

Oliver excused himself to keep an engagement, and soon afterward Beryl, with a sugary smile, announced she would leave Jerrold and her husband to have a man-to-man chat. Jerrold immediately suspected that a request was about to be made to him, probably for money. Rupert had a generous Layton family allowance, and his wife also had an income, but there never seemed to be enough money to support an ambitious political couple in style.

However, Rupert's remarks at first were purely conversational. "These are exciting times in the world, my boy. At the Foreign Office yesterday they told me that Napoleon had signed the articles of abdication."

"Yes. I saw the announcement in *The Times* this morning. Napoleon will soon be off to rule over his new empire of Elba."

Rupert eyed his nephew sympathetically. "Will you miss not serving in the House?"

"Oh, yes. Unfortunately, there's no help for it. Peers can't sit in Commons." Jerrold grinned. "I'll just have to make do with the House of Lords, Uncle Rupert."

Turning thoughtful, Rupert observed, "Perhaps we could interest Oliver in replacing you in the family seat."

Unable to keep the edge out of his voice, Jerrold snapped, "I don't think Oliver has much interest in politics."

"No, I daresay you're right," Rupert agreed regretfully. He cleared his throat. "Speaking of Oliver, would you consider giving him an allowance, as a first step in acknowledging him as your eventual heir? Because let's face it, my boy, I'm getting to be an old man. Almost certainly I shan't survive you!"

Raising his eyebrow, Jerrold said, "Aren't you being somewhat premature, sir? At the moment you, and after you, Oliver, are my heirs, yes, but—"

"Oh, come now, you're not suggesting you intend to

have children of your own—" Rupert broke off, looking discomfited.

Jerrold stared at his uncle. "Perhaps you should explain that remark."

"I was merely being realistic," Rupert said defensively. "In view of your physical condition—you contracted the mumps some years ago—it's unlikely that you'll father any children."

"You seem very knowledgeable about my health. Uncle Rupert."

"I . . ." Rupert bit his lip.

"I came down with the mumps when I was paying a quiet family visit to Malvern Hall," Jerrold went on. "So far as I was aware, the only people who knew about my illness—which I wasn't anxious to inform the world about!—were Papa, several of the servants, and Dr. Gates."

At the mention of Dr. Gates, Rupert's expression changed perceptibly. Jerrold paused. Of course. Dr. Gates, conscientious practitioner though he was, had probably not considered it a breach of medical ethics to mention Jerrold's illness, and its possible consequences, to a close relative like Rupert Layton.

Jerrold rose, saying coolly, "At the risk of disappointing you, Uncle Rupert, I'm not prepared at this point to groom Oliver as my eventual heir. I'm still a young man. Who knows? I may decide to marry and take my chances about siring a child."

As Jerrold drove off in the hackney cab waiting for him in front of his uncle's house, he reflected that, while he might have put a temporary spoke in Rupert's wheel of ambition, his triumph was very shallow. The facts were inexorable. He was sterile, and unless he managed to outlive Oliver, his cousin *was* his heir.

Another disquieting thought struck him. Had Rupert been discreet with his knowledge? Jerrold squirmed at the idea that his sexual life might be the subject of bawdy speculation among his acquaintances in the *ton*. But no. Surely in the past five years he would have become aware of such sniggering gossip. Rupert had had the good sense to keep his nephew's medical condition to himself.

The hackney stopped in Grafton Street. Instructing the coachman to wait for him, Jerrold walked around the corner to the trim little house in Albemarle Street. "Oh, yes, my lord, her ladyship is at home," said the smiling maid who answered the knock. "I'll tell her ladyship that ye're here."

Dorothea received him, not as she usually did, in her boudoir, but in her cozy morning room. "Well, Jerrold, it's been a long time," she said with a brittle smile. "I vow, I very nearly didn't recognize you!"

She was as beautiful as he remembered her, Jerrold thought, as he gazed at the opulent figure and the luxuriant Titian curls framing the exquisite face. But for the first time in their association, his pulses remained unstirred at the sight of her. At the moment he felt not the slightest urge to make love to her.

"I didn't neglect you deliberately, Dorothea," he said coolly. "You'll recall that I was in Herefordshire, burying my brother. And after that I spent a few days in Cumberland with my cousin, Lady Rosedale, who recently returned to England after her husband's death in Vienna."

"You might have written. Even a line or two, to let me know that I was occasionally in your thoughts."

"I'm sorry. I really didn't feel up to writing. Perhaps

you didn't realize what a crushing loss my brother's death was to me. We were very close, you know."

Dorothea's expression softened. "I do know. I'm sorry, too. I didn't mean to reproach you." She paused, obviously choosing her next words carefully. "While you've been gone, I've been thinking about our situation. Jerrold, I want to get married."

Stiffening, Jerrold replied, "I thought we'd settled this marriage question the last time we talked. I haven't changed my mind. We agreed when we began our affair that marriage wasn't an option."

"But now everything is changed," she argued. "Then you were the Honorable Jerrold Layton, a bachelor with no family obligations. Now you're the Earl of Woodforde. You need a wife, if only to act as your official hostess. I would make a splendid hostess."

"Dorothea, please listen to me. At this stage in my life, my only reasons for marrying would be if I fell madly in love *or* if I wanted to produce an heir. Well, you know about my medical situation. I'm not likely to have an heir. As for love, you've always understood our relationship. We satisfy each other sexually. You inflame me, you intoxicate me, more than any woman I've ever known—but I don't love you."

Her beautiful features hardening, Dorothea said, "That's your last word? You refuse to get married?"

"Yes. I see no point in marrying."

"Then I trust you won't object if I make other plans for myself. *You* may not wish to marry me, but other men have definitely expressed an interest. Lord Windermere, for example."

"Windermere! Good God, Dorothea, the man's practically doddering. I doubt that he's physically capable of performing—" Jerrold broke off, biting his lip.

"He may not perform like an acrobat in bed, my dear, but at least he's prepared to put a wedding ring on my finger while he makes the effort," Dorothea retorted, tossing her head.

Drawing a deep breath, Jerrold said, "Yes, of course. Forgive me. I had no right to interfere in your private affairs. Goodbye, Dorothea. I wish you nothing but happiness."

As he left Dorothea's house and walked along Albemarle Street on his way to join his hackney cab and driver in the adjoining street, Jerrold examined his feelings and was conscious of nothing but relief. He and Dorothea had broken off a relationship that had disintegrated into little more than occasional bouts of physical passion. They would both be better off without each other. But even as he acknowledged his relief, Jerrold had another thought. Over the years he and Dorothea had achieved a certain closeness, even if it was mostly physical. Now there was a void. With the exception of Melicent, there wasn't a person in the world with whom he felt close.

Reaching the waiting carriage, he called to the coachman, "Take me to the Pulteney Hotel in Piccadilly."

A little later, as he climbed up the steps of the hotel, he reflected that the Pulteney was becoming increasingly fashionable. For one thing, it had a pleasing location, opposite the verdant reaches of the Green Park, where cows grazed contentedly. The establishment was also noted for its excellent service and, especially appealing to female guests, its newly installed water closets.

A porter directed him to the second floor, where "Mrs. Manning has engaged a suite, sir." The door to the suite was open. The small sitting room had been converted to an office by the addition of a businesslike desk, behind which sat a fresh-faced young woman in a conservative dark gown. "Good afternoon, sir. How can I help ye?" she inquired in a voice tinged with a country accent that reminded him of Melicent's servants at Merefield Park. He suspected that the young woman was probably one of the rectory servants from Heathfield.

"I'd like to speak to Mrs. Manning. Will you tell her Lord Woodforde is here?"

"She has a sitting now, my lord. If ye'll wait until she's finished, I'll tell her ye're here."

"Thank you." Jerrold sat down in a comfortable chair. Zoë Manning must be doing very well with her painting, he mused. Renting a suite at the Pulteney for a number of days must cost a pretty penny. He remarked to the receptionist, "Mrs. Manning is becoming so well known that she must be very busy when she comes to London for these portrait sittings."

"Oh, indeed, my lord. She has appointments from early morning until late afternoon." A faintly puzzled expression crossed the girl's face. "I must say, though, it was a little harder than usual for Mrs. Manning to make the arrangements for this trip. She hadn't planned to come to London until next month, so of course she had to write to all her clients, changing the times for their appointments."

"Really?" Jerrold assumed an air of polite interest, but his mind was working busily. So Zoë Manning, to the mystification of her young servant, had suddenly advanced the time of her visit to London by a full month. Why? There might be a number of reasons, but it seemed to Jerrold most likely that she'd left Heathfield so precipitously in order to avoid an encounter with him. He clenched his jaw. She would soon learn he couldn't be avoided forever, and then, finally, he would discover why Zoë Manning was so desperate to keep her distance from him.

The door of the inner room opened and a fashionably dressed woman emerged in the company of a little girl and a nursemaid. The receptionist slipped into the inner room and closed the door behind her.

The woman, a tall, vivacious-looking brunette, exclaimed, "Jerrold Layton—I'm sorry, Lord Woodforde—how good to see you." She told the nursemaid, "Take Maria to the carriage. I'll be with you shortly." Turning back to Jerrold, she said, "I must offer my condolences on the death of your brother."

"Thank you, Lady Bradford. It was a great loss."

"Yes. All your friends feel for you." The formal expression of sympathy on Lady Bradford's face changed to one of curiosity. "Surely you're not planning to ask Mrs. Manning to paint your portrait? I assure you that she only paints females and young children."

Jerrold thought fast. Certainly he wanted no speculation about his reasons for associating with Zoë Manning. He smiled at Lady Bradford, saying carelessly, "Well, yes, I did know that Mrs. Manning specializes in painting females and children, but I've heard so many favorable comments about her skills that I determined to try my luck and ask her to do my portrait."

Lady Bradford laughed. "You may try, Lord Woodforde, but I doubt you'll succeed. I don't think she's ever painted a gentleman." She knit her brows. "Perhaps I can help. Why don't you come to dinner tonight? Mrs. Manning has already accepted the invitation. It's not a large party. The Season hasn't started yet, and London is still thin of company. In a small group you can talk more intimately, and you may be able to persuade Mrs. Manning to do your portrait."

"Why, thank you, Lady Bradford. I'd be delighted."

"Until this evening, then."

As Lady Bradford went out the door of the suite, the young receptionist emerged from the inner room. She seemed faintly embarrassed. She said in her marked country accent, "I'm very sorry, my lord, but Mrs. Manning won't be able to see ye. As I told ye, she's very busy."

"Yes, I appreciate that. On the other hand, I have something rather important to discuss with her. I'd be very willing to wait until the she finished her appointments today. Or perhaps I might visit her this evening? Or tomorrow or the next day. I believe Mrs. Manning plans to be in London for several days."

Looking harassed, the girl said, "I spoke to Mrs. Manning about an appointment to see ye at some other time, but she said her schedule was completely filled for the rest of her stay in London. I'm that sorry, my lord."

"I, too." Jerrold smiled at the girl. "I'm sure you did your best for me. Goodbye."

As Jerrold left the suite, he wondered ironically what Zoë Manning's reactions would be when she saw him that evening in Lady Bradford's drawing room.

Chapter Five

Zoë stood on her balcony, gazing abstractedly at the luxuriant greenery of the park opposite the hotel. Her mind was chaotic. She thought she'd escaped Jerrold Layton's unwelcome presence by coming to London, but only moments ago she'd learned that her nemesis was still pursing her. Meg Brant, the young rectory servant whom she'd brought with her as a combined chaperon and assistant, had told her that Jerrold Layton was even then sitting in her reception room, demanding to see her.

Perhaps her luck had simply run out, she thought. In the last seven years she'd managed to salvage her life from the consequences of the disastrous elopement to Gretna Green. She'd successfully concealed the experience from friends and family, she'd arranged for Philip a believable legitimacy, and she'd been able to assure him a secure life with her painting. Now a series of unfortunate coincidences had combined to threaten the existence she had painstakingly stitched together. Lady Rosedale's husband had died on the Continent, and so she had come home at last to Cumberland. Jerrold Layton had then paid his first visit to Merefield Park in many years. And on one unlucky afternoon he had just happened to encounter Philip on the road.

Disturbing Zoë's bitter thougths, Meg Brant poked her head around the doorway to announce, "Mrs. Braddock and her son are here for their sitting, ma'am."

"Send them in." Her jaw set, Zoë left the balcony and went to her easel. She wouldn't allow Jerrold Layton to interfere with her work. Nor would she, in the end, allow him to invade her privacy. He couldn't force her to receive him . If she simply continued her refusals to see him, he might well grow tired of his attempts and leave her alone.

"You look lovely, ma'am," offered Meg Brant as she watched Zoë complete her toilet by fastening a fillet of green ribbon in her hair, arranged *à la Grecque,* with curls in the front and ringlets falling behind.

"Thank you." Zoë glanced down at her gown of white lace over a green satin slip. She knew it was becoming, and she stifled a slight feeling of guilt over its purchase. It had been expensive, but then she so seldom bought any new clothes for herself. She could certainly afford one new gown.

As she took the shawl of Indian worsted that Meg was holding out to her and draped it around her shoulders, Zoë was suddenly conscious of a feeling of anticipation for the evening ahead at Lady Bradford's house. Her social life in Heathfield was very quiet, restricted to an occasional small dinner at the home of Mrs. Randolph or another of the neighbors. A London dinner party would be a real event.

Accompanied by Meg, Zoë rode in a hackney cab the short distance from the hotel to St. James's Square. The cab circled the equestrian statue of William III in the center of the square and paused before a substantial red-brick house, where Meg was whisked away by a footman to spend the evening in the servants' hall. Another footman escorted Zoë to the drawing room, where Lady Bradford came forward to take her hand and lead her around the small circle of perhaps twenty guests to introduce her.

"And here, my dear, is someone who is *most* anxious to meet you," said Lady Bradford with a bright smile. "Mrs. Manning, may I present Lord Woodforde?"

Zoë stared into Jerrold Layton's intensely blue eyes and said between stiff lips, "How do you do." Apparently Lady Bradford didn't know that she and Woodforde were already acquainted, and Zoë chose not to enlighten her.

"I'm enchanted to meet you, Mrs. Manning," said Woodforde. "I'm a great admirer of your painting. Won't you sit here with me so we can chat?"

Trapped, thought Zoë, trying to curb her panic. She glanced around helplessly, but there seemed to be no way of refusing the offered chair without creating a scene. She sat down.

Woodforde smiled at her—a smile, Zoë noticed, that didn't quite meet his eyes. He was looking impossibly handsome this evening in his impeccably tailored black coat and breeches, elaborately tied cravat, and white silk stockings and slippers. He looked, as a matter of fact, very much as he had looked on that fatal evening seven years ago. Zoë's heart felt like a stone in her breast.

"You're so phenomenally busy, Mrs. Manning, that I was beginning to despair of ever having the opportunity to speak to you," said the earl smoothly. "So, when Lady Bradford mentioned you would be her guest this evening, I was delighted to accept her dinner invitation."

Zoë glanced across the room at her hostess's good-natured face and narrowly suppressed a murderous urge to scratch out Lady Bradford's eyes. She turned her attention back to the earl and, out of desperation, made a frontal attack. "Well, for what it's worth, Lord Woodforde, you've achieved your goal. Here I am. What did you wish to speak to me about?"

Seemingly taken aback for a moment, he said, lowering his voice, "Er—actually, what I wish to discuss is—is of a somewhat delicate nature."

Zoë looked him straight in the eye. "Frankly, I find it hard to believe that you and I could have anything of a delicate nature to discuss."

Woodforde had recovered his composure. "Oh, I think we do, Mrs. Manning. Perhaps, if we can find a private moment to speak together later in the evening, I can explain the matter to you."

Zoë gave him a noncommittal look and changed the subject. "What a lovely room," she observed, gazing around her. "Lady Bradford has splendid taste."

She had no intention of spending a private moment alone with Jerrold Layton. No, the Earl of Woodforde. She might as well start thinking of him as the earl. He'd cornered her at last with Lady Bradford's help, but she could still retrieve the situation. For a moment she toyed with the notion of falling suddenly ill. She shook her head mentally. It wouldn't do. Very likely Woodforde would gallantly insist on escorting her to her hotel. No, she should simply remain on her guard, refusing any attempt by Woodforde to speak to her privately, and she would leave Bradford House immediately after dinner, pleading a sudden headache.

For most of the evening her plan seemed to be succeeding, though Woodforde remained pinned to her side before dinner, causing her extreme discomfort by his questions and comments about Philip and her life in Heathfield.

"Your son is recovered, I trust, from his accident?" Woodforde inquired politely.

"Yes, quite."

"Splendid. He's a fine-looking child. He doesn't much resemble you or your brother. Does he take his looks from his father?"

Zoë clenched her hands together in her lap and quickly unclenched them, hoping that the earl hadn't noticed the telltale movement. On the surface the earl's question sounded so innocuous. If any of the other guests had heard it, they would have assumed he was merely being polite. But she understood perfectly. Woodforde was trying to throw her off balance.

Keeping her voice calm, she replied, "Why, yes, Philip does resemble his father. He looks like all the Mannings. My husband once told me that most members of his family have blue eyes and dark hair."

The earl raised an eyebrow "Really? I understand physical traits do run in families. Mrs. Manning, my cousin, Lady Rosedale, told me your late husband was an American. Where in the colonies did he hail from?"

If Woodforde had hoped to disconcert her, Zoë was prepared for him. She and Cousin Augusta had worked out a complete biography for David Manning. "My husband's people live in Massachusetts, near the city of Boston," she said composedly. "Incidentally, Lord Woodforde, Massachusetts isn't a colony any longer. It's part of the new United States."

"Of course it is." The earl grimaced. "That was a real

slip of the tongue. As a member of the House of Commons until recently, I assure you that I'm very much aware that we're at war with the new United States."

If Zoë thought she had finally scored a point against the earl, her satisfaction was short-lived. A moment later Woodforde remarked, "My memory must be failing me prematurely. I thought I was meeting you for the first time several weeks ago when I had the privilege of helping your son that day on the road near Heathfield. But my cousin Melicent has assured me that you and I actually met some years ago at a ball at Merefield Park. She says she introduced us to each other."

Steady, Zoë told herself. "Lady Rosedale thinks we met at a ball at Merefield Park?" she asked with an air of polite surprise. She paused, as if she were thinking deeply. "I did attend a ball at Merefield Park some years ago," she mused. "I'm trying to recall . . . why, of course." She gave him a friendly nod. "I remember now. Lady Rosedale was quite right. She did introduce us, and you asked me to dance."

"I don't remember meeting you at all," Woodforde blurted. The words seemed to slip out involuntarily.

"That's quite understandable. At the time I was a most uninteresting sixteen-year-old. It was my first ball. Why should you remember me?"

Before Woodforde could reply, the butler announced dinner, and Zoë felt a stab of annoyance when she discovered that Lady Bradford had seated her and the earl together at the table. During dinner, however, she was able to relax a little, because good manners prevented Woodforde from talking exclusively to her. Nevertheless, at the end of the elaborate meal she sighed with relief when Lady Bradford gathered the ladies with her eyes and rose to lead the way out of the dining room, leaving the gentlemen to their port.

Detaining her hostess at the door of the drawing room, Zoë said, "Dear Lady Bradford, it's been such an enjoyable evening, but I fear I must ask you to excuse me now. I've suddenly developed a dreadful headache. Will you ask one of your servants to engage a hackney cab for me?"

Lady Bradford's face fell. "Must you really leave so early? Well, of course you must, if you have the headache. However, I won't hear of a hackney cab. I'll send you home in my carriage. While you're waiting for the horses to be put to, won't you come to the library? My heart was quite set on showing you a set of miniatures that have been in my husband's family for many years. They're quite exquisite, but only a painter like yourself could really appreciate them."

"Certainly. I'd love to see the miniatures." As Lady Bradford led the way to the library, Zoë's spirits lifted. A few more minutes and this interminable evening would be over. She would be out of danger from the Earl of Woodforde, who was at the moment safely pent up, guzzling port with his host and the other gentlemen.

Bending over to examine the miniatures, which had been arranged under the glass on a pedestal table, Zoë heard the door of the library open behind her and turned, saying, "The carriage is ready—" She broke off with a gasp. The earl stood in the doorway. He shut the door behind him and advanced toward her.

"Now, Mrs. Manning, thanks to Lady Bradford's good offices, we can have the talk that you've been evading for so long." His voice was harsh.

"I have nothing to say to you," she snapped, and

headed for the door. He placed his hand on her arm as she attempted to pass him, and forced her to face him.

"Let me go," she said sharply.

He shook his head. "I'm sorry. You don't leave this room until you give me the information I want."

"What information is that? It must be a matter of life and death to you, to cause you to lose all the instincts of a gentleman."

Zoë's scornful words had no effect on Woodforde. His handsome face set, he said quietly, "I want to know if your son Philip is also my son."

Though she had lived in dread for weeks about the direction in which Jerrold Layton's suspicions seemed to be leading him, the moment of confrontation came as an excruciating shock to Zoë. Between stiff lips she barely managed to say, "That's an insulting thing to say, Lord Woodforde. My son's father is David Manning."

"I don't think so." Maintaining his hold on her arm, he went on, "When I met your son, I was reminded of a picture that has hung in the drawing room of my family's London house for many years, a portrait of me and my brother Trevor with my mother. Your son bears an extraordinary resemblance to me at about the same age."

"That's sheer coincidence, and hardly a reason to insult me like this!"

"A coincidence? Yes, possibly. Perhaps even probably. However, my cousin informed me that some years ago you and I met at a ball at Merefield Park, on an evening that remains a complete blank in my memory. I was drunk, disgustingly so. I make no excuses for my behavior. The next morning I awoke in an inn in Gretna Green, a few miles from Merefield Park, in the company of a young woman who was a stranger to me.

Were you that woman, Mrs. Manning? And if you were, did you later discover you were pregnant with my child?"

Zoë felt a wave of hot crimson flood her cheeks. "No—no. How can you speak to me like this?"

A muscle twitched in his cheek. "I'm sorry," he said again. "If this wasn't so important to me . . . Mrs. Manning, believe me, long before this I would have concluded that my fancies about your son Philip were just that, pure fancies, if you hadn't started avoiding me. You repeatedly refused to see me in Heathfield. This afternoon your servant told me that you abruptly moved up the date of your visit to London by a full month, in what I can conceive as a further effort to avoid talking to me. Today at your hotel you again refused to receive me. Lady Bradford tells me you were about to leave her house this evening before the gentlemen joined the ladies in the drawing room."

Drawing a ragged breath, Zoë said, "Has it occurred to you that I might have taken an instant dislike to you and had no wish to be in your company?"

"A possibility, certainly," Woodforde agreed, "but it didn't explain the rudeness, in a lady of your sensibilities, with which you refused my attempts to visit you." His expression hardened. "Enough of this. It's struck me as highly convenient that David Manning is dead, and that, moreover, he was a foreigner with no kin in England. This is the man you claim is the father of a child who closely resembles me, and who is approximately the right age for me to have fathered him on the night of the Merefield Park ball so many years ago. Did David Manning even exist? We can settle the matter easily. Show me your marriage lines."

"How dare you make such an outrageous request?" Zoë flared. "I think you must be mad."

"If you won't show me your marriage lines, you force me into further intrusion on your privacy. I'll write to David Manning's family in Massachusetts for confirmation of the marriage. That is, if such a family actually exists."

"You can't do that," Zoë blurted. "The United States is at war with England. You can't communicate with Massachusetts."

Woodforde smiled thinly. "You forget, I think, that until I succeeded to the earldom I was a member of the House of Commons. I have friends in the Foreign Secretary's office. They can make inquiries for me, they can send letters, through the embassies of countries that are *not* at war with the United States."

Her knees suddenly weak, Zoë felt herself swaying. She'd fought for so long, and so hard, and now, as a result of Jerrold Layton's relentless probing, she had reached the end of her tether.

"Here—sit down. You look ill." Woodforde guided her to a chair. He stood staring down at her, his expression of concern giving way to a faint smile of triumph. "I don't want to press you unduly, Mrs. Manning, but are you now prepared to tell me the truth about Philip?"

Zoë looked up into that handsome, assured face, and his expression of triumph suddenly made her backbone stiffen. "You want the truth?" she said defiantly. "I'll give it to you. Yes, you're Philip's father. That night at the Merefield ball you convinced an incredibly naive sixteen-year-old girl that you loved her and wanted to marry her, and you eloped with her across the border to Gretna Green. Philip was born nine months later."

The earl's eyes widened. "You say we eloped? Does that mean . . . ?"

"It means we went through a marriage ceremony, yes. Oh, unlike so many vulgar couples before us, we weren't married by the tollhouse keeper at the Gretna Green bridge. As a clergyman's daughter, I insisted on the services of a clergyman."

Even before the words were out of her mouth, Zoë had seen the pitfall into which she had fallen. By admitting there had been a ceremony, she was in danger of giving herself over into Woodforde's hands. She clamped her lips firmly together.

"Oh, my God." The color drained from the earl's face. He sat down abruptly in a chair opposite her. He stammered, "But this means that Philip is not only my son, he's my legitimate son. He's the heir to Woodforde. In heaven's name, why didn't you tell me about this marriage years ago?"

In a voice as frigid as the icy cold that was spreading over her body, Zoë said, "When you awoke that morning in the inn at Gretna Green, you assumed I was a lightskirt you'd hired for the evening. As a matter of fact, you offered me a handsome payment. Under those circumstances I think you can understand why I didn't inform you about the marriage. I wanted only to get away from you and Gretna Green as soon as possible. I never wanted to see or hear from you again. I hated you more than I've ever hated anyone, before or since."

"God . . ." The earl buried his face in his hands for a long moment. Then he looked up, saying, "I don't fault you for feeling as you did. I treated you shamefully. Nothing can excuse my behavior. But after you discovered you were increasing . . ."

Zoë's voice had grown even colder. "I still wanted

nothing to do with you. I didn't want my child to have a father like you. I gave Philip a name and a background, I was able to support him adequately. I didn't need you."

Though he still looked shaken, the earl began speaking in a calm, reasonable tone. "As I told you, I understand why, at the time, you felt and acted as you did. But surely you must now see that you also acted unwisely. You and I were legally married. We had a son who is my legitimate heir. You simply ignored those facts, you brushed them under the carpet. We can't go on doing that. I'll immediately acknowledge you as my wife, and Philip as my son."

"You'll do nothing of the kind." Rising, Zoë stared down at the earl, saying, "If you make any such announcement I'll deny everything I told you tonight, and you have no way of proving the truth of what you say. I meant what I said. I want nothing to do with you, now or in the future. I don't want Philip ever to know that you're his father. Good night, Lord Woodforde."

Zoë stalked out of the library.

Chapter Six

As the carriage rolled to a stop in front of the gate, a small boy erupted out of the front door of the rectory. He reached the carriage just as the coachman handed Zoë down the steps.

"Mama! You're home at last. I thought you'd never come back."

Bending to hug her son, Zoë exclaimed, laughing, "Oh, what a bouncer, Philip. You *knew* I was coming back. I told you I'd be gone ten days, and here I am in Heathfield, exactly ten days from the time I left."

Philip grinned at his mother. "It seemed *much* longer than that. I missed you, Mama."

Hugging Philip again, Zoë said fervently, "I missed you too, every minute I was away." As she took his hand and began walking toward the house, she shivered at the thought of how empty her homecoming would have been without Philip's eager welcoming presence, of how empty future homecomings might be if she allowed the Earl of Woodforde any share in Philip's life.

Edmund was waiting to greet her in the foyer. "Welcome home," he said with an affectionate smile. "Did the carriage meet you on time in Carlisle?"

"Indeed, yes. The moment Meg and I stepped down from the mail coach, we saw the rectory carriage waiting."

'I still think you should have gone to London by post chaise. Fifty hours each way in a mail coach must have been very wearying."

"So it was. I think I've developed a permanent crick in my back from sitting still for so long," said Zoë ruefully. "But traveling by the mail was much cheaper than a post chaise would have been. Remember, Edmund, I have school fees to think of next year." She turned to Philip. "I know you're dying to ask, love, and the answer is yes, of course, I brought you something from London."

"What did you bring me, Mama?" Philip's blue eyes sparkled with anticipation.

"A box of sweetmeats from Gunther's, and some books, and fabric to make you new clothes, because you're shooting up like a weed and outgrowing every garment you own, and a game of draughts. I think you're old enough to learn to play draughts, and your Uncle Edmund is a dab person at the game. He'll teach you."

"Today, Uncle Edmund?" said Philip eagerly.

"Well, if not today, then tomorrow," the rector replied, smiling.

Zoë had no opportunity to talk to her brother privately until later that evening. She sat with Philip while he had his supper and read him a bedtime story, and she chatted impersonally with Edmund over a simple supper until the servants retired from the dining room, leaving brother and sister to drink their coffee together.

Edmund gave Zoë a keen glance over his coffee cup. "I wish I could say you look in prime twig, my dear, but

I can't. You seem a trifle hagged. Didn't your trip go well?"

"Oh, yes. It was a very successful trip. I have more new commissions that I can easily deal with. I'll have to work very hard to complete them."

Edmund raised an eyebrow. "Well, then?"

"Well, what?"

Falling silent for a moment, Edmund said at last, seemingly at a tangent, "Zoë, the Earl of Woodforde came to see me the day after you left for London. He asked me where you would be staying, and I could think of no reason, short of actual rudeness, not to tell him. Shortly afterwards I heard that he had left Merefield Park to return to London. Did he come to visit you there?"

"Yes, he did."

"And?"

Zoë's lip curled. "I refused to see him, of course. Finally he cornered me at a dinner party. For the life of me, I don't understand how it happened, but somehow he inveigled me into telling him about the Gretna Green ceremony." Zoë shook her head, saying bitterly. "How could I have been so weak—so stupid?"

"May I remind you that you were simply telling the truth?" At Zoë's resentful look, Edmund hastened to add, "How did the earl receive the news of the ceremony?"

"He told me he intended to acknowledge the marriage and the fact that Philip was his heir."

Edmund's face relaxed in an expression of sheer relief. "Thank God," he murmured. "You and the earl are doing the right thing, the only possible thing."

"No, we aren't. Not if you mean that I'm going to allow Woodforde to claim Philip as his son. I told the earl that, if he made a move to acknowledge Philip, I would deny there was ever a legal ceremony of marriage. Let him deal with that if he can."

Throwing up his hands, Edmund exclaimed, "Zoë, you're making such a great mistake. At some point you simply must deal realistically with this situation between you and the Earl of Woodforde."

Zoë pushed aside her coffee cup and rose from the table. "If I'm making a mistake, please remember that it's *my* mistake, and I'll deal with the consequences. Good night, Edmund."

Feeling mildly ashamed of herself—she'd been rude, taking out her fears and frustrations on her long-suffering brother—Zoë walked slowly up the stairs. She looked into Philip's room, reassuring herself that he was soundly asleep, and then went to her own bedchamber. There she stood at her window for some time, gazing blindly down at the village street in the gathering spring twilight.

For so long, her only aim in life had been to safeguard the future of the little boy sleeping so peacefully in the adjoining room. Until a few weeks ago, she'd considered herself successful. Then Jerrold Layton had re-entered the picture, and though she'd blocked his attempt last week in London to claim Philip, the doubts were creeping in. Was Edmund right? At some point would it be necessary for her to have a final decisive struggle with the Earl of Woodforde?

"Look, Mama. The black lamb has grown twice as big as he was before you went off to London."

"Well, I don't know that he's grown quite that much, but he's certainly bigger," Zoë agreed as she stood beside Philip gazing over the stone fence at the sheep grazing in the field. She drew a deep, pleasure-filled breath. It was so good to resume her late afternoon walks with Philip after her absence in London. In addition, the late April sun shone with a delightful warmth, her painting that day had gone very well, and during the preceding night she'd succeeded in pushing to the back of her mind her nagging fears about the future. After all, here she was, back in the security of her ordered life in Heathfield, and her nemesis, the Earl of Woodforde, was far off in London, where he couldn't do any harm.

"Good afternoon, Mrs. Manning, Philip."

At the sound of the earl's voice, Zoë whirled about, her eyes wide with shock. He cantered up to them and dismounted, leading his horse as he walked over to them. He touched his hat.

"Good afternoon," Zoë said between stiff lips. Innate good manners carried her over the moment, as well as a desire to prevent any signs of strain from becoming evident to her son. "Philip, you remember Lord Woodforde, I'm sure."

"You let me ride your horse," said Philip with a longing glance at the earl's mount.

Woodforde flashed the child an understanding smile. "Would you like to ride again today? Here we go." He lifted Philip into the saddle. "You know what to do. Just hold on to the pommel. That's it. You're doing splendidly, Philip. You'll be a rider in no time at all." Slowly the earl began leading the horse down the road.

Walking beside him, Zoë said in a low voice, "I thought you were still in London."

"I had more important concerns to take care of here in Heathfield," the earl replied calmly.

Zoë bit her lip.

The earl went on, "Philip seems very interested in riding. Have you thought of giving him lessons?"

Knowing that Philip was listening, Zoë tried to keep the resentment out of her tone. "Not at the present time. Philip and I live on my earnings from portrait work. My income doesn't extend to keeping riding horses."

"Perhaps, if you'll allow me, I might be of some help there—"

Zoë cut him off. "I thank you, Lord Woodforde, but I must decline your help."

The earl shrugged without replying. They had reached the rectory gate by this time, and the earl lifted Philip down from his perch. "Until next time, lad," Woodforde said, smiling.

"I hope there will be a next time," Philip replied shyly. "Thank you, sir—my lord. Goodbye."

Watching as Philip scampered up the path to the door, Zoë drew a deep breath and said to the earl, "There won't be a next time. I can't prevent you from visiting your cousin in Heathfield, but I insist that you stop accosting me and Philip."

Woodforde raised an eyebrow. "The public roads are free to everyone."

"Then you force me to deprive my son of healthful exercise in the open air. For now on you won't encounter us on the 'public roads.' Good day, my lord."

As Zoë turned to go, the earl said, "One moment. We haven't finished our conversation."

Facing him, Zoë said with a cold finality, "We've finished as far as I'm concerned. A few days ago in London I told you I wouldn't allow you to claim you were Philip's father, even if I had to deny that an elopement to Gretna Green had ever taken place. I meant what I said. It's my last word on the subject. You may as well return to London."

Beneath the brim of the beaver hat the blue eyes blazed angrily. "Your pardon, my dear, but I haven't said *my* last word. Philip is my legitimate heir. If you won't permit me to acknowledge him and provide for his future, I'll go to the law. Will you enjoy standing in the dock? Are you prepared to commit perjury by denying the truth of Philip's paternity?"

"You wouldn't do such a thing. . . . You have no proof of any claim," said Zoë in a strangled half-whisper.

"By the time we get to court, I'll have investigated your putative husband, David Manning. I believe his purely imaginary status might constitute proof of a sort. I'll have gone up to Gretna Green to look for the clergyman you say married us. If I find him, and if he kept a register of his clients, that will be proof. And I intend to call the Reverend Edmund Bennett as a witness. I think your brother knows all about our elopement to Scotland. I suspect a clergyman of his standing might be reluctant to support his sister's cause by committing perjury."

The earl swung himself into the saddle and sat looking at Zoë with hostile eyes. "Think about it, Zoë Manning. If you make it necessary for me to go to court, and I then win my case, I'll take Philip away from you. I'll be staying with my cousin for the next few days. If you come to see reason, you can communicate with me at Merefield Park." He touched his hand in a brief, curt gesture to his hat, and trotted off.

In her sitting room that evening after dinner, Lady Rosedale poured a cup of coffee and handed it to her cousin, saying with a quizzical smile, "Delighted as I am to welcome you back to Merefield Park, Jerry, I must confess that I'm a little puzzled to see you here again so soon. When you left here to return to London, I had the distinct impression that you intended to plunge into your new duties in the House of Lords. Is there some attraction for you in the wilds of Cumberland that I'm unaware of?"

Woodforde sipped his coffee. "Come now, Melicent, you know you've always been a prime attraction for me. I enjoy your company."

The countess's eyes twinkled. "And I yours. I did notice, however, that you didn't press me very hard to go riding with you this afternoon."

Setting down his coffee cup, the earl said ruefully, "I never could keep anything secret from you, could I? I remember how you inveigled me into telling you how I stole a kiss from Lady Anne Somerset in her father's conservatory. How old were we when that happened? Fourteen, fifteen, no more." He sighed. "You're right. I didn't come back here merely to enjoy the pleasure of your company."

"Do you want to talk about it?" Melicent added hastily, "Don't, if you'd rather not."

Falling silent for a few moments, Woodforde said at last, "No, I think I'd like to talk about it. I'm confused, Melicent. I have a problem, and I really don't know how to solve it." He paused, gazing at his cousin's sympathetic face as he tried to formulate his thoughts. Finally he said abruptly, "There's something you don't know about me. I can't have children."

The countess looked aghast. She faltered, "Jerry, how can that be, how do you know . . . ?"

Briefly he explained about his bout of illness with the mumps.

"But that means . . ."

Woodforde nodded. "Until I few weeks ago I was convinced that Oliver would succeed me, if I didn't outlive him. The thought crucifies me. He's a disaster of a human being."

"Until a few weeks ago . . .?"

"Melicent, I've just discovered I have a son, a son I believe to be legitimate." At the countess's look of blank amazement, Woodforde went on: "You told me recently that I met and danced with Zoë Bennett years ago at a ball here at Merefield Park. I still don't remember meeting her. In fact, I don't remember anything about that evening. I was too drunk. But Mrs. Manning has admitted to me that she and I eloped to Gretna Green that night and were married. Nine months later she bore my son."

"Jerry! You and Zoë Manning! I can't believe . . . do *you* believe her story? Have you seen the marriage lines?"

"Yes, I believe her. No, I haven't seen the marriage lines. Perhaps there aren't any. I understand that in Scotland you can contract a valid marriage merely by declaring your intent, with or without witnesses. A parson performing a ceremony may or may not give the couple a certificate, or record the marriage in a private register."

Frowning, Melicent said, "But . . . if there really was a ceremony, why did she keep the marriage secret? Why, at the very least, didn't she come to you when she discovered she was increasing?"

Staring down at his clasped hands, Woodforde said in a low voice, "She had her reasons." After a pause he looked up, his face strained, and told Melicent how, awakening on the morning after the elopement with no recollection of what had happened, he'd assumed that Zoë was a lightskirt, hired for the night. "Mrs. Manning, who apparently had taken part in the elopement in good faith, was outraged to learn that I'd taken her for a prostitute. She left Gretna Green never wanting to see me or hear from me again. All she wanted to do was to forget I'd ever touched her life. She hated me. She still does."

Melicent's expression altered. "Oh, Jerry. That poor child," she murmured. "She was like a wounded animal, I think, creeping away to recover in solitude. I really can't find it in me to blame her for concealing the marriage from you. However, she shouldn't have married that fellow Manning. Why, that made her a bigamist!"

"I'm convinced there never was a second husband. Mrs. Manning simply invented him to give her child a name. And I don't blame her, either, for acting as she did. I blame myself. All I want is to put the situation right. Unfortunately, Zoë Manning still hates me so much that she won't allow me to acknowledge little Philip as my son."

Woodforde stared at his cousin, misery in his eyes. "I'll tell you frankly, I'm at my wit's end. I'm sterile. Philip is the only child I will ever have. I want to claim him as my heir. His mother won't let me. So today I told her that I was prepared to go to law for custody of the boy."

Melicent flushed with indignation. "Jerry! How could you? I know how I'd feel if someone threatened to take away my son. Mrs. Manning is a wonderful mother. She adores that little boy."

"Well, then, what do you suggest I do? Help me, Melicent. Philip is my son, too. I can't lose him."

The countess eyed her cousin compassionately. "I don't know. . . . Perhaps I could talk to Mrs. Manning's brother. The Reverend Bennett has always seemed to me to be a sensible sort of man."

Zoë stared at the blank canvas. She'd been sitting in front of her easel since midmorning—it was now close to noon—and in all that time she hadn't touched brush to canvas. It was as if both her mind and her hand had been paralyzed by her brooding thoughts about Jerrold Layton's chilling pronouncement of the day before. He'd threatened to take Philip away from her. She would fight him to the death before she would give Philip up, of course, but . . . was there even a possibility that he could make good his threat?

She turned away from the easel as Edmund entered the studio after a perfunctory knock.

"Zoë, I've just had a visitor," he said. "It was Lady Rosedale. Lord Woodforde has taken her into his confidence about your—your problem. She agrees with me that something must be done to resolve this impasse. She's invited both of us to come to Merefield Park this afternoon to discuss the situation."

Zoë recoiled. "I won't go. There's no need to 'discuss the situation.' I've told you—I've told Woodforde—that I refuse to allow any connection between him and Philip. I mean it. Nothing will ever change my mind." She glared at Edmund. "Do you have any idea of what kind of a man the earl really is? Yesterday he threatened to institute proceedings in a court of law to take Philip away from me. And you want me to have a discussion with him?"

"It just proves my point, that matters are going from bad to worse," Edmund exclaimed in dismay. His face hardened. "I'm sorry, Zoë. I can't support you unconditionally any longer. I've provided a home for you for many years, partly because I've felt it was my Christian duty to do so, mostly because I love you, and I love Philip. But if you become embroiled in a notorious court case over Philip's paternity, you must see that I couldn't allow you to remain at the rectory. I would be obliged to disown you. A clergyman must be like Caesar's wife. His family life must be beyond reproach."

Almost speechless from shock, Zoë stared at Edmund. Could this grim-faced man be the good-natured, affectionate brother who had always come to her aid when she needed him? Then she noticed that the fingers of his hand were knotted so tightly together that his knuckles showed white. She guessed that his threat to sever their family ties by banishing her and Philip from the rectory was simply a bluff, designed to force her to reconsider her position. On the other hand, the very fact that he'd been impelled to deliver his ultimatum was proof of how strongly he felt about the situation.

She drew a deep breath. "I don't want you to think I'm totally unreasonable. Yes, I'll go with you to Merefield Park this afternoon. I promise to listen to what the Earl of Woodforde has to say. I *don't* promise to change my mind about allowing Jerrold Layton to claim paternity rights over my son."

"That's fair enough, Zoë. That's all Lady Rosedale and I are asking of you: to listen to Lord Woodforde."

Trying to appear as usual, Zoë sat with Philip while he ate his lunch in the nursery, and later she shared a largely silent luncheon with Edmund. Then it was time to put on her bonnet and pelisse and climb into the rectory carriage with Edmund for the drive to Merefield Park.

Lady Rosedale and Woodforde rose as the footman ushered Zoë and Edmund into the drawing room. The countess flashed brother and sister a rather strained smile and murmured a greeting. The earl crossed the room to Zoë. His face looked drawn, and she felt a fleeting sense of satisfaction. Apparently he wasn't finding the situation easy, either. He said in a low voice, "I wasn't sure you would come."

"I came because my brother asked me to do so. Edmund thought you had the right to a hearing."

"Well . . . I thank you. Won't you sit down?"

Edmund took a seat beside Lady Rosedale on a sofa, but Zoë, glancing about her, deliberately chose a chair some distance away. After a brief hesitation, Woodforde sat down near his cousin and Edmund. Gazing at the three of them, seated so closely together, looking at her with a concentrated attention, Zoë had the uncomfortable sensation that she was facing, all alone, a disapproving jury of her peers. Her backbone stiffened. She might be outnumbered three to one, but she wasn't going to be cowed.

For several moments no one spoke. The silence deepened. Finally Woodforde cleared his throat. "I want to start by saying something I should have said long go. Zoë—Mrs. Manning—I accept full responsibility for what happened at that ball so many years ago. I was dead drunk, but that doesn't excuse me. I took advantage of a very young and innocent girl. And I don't blame you for your later actions. When you invented an imaginary marriage to Manning, I'm sure you thought you were protecting yourself and your child in the only way open to you."

Zoë felt a cold anger rising within her. Oh, she knew what he was about. He was so devious. By admitting his faults, by expressing his regret for his actions on that long ago, disastrous night, he was hoping to soften her opposition to his demands. She stared at him without replying, her lips pressed stubbornly together.

He shrugged. Obviously his apology hadn't achieved the reaction he'd hoped for, but he went on, speaking calmly. "The issue of blame isn't really what concerns us here, however. Zoë—Mrs. Manning—you told me that we eloped to Gretna Green and were married. I believe you. In that case you and I are still legally married. Philip is my legitimate son. However much you may dislike those facts, they happen to be realities. You—we—can't change what happened. We can only deal with the consequences."

Despite herself, listening to the earl's quiet, reasoned voice, Zoë for the first time in seven long years began to feel the bonds of her denial loosen. From the beginning, in her desperation, she'd convinced herself that no real marriage had taken place in Gretna Green. She'd continued to strengthen her feelings of denial with the story, which, over time, she'd virtually come to believe, that she was truly Mrs. David Manning, and Philip was his son. Now, in a sudden flash of insight, she felt impelled to confront the reality of which Woodforde had spoken.

Her warring, indecisive feelings must have been reflected in her face. Lady Rosedale said quietly, "Jerry hasn't mentioned this, Mrs. Manning, but have you considered that the Gretna Green ceremony has made it impossible for either of you to marry anyone else?"

"I have no intention of getting married," Zoë snapped.

"All well and good," Lady Rosedale replied. "But supposing Jerry wanted to marry? He'd be committing bigamy, unless he obtained an annulment or a divorce. That's scarcely fair to him, is it? In any case, whatever his marital situation, little Philip would still remain his first-born son and his heir."

Edmund joined the attack. "I think you're forgetting something else, Zoë. Before very long you may find it difficult to maintain the fiction that you married an American. Lord Woodforde, as a member of Parliament, will know more about this than I do, of course, but I believe there will be a meeting of American and English commissioners sometime soon to negotiate a treaty ending the war with the United States."

Woodforde nodded. "The negotiations will take place in August, I believe."

"There you are, Zoë," Edmund commented. "Before very long, communications will open between England and America. People may start wondering why you don't receive visits or letters from Philip's father's family."

Zoë's shoulders slumped. "Very well," she said. "I give in. I concede that Lord Woodforde should recognize Philip as his legitimate son and heir."

The three other people in the room looked dumbstruck, too paralyzed by surprise to answer immediately.

"Thank God," Lady Rosedale said at last.

"Yes, thank God," Edmund agreed fervently.

His voice betraying his relief, the earl said, "Thank *you*, Zoë. You've done the right thing."

Zoë gave him a long look. "Perhaps so," she said

somberly. "I wonder, though, if you'll still think the same when the scandal breaks."

"Scandal?" he questioned.

"Yes, scandal. What will your friends in the *ton* think—for that matter, what will my friends in the neighborhood of Heathfield think—when you suddenly announce that, far from being a bachelor, you've been married for seven years, and your son and heir has been living in the rectory of St. Bride's under the name of Philip Manning?"

Lady Rosedale drew a quick breath. "I hadn't thought . . . Jerry, Mrs. Manning is right. The gossip—"

"Hang the gossip," the earl exclaimed defiantly. "My private life, and yours, Zoë, are none of the public's affair. I will simply say that you and I had a falling out soon after our secret marriage in Scotland, and you chose to live quietly apart from me under an assumed name. That is still your preference, but from now on you will rear Philip as my acknowledged heir."

Shaking her head, Lady Rosedale said to Woodforde, "I fear that won't be good enough. If Zoë and little Philip continue to live at the rectory under the name of Manning, there will always be people who won't believe your secret marriage actually took place. Philip's claim to your name would be clouded. No, Jerry. You must do more than acknowledge that Philip is your son and heir. You and Zoë must live together as the Earl and Countess of Woodforde."

"No!" Zoë exclaimed sharply.

The earl looked dazed.

Lady Rosedale pressed her arguments. "I'm not talking about a real marriage. It would be one in name only. Both of you could continue to live separate lives while residing under the same roof. I'm sure Jerry can name many couples among his acquaintance who have such an arrangement! But by sacrificing your personal inclinations to some extent, you could ensure that Philip would grow up without a hint of scandal as the future Earl of Woodforde."

The countess eyed the earl and Zoë challengingly. "Well? Zoë, I presume that Philip's welfare is the most important consideration in your life. Jerry, I know that you believe your principal duty is to provide an heir for your family line. Won't both of you do what's best for Philip?"

After a long moment Woodforde said with a dragging reluctance, "I think you're right, Melicent. The gossip would be too damaging if Philip remained at the rectory." He looked at Zoë. "For our son's sake I'm willing to set up household with you."

Zoë fought an agonizing inner battle, her hatred and resentment of Woodforde warring against her love for her son. She looked beseechingly at her brother. "Edmund? What do you think I should do?"

"My dear, I can't decide for you. I think you know that you should act according to Philip's best interests," said Edmund.

For a little while longer Zoë's struggle continued. Finally, gazing directly into Woodforde's eyes, she said in a strangled voice. "I agree. We should live together for Philip's sake. But you needn't expect that my opinion of you will change one iota. I'll despise you to my dying day."

Chapter Seven

Mrs. Randolph poured a cup of tea and handed it to Zoë. saying with a beaming smile, "I'm so glad you decided to pay me a visit, my dear. Before you arrived, the morning promised to be so dull. I'd planned to examine the housekeeper's monthly accounts, and you know how I hate figures. They never seem to add up properly! But I must confess I was a trifle surprised to see you. You're so busy with your painting career these days that you have little time for purely social calls."

"Well, perhaps I've been a little too busy with my painting. Perhaps I need to see more of my friends," said Zoë lightly. But as she gazed over the rim of her teacup at her old friend's plump, good-natured face, she felt a pang of guilt. She'd fibbed to Mrs. Randolph. Her visit this morning was far from being a "purely social call."

Yesterday at Merefield Park Zoë had reluctantly and painfully agreed to decisions that would overturn the foundations of her life. After a sleepless night, pursued by agonizing doubt, she still recognized the necessity of making public Philip's true status as heir to an earldom, and of her own as the Countess of Woodforde. But her fears of the scandal the announcement would provoke had multiplied. From now on, she was convinced, speculation and gossip would dog her every step. Human nature was human nature. People would find it hard to understand why she'd kept her marriage secret for seven years, and why she and Philip had lived under an assumed name.

She was here at Mrs. Randolph's house this morning to test the waters. Her friends and acquaintances in the neighborhood of Heathfield would be the first to know about her changed situation. How Mrs. Randolph reacted to the revelation might indicate how the other people in the locality would receive the news. During the first minutes of her visit, however, Zoë was tongue-tied, unable to think of the proper words to introduce the subject of her marriage.

Oblivious to Zoë's mental discomfort, Mrs. Randolph chattered happily. "You're just back from your London trip, I hear. Was it exciting? Did you meet the Prince Regent?"

Zoë laughed. "No, indeed. I don't travel in the Prince's social circles. I did go to a dinner party at the home of Lady Bradford." She paused, remembering her confrontation with Woodforde at Lady Bradford's house, when he had finally unmasked Philip's identity. She began hesitantly, "Mrs. Randolph, I have some rather surprising news for you. Do you remember that ball so many years ago at Merefield Park, when I danced with Lady Rosedale's cousin, Jerrold Layton?"

"Why, yes." Mrs. Randolph chuckled. "Little did you know that you were dancing with a future peer. He succeeded his brother recently, I believe."

"Yes. He's Lord Woodforde now. Well . . ." Zoë's voice trailed away. She resumed abruptly. "Jerrold

Layton and I eloped to Gretna Green that night. We quarreled and parted the next morning. I was still angry with him when I discovered I was increasing, so I—I simply invented another husband. There never was a David Manning, and Jerrold Layton never knew he had a son. Then, recently, we met again when he visited Lady Rosedale at Merefield Park, and we realized that our original quarrel had been foolish to the point of being meaningless. In fact, we couldn't remember what the quarrel had been about!"

Zoë felt an extra pang of guilt at this latest bit of invention, but she knew instinctively that public acceptance of her new situation would stand or fall on the issue of youthful romance. Under no circumstances could she reveal the actual sordid details of her elopement.

Gazing at her hostess with the brightest smile she could summon up, she said, "So now, Mrs. Randolph, the earl and I have reconciled, and we've decided to resume our marriage. I daresay it will take some time for you to become accustomed to thinking of me as the Countess of Woodforde!"

The silence in the room was so profound that the ticking of the clock on the mantelpiece sounded intrusively loud. Mrs. Randolph appeared to be in shock. Her rather prominent eyes were almost bulging. Her mouth opened, but she seemed incapable of talking.

"I hoped you would wish me happy," Zoë faltered.

Mrs. Randolph spoke at last. "My dear, I want so much to wish you happy," she said in a bewildered voice. "However, I must confess I don't understand how you and Lord Woodforde could simply ignore for seven years the fact that you were really married. Of course, I know that divorce or annulment can cause so much unpleasantness that no genteel female would care to embark on either course, but ... supposing that either of you had wished to marry someone else during those years?"

"Perhaps we were fortunate. I had no wish to marry. Neither, apparently, did Lord Woodforde."

Mrs. Randolph relaxed slightly. An understanding gleam came into her eyes. "Oh, I daresay he was in no hurry to get married," she said indulgently. "Well, you know there were all those rumors about what a dreadful flirt he was, practically a rake, in fact! And before he succeeded to the title, there was no real need for him to marry."

Mrs. Randolph fell silent, looking thoughtfully at Zoë. A smile curved her lips. "I won't deny that I was a bit taken aback by your news, it was *so* unexpected, but now I've had a moment to think about it ... Zoë Manning, I mean Lady Woodforde, I do truly wish you happy."

"Thank you." Zoë's rigidly held shoulders relaxed slightly. She had cleared her first hurdle.

"And to think, all it took to revive your earlier romantic feelings for each other was to meet again in Heathfield," marveled Mrs. Randolph. "It's almost like those fairy tales I was used to read to you and Charlotte when you were little girls. Why, Lord Woodforde was really your Prince Charming, wasn't he?"

Bemused, Zoë thought grimly that "Cinderella" was the last fairy tale she would choose as an analogy for her relations with Woodforde. "Beauty and the Beast" was more like it, at least up to the point where the heroine tamed the beast.

"Not only will I have difficulty at first remembering you're a countess, my dear," declared Mrs. Randolph, "but there's also little Philip. He'll be Philip Layton, of course. . . . No, that isn't right. He'll take his father's courtesy title, naturally. Now, what would that be?"

"I don't know," said Zoë blankly.

Mrs. Randolph knit her brow in thought. "I have it," she announced. "It's Silverbridge. Philip will be Lord Silverbridge."

"Oh," said Zoë, even more blankly. A short while later, she managed to drag herself away from Mrs. Randolph, who had progressed from excited comment on the news to questions about plans for the future, questions for which Zoë as yet had no answers. As she drove back to the rectory, she reflected on the result of her first announcement of her new status, and she felt far from reassured. If Mrs. Randolph, an old and dear friend who was devoted to her, had experienced difficulty in understanding or accepting Zoë's secret marriage, how would more distant friends and acquaintances, or strangers, react?

Arrived at the rectory, she went straight to her studio. Regardless of the turmoil in her personal life, she had resolved not to neglect her work. This morning she must begin the portrait of Lady Bradford and her daughter. Rather to Zoë's surprise, she was able to concentrate on her painting. She was deep in the process of transferring her initial sketches to canvas when a knock sounded at the door.

Zoë sighed in vexation. "Come."

"Excuse me fer interrupting ye, ma'am," said the chambermaid who opened the door. "Ye have a caller."

"Yes?"

"It's Lord Woodforde, ma'am. The Reverend, he thought as how ye would wish ter see his lordship."

The chambermaid's voice was politely noncommittal, almost too much so, because she couldn't suppress entirely an expression of lively curiosity. Zoë knew the girl was thinking of the numerous occasions during the past weeks when Woodforde had called to see her and had been unceremoniously turned away.

For a moment Zoë was strongly tempted to repeat her actions. But no. The time was past when she could turn away Woodforde. She said, "Bring Lord Woodforde to the studio, please. And ask Cook to send up a bottle of Madeira."

The chambermaid's mouth gaped open in surprise. Then, rolling her eyes, she murmured, "Very well, ma'am," and scurried out of the door. In a few moments she returned to announce, "Lord Woodforde, ma'am."

Zoë had risen from her easel and was standing in the center of the room when the earl entered. As she murmured a cool "Good morning," she had the strange impression that she was seeing him for the first time, as indeed she was, in a sense. The impression had nothing to do with his appearance. The handsome, assured face, the elegant figure in the superbly tailored clothes, were perfectly familiar. Rather, Zoë realized that, for the first time in their acquaintance, she was obliged to deal with him, not as an adversary in an ongoing struggle, but as a person who would henceforward be a dominating element in her life. Suddenly she felt excruciatingly nervous, uncertain of what to say or how to act.

"So this is your studio," he observed. He strolled around the room, glancing at several of the finished paintings, as yet unframed, and coming to a stop beside the easel. "I see you're working on Lady Bradford's portrait," he said, examining the canvas Zoë had begun that morning. "Already it looks like a speaking image."

He spoke with a certain stiffness, and in that moment

Zoë discerned that the earl felt as awkward in their new relationship as she did. Some of her tension evaporated. "Please sit down," she said, indicating a chair and taking a seat beside her easel. She gave him a composed look. "You wanted to see me about . . ."

"I hesitated to disturb you, but I think we should discuss what we're going to do about our situation as soon as possible." He cleared his throat. "To start, may I suggest that we use our Christian names? Will you allow me to call you Zoë? And my name, in case you've forgotten, is Jerrold."

"Yes. I agree," said Zoë after a moment of reluctance. She would have preferred to keep a barrier of formality between them, but she realized that such formality might destroy the illusion of marital closeness they had decided to convey to the world.

"Thank you, Zoë." Jerrold motioned to the easel. "Another thing. Will you tell me if you intend to continue your painting?"

She looked at him with narrowed eyes. "Certainly. Painting is my profession. I enjoy doing it, and I enjoy the money I make from it. I didn't inherit a fortune, you know. Papa was able to leave me only a small sum invested in the Funds, which yields about fifty pounds a year."

"But money, surely, shouldn't ever be a problem for you. My income is ample—"

Zoë cut him off. "You don't understand. It's not just a question of money. It's a question of independence. You, of course, now have the right and the duty to provide for Philip's support. As much as possible, at least as far as my personal needs are concerned, I would prefer to provide for my own support."

His brows drawn together, Jerrold studied her for a

long moment. "Continuing with your **career** after you become the Countess of Woodforde might cause raised eyebrows," he commented. "It's certainly not customary for married ladies of your rank to have separate careers."

"But then our entire situation is far from being customary, isn't it?"

He looked startled. "You have a point," he admitted. After a brief pause he said, "I've no wish to quarrel with you about your career. By all means, continue with it if you like."

"Thank you." Zoë felt relieved that she didn't have to fight yet another battle with Jerrold. Her painting was more than a satisfying profession to her. In this new life which she was about to enter, having a career would allow her to remain a person in her own right. As a recognized professional, she couldn't be swallowed entirely by the Layton family and their highborn circle of friends.

"I've been thinking of Philip's state of mind," said Jerrold after a brief pause. "Have you told him that I'm his father?"

"I—no." Zoë thought of the previous evening, after her return from the conference with Woodforde at Merefield Park. Sitting with Philip as he ate his supper, she had fully intended to broach the subject of his parentage, but the words had caught in her throat. How could she tell her son that his name, his very identity, were false?

"Don't you think we should tell Philip who he really is?" Jerrold asked. "Before he learns about it from idle gossip? Perhaps we could talk to him together."

Zoë bit her lip. "You're quite right, of course." She crossed the room to the bellrope. When a chambermaid appeared, Zoë said, "Ask Sarah to bring Master Philip here, please."

When his nursemaid brought Philip to the studio, he seemed a little perplexed. "Why did you want to see me now, Mama?" he asked. "You're usually working at this time of day." He caught sight of Woodforde. "Oh, good morning, sir—my lord. Did you ride here on your wonderful horse?"

"I did, indeed. And someday, Philip, you'll be riding that horse yourself, or one like it."

"Do you really think so?" Philip asked, a glimmer of bliss crossing his face.

"I'm sure of it." Jerrold flicked Zoë an inquiring glance.

Her mouth felt suddenly dry. "Philip, Lord Woodforde and I have something to tell you."

"About a horse, Mama? You're going to buy me a horse?"

"No—not just now, at any rate." Zoë could feel a light film of perspiration gathering on her forehead. "My darling, I think you should know that Lord Woodforde and I have been acquainted for many years. In fact . . ." She groped for words. "In fact, Lord Woodforde is your father," she blurted.

"No—no, he can't be," Philip stammered. "My papa is dead. He went down with his ship before I was born. That's what you've always told me."

In desperation, Zoë hurried on. "I know that's what I told you, dearest, but it wasn't true. You see, shortly after Lord Woodforde and I were married, we quarreled and decided never to see each other again. So then, later, when I knew you were on the way, I thought you should have some—some knowledge of a father, so I made up an American sea captain named Manning and told you he was dead. But now that Lord Woodforde and I have met again after all these years, we've decided we should be a real family. So we're all going to live together, and you must learn to call Lord Woodforde your papa."

The inadequacy of Zoë's explanation was visible in Philip's face and figure. He was rigid with shock. "No—I don't believe what you're saying . . ."

Jerrold, who until then had been standing silently apart from mother and son, came forward and dropped to one knee beside Philip, placing a hand lightly on the child's shoulder. Looking deep into Philip's eyes, he said, "I know this news must be different to grasp all at once, but I *am* your father. Oh, I know I'm not as heroic and dashing as a sea captain. However, I'll do my best to be a good father to you. Will you let me try?"

The moments passed. Philip's sturdy little frame remained rigid, his face blank.

"Philip? Will you let me try?" Jerrold repeated gently.

Finally Philip stirred. "All right," he muttered, his lower lip trembling. "I guess you can try." He shrugged away from Jerrold, who slowly rose to his feet. "Mama? Can I go?"

"Yes, darling." But as Philip darted out of the studio, slamming the door behind him, Zoë made an instinctive move to follow him.

"Zoë." Jerrold's voice was sharp with authority. "Let the child be. He needs to be by himself right now."

Her legs suddenly feeling weak, Zoë sank into a chair. She stared dully down at the floor. Had she destroyed Philip's love for her? Would he ever trust her again? Slowly she was beginning to realize the enormity of the mistake she'd made seven years ago when she had refused to recognize the reality of her ill-fated marriage and Philip's paternity. In a fit of anger and revulsion against Jerrold Layton she had invented David Manning, and now the foolish lie had caught up to her, as she should have known it would.

"Zoë, I think you're worrying too much about Philip."

Her eyes blazing, Zoë shoved aside the comforting hand Jerrold had placed on her shoulder. She blamed herself bitterly for the life of lies she'd foisted on Philip, which might poison forever her relationship with her son, but she refused to absolve Jerrold Layton from a major part of the blame. If it hadn't been for his brutish behavior, she would never have initiated the deception. Suddenly a wave of renewed resentment against him surged over her.

Jerrold stepped back, his mouth tightening at the rebuff. After a moment he said quietly, "I realize how difficult it was for you to speak to Philip. However, I repeat, I think you're overly concerned. Oh, your news shocked and angered him. That was only to be expected. In the end, though, he'll come around, I'm convinced of it. Meanwhile, we have plans to make. About where we will live, for example."

Drawing a deep breath, Zoë tried to compose herself. She knew she couldn't afford to indulge her resentment of Jerrold. She rose to face him, saying, "I presume you won't wish to live here at the rectory. I believe your family estate is in Herefordshire."

"It is, yes. Though I don't believe we should reside there immediately. The Season is just starting. My cousin Melicent thinks—and I agree—that we should live at Woodforde House in London during the Season."

"No!" Zoë's response was instinctive. She shrank at the thought of having the details of her personal life exposed to the curious, gossipy eyes of the London *ton*.

"Think about it," Jerrold urged. "I know you're concerned about scandal. You're afraid that people will question why we concealed this marriage for so many years. Melicent is convinced—and again I agree—that by establishing ourselves boldly in London at the height of the social season, when everybody of any consequence in the kingdom will be there, we'll be declaring, in effect, that we have nothing to hide. Such a move could cut off scandalous rumors before they even start."

After several moments of thought, Zoë said with a shrug, "I daresay there's some merit in what you say. Very well. We'll live in London during the Season."

"Good." Jerrold sounded relieved. "Now, as to the immediate present. Melicent wants to invite the local gentry to an evening reception at Merefield Park in my honor. At some point in the evening she would announce that you and I wish to make public a secret marriage dating back seven years. I'm in favor of this reception. It might serve as a trial run, for example, as to how people will receive the news of our marriage in the larger context of London society." Jerrold paused, gazing at Zoë, a question in his eyes. "Do you approve of the idea?"

Zoë considered the proposal. At last she said, "Yes. A party might be the best way to acquaint the neighborhood with our circumstances." The reluctance in her voice, however, echoed the reluctance in her mind. Lady Rosedale's reception *was* the best way to announce the marriage to the countryside, but Zoë cringed at the prospect of the public exposure. Resentfully she reflected that, although this was only the first day of her newly married life, she had already engaged in a shattering interview with her son, and she'd been forced to agree to decisions that would drastically disrupt the ordered arrangements of her life.

Jerrold broke into her thoughts. "I'm glad you think the reception is a good idea. I won't take up any more of your time, then. I've covered all the points I wanted to make. Except . . ."

Zoë gave him an intent look. He sounded, suddenly, very unsure of himself. "Yes?" she inquired.

"I, er, last night we agreed to a marriage of convenience. I want you to know I fully intend to honor the terms of that agreement. That is to say, I will make no demands of a—a personal nature upon you at any time."

Lifting her chin, Zoë replied, "Thank you, but your assurance was quite unnecessary. I presumed you understood that I wouldn't have agreed to any arrangement except a marriage in name only."

"Er, quite. Until Friday, then. Seven o'clock at Merefield Park. Goodbye, Zoë."

After Jerrold was safely out of the way, Zoë left the studio to walk swiftly toward the nursery. She knew Philip was disturbed, and she yearned to comfort him. Halfway down the corridor she paused. Jerrold had urged her to leave Philip to himself for a while, to give their son time to sort out his thoughts and feelings. Perhaps Jerrold was right. She turned back to her studio.

Meg Brant, the young servant she had drafted to be her clerical assistant, was just coming up the stairs. "Oh, good, ye're not working now, so I'll not be disturbing ye," she said. "Could I talk to ye for a moment?"

"Yes, of course. Come into the studio."

"It's this letter, ma'am," Meg said a moment later. "I didn't quite know how to answer it. It's from a Lady Wetherby in Chester. Since she lives not too far from here, she wants to know if she can come to Heathfield for a sitting instead of waiting until your next trip to London."

Zoë hesitated, studying Meg Brant. She had selected Meg from among the rectory servants to assist her because of the girl's quick intelligence and beautiful handwriting, and the arrangement had worked well. Zoë came to a quick decision. "Write Lady Wetherby, Meg, that I won't be able to see her here in Heathfield."

"But . . . when can you see her, then? It will be six months or more before you go to London again to take appointments."

"As a matter of fact, I'll be going to London shortly to spend the next three months." Zoë paused. "Meg, I have something to tell you. Lord Woodforde and I were married many years ago. Philip is our son. We'll all be going to London together as a family."

Meg looked stupefied.

Continuing, Zoë said, "Will you do something for me? I'd like you to inform the servants about my marriage. The housekeeper first, please. We don't want to offend Mrs. Humphries. Tell her I gave you permission to spread the news. Then talk to the other servants."

"Yes, ma'am." Meg had recovered the ability to speak, though she still seemed to be in shock.

"One more thing, Meg. I daresay, now that I'm a countess I'll be expected to have an abigail. How would you like to be my combined abigail-secretary?"

"Me, ma'am?"

"You, indeed. I intend to continue my painting, so I'll also continue to need someone to take care of my appointments and correspondence. And during our recent trip to London, when you helped me dress for Lady Bradford's dinner party, I noticed you were quite a skillful hairdresser. I think you'll make a splendid abigail."

* * *

Meg Brant arranged a circlet of tiny white roses tied with green ribbons around the topknot of curls on the crown of Zoë's head and stepped back to examine her handiwork in the mirror of the dressing table. "I like the circlet of roses better than the satin bandeau, ma'am—I mean my lady," she ventured.

"Yes, so do I. My hair looks very nice, Meg. Thank you." Zoë smiled at Meg's stumble over the proper style of address. It was only two days since she'd revealed her new identity to the rectory household, and Meg and the other servants were still finding it difficult to remember her title.

Zoë's smile faded as she stood to look at her reflection in the cheval glass. Tonight she would be attending the announcement party of her new status at Merefield Park, and to give herself a little moral courage she had decided to wear the expensive white lace over green satin gown she had bought in London on her recent trip. She looked well, she mused as she slowly revolved in front of the glass, but somehow the knowledge wasn't of much comfort. She still dreaded the evening that lay ahead of her.

Turning away from the cheval glass, she said to Meg, "Tell Mr. Bennett I will be ready to leave in fifteen minutes. I'm just going up to Master Philip's bedchamber to read him his bedtime story."

Philip was already in bed when Zoë, carrying a book of fairy tales in her hand, entered his bedchamber. His eyes widened as he gazed at his mother. "You look like a fairy princess, Mama."

"Do you think so, love? Thank you very much." Zoë sat down beside the bed. She looked at Philip with a great feeling of inner relief. He was, if not thoroughly reconciled to his new identity, at least part way on the road to accepting it. Yesterday, and again today, she'd spent hours talking to him, reassuring him that, although their lives would now be different, her feelings for him would never change. He would always be the most important person in her life.

After she read several fairy tales to Philip, she sat back in her chair, saying with a smile, "I hear you received a surprise gift today."

Philip's eyes sparkled. "Lord Woodforde . . ." He broke off, frowning. "I expect I should call him Papa now."

"Yes, love. I think you should."

"I'll try to remember." The animation returned to Philip's face. "Well, Lord Woodforde—I mean Papa—brought over the most splendid pony this afternoon. Lord—Papa—said the pony was to be mine, and I could name him anything I liked. So I decided to call him Robin, because I like those stories you read to me about Robin Hood so much. And then Lord—Papa—gave me my first riding lesson, and would you believe it, Mama, I didn't fall off even once!"

Blinking away a sudden tear, Zoë breathed a brief prayer of thanks. She was certain that she herself would never feel anything for Jerrold except dislike and distrust, but it was important for Philip's happiness that he develop some kind of benign relationship with his newly found father. She could at least be grateful to Jerrold for making an attempt to be friends with their son.

A little later she set out with Edmund in the rectory carriage for Merefield Park.

"You look charming, Zoë," Edmund remarked. "Is that a new gown? I don't recall seeing it before."

"Yes, I bought the gown in London. Edmund, I may *look* charming, but I don't *feel* charming. I'm in a panic about this party. What will all these people, people I've known for years, think of this secret marriage?"

"You've done nothing wrong. You're legally married to Lord Woodforde."

"Nothing wrong?" Zoë repeated in a low voice. "What do you call living a lie for seven years? Edmund, how could I ever have thought I was solving my problems by inventing a husband? I must have been mad."

Placing a comforting hand on her arm, Edmund sat beside Zoë in silence as the carriage turned into the driveway of Merefield Park.

Zoë and Edmund were the first guests to arrive in the drawing room.

"What a lovely gown, Zoë," Melicent said approvingly. She herself was wearing a clinging silk gown in a lavender shade of late mourning.

"Thank you. It's very kind of you, Lady Rosedale, to give this party."

"Nonsense. I love giving parties. And please call me Melicent. After all, we're cousins now!"

Jerrold, who had been greeting Edmund, spoke up. "Melicent is quite right, Zoë. You look lovely."

For a moment Zoë looked at Jerrold, not through the filter of her dislike, but seeing him as his London friends would have seen him: handsome, superbly groomed, utterly at ease in his faultlessly tailored black evening dress. For a fleeting second her heart recaptured the yearning that a sixteen-year-old had once felt at her first glimpse of Jerrold Layton.

His eyes flicked to her hands, which she held tensely clenched together. "Relax, Zoë," he advised. "There's nothing to be nervous about."

He was wrong, as Zoë discovered even before the last of the guests had arrived. As she stood with Edmund, watching the gentry of Heathfield file past Melicent and Jerrold at the door of the drawing room, Zoë gradually became uncomfortably aware that she was the object of intense scrutiny, especially among the female guests. Old acquaintances flocked to greet her and Edmund, and though their remarks were commonplace enough, the avid curiosity in their eyes was almost palpable.

This assembly in Melicent's drawing room is quite unnecessary, Zoë thought suddenly. Most of the people in this room have already heard some kind of rumor about me and Jerrold.

Her suspicions were confirmed a little later when Mrs. Randolph came up to her, saying in a low, conspiratorial voice, "Well, my dear, are we all gathered here tonight to hear a very important announcement?"

Of course, Zoë thought morosely. Mrs. Randolph has been talking. I should have guessed. I didn't think to ask her to keep my news secret from her friends and neighbors, since my marriage was soon going to be common knowledge. In any case, the rectory servants would have gossiped about my situation with their cronies in the village, and from there the titillating news would have spread quickly to all the servants' halls in the area.

"Yes, there will be an announcement tonight, after supper, I believe," Zoë told Mrs. Randolph resignedly. She continued, with a kind of numb endurance, to chatter meaninglessly with her old friend and with other acquaintances until supper was served in the ballroom, where numerous tables had been set up to accommodate the large number of guests. Zoë and Jerrold were at Melicent's table, seated on either side of her.

"Everyone I invited is here, despite the short notice," Melicent murmured to Jerrold and Zoë with a satisfied air.

Jerrold smiled at his cousin. "This reception was a splendid idea, Melicent. Zoë and I will be able with one stroke to make our marriage public to the entire gentry of Heathfield, before gossip or speculation has had a chance to spread."

Zoë kept her thoughts to herself.

At the end of the second course, Melicent rose from her chair. Waiting until she had the attention of her guests, she said, "I know I mentioned in my invitation that I wanted my friends in the county to make the acquaintance of my cousin, Lord Woodforde. That's true, but I had another reason for asking you here. I wish to make an announcement of the marriage of Lord Woodforde to the former Miss Zoë Bennett of Heathfield. The event occurred some years ago, although they chose not to make their marriage public at the time. Indeed, Lady Woodforde preferred to live anonymously as Mrs. Manning. Now, however, they have decided to establish a household, together with their son, Philip, the new Lord Silverbridge. I hope you will all wish Lord and Lady Woodforde happy."

Zoë shot a quick sideways glance at Melicent as she finished her graceful little speech. Melicent looked faintly baffled. There had been no collective gasp of surprise from the assembly, no expression of surprise on any of the guests' faces. It was obvious to Zoë that her suspicions had been correct. These people were already familiar with the gist of Melicent's announcement.

Later, when the ladies retired to the drawing room to drink their coffee, Zoë's discomfort intensified. Freed by Melicent's announcement to discuss Zoë's affairs, the ladies swarmed around her chair with curious comments and questions. Those who could not reach Zoë immediately clustered around Melicent.

Some of the comments were innocuous, if embarrassing. One very young woman said, blushing and giggling, "I heard that you eloped to Gretna Green, Lady Woodforde. That must have been so romantic. Did your papa pursue you to the border? Were you married by the toll-keeper?"

"Actually, Lord Woodforde and I were married by a clergyman," said Zoë coolly, amused at the look of disappointment on the girl's face. "And no, my father didn't pursue us."

Other comments weren't so innocuous. One lady, an elderly spinster with a nose as long as her curiosity, pounced on Zoë with the question, "When was it exactly that you and Lord Woodforde were married? Seven years ago? And how old is your son, dear little Lord Silverbridge? Six years of age. I see." But her expression plainly indicated that, if she saw, she didn't believe.

Another woman, a baronet's wife locally noted for her love of gossip, disguised her normally acid tongue beneath a sugary manner as she remarked, "All your friends are delighted that you've been reunited with your husband. Some of us, however, do wonder why you called yourself Manning. Does the name have something to do, perhaps, with one of your husband's secondary titles?"

Scarcely bothering to conceal her irritation, Zoë replied, "No, Lady Wheele, the name 'Manning' has nothing to do with any of Lord Woodforde's secondary titles. I chose to use the name simply because it suited my purpose at the time."

Lady Wheele looked distinctly affronted.

By the time the gentlemen appeared in the drawing

room, Zoë felt physically weary from the effort of coping with the torrent of questions, some well-meaning, others purely inquisitive. While the gentlemen drank their coffee, she waited with a mounting impatience for the moment when she could stand beside Melicent and Jerrold at the door of the drawing room to say goodbye to the guests.

"Well, I think the evening went very well," Jerrold observed to Zoë and Melicent and Edmund after the last guest had made his exit. "Don't you think so?" he added with an inquiring glance as Melicent and Zoë stood silently looking at him.

"No," said Melicent, sighing. "Zoë and I have just been deluged with questions about your marriage. Judging from the remarks addressed to me, I gather that many of the local ladies are unable to understand why you kept the marriage secret for so long, and especially they're puzzled by Zoë's use of another man's name and family history. Would you agree, Zoë?"

"Yes." Her lip curling, Zoë looked straight into Jerrold's eyes. "If people I've known all my life react to the news of our marriage with such skepticism, I shudder to think how the London *ton* will receive our announcement." She swallowed hard. "Jerrold, I've changed my mind about going to London. I don't wish to live there."

The blue eyes became cold. "I'm sorry. I understand your distress, but I must insist we spend the Season in London. If we avoid going there, we might raise questions in society's mind about the legitimacy of Philip's position as my heir. No, Zoë, we must simply brazen through any suggestion of scandal."

"That's easy enough for you to say," Zoë burst out. "Doubtless you don't mind raised eyebrows or smirking remarks or gossip behind your back."

Melicent said quickly, "Zoë, perhaps we've both been a bit cavalier. Look, I think I can help. I've been in mourning for very nearly a year, as near as makes no difference. I hadn't planned to take part in the London Season this year, but now I think I should go to London ahead of you and Jerry. I'll open Rosedale House and start spreading the story of the greatest love story of this generation. If we can convince the romantics in the *ton*— meaning the ladies, mostly!—that two star-crossed lovers have been reunited, perhaps they won't bother to ask questions about why Zoë invented another husband."

His voice urgent, Edmund said, "Lady Rosedale has great good sense, Zoë. Please listen to her."

For several moments Zoë struggled with her feelings. Her eyes moved from the concerned faces of Edmund and Melicent and Jerrold, who all stared at her with expressions of intense anxiety. Finally she shrugged, saying, "Once more I seem to be in the minority, being urged to do something I don't wish to do. Very well. You've all convinced me. I'll go to London."

Jerrold said quickly, "Thank you, Zoë. I know that was a difficult decision for you to make. I have one more suggestion. I think that I should either move into the rectory, or you and Philip should come to stay at Merefield Park, until we make the move to London. Either alternative should convince the local gossips that ours is a real marriage."

"No." Zoë tossed her head. "I've made enough concessions. I won't live in the same household with you a minute sooner than absolutely necessary."

Reddening, Jerrold stared at Zoë for several moments. Then it was his turn to acquiesce. "As you wish. I won't insist."

Chapter Eight

On the morning of her departure from Heathfield for London, Zoë walked into the nursery, where Philip's nursemaid was trying without much success to brush his hair. Zoë told her squirming son, "Stand still, you goose. Don't you wish to look presentable when you start out on our journey to London?"

"Yes, Mama." Doing his best to stand quietly, Philip submitted to the nursemaid's hairbrush.

"Shall I see that all of Master Philip's luggage is in the fourgon, my lady?" the nursemaid inquired.

"Yes, do that, Sarah."

When the nursemaid had left, Zoë said to Philip with a sudden catch in her throat, "We're about to start a whole new life, darling. How do you feel about it?"

Philip looked surprised. "What do you mean, Mama?"

Zoë said, floundering, "Oh, I don't really know what I mean. . . . Are you sad to be leaving Heathfield? You've spent your whole life here. You'll be leaving your Uncle Edmund, everybody you've known and loved."

"Except you, Mama—and Sarah, of course. And Papa." Philip's eyes sparkled. "I'll miss Uncle Edmund, of course, and everyone at the rectory, but if Papa thinks we ought to go to London, I'm sure he's right. Papa says London will be a whole new world for me."

Zoë sighed. She had no right to reveal her qualms about this journey to London to Philip, any more than she had any right to fault her son's devotion to his father. "Run along, Philip. Papa's carriage will arrive soon."

"Mama! The carriages are here," exclaimed Philip a little later. He had been standing at the window of the rectory drawing room for the past half hour, his eyes glued to the village street in front of the house.

"Oh, dear, so soon?" said Mrs. Randolph with a sigh, rising from her chair. "Then it's time to say goodbye to you and Philip, Zoë."

Zoë hugged her old friend, saying, "I'm afraid it is time. Thank you for coming out so early in the morning to bid us a *bon voyage*." She was already dressed for the long journey ahead of her in an unlined gray muslin pelisse, worn with a straw cottage bonnet trimmed with small yellow roses. It was the middle of May. Today she and Philip would travel with Jerrold to London to begin their new life together.

Wiping a tear from the corner of her eye, Mrs. Randolph said, "Lord, I wonder how long it will be before I see you again? After the Season in London you'll no doubt be going to Lord Woodforde's estates in Herefordshire."

"You've always said you wanted to see London again. Come visit us in Bedford Square," Zoë urged.

Mrs. Randolph looked wistful. "I'd love to visit you, but you know how Mr. Randolph is. He hates to travel."

"Persuade him," Zoë said with a smile.

Edmund appeared in the door of the drawing room. "Zoë, the carriages are here. The servants have begun to carry out your luggage."

Zoë drew a deep breath. "Coming, Edmund. Philip?" But the child had already bolted out of the drawing room, and Zoë could hear his feet clattering down the hallway toward the front door. Zoë said to Mrs. Randolph, "Please excuse Philip. This will be his first real journey away from the village, and for several days he's practically been bursting from excitement."

As Zoë emerged from the door of the rectory, followed by Mrs. Randolph and Edmund, she saw drawn up beside the rectory gate a traveling coach and a fourgon. Jerrold was advancing up the pathway from the gate with a grinning Philip perched on his shoulder. As he reached Zoë, he swung Philip to the ground, saying, "I'm glad to see you're both ready to the minute. In fact, I think Philip was prepared to make the journey on foot!"

"Oh, we've been ready for almost an hour, Papa," Philip assured him.

Jerrold smiled, giving Philip a playful poke on the top of the boy's low-crowned hat. As usual, he himself was superbly dressed in a beaver hat and a caped greatcoat worn over a coat and leather breeches and top boots. Addressing Zoë, he said, "I think you'll be comfortable in the coach. It's quite new—my father bought it shortly before he died a few years ago—and it's very well sprung."

"I daresay we'll be most comfortable," said Zoë politely. Gazing at the coach, painted a dark blue to match the liveries of the white-wigged coachman and the two footmen on the rear platform, with shining gilt door handles and lamps and the Woodforde crest on the door, she reflected that she would be traveling to London on this occasion in far more luxury than she had enjoyed on her previous journeys. On this occasion there would be no ride in the rectory carriage to Carlisle to meet the mail, followed by a grueling fifty-hour drive to London, broken only by stops for meals and to change horses. This time she would be traveling in a private carriage, with overnight stops at the end of each day in comfortable inns. It would take the newly united Woodforde family almost five days to reach London.

Jerrold glanced at the fourgon, over the rear half of which the rectory servants, having loaded the various portmanteaus and valises, were drawing a waterproof tarpaulin. Jerrold's valet, Philip's nursemaid, and Meg Brant, now officially Zoë's abigail, would ride in the front part of the fourgon, fitted with a folded hood to protect them from the elements.

"The fourgon is loaded. Shall we start?" Jerrold asked.

"Oh. Yes." Zoë turned to give another hug to a tearful Mrs. Randolph and a fervent embrace to Edmund. "I've already invited Mrs. Randolph to visit us in London, Edmund. I *insist* that you come, no excuses accepted. And thank you for everything."

"You and Philip will be constantly in my thoughts and prayers," replied Edmund affectionately. "I wish you every blessing and happiness."

A few moments later Jerrold handed Zoë up the steps of the carriage, Philip scrambled in after her, and Jerrold took his place beside his son. A footman let up the steps and closed the door, and the little procession rolled down the main street of Heathfield. Most of the population of the village lined the streets, waving goodbyes. Zoë felt a pang of sadness. She had spent virtually the whole of her twenty-three years of life in Heathfield, and for the past seven years the place had been a haven of refuge. In the future she would rarely see the village again.

As they drove into the open country beyond the village, Philip pointed out the window, exclaiming, "Look, Mama, there's the black lamb, only I daresay we should call him a sheep now, he's getting so big." To Jerrold he said, "Do *you* know why some lambs are black, Papa? I've asked Mama and Uncle Edmund, and they can't tell me."

"Well, I can't tell you either, my boy, even though we raise a great many sheep on my estate."

"You raise sheep, Papa? Can I see them sometime?"

"Certainly. You'll be seeing them every day when we move to Herefordshire after the London Season is over. I'll give you one for your very own."

"Do you really mean it? Can I have a black one?"

"Yes, of course," Jerrold replied, laughing. "Provided there's a black sheep available. I expect there will be. The world seems to be full of them." He flicked a sideways glance at Zoë. She ignored the last remark. If it was intended to be an amusing overture to her, or even some form of apology for their disastrous beginnings, she wasn't interested. It was too late for apologies.

Philip looked delighted at the promise of a sheep, but soon his expression changed to one of concern. "You know, Papa, I was so happy when you promised to send my pony Robin to London so I could ride him there, but . . . London is very far from here, isn't it? Won't Robin get very tired, walking all that way?"

"As a matter of fact, he won't. I've arranged for him to be taken to London in a bullock cart. I got the idea from one of my friends who does a good deal of racing.

He told me not long ago that he was thinking of transporting his horses in carts from one racecourse to another, so that they would arrive unfatigued for the next race. So rest easy, Philip. Robin won't get too tired."

Listening to the interplay between father and son, Zoë had to suppress a momentary twinge of jealousy. Until recently she and Edmund had been the important people in Philip's life. Now they had to make room for Jerrold. During the past two weeks he had completely won over Philip in his daily visits to the rectory, which always ended in a riding lesson.

Zoë knew very well that most fathers didn't give the time and attention to their young children that Jerrold was bestowing on Philip. Her own well-loved father, indeed, had been rather a distant figure to her and Edmund until they entered their teens and were able to talk to him on an adult level. Whatever Jerrold's motives were—and he may have decided to cultivate Philip's affections only to make smoother the task of convincing the public that his long-secret marriage was legitimate— Zoë was grateful. Philip's warm association with his newly discovered father had made it easier for the child to adapt to the drastic changes in his life.

For herself, this move to London filled Zoë with foreboding. From now on, she would be in intimate daily contact with a man she had despised and distrusted for seven years. Jerrold's recent behavior had given her no reason to change her opinion of him. Oh, he was now being respectful and considerate, he'd abided by her wish that they continue to lead separate lives—he at Merefield Park, she at the rectory—until the actual move to London, but she knew that his actions were motivated by the one inescapable fact: Philip was his legitimate heir, and the world must be made to accept that fact. Even though their marital relationship would be strictly a platonic one, Zoë wasn't sure she could maintain the calm civility necessary to make it possible for her and Jerrold to live together under the same roof.

"I received a letter from Melicent yesterday," Jerrold remarked as the coach rolled along. "She reports that she's well established at Rosedale House, and has already been doing some entertaining. However, she says company is a bit thin in London. So many of the *ton* have gone off to Paris to see the sights now that Napoleon is gone."

Zoë murmured a polite expression of interest. True to her word, Melicent had gone to London two weeks earlier to prepare the ground for the entry of her cousin and his wife into society. Her lip curling, Zoë wondered silently if Melicent had succeeded in persuading her friends that the Earl and Countess of Woodforde were the "star-crossed" lovers of this generation.

At the very first stop to change horses, Zoë became aware of the contrast between travel by mail and travel by private coach. Swarms of hostlers surrounded the carriage the moment it entered the inn yard; they changed the team so quickly it smacked of magic. Inn servants came to the door of the coach, solicitously offering to bring tea or coffee or wine or any refreshment the occupants might desire.

The journey continued smoothly throughout the cool, bright May day, as the county of Cumberland merged into Westmorland. At noon they stopped for luncheon at the Queen's Arms in Brough, and here Zoë once again appreciated the advantages of traveling by private coach. The landlord of the inn himself greeted Jerrold and his family at the door and ushered them into a private dining parlor.

Philip was immensely intrigued by every aspect of the trip, peering out the carriage windows with wide-eyed interest at the passing countryside, enjoying the novelty of dining at a public inn, but toward the middle of the afternoon his energy flagged. Soon he fell sleep in the curve of Zoë's arm.

Gazing intently at Philip's sleeping face, Jerrold started to observe, "He's a—" He broke off, looking a little foolish. Then, with a wry smile, he continued, "I was about to remark that Philip is an exceptionally handsome child, but then I remembered that I've told you several times how much Philip resembles portraits of myself painted at the same age. I can assure you that I never thought of myself as an exceptionally handsome child!"

With some surprise, Zoë realized that Jerrold was embarrassed at the thought that she might think he was conceited about his own looks. She couldn't imagine why her opinion would matter to him. She said coolly, "No one with normal eyesight would deny that you and Philip strongly resemble each other."

"Er . . . yes, I daresay that's true." Jerrold still looked ill at ease. After a moment, changing the subject, he said, "It seems to me that Philip is adjusting well to his new circumstances. What do you think?"

"Oh, I agree. He's accepted you completely, and he's excited about living in new places." Rather grudgingly—because it went against the grain to acknowledge that Jerrold could be right in anything—she added, "You helped Philip to adjust by spending so much time with him. Thank you."

"Not at all. It was the least I could do." Jerrold seemed mildly embarrassed again.

An awkward silence descended on the coach, broken

only by the faint sound of Philip's even breathing. Zoë reflected that this was the first occasion in which she and Jerrold had been alone together since they had made their marriage public, and it appeared that they had nothing to say to each other. Philip woke up shortly, and his lively questions and comments to both parents gave the illusion of a general conversation.

In late afternoon Jerrold leaned forward to look out the window, saying, "There's the River Lune. We're on the outskirts of Lancaster." He took out his watch. "A little past five. We've made very good time today— we've driven seventy-five miles from Heathfield—thanks to the good weather. We'll stay the night in Lancaster. I've reserved rooms for us at the Royal Oak."

Zoë smiled at her son. "You're having a living geography lesson on this journey, Philip. Now we're in still another county of England. This is Lancashire."

The carriage stopped in the courtyard of the inn and the Woodforde party was immediately enveloped in the attentive services Zoë was beginning to perceive as routine. Hostlers surrounded the carriage and inn servants swarmed to remove baggage from the fourgon. The proprietor of the Royal Oak bustled across the courtyard, greeting Jerrold with a deep bow. "It's a great pleasure to welcome ye again, my lord. Yer rooms are ready." He beamed at Zoë and Philip. "Welcome to ye also, my lady, and the young master."

As they walked into the entrance hall of the inn, Jerrold said to Zoë, "Come down to supper whenever you're ready. I've engaged a private parlor."

Zoë nodded. "I'll just see that Philip is settled. Then I'll be down."

Following the inn servant up the stairs, Zoë went first to Philip's bedchamber, where she satisfied herself that her son would be comfortable and ordered supper brought up to the room. Then she went to her own bedchamber. Servants were bringing in hot water and fresh towels, and Meg Brant was already there, preparing to unpack one of the valises.

"This seems like a very old town indeed, my lady," Meg observed. "There's a huge castle up there on the hill."

Zoë crossed to the window to gaze up at the hulking ruins on the steep hill above the town. "Yes, I believe that's one of John of Gaunt's castles. You're right, Meg. It's centuries old."

As she turned away from the window, Zoë stopped short, her eyes narrowing. On the floor in the center of the large room, which she suspected was the best bedchamber in the inn, the servants had deposited, not only a large portmanteau and a valise belonging to her, but several other pieces of luggage.

Following her mistress's gaze, Meg said in a tone carefully devoid of expression, "Those are his lordship's bags."

"I see." Zoë removed her pelisse and bonnet and laid them on the bed. She washed her hands and face and sat down at the dressing table, saying, "My hair is sadly in need of repair, Meg, after such a long day." Her voice was calm, but she had a hollow feeling in the pit of her stomach. Why was Jerrold's luggage in her bedchamber? Surely there was no possibility that Jerrold intended to share a room with her. Had the inn servants made a mistake? Apparently Meg was wondering, too. The young abigail knew quite well that, in the weeks since Jerrold and Zoë had announced their earlier marriage, they had never spent a night under the same roof. Zoë presumed that Meg, bright and intelligent, had drawn her own conclusions about the state of the Woodforde marriage.

Controlling her impatience, Zoë sat quietly while Meg arranged her hair. Then, after smoothing her figured muslin gown and arranging a lace shawl around her shoulders, she walked quickly down the stairs. A servant directed her to the private dining parlor. "The first door on yer right, my lady."

As she entered the parlor, Jerrold rose from a chair near the fireplace, where banked coals took an edge from the chill of a May evening. He held a glass of wine in his hand, and he said politely, "May I pour you a glass of Madeira? It would help you to relax after a long, tiring day."

"Yes. Thank you." As she accepted the wine, Zoë felt a sense of unreality. Here they were, she and Jerrold, linked together in the closest of human bonds as husband and wife, yet speaking in the careful tones of formality which concealed, at least on her part, a feeling of acute constraint. On Jerrold's part, too, she decided, judging by the slight stiffness in his manner.

Pulling out a chair for her, Jerrold asked, "Is Philip settled in?"

"Oh, yes. He feels quite grown up to be staying in an inn. In fact, he told me it wasn't necessary for his nursemaid to sleep with him in his bedchamber. He's not a baby anymore, he informed me."

An amused smile kindled Jerrold's eyes. "Good for Philip. He has backbone. He reminds me of my brother Trevor when he was a boy." Jerrold broke off, his face turning somber. Zoë remembered that Jerrold's older brother had died only recently. Evidently the brothers had been close.

About to ask him about the presence of his luggage in

her bedchamber, Zoë hesitated, unwilling to intrude on his memories. A knock sounded at the door and their landlord arrived to reel off a long menu which included venison, ham, capon, a jugged hare, and stewed eels. He ended in a burst of enthusiasm. "And if there's anything else ye'd fancy, my lord, my lady, ye have only to say the word."

"Don't concern yourself, landlord. I daresay Lady Woodforde and I can find something to tempt our palates from among the dishes you mentioned," said Jerrold gravely.

As they served the dinner, waiters entered and left the parlor in a constant parade, so that any conversation between Jerrold and Zoë about personal matters was impossible. She would have to wait until after dinner to pose her question.

During the meal Jerrold kept up a stilted small talk. "I hope you'll be comfortable at the inn. I've stayed at the Royal Oak on a number of occasions and they've always treated me well."

"Oh, I'm sure I'll have no complaints," Zoë assured him. She wondered silently if they would ever be at ease with one another.

Jerrold tried again. "If we continue to have as smooth traveling as we had today, we should reach Dunstable in three more days, with overnight stops at Macclesfield and Leicester. From Dunstable we can drive to London in half a day."

"I've no doubt you've arranged a very suitable itinerary," said Zoë. Lord, she thought, I sound completely vacuous. He must think me a buffle-headed female.

At last the servants cleared the table and brought in a coffee service and a bottle of port before withdrawing. Acting the hostess, Zoë poured the coffee, and then, as

Jerrold lifted his cup to his lips, she blurted, "The servants put your luggage in my bedchamber. That was a mistake, surely."

He put down his cup untasted. "Actually, it wasn't a mistake. The inn servants naturally assumed that you and I would be sharing a bedchamber."

Zoë gasped. "Then pray inform them immediately that their assumptions were wrong!"

Shaking his head, Jerrold replied, "I can't do that. Until we reach London, Zoë, you and I will sleep in the same room."

Zoë jumped to her feet and headed for the door. Jerrold intercepted her before she could reach it. Holding her arm, he said, "Wait, Zoë. We must talk."

The touch of his hand and his close proximity caused Zoë's heart to pound and her breath to quicken, reviving shameful sensual memories she had buried years before. "Let me go, Jerrold."

"Not until we come to an understanding."

"Oh, I think we understand each other very well," Zoë snapped. "You've broken your promise, so you can hardly blame me for breaking mine. I won't travel another mile with you on this journey to London. As soon as I can hire a carriage and driver, Philip and I and my servants will be on our way back to Heathfield."

Grasping her by her shoulders, Jerrold gave her a slight shake. The blue of his eyes intensified almost to black. "Listen to me. I haven't broken promises to you, nor will I. I don't propose to share your bed, only your bedchamber." Belatedly he noticed that his fingers were digging into her flesh, and he dropped his hands. "I'm sorry. Did I hurt you?"

"No . . ." Confused as well as angry, Zoë drew back

a step, looking searchingly at Jerrold. "What did you mean, that you didn't want to share my bed?"

Jerrold motioned to the dining table. "Come finish your coffee, and I'll explain. Please, Zoë."

She stared at him for a long, uncertain moment. Then, reluctantly, and yet with a growing curiosity, Zoë walked back to the table and sat down. "Well?" she inquired as he took a seat opposite her.

He began obliquely. "We agreed to establish a household together for one reason only, to preserve our son's heritage. Because we concealed the fact of our marriage for so long, some people may doubt that it ever took place, thereby putting Philip's legitimacy into question. I suggest to you, Zoë, that we should do everything possible to convince the doubters that we have a real marriage."

"Well, but . . . aren't we doing that? Isn't that why we decided to live together? To show the world, to quote your cousin Melicent, that we were"—Zoë flushed—"that we were reunited lovers?"

"Exactly. That being the case, don't you agree that 'reunited lovers' would share a bedchamber while traveling? Only the bedchamber, Zoë," Jerrold added quickly. "Once the door closes behind us, no one will know that you're sleeping chastely in the bed and I'm reclining in an armchair."

"But—this is a public inn. Who would ever know if we occupied separate bedchambers?"

"The innkeeper would know. The servants would know. They might gossip. I'm a fairly well-known figure, and many of my friends and acquaintances patronize the same establishments that I do. Rumors of our separate sleeping quarters could spread."

"Oh. Yes, I see." Zoë hesitated. Her anger had dissipated, but she still rebelled at the thought of being drawn into any closer relationship with Jerrold. Finally she said, "Very well. To avoid gossip, I agree to a joint bedchamber on this journey to London." She frowned suddenly. "Later? Are you saying we must also share bedchambers in London and at your estate in Herefordshire?"

"No. At Bedford House and at Malvern Hall master and mistress occupy separate bedchambers." Jerrold smiled wryly. "Under normal circumstances, of course, master and mistress would sleep in the same room more often than not, but ours aren't normal circumstances, are they?"

"No." Zoë looked away, feeling a wave of embarrassment.

"I'll try to inconvenience you as little as possible," Jerrold went on. "Tonight, for example, when you go up to the bedchamber, you can count on a good hour's privacy." With a faint smile, he nodded at the bottle of port. "As you can see, our landlord has provided me with a companion to while away the time until I can join my eager bride. And after that I'll go for an evening stroll to walk off any adverse effects of the port."

Zoë eyed him uncertainly. Was he making subtle fun of her? She rose, saying, "If you'll excuse me, I'll go up to bed now. I'm quite tired."

Standing up politely, Jerrold said, "Good night. Sleep well."

Chapter Nine

Sleep well, indeed, fumed Zoë to herself as she swept out of the dining parlor and walked up the stairs. She doubted she would sleep a wink tonight, occupying a room with a man whose dark memory had haunted her dreams for so many years. Her sense of grievance intensified as she reflected that, once again, in allowing Jerrold to sleep in her bedchamber, she had been forced to make a concession in order to ensure that their bizarre marital arrangement would pass public scrutiny.

In her bedchamber she found that Meg had not only unpacked her needs for the night and was waiting to help her get ready for bed, but there were also traces of another presence in the room. Someone had neatly arranged articles of shaving gear on the washstand, and had draped an obviously masculine silk brocade dressing gown and a linen nightshirt over the bed.

"His lordship's valet was here a bit ago, unpacking his lordship's valise," Meg observed.

Ignoring the hint of inquiry in the girl's voice. Zoë said, "Put his lordship's dressing gown and nightshirt on that chair over there, Meg. He'll not be up for some time, and I'd like to go to bed now."

"Yes, ma'am." Meg cleared her throat. "Will you wear your new nightdress, the pink silk one you bought in London?"

About to say no, Zoë changed her mind. If the object of this charade of sharing a bedchamber was to create the impression with the inn servants that she and Jerrold were sleeping together, then it might be as well to allow her own servants to think the same. "Yes, Meg, I'll wear the pink silk."

After Meg left the bedchamber, having helped her mistress into the silk nightdress and a peignoir and brushed out her tawny hair, Zoë smiled wryly to herself, thinking how easily she had slipped into the routine of having an abigail assist her with her toilet, now that she was a countess. For all the years before, as the presumed widow of an ordinary American seaman and the sister of the rector, she had taken care of her personal needs herself.

Though it was still quite light in the room despite the deepening spring twilight, Zoë lit a lamp and sat down in an armchair to read, as she often did before retiring for the night. But after a few moments she put the book down. The thought of facing Jerrold when he appeared in the bedchamber filled her with panic. Better to be in bed and asleep before he arrived. About to blow out the lamp, she paused. No, she would turn down the flame, leaving a dim light and allowing Jerrold to come into the room without stumbling into the furniture.

She discarded her peignoir and got into bed, pulling the coverlets up over her head and face so that only her nose was exposed. Weary though she was from the long day of travel, sleep would not come. She lay tense and wide awake, waiting for the sound of an opening door. Finally it came. She held her breath. Jerrold had promised that their marriage would be a platonic one, and in any case she had no reason to believe he had any sensual interest in her. Nevertheless, his presence in her bedchamber filled her with apprehension.

He paused inside the door and then slowly entered the room. Skirting the bed, he walked to the side of the bedchamber opposite the door. Soon she heard a rustling sound, as if he was removing his coat, followed by a faint double thump, probably his boots being deposited on the floor, and after that a faint creaking noise as he settled himself into an armchair. Still tense, Zoë waited sleepless as the minutes dragged by. At length, hearing Jerrold's breathing change to a deep, regular rhythm, she began to relax.

Hours later, she awakened slowly, vaguely aware that she was in a strange place and not in her familiar bedchamber in the rectory. A faint groaning sound brought her to complete wakefulness. She sat up abruptly, looking at her husband in the chair on the other side of the bed. He was stirring uneasily. Probably he was cold. Dawn was just breaking, and the early morning May temperature was frigid. Jerrold clutched his dressing gown more closely around him in his sleep. Despite her normally kindly instincts, Zoë rather enjoyed looking at the signs of his discomfort.

She stared at his sleeping face. His black hair was tousled into ringlets, and the closed eyelids with the absurdly long lashes concealed the arrogant blue eyes. Sleep had softened his features, making him look younger, as young as the dashing Jerrold Layton who had ensnared her heart at the long-ago ball at Merefield Park. Suddenly her entire body felt aflame with desire as the memories of that one searing night of physical love surfaced. She remembered her eager response to Jerrold's kisses and the touch of his roving hands, and the aching pleasure of feeling his hard body pressed against hers.

Overcome with humiliation, she sank back against the pillows and pulled the blankets over her head, as if to shield herself from any inquisitive eyes. For years she had fought against remembering the details of what had been for her a night of romantic love, but which had been for Jerrold merely a rake's need to satisfy his sexual lust.

The Earl of Woodforde and his family stepped out of the door of the Red Lion Inn in Dunstable on the fifth morning of their journey from Heathfield. As they walked to their carriage waiting in the courtyard, Philip remarked with an air of importance, "Mama, did you know that this is a very old inn? The chambermaid told me this morning that King Charles stayed here on his way to the Battle of. . ." He paused, frowning in concentration.

"The Battle of Naseby," Jerrold finished for him, smiling. "Dunstable itself is very old too, you know. The main street for a full mile follows exactly the old Roman road, Watling Street."

As the carriage moved out of the courtyard of the inn, Jerrold observed, "Dunstable is little more than thirty miles from London. We should be in Bedford Square by midafternoon.

"That's good to hear. It's been a long journey," Zoë replied. Her response was a mild reflection of her feelings. Her enforced association with Jerrold, day and night for four long days, had created such a strain that she could almost imagine her nerves dancing on the surface of her skin. She didn't think she could endure one more day of searching her mind for safe, dull topics of conversation, both in the cramped confines of the carriage and during meals at the various inns. She and Jerrold had nothing in common except Philip.

Most of all during this journey Zoë had come to dread the nights, when she and Jerrold shared a bedchamber. Simply knowing he was in the same room had caused her to sleep badly, awakening countless times during the night to listen apprehensively for the sound of his deep breathing. She had to admit, grudgingly, that he had kept to his promise to inconvenience her a as little as possible. Each morning he had left the bedchamber before she was fully awake, allowing her privacy to dress for the day. But she longed desperately for the luxury of sleeping alone in her bedchamber, free of Jerrold's disturbing male presence. Soon now, at Woodforde House in Bedford Square, she would have it.

"We're almost at journey's end," Jerrold assured his son some hours later over lunch at the Angel Inn in Islington. "This is the last coach stop before London."

Apparently unaware of the strain between his parents, and unfatigued by the long journey, Philip was still intrigued by every aspect of their travel. As the fields and farmlands along the New Road merged into the built-up areas of Somers Town and Pentonville, the stream of vehicular traffic thickened, and Philip turned to his father, wide-eyed, saying, "Papa, I've never seen so many carts and wagons and carriages and stagecoaches in my whole life."

Jerrold laughed. "Wait until we take a drive into the City. Then you'll really see traffic. Pedestrians cross streets at peril of life and limb."

Philip clutched Jerrold's arm. "Papa, look over there at that basket hanging on the walls of the church. The lady has birds for sale in the basket. Could I have a bird, please?"

"Of course. But we'll go to Spitalfields market to buy one. There we'll find the best selection of singing birds in London—linnets, woodlarks, goldfinches, greenfinches. And no," Jerrold added firmly as Philip peered excitedly out the carriage window at an organ grinder playing beside the road, "you cannot have a monkey."

Philip flashed his father a cheerful grin of acceptance, and once again Zoë had to suppress a pang of jealousy. Jerrold was fast winning her son's heart.

The carriage swung out of the New Road into the Tottenham Court Road and thence into a large square lined on four sides with handsome houses, each three bays wide, of brick construction with wrought iron balconies and decorations of Coade stone. The middle houses on each side, stuccoed and pilastered, were more impressive. The carriage stopped in front of the middle house on the east side, and the footmen opened the door and let down the steps.

"Welcome to Woodforde House," Jerrold said as he stood on the pavement with his hand raised to help Zoë down. "The Lord Chancellor lives across the way, and almost immediately behind us is Montague House, the British Museum."

A stately butler followed by a cohort of white-wigged footmen swarmed out of the house to greet their master and to conduct his lady and his heir into their new home. Zoë walked into the foyer, feeling a hollow void in the pit of her stomach. Now she was the mistress of a great London mansion staffed by an army of servants, and she wasn't sure she was equal to her new responsibilities.

* * *

"Will you wear the blue silk for dinner, ma'am?" Meg inquired.

"Yes, that will be fine," Zoë replied. She walked to the large dressing room connecting the master's and mistress's bedchambers and gazed rather dubiously at the gowns Meg had hung in the wardrobe. She would need more clothes, many more clothes, she now realized, in order to participate in the events of a London Season. Why hadn't it long since occurred to her that her Heathfield wardrobe would be inadequate?

Sighing, she went back into the bedchamber, eyeing the spacious, sunny room with pleasure. It was furnished with delicate satinwood furniture embellished with gilt inlays and upholstered in muted pastel blue and rose colors that echoed the jewel-like hues in the rug. It was the most beautiful bedchamber she had ever occupied.

While Meg was arranging her hair, Zoë recalled her encounter with the Woodforde House housekeeper, who had come up a little earlier to introduce herself.

"Do you like your bedchamber, my lady?" the housekeeper had inquired. Mrs. Kenton was a stout, dignified woman dressed in impeccable black.

"Yes, it's lovely."

"Her late ladyship, the present earl's mother, had the room redecorated shortly before her death. Blue and pink were her favorite colors," Mrs. Kenton volunteered. "And the young master's—Lord Silverbridge's—rooms, are they satisfactory?"

"Yes, quite."

"His lordship sent word that you were a painter, my lady, and would require a studio with a strong north light. I have had the furniture removed from a bedchamber on this floor that I trust will serve your purposes."

"Thank you, Mrs. Kenton." While the housekeeper was talking, though her manner was completely respectful and indicative of a desire to please, Zoë had been uncomfortably aware that the woman's eyes were boring into her with an avid curiosity. Probably the announcement that their new earl had a hitherto unknown wife and son had astonished his servants as much as it had shocked the countryside around Heathfield. Zoë had wondered uneasily if she would be the object of such acute scrutiny by all her new servants.

Changed into her blue silk gown, with a lace shawl around her shoulders and a wisp of lace topping her curls, Zoë walked down the great divided staircase to the ground floor. She paused uncertainly in the foyer, floored in black and white marble. A young footman materialized as if from nowhere. "His lordship is waiting for you in the drawing room, my lady. Please follow me."

Before the footman turned away, Zoë caught the flash of curiosity in his face, and shrugged resignedly. She would simply have to grow used to the interest she was arousing in Jerrold's servants.

Jerrold came forward to meet her as she entered the drawing room, opulently furnished with rather heavy, formal pieces, a large glittering chandelier, and elaborately draped windows. Zoë gazed with delight at the painted figures in the octagon-shaped inserts in the plaster ceiling. "Are they . . .?"

Jerrold nodded. "Yes, the paterae are by Angelica Kauffman. I thought you might like to see them. When there are no guests, the family usually meets in the morning room before dinner, but tonight I also wanted to show you this." He motioned to a large portrait over the mantelpiece.

Zoë walked toward the fireplace for a closer look. The portrait was of a dark, slender young woman, dressed in a yellow satin gown in the style of the nineties of the last century. She was sitting in an armchair, on either side of which stood a small boy. The children closely resembled each other and the woman, who was obviously their mother. The younger boy, who appeared to be five or six years old, could have been a mirror image of Philip.

"My mother with my brother Trevor and me," said Jerrold quietly as he stood beside her. "You see the resemblance?"

Zoë nodded, feeling rather deflated. Her scheme to keep Philip's identity secret had been doomed from the moment Jerrold had laid his eyes on his son. No one who had seen the portrait could have denied the relationship.

A footman appeared in the doorway. "Mr. Layton is here, my lord. Will you see him?"

The large figure of Rupert Layton pushed past the footman and bustled into the drawing room. "I was sure you would see me, Jerry. No need to stand on ceremony with you, eh?"

"No, not at all. I'm happy to see you. Zoë, may I present to you my uncle, Rupert Layton? Uncle Rupert, my wife."

The tall man stared down at Zoë with an intentness that she found unnerving. At length he said, smiling broadly, "Well, well, my dear Zoë, so we meet at last. Welcome to the Layton family."

"Thank you."

The smile fading, Rupert turned back to Jerrold. "My

boy, I dislike bringing you bad news on your first day in London, but I think you should know that you and Zoë are the subject of some very unpleasant rumors."

"Rumors?"

"Yes, about your marriage. Well, in the first place, everyone in the *ton* now seems to know you and Zoë are married, which isn't surprising. Your cousin Melicent and I have been quietly spreading the word for several weeks. Naturally, the news has occasioned a great deal of comment. A nine days' wonder and all that. Again, not surprising. But during the past few days I've been hearing reports that people are wondering *why* you kept the marriage secret for so long. They are questioning whether there was ever really a marriage, or are you simply claiming it took place because you wish to legitimize your by-blow."

Zoë gasped. She could feel the blood draining from her face.

Patting her shoulder, Rupert murmured, "I'm sorry, my dear. This must be difficult for you." To Jerrold he said, "One story I've heard speculates that you and Zoë had an illicit affair years ago, and that you met again recently. At that time you became so taken with Philip that you decided to make him your heir. In order to do that, you had to claim that a marriage had taken place." Rupert spread his hands. "I regret very much to tell you this, Jerry, but Melicent suspects that the source of some of these scurrilous rumors is Lady Harlow."

"Dorothea?" Jerrold exclaimed incredulously. "Why . . . ?" He cut himself off, his mouth set in a grim line.

Rupert gave him a sympathetic look. "The thing to do is to ignore the rumors. As you and Zoë take your rightful place in the *ton*, I think—I hope—the rumors will die away. Your family will indicate by our support that we believe the rumors to be false. To start, Beryl and I want you to come to dinner on Saturday. Not a large party, our house is too small, but I hope to invite some influential people. And Melicent will entertain for you as well. And now I must be off, or I'll be late to a supper meeting at White's to discuss an important by-election in the West Country."

After Rupert had left, Jerrold explained his uncle's parting remark to Zoë: "Uncle Rupert is a mover in the inner circles of the Tory party." As he looked at her troubled face, he added, "My uncle is right, you know. These rumors will eventually fade away. Don't bother your head about them."

He sounded entirely too unconcerned to suit Zoë's agitated state of mind, but for the moment she was unable to talk to Jerrold any further about Rupert Layton's unsettling news. A footman announced dinner, and she and Jerrold, sitting at opposite ends of the long table in the cavernous dining room, ate a subdued meal, making occasional commonplace remarks for the benefit of the attentive ears of the servants. Zoë excused herself after the dessert course and went to her bedchamber.

As Meg Brant was brushing out Zoë's hair, the abigail remarked, "I've unpacked all your painting equipment, ma'am. Ye can start working in the new studio tomorrow if ye like."

"Thank you, Meg. I'll need to make up for lost time, won't I?" Briefly the prospect of throwing herself into the work she loved lifted Zoë's spirits, but after Meg left the bedchamber, the nagging doubts resurfaced.

Dressed in her nightdress and peignoir, Zoë stood at her window, looking abstractedly down at the square below, where a carriage, its lamps glowing brightly in the deepening twilight, had just stopped before a house on the opposite side of the square. Was it the Lord Chancellor's house, she wondered idly, and then her harried thoughts caught up with her again. She cringed as she recalled Rupert Layton's conversation. If even a portion of the London *ton* believed that Jerrold was trying to foist his paramour and his bastard on society, she doubted both her courage and her ability to carry off the pretense that she and Jerrold were a happily married couple.

A light knock sounded on the dressing room door, which Meg had closed before she left. Zoë gazed at the door uncertainly. Finally she said, "Come."

Jerrold entered the bedchamber. He was still fully dressed. "I apologize for disturbing you. However, in view of my Uncle Rupert's visit tonight, there's something we should discuss." Hesitating a moment, he said abruptly, "Do you have your marriage lines? I recall that you told me a clergyman performed the wedding ceremony—"

Zoë interrupted him. "Are you implying that there *are* no marriage lines, because no marriage ceremony was performed?" she asked coldly.

Jerrold looked dumfounded. "No, certainly not. Sometimes the recording of Scottish marriages is irregular to nonexistent, but clergymen are usually more methodical."

"Oh." Zoë bit her lip. After a moment she went to her dressing table and opened her jewelry case, removing a piece of paper from a compartment at the bottom of the case. She brought the paper to Jerrold.

He unfolded the certificate and scanned it quickly. "May I keep this?"

"Why?" Zoë stared at her marriage lines. Though she

had tried for so many years to deny the reality of her elopement to Gretna Green, she had, for a reason she had never explained to herself, guarded carefully the document that proved the truth of that secret marriage.

"I want to take the certificate to my solicitor to be locked in his files," Jerrold explained. "In the event I die or am killed while Philip is still a minor, the certificate will ensure that no one can dispute his claim to my title and estates."

"I see. Yes, you may keep the marriage lines."

"Thank you." As Jerrold turned to go, he paused, saying, "You're not still disturbed about Uncle Rupert's rumors, are you?"

Zoë gave him a direct look. "I am, yes. I don't feel comfortable with the thought that I'll be the object of venomous gossip each time I step out in public. Apparently you're somewhat disturbed yourself. Otherwise you wouldn't be so concerned about the safekeeping of our marriage lines."

Shrugging, Jerrold replied, "Oh, I'm not comfortable with gossip, either, but I assure you, Zoë, that all we need do is ignore these rumors, keep our heads high with grace and dignity, and the prattleboxes will eventually find something else to occupy their minds."

A thought struck Zoë. "Just who is this woman your uncle thinks is responsible for the worst of these rumors? A Lady—Lady Harlow, I believe her name was."

"She's a—she was a friend."

"A friend?" Zoë stared at Jerrold. "A *friend* is spreading scandalous rumors about you?"

He bit his lip. "Well, if you must have it, Lady Harlow was my mistress until recently. We decided that we, er, no longer suited."

"Perhaps your decision was one-sided, on your part

only. That would explain Lady Harlow's rumor-mongering," Zoë exclaimed. This news of a spiteful mistress, added to the fatigue and strain of her long journey from Heathfield and Rupert Layton's report of worrying gossip, brought her temper to the boiling point. She glared at Jerrold. "Oh, just go away. I've been longing for a little peace and privacy in my own bedchamber for five whole days. Is that too much to ask?"

He bowed stiffly. "No, not at all. I apologize for disturbing you. Good night, Zoë."

Chapter Ten

Zoë stirred, opening her eyes drowsily as a ray of bright May sunshine slanted in through the bed curtains. Momentarily confused about where she was, she soon realized she was in the elegant blue and rose bedchamber in Woodforde House, Bedford Square, once occupied by Jerrold's mother. As she sat up, yawning, the bedchamber door opened a crack and Meg Brant's voice said briskly, "Oh, good, ye're awake, my lady. I've brought yer tea. Would ye like me to bring up yer breakfast too?"

"Oh, yes, thank you, Meg," Zoë replied in relief. After last night's rancorous encounter, during the course of which she'd virtually chased Jerrold from her bedchamber, Zoë didn't relish the thought of eating breakfast with her husband.

A little later, propped up by a myriad of pillows, Zoë luxuriated in eating her breakfast in bed, one of the very few advantages, she thought wryly, of being the Countess of Woodforde. Sipping her tea, she leafed through the pages of the *Morning Post*, which Meg had brought up with her tray. She read the latest foreign news—the new French king had hosted a grand reception for foreign dignitaries at the Tuileries—and noted the theatrical announcements, thinking she might take Philip to an equestrian performance at Astley's Amphitheatre. Then, glancing idly at the society anecdotes, she froze.

"Lord and Lady W. have taken up residence in London. Friends of Lord W., who only recently was considered the most eligible bachelor in England, are waiting eagerly to make the acquaintance of the hitherto unknown Lady W. We are told that Lord and Lady W. were married some years ago, but chose, doubtless for good and sufficient reasons, not to make their union public. They are said to have a son."

Zoë slammed the newspaper down on her tray so hard that she knocked over her pot of tea. As she mopped ineffectually at the spilled liquid with her napkin, her apprehensions of the previous evening revived. Now she was not only the subject of scurrilous anonymous rumors, she was also being pilloried in the public press. The writer of the gossipy tidbit in the *Morning Post* had clearly implied that there was some irregularity in the Woodforde marriage.

She pressed her lips firmly together. She couldn't allow rumors, even published ones, to paralyze her every action. She would get dressed, take Philip to play in the Bedford Square garden, and then get on with her painting.

But Philip had other plans. When she arrived in his bedchamber, she found Jerrold with him.

"Mama, guess what?" Bubbling with excitement, Philip exclaimed, "Papa is taking me to that market with the funny name—you remember, Spit or something like that—to buy me a bird. We'll drive to the market in a curricle, think of that. And Papa says, after we choose a bird, he'll buy me an ice at—at . . ."

"At Gunther's sweet shop in Berkeley Square," finished Jerrold with an amused smile. "Doubtless, during the next few months, Philip, you'll become a regular customer, once you taste their black currant ice."

"I daresay you'll have a most enjoyable time, Philip," Zoë said rather stiffly.

Flicking her a quick glance, Jerrold said to Philip, "Go downstairs and wait for me in the foyer. I want a word with your mother." He nodded a dismissal to Philip's nursemaid. "I hope you won't think I'm being high-handed, Zoë," he said with a touch of apology. "I intended to inform you that I was taking Philip out this morning. I know how carefully you supervise his daily activities."

"Thank you. I do like to know where Philip is at all times," Zoë replied, still stiffly, and turned to go.

"Wait, please."

Zoë turned around, her eyebrows lifted interrogatively as she gazed at Jerrold. He was well turned out, as usual, in town garb of blue coat, red waistcoat, tight beige pantaloons, and shining Hessians.

He said, almost diffidently, "I wanted to tell you I'm sorry Uncle Rupert distressed you last night. Naturally you were overset by his account of the rumors floating about London. I wish my uncle had kept his news to himself. Possibly the rumors would never have come to your attention otherwise."

"Oh, but they would. The paragraph in the *Post* this morning took care of that. The *Post* strongly intimates that there is something havey-cavey about our marriage."

A crease formed between Jerrold's brows, and his hands clenched. "I'm sorry," he said again. "I hoped the item wouldn't come to your attention. It must have been distressing for you to see your story in the public prints."

Zoë blurted, "I feel as if I'm exposed in an open field, with lightning striking all around me. I keep wondering what catastrophe will happen next."

He hesitated, as if seeking for the right words. "Zoë, this situation has been difficult for both of us. We've been forced to live together when we're really strangers to each other. We've been uncomfortable and prickly with each other. We can't talk normally, for fear of saying the wrong thing. Don't you think our lives would be easier if we were friends, or at least pretended to be?"

He looked and sounded so earnest and reasonable, Zoë thought. But the Earl of Woodforde was the same Jerrold Layton who had poisoned her girlhood, and she couldn't believe his character had really changed. For her he would always be the arrogant rake who had mistaken her for a strumpet on the morning after their elopement. He was being sympathetic and understanding now only because he needed her cooperation to preserve his ancestral line. For the safety of her peace of mind, she had to keep up her guard against any intimacy.

Edging away from him, she said, "Apparently I still haven't made my position clear to you. I can't pretend to a friendship I don't feel. In public, of course, I'll be polite, dutiful, whatever the occasion demands. However, in private I would prefer to have as little personal contact with you as possible."

A curtain descended over his face, leaving it devoid of expression. "As you will, naturally." Stony-faced, he turned away and walked out of the room.

* * *

As Jerrold took the reins of the curricle, the tiger moved away from the horses' heads and climbed on his perch at the rear of the vehicle. At the entrance of the square, the tiger jumped down to open the gates to allow the curricle to pass through.

As Jerrold turned into Holborn, he glanced sideways at Philip. "Mind you sit still," he warned the boy. "I can't have you falling out under the wheels to be crushed to death."

"Oh, I promise, Papa. I'll be as still as a statue." A smile of blissful enjoyment curved Philip's lips during the drive westward into Newgate and Bishopsgate. Jerrold pointed out to him the principal sights—Grey's Inn, the Fleet Prison, St. Paul's. But Philip was more interested in the teeming life of the streets, the strolling ballad singers, the milkmaids with their pails suspended from yokes worn across their shoulders, the bakers in their white aprons shouting "Hot loaves," the news vendors blowing their horns.

In Spitalfields market father and son wandered among the booths selling fruits and vegetables and fresh meat, stopped at one booth to enjoy a cup of the famous oxtail soup, and finally settled into the serious business of the morning, choosing a singing bird. Jerrold stood behind Philip, waiting patiently while the boy agonized between a linnet and a goldfinch.

Finally Philip turned to his father. "Papa, couldn't I—"

"No, you can't have both birds," Jerrold interrupted him. Hardening his heart, Jerrold said, "You must choose one or the other.'

After another few moments of indecision Philip picked a plump goldfinch.

"An excellent choice," Jerrold commented as they

walked back to the curricle, with Philip holding the wicker cage carefully. As he took the reins, Jerrold said, "Now then, if you're not tired, we'll be off to Gunther's for that ice I promised you."

Philip looked indignant. "Papa! I'm not a baby. I'm six years old. Of course I'm not tired."

A little later, sitting in the curricle under the plane trees of Berkeley Square, surrounded by carriages whose occupants waited to be served by the scurrying waiters from the sweet shop, Jerrold watched Philip as the child dug his spoon enthusiastically into a second ice. Only a few short weeks ago, Jerrold reflected, he couldn't have conceived of this visit to Gunther's with a small boy in tow, and that boy his own son.

Until now, he had never had any interest in children, or indeed, any real contact with them since his own childhood. Siring a child to carry on his name had been of no importance to him while Trevor was alive. There had been no need for him to procreate and provide for the succession, and he had received his doctor's pronouncement that he was probably sterile as a result of his siege of the mumps with scarcely a twinge of disappointment. Being sterile had certainly simplified his relationship with Dorothea. But Trevor's death had changed his indifferent attitude toward children to one of bitter regret. When his brother was killed, he would have paid any price to reverse his sterility and thus preclude any possibility that Oliver Layton might inherit the family estates. He had greeted the discovery that he had a legitimate son with exultant joy, though not because of the fact of fatherhood itself. At the very beginning, his relationship with Philip had been quite impersonal. He thought of the boy merely as the instrument to bar Oliver from the succession, and he'd cultivated the child's regard more in the hope that the effort would help persuade Zoë Manning to agree to make their marriage public than from any interest in Philip himself.

Now ... Jerrold felt an overwhelming rush of affection as he watched his son spoon up the last mouthful of black currant ice. Almost from that first meeting on the road outside Heathfield, Philip had begun to conquer his father's heart, until now Jerrold couldn't conceive of a time when this small person, this miniature of himself, hadn't been a part of his life. He took out his handkerchief and handed it to Philip. "Here, wipe your mouth. We don't want your mama to think I'm not taking good care of you."

As Philip was obediently mopping his face, Jerrold flicked his reins and put his team in motion. "Time to go home."

"Oh, Papa, must we go so soon?"

Squeezing Philip's arm, Jerrold smiled saying, "There will be other days, you know. We'll go see the animals in the Tower, and sail a boat on the Serpentine. But for now I have business to take care of, and your mama will worry if I keep you out too long."

Driving along New Bond Street and making the turn into Oxford Street, Jerrold listened, amused, to Philip's artless chatter and answered the boy's questions with only one part of his mind engaged, while at the same time he reflected on the contrast between his son's attitude toward him and that of the boy's mother.

Zoë's life had been torn asunder by their elopement to Gretna Green—he understood that. She had never forgiven him for what had happened that night, and he understood that, too. And God knew he hadn't expected or wanted a real marriage when he persuaded Zoë to set up a household with him for their son's sake, but he certainly expected more than the chill, almost shrinking aversion that Zoë had shown him this morning when he offered her his friendship. He sighed. They were bound together for the immediate future, at least until Philip's majority. He didn't look forward to sharing a house and a life with a woman who, he now realized, had to make a great effort to treat him with even a modicum of civility.

After depositing Philip in the care of a footman at Woodforde House, Jerrold drove to his solicitor's office in Grey's Inn, where he deposited the precious marriage lines that proved his son's legitimacy.

"Mind, if you have a fire on the premises, you're to retrieve this certificate even if it means you don't save another scrap of paper from your file boxes," Jerrold told the solicitor's clerk, only half in jest.

The young man's eyes grew round. "To be sure, my lord."

From Grey's Inn, Jerrold drove toward Mayfair. In Grafton Street he left the curricle with his tiger and walked to Albemarle Street. As he went up the steps of the familiar small fashionable house, his feet dragged with reluctance, and he smiled wryly, remembering all the other times when he'd taken those same steps two at a time in his eagerness to bury himself in Dorothea's warm voluptuous embrace.

The maid who answered the door greeted him with less than her usual warmth. Had Dorothea informed the girl that he would no longer be a regular visitor? "If ye'll wait in the morning room, my lord, I'll inquire if her ladyship is to home."

Dorothea kept him waiting. And waiting. Shifting his

long body uncomfortably in one of Dorothea's spindly gilt chairs, Jerrold was sure the wait was intentional.

He rose when she finally entered the room in a cloud of scent, every Titian curl in place, her ample bosom barely veiled by her low-cut bodice. "Well, Jerry, this is a surprise," she said as she sat down and waved him to a chair. She raised an eyebrow. "According to the *on dit*, you've acquired both a wife and a son since we last met. Tell me, how do you like being a father?"

"Actually, I'm finding the experience very rewarding. Today, for example, Philip and I shopped in Spitalfields market for a singing bird, and afterwards we went to Gunther's for an ice.'

Dorothea burst out laughing. "Jerry, you didn't! What a perfect guy you must have looked, bear-leading a small child around London at the height of the Season. Why didn't you leave your son in the country in the care of a tutor or a nanny, like any normal parent?"

"I happen to enjoy Philip's company, that's why. Dorothea, I didn't come here to discuss parenthood."

"No? Then why did you come? Can it be that you've tired of domesticity so quickly and want to share my bed once more?"

Ignoring Dorothea's mocking smile, Jerrold said coolly, "You're all abroad, my dear. Zoë and I are perfectly happy. Or we would be if it weren't for the gabblemongers who are spreading false rumors about our marriage. Rumors I understand originated with you."

"With me?" Dorothea tossed her head. "Why would I circulate scandalous rumors about you and your new wife?"

"Zoë isn't my new wife, you know. We've been married for seven years."

"Seven years? Fancy that. And why, pray, have you been so secretive about the happy event?"

"We had our reasons."

"Oh? And what might those reasons be?"

Jerrold looked at her composedly. "I don't believe I'm under any obligation to explain my marriage to you, Dorothea."

Her bosom heaved, and the violet eyes flashed in fury. "Don't speak to me about marriage, you hypocrite. Only a few weeks ago—scarcely a month, if that—you carefully explained to me your reasons for wishing to remain a bachelor. And all the while you were planning to announce that you were already married, had been for seven years. Was it really that long, Jerry? Or did you decide to marry the mother of one of your by-blows and pass the boy off as legitimate after your brother died and you needed an heir? An heir you could no longer father because of that childish ailment you contracted a few years ago."

His temper rising, Jerrold snapped, "If you care to accompany me to my solicitor's office, I'll show you my marriage lines—duly dated seven years ago." He broke off, clamping his lips shut. Dorothea had some justification for being angry, though it didn't excuse her malicious attempt to cast doubt on the legitimacy of his marriage. And he couldn't tell her the truth in an attempt to placate her. He couldn't explain to her that at the time he refused to marry her he himself was in ignorance about his marital status.

He rose, saying, "I daresay you'll find it hard to believe, but I never had any intention of injuring you."

"You're quite right. I do find it hard to believe. You've made a perfect gull of me."

Jerrold's mouth hardened. "I'm sorry you feel that

way. I came here hoping to persuade you to drop this vendetta of gossip, but I see now that more extreme measures are indicated. Stop spreading these rumors, Dorothea. Don't discuss my affairs at all, and that includes any speculation about my possible sterility. Otherwise, suppressing every gentlemanly instinct I ever possessed, I'll be obliged to spread a few rumors myself."

At Dorothea's quick affronted frown, Jerrold nodded, saying, "We were very discreet during our affair. Perhaps a number of people guessed we were lovers, but no one knew for sure. There was never any scandal to sully your pristine reputation. I fancy you wouldn't enjoy having it open knowledge that you and I had a passionate affair, and then, when I threw you over for my long-lost wife, you fell into a fit of the jealous megrims. That would put you into the category, not just of a loose woman, but of a woman scorned. Not a comfortable position for you to be in at this present, since, as you informed me recently, you're on the catch for another husband."

Her face contorted so that all its delicate prettiness disappeared, Dorothea expressed herself with an earthy vocabulary that would have done justice to a Billingsgate fishwife.

Picking up his hat and stick, Jerrold said, "Exactly. We understand each other, then. Goodbye, Dorothea."

That morning, after Jerrold's departure to take Philip shopping for a singing bird, Zoë, more disturbed than she would have cared to admit, tried to put her latest clash with her husband out of her mind by going to her new studio to resume work on Lady Bradford's portrait.

But as she left the room, a footman intercepted her. "Lady Rosedale is here, my lady. Will you see her?"

"Yes, of course. I'll come right down."

In the drawing room, Zoë greeted Melicent with a warm handshake. "I'm so glad to see you." She glanced questioningly at the tall young man who had risen at her entrance.

Melicent smiled. "Jerry sent word you'd arrived, so I came right over. I also brought another relative to meet you. Zoë, this is Oliver Layton, Uncle Rupert's son."

The young man, who strongly reminded Zoë of Jerrold, except that his eyes weren't as intensely blue and his shoulders weren't as broad, seized both her hands and leaned down to kiss her cheek lightly. "Pray excuse such an early call," he said with an easy grin. "M'father told me you and Jerry were in town, and I couldn't wait to meet old Jerry's bride." He looked at her closely. "That nodcock, Jerry. Deuced if I can imagine why he elected to keep an Incomparable like you a secret for so long."

"Stop doing the pretty, Oliver," Melicent ordered. "You're embarrassing Zoë."

Oliver subsided, grinning even more widely.

"It occurred to me you might wish to go shopping this morning, Zoë," Melicent went on. "When I arrived in town several weeks ago, I discovered that my wardrobe sadly needed replenishing after a year of wearing nothing but mourning." She herself looked striking in a pelisse of coral-colored muslin that set off her dark prettiness, worn with a straw bonnet trimmed with matching ribbon.

"I decided last night that my wardrobe would never do for a London Season," said Zoë ruefully. "Thank you, I'd like to go shopping."

"At your service," said Oliver, bowing. "Happy to escort both you ladies. Take you in my curricle, if you like."

"No, thank you, Oliver. I've no wish to sit crowded three to a seat in your curricle, with my hair and my bonnet blowing in the breeze," said Melicent firmly. "And no offense meant, but I prefer not to have gentlemen underfoot when I'm choosing a new gown."

"Well, then, if I'm to be rebuffed, I'll take my leave," said Oliver mournfully. "Goodbye, Melicent, Cousin Zoë."

Later, driving with Melicent in the elegant Rosedale town coach, Zoë remarked, "Oliver Layton seems very friendly."

Melicent made a face. "Perhaps a little too much so. He's been underfoot since I came to London, offering to escort me here and there, inviting me to ride in the Park or attend the theater. Incidentally, Jerry dislikes him intensely, and I must confess that I never cared very much for Oliver when we were growing up. However, I've no intention of discouraging him. At this time I think a show of family solidarity is important." She paused, looking closely at Zoë. "And how has it been going with you, my dear?"

"If you mean, are Jerrold and I dealing together without bloodshed, the answer is yes. We've succeeded in being tolerably polite to each other."

"You'll have to do better than that, you know, at least in public. As your advance messenger, so to speak, I've been telling everyone I meet about your romantic love story."

"Star-crossed lovers?" Zoë grimaced. "I know you want to help, Melicent, and I'm grateful, but is there really anything we can do to avoid scandal? Jerrold's uncle told us last night about the rumors circulating in London concerning our secret marriage. And then this morning there was that paragraph in the newspaper.

"I saw it. It was quite dreadful." Melicent set her jaw. "You can't let it affect you. Simply put it out of your mind. Remember, in the end it's how you and Jerry conduct yourselves that will convince people you have a solid, respectable marriage." Melicent grinned. "For example, this morning we'll not be merely shopping for a new wardrobe for you. We'll be adding to your image, showing the *ton* that a dazzling Countess of Woodforde has arrived on the scene, and that Jerry displayed excellent taste in choosing you."

Raising an eyebrow, Zoë said, "Dazzling? Coming it too strong, Melicent. "I've never been dazzling in my life." But the nonsense raised her spirits a little.

During her brief previous visits to London, Zoë had never been able to spare the time from her painting appointments for leisurely shopping trips. Today she was caught up in the bustle and excitement of Oxford Street, with its double row of elegant lampposts, the long line of waiting carriages ranged in the middle of its wide expanse and above all the myriad of shops selling every imaginable commodity: silver and china, wines and fruits, lamps and crystal and fans, linens and shoes and fabrics of every description. Melicent did not allow Zoë to linger in front of any of the enticing shop fronts, but dragged her ruthlessly to the establishment of Madame Leclerc.

Madame was charmed to meet a new customer of the social status of the Countess of Woodforde. She urged Zoë to examine the fashion magazines strewn on a long table: the *Lady's Magazine, Ackermann's Repository,* the *Lady's Monthly Museum, La Belle Assemblée,* and when Zoë had finished poring through the periodicals, Madame unrolled bolt after bolt of exquisite material in silk, crape, muslin, jaconet, satin, sarcenet, velvet, and gauze.

"You'll need a minimum of ten gowns for evening, and at least that many morning dresses and carriage dresses," pronounced Melicent. "And a sufficient number of pelisses and bonnets and shawls, of course."

Zoë gazed at Madame's smiling face and avaricious eyes and succumbed to a wave of panic. She pulled Melicent aside and half whispered, "I can't possibly afford that many new clothes at the prices this woman must charge."

Patting her arm, Melicent murmured, "Don't be ridiculous. You could buy the entire shop if you had a mind to. Or Jerry could. His income must be well over forty thousand a year."

"Pounds?" gasped Zoë.

Melicent smiled. "Pounds, certainly, you goose. Jerry is the largest landowner in Herefordshire." She raised her voice. "Now, then, you must start making some decisions. What about that blue aërophone crape over a white satin slip? The pale yellow mull is very nice, too, and I like the peach-colored *soie de Londres.*"

While Zoë, still somewhat befuddled, was making her choices of patterns and fabrics, Madame disappeared into an inner room, returning shortly with a gown made of sheerest *crêpe lisse* in a shade of emerald green. Its brief bodice and tiny puff sleeves were embroidered in gleaming seed pearls in an intricate pattern. Zoë fell in love with the gown the instant she saw it.

"Lady Wantage ordered this gown just before her husband dropped dead," reported Madame. "Heart, I think it was, poor man. Of course, the dress is of no use to her ladyship now that she's in mourning, and she sent it back." Madame held up the garment invitingly. "The color exactly matches your eyes, my lady, and I think the gown is very close to your size. Do you care to try it on? Naturally, I would be prepared to make an adjustment in the price."

"Do try on the gown, Zoë," urged Melicent. "It looks perfect for you."

Zoë needed no urging. In the dressing room the modiste's assistant circled her slowly, saying, "The gown might have been made for you, my lady. It needs practically no alteration."

Eyeing herself in the cheval glass, Zoë knew that she had never owned a dress that was more becoming. Her cheeks pink with pleasure, she left the dressing room to show herself off to Melicent. At the door leading into the show room, she paused, hearing her name.

"Countess of Woodforde," a voice said scathingly. "Countess of Woodforde, indeed! My dear Melicent, where has this woman been for all these years? Has your cousin kept her hidden away for some dark reason? Is she unpresentable? Deformed, perhaps, or—mad? I actually heard, you know, that she'd been living in some parson's house under a false name!"

"Don't talk fustian, Annabel," came Melicent's crisp reply. "Zoë is a lovely woman. I predict she'll take London by storm. And she wasn't living in 'some parson's house.' She was residing with her brother, the highly respected rector of my home parish. She changed her name because she, er, she wished for privacy. There's no mystery about her situation at all. The simple truth is what I've been trying to tell you. My cousin Jerry and Zoë fell in love and eloped to Gretna Green. Shortly afterwards they had a violent quarrel and went their separate ways. Recently they met again and realized they had never stopped caring for each other."

"Very romantic, I'm sure," sniffed the unseen speaker. "I must say, however, that the young woman's behavior makes her seem a little common. What are her connections?"

"Her father was the former rector of our parish. He was a younger son of the Marquess of Kilburn."

"I see." After a pause the speaker said grudgingly, "Well, Melicent, we've been friends for a long time, and I daresay I must take your word for your cousin's wife."

Zoë went back to the dressing room. She had heard enough. Melicent joined her as the dressmaker's assistant was helping her out of the pearl-embroidered gown. After she had nodded a dismissal to the assistant, Melicent said, "You never came out to show me the gown, so I assume you heard me talking to Annabel Sykes."

"I did, yes. Doubtless she was only repeating what a great many other people in London are saying."

"Don't pay Annabel any mind, Zoë. She was always a prattle box. She'll come around when she actually meets you. Everyone will."

"I hope you're right," said Zoë, attempting a smile. "We'll soon find out, won't we?" Her pleasure in selecting a pretty new wardrobe had evaporated.

Chapter Eleven

Zoë's dispirited mood persisted after she returned to Bedford Square, as her thoughts lingered on the spiteful comments of Melicent's friend, Annabel Sykes, at the modiste's shop. With each passing day she was beginning to realize how naively, how stupidly, she had dealt with the consequences of her elopement to Gretna Green. She could understand why strangers like Annabel Sykes would question why she and Jerrold had concealed the fact of their marriage for so many years, and why, especially, they would look askance at her assumption of a false identity. In their place she would have reacted in much the same way.

She set her mouth. There was no help for it. For Philip's sake, she and Jerrold would simply have to brazen the situation out. And their task would be infinitely more difficult in the present strained state of their relations, she reminded herself, thinking back to their difficult scene of this morning.

Now that she was calmer, she realized that she shouldn't have rejected Jerrold's offer of "friendship" so impulsively. No, not friendship, merely the pretense of friendship. He'd meant only that such a pretense might smooth the awkward edges of their enforced relationship, and he was right. She should have agreed with him, simply to ease the daily strain in her dealings with him. Instead, angered and distressed by Rupert Layton's disclosure last night that Jerrold's former mistress was spreading rumors about her and Jerrold, and further overset this morning by the malicious paragraph in the *Morning Post,* she had childishly lashed out at him, and now they were back in their old prickly impasse.

Well, so she'd made a mistake. She could correct that mistake, she supposed, if she were willing to sacrifice her personal pride, but . . . . Shying away from the thought, she took refuge in a painting session that afternoon, and as usual while she was working, she was able to put her problems out of her mind. When Meg Brant came to the studio in late afternoon, carrying a tray piled with calling cards, the abigail peered at the partly finished portrait and said appreciatively, "That's Lady Bradford, isn't it? Ye've caught that sort of bright, inquisitive look she always has."

Inquisitive was exactly the right word for Lady Bradford, and doubtless it was also the right word to describe all the people who had left calling cards at Woodforde House today, Zoë thought wryly as she turned over the cards on the tray. She didn't recognize any of the printed names. She groaned inwardly as she realized she would be required to return the calls.

She cleaned her brushes and draped a cloth over her easel and went down the corridor to check on Philip before she dressed for dinner. Her son was eating his supper at a small table, spooning a pudding into his mouth absent-mindedly as he kept his eyes fixed raptly on the wicker bird cage hanging from the ceiling.

"Master Philip ain't hardly taken his eyes off that bird

since he brought it home," reported the nursemaid, Sarah, in a smiling aside. "He fair dotes on the creature."

Catching sight of his mother, Philip exclaimed, "Listen to Sunshine, Mama. Have you ever heard such singing?"

"No, never," Zoë agreed, gazing admiringly at the plump gold and black bird. "He's very handsome, too. And I like the name you've given him."

"It was hard to choose between Sunshine and another bird," Philip confided. "I would have liked to have both birds, really, but Papa said no."

"Perhaps your papa feared the two birds might become jealous of each other. And so, I gather you enjoyed your excursion today?"

"Oh, yes, Mama. After we bought the bird, we went to a sweet shop. I had two ices . . ." Philip's voice trailed away. He gave Zoë a guilty look. "Papa thought perhaps I shouldn't tell you about the second ice. He was afraid it would spoil my appetite for lunch."

"Which it did, too, my lady," said the nursemaid, smiling broadly.

"Oh, well." Zoë ruffled Philip's curls. "Just once, I daresay an overindulgence won't hurt you."

He was so happy, she thought with a catch in her throat. Whatever the cost, she had to do everything she could do to preserve that happiness.

In the morning room a little later, waiting for Jerrold to join her for dinner, Zoë gazed about her with a feeling of pleasure. It was a comfortable, lived-in room, furnished by her late mother-in-law with unpretentious pieces that contrasted with the heavy magnificence of the rest of the house. It was a room that Zoë could relax in, though, as Jerrold entered, she could feel her nerves tightening as she recalled the decision she had made, while dressing for dinner, to mend the fences between them.

"Good evening," he said, his voice conveying a certain aloofness that Zoë recognized was the result of their confrontation that morning. He went to a small table at the side of the room and poured two glasses of wine. Presenting one to Zoë, he sat down in a chair near her. "Did you have a pleasant day?"

"Very much so," Zoë said, trying to convey a casual ease. "Your cousin Melicent called to take me shopping for a new wardrobe." She smiled at him, hoping the smile didn't appear artificial. "Apparently Philip's day was memorable, too. Thank you. I realize fathers don't usually spend much time with small children."

"I enjoy being with Philip." Jerrold looked wary, as if he wasn't quite sure what Zoë's unexpectedly cordial overture might mean. He cleared his throat. "Ah—I trust the shopping expedition was successful?"

"Oh, indeed. I took Melicent's advice and ordered a grand new wardrobe." Zoë cocked her head at him. "The clothes were very expensive. I hope you won't think I was extravagant. I charged my purchases to your account."

"Naturally," said Jerrold a little stiffly. "You're my wife."

"I felt guilty, spending so much money," Zoë went on, "but then Melicent assured me you could afford the cost. Is that true?"

"Of course I can afford the cost. My wife must be suitably dressed," Jerrold said testily. Then he stopped, observing the faint smile at the corners of Zoë's mouth. "You're bamming me," he accused her.

"Well, perhaps I was teasing you, just a little," she admitted. "Melicent did say that you were the richest landowner in Herefordshire."

He burst out laughing, and Zoë felt the tension lessening between them as the result of her rather labored little joke. Taking a deep breath, she said, "Jerrold, I want to apologize. This morning you made a perfectly sensible suggestion, and I turned thumbs down on it. I've changed my mind. I think we should behave to each other in a friendlier fashion. It will make life easier for both of us if we aren't engaged in a constant sparring match."

An expression of relief spread over Jerrold's face. "Thank you, Zoë. I'm sure you won't regret this." Visibly relaxed, he sipped at his wine. "Well, now, tell me about your new wardrobe."

He listened attentively as Zoë described the gowns she had ordered, asking an occasional knowledgeable question. Yes, knowledgeable, Zoë reflected with a sudden illogical prick of anger. Doubtless he'd accompanied numerous females, respectable or otherwise, to modistes' salons. Hastily suppressing the thought, she began to describe the emerald green dress with the pearl beading and paused in midsentence, remembering the conversation upon which she'd eavesdropped at Madame Leclerc's shop.

"What is it?" asked Jerrold.

"I—it's nothing."

"What kind of a nothing, exactly?"

"Oh . . . at the dress shop I overheard one of Melicent's friends speculating to her about the new Countess of Woodforde. The woman seemed to think you had made a dreadful mesalliance. She assumed you wouldn't have hidden me away for all these years unless I was either mad or common."

A muscle twitched in Jerrold's cheek. "I'm so sorry you were exposed to such unfeeling cruelty," he exclaimed. "I'm convinced, though, that remarks like that will cease when people really know you."

"That's what Melicent says."

"She's right. She usually is." After a moment Jerrold added, clearing his throat, "For what it's worth, I believe I've silenced the source of the worst of the gossip. I went to see Lady Harlow today. I think she understands now that it's in her own best interests to stop spreading untrue rumors.

Zoë looked fixedly at Jerrold. She couldn't tell from his expression what his feelings might be. Had he disliked visiting his ex-mistress? Was the woman really an "ex"? What did she look like? Was she beautiful? Had Jerrold ever gone shopping with her for new gowns? Feeling the color rising in her cheeks, Zoë tried to jerk her thoughts away from Lady Harlow. She was relieved when the butler appeared in the doorway to announce dinner.

Rather to her surprise, Zoë found that she was able to maintain her newfound truce with Jerrold more easily than she might have imagined. It was as if her mind had two compartments. In the one, she could tuck away her past feelings of resentment and dislike for Jerrold and not dwell on them. In the other, she could begin to think of him as merely a friendly acquaintance who lived in the same house with her and shared with her the care of her son.

However, even if she was more comfortable in her domestic life with Jerrold, Zoë still sank into a state of nerves several days later, as she prepared for the dinner hosted in their honor by Rupert Layton and his wife. Zoë dressed for the occasion with considerable trepidation. For the first time she would be meeting Jerrold's friends and acquaintances as his wife. Her stomach was already in knots at the thought of being the center of attention of a curious and possibly critical audience.

"Oh, ma'am—my lady—ye look perfectly beautiful," breathed Meg as Zoë turned slowly before the cheval glass in the emerald green *crêpe lisse* gown with its pearl embroidery, delivered from Madame Leclerc's shop only that afternoon.

"It looks a little bare," fretted Zoë. She possessed no real jewelry save her mother's modest string of pearls, which hadn't looked quite right with the intricate pearl beading of the bodice, and which she'd entwined instead in the curls of her topknot.

"Ye really don't need a necklace with that lovely beaded bodice," Meg assured her, and, though Zoë didn't agree, she nodded resignedly, slipping a silvery lace shawl around her shoulders and walking out into the corridor.

Jerrold met her outside her door. He cocked his head, eyeing her slowly from head to toe, his lips gradually curving in an approving smile. "So this is the gown you were telling me about. It's quite lovely. You have excellent taste." He paused, his brows drawing together. "By Jove, I almost forgot. . . . Wait." He turned, walking swiftly down the corridor. In a few moments he returned with a worn velvet-covered box in his hand. He opened the box and held it out to her. "I went to the bank today to retrieve my mother's jewels. I think these will go well with your gown."

Zoë gasped as she gazed at "these," which consisted of an exquisite necklace of pearls, emeralds, and diamonds with matching earrings. "I can't possibly accept such a gift . . ." His eyebrows raised, and suddenly feeling like an idiot, she floundered, "That is, I assume you meant the jewelry as a loan . . ."

"On the contrary," Jerrold retorted. "The necklace and earrings are neither a gift or a loan. They belong to you. They're part of the jewelry collection of the Countess of Woodforde. You're the Countess of Woodforde. Here, hold the box and turn around."

Before Zoë quite realized what he was doing, he had fastened the necklace around her neck. She drew a quick sharp breath as the gentle brush of his fingers caused her bare skin to feel excruciatingly sensitive. Moving away, she said hastily, "Do you mind? I'd like to see myself in the glass."

Seated before her dressing table, Zoë stared at her image in the mirror. The magnificent necklace blazed at her throat, complementing the gown so perfectly that the two might have been designed for each other. "Oh, my lady, ye remind me of a queen," exclaimed Meg admiringly.

With nervous fingers, Zoë fastened the earrings in her ears and looked back in the mirror. She did look—well, not queenly, exactly, but more impressive than she had ever appeared in her life. In some mysterious way the jewels fortified her self-confidence. Perhaps this dinner wouldn't prove as much of an ordeal as she had feared.

She joined the waiting Jerrold in the corridor.

"Well?" he asked. "Did you like the effect?"

"Very much. And my abigail think I look like a queen. Thank you."

"Tomorrow you can look through my mother's collection and choose any pieces that appeal to you."

"I—" She closed her mouth on her refusal. There was no need for her to feel either embarrassed or grateful. He was presenting the jewelry to her, not as a personal gift, but as an accessory to bolster her image as Countess of Woodforde.

Rupert Layton had described his dinner party as a small affair, limited in the number of guests he could invite by the small size of his house. When she arrived in

Bruton Street, Zoë realized that Jerrold's uncle had been overly modest in describing his residence. He lived in a substantial house, what Zoë, in her provincial ignorance, would earlier have styled a mansion. The large drawing room was crowded to capacity with well-dressed guests, all of whom, to Zoë's dismay, seemed to cease talking and turn their heads to stare at her and Jerrold when they were announced by the butler.

His hands outstretched, his face wreathed in a beaming smile, Rupert hurried up to them, followed by his wife. "Welcome, welcome," he exclaimed. "My dear Zoë, you're quite enchanting tonight. Don't you agree, Beryl?"

His wife, a stringy, rather dour-faced woman, nodded her head. "Indeed, yes, you look charmingly," she told Zoë. Her eyes narrowed. "I see you're wearing the Woodforde emeralds."

Her tone puzzled Zoë. It sounded vaguely accusatory, almost as if Zoë had no right to wear the emeralds.

Jerrold said promptly, "Well, of course Zoë is wearing the Woodforde emeralds, my dear Beryl. She is, after all, the Countess of Woodforde."

"Quite right, my boy, and an uncommonly lovely countess to boot," said Rupert jovially. "Now then, Jerry, you're acquainted with everyone here. You must make them known to your bride."

The next few minutes were a nerve-racking blur to Zoë as person after person came up to her, were introduced by Jerrold, said a few words, and departed. She recognized a few names as prominent Tory politicians—was that really Lord Liverpool, the prime minister?—but the identity of the other people didn't register with her. Everyone spoke graciously, but Zoë was conscious of an atmosphere of intense curiosity that made her uncomfortable.

Evidently recognizing the strain she was under,

Jerrold said beneath his breath, "Try to relax, Zoë. There's no need to be nervous. Everyone here wants to be friendly."

"Yes, I'm sure they do," Zoë murmured, but she couldn't quite believe it.

Blessedly, a familiar face appeared. Melicent kissed her, murmuring, "You look in prime twig, my dear. I knew how it would be." Aloud she said, "Jerry, I'm taking your bride away to meet an old friend I particularly asked Uncle Rupert to invite here tonight."

Mystified, Zoë allowed Melicent to guide her to a seat on a settee next to a slender attractive woman of about thirty. "Sally, this is Zoë, my favorite cousin's wife. Zoë, my dear friend, Lady Jersey."

Zoë gazed rather apprehensively at the powerful and legendary patroness of Almack's assembly rooms, who had fixed her with a penetrating and decidedly intimidating stare.

"Well, my dear, I've been hearing a great deal about you," said Lady Jersey dryly. "Apparently you've been leading a highly romantic and unconventional life."

Zoë raised her chin, suddenly irked at being judged by a complete stranger. "I see nothing unconventional about being a wife and mother, Lady Jersey," she said coolly. "Unless—perhaps you're referring to my profession? I assure you, I paint only mothers and their children in the most innocent and chaste of poses."

Looking taken aback for a moment, Lady Jersey broke into a chuckle. "Well done, Lady Woodforde. That put me nicely in my place."

Aghast, Zoë said, "I didn't mean to be rude—"

"No, no, don't apologize. I like a woman with some spirit. Melicent told me you were out of the common way, a female with a mind of her own, and she was right." Lady Jersey eyed Zoë with a quizzical smile. "I was right, too, when I accused you of being a romantic. After all, you eloped to Gretna Green."

"As many another couple has done, surely," Zoë said, with a return of her defensiveness.

Lady Jersey laughed outright. "Truly, I meant no criticism. After all, my own mother eloped to Gretna Green." At Zoë's look of surprise, Lady Jersey nodded, saying, "Yes, indeed. My grandfather was Mr. Child, the banker, and my mama was his only daughter. He had no sons. Mama fell in love with my papa, who wasn't yet Earl of Westmorland, only Lord Berghersh, and then, when her father disapproved of the match, she eloped with Papa to Gretna Green. Attempting to prevent the marriage, Grandfather followed in close pursuit. He arrived only minutes after the ceremony was performed. Of course, he never forgave Mama. That's why he left me all his money."

Zoë looked at Lady Jersey's smiling face, and began to smile in her turn. "The rewards of virtue, no doubt," she said daringly.

Lady Jersey laughed again. "Exactly so." Sobering, she said, "Now, then, Melicent has been telling me something of the hurtful gossip that's been circulating about the town. I sympathize with your situation, and I'd very much like to help. Please consider me your friend. I'll send you vouchers admitting you to Almack's. That should satisfy everyone that you're eminently respectable! And I'll do my best to secure you an invitation to one of the Drawing Rooms the Queen will be hosting in honor of the visit of the Allied sovereigns next month."

Zoë swallowed a lump in her throat. Although she had never enjoyed a come-out during the London Season, she knew both the value of a voucher to Almack's and the prestige that would accrue to her in attending a royal Drawing Room. "Thank you, Lady Jersey. You're most kind."

Sally Jersey patted her arm. "Not at all. I'm really an old romantic at heart. And now, my dear, I must ask you to excuse me. I must have a word with the prime minister."

Melicent slipped into Lady Jersey's place on the settee. "I knew Sally would offer to help," Melicent said with satisfaction. "She has the kindest heart."

"Did you know about her mother's elopement to Gretna Green?"

"Well, of course, everyone knows."

"And you considered that her mother's example would make her favorably disposed toward my situation?"

Melicent's eyes twinkled. "I had hopes, yes."

Rupert Layton's son Oliver came up to them. "You were surrounded by such a crush I feared I would never have the opportunity to say hello," he complained to Zoë. "I say, cousin, you look complete to a shade. I predict you'll be the toast of the Season."

"Thank you." Zoë's reply was a little guarded. She considered Oliver's compliment entirely too fulsome.

"Next time I visit Woodforde House, I insist on meeting your son, Cousin," Oliver went on. "Jerry's son too, of course!" He grinned. "I'll admit to being a mite jealous. Until your son—Philip, is that his name?— appeared on the scene, my papa, and myself after him, were the next heirs to the estate, you know."

Zoë felt uncomfortable. Oliver's grin didn't quite extend to his eyes, and she remembered his mother's comment about the Woodforde emeralds. Suddenly it occurred to her that, when Jerrold produced a newly discovered son, he might have disturbed the expectations of Rupert Layton and his family. But no, how could that be? Only a short time previously, before his accidental death in a duel, Jerrold's brother Trevor had been alive and well, about to marry and produce an heir. And surely Rupert must have assumed that Jerrold, in time, would also marry and father a child.

In a few moments, as Oliver plunged into an animated conversation with Melicent, virtually ignoring Zoë, she began to suspect that his manner was more than cousinly. Was Oliver actively courting Melicent?

The butler appeared in the doorway of the drawing room, and waiting until he caught the eye of Rupert's wife, he announced, "Dinner is served."

Jerrold arrived at Zoë's side just as Oliver extended his hand to Melicent, saying with a cajoling smile. "You'll allow me to take you in?" Flashing a rather resigned look at Jerrold and Zoë, Melicent rose, taking his arm.

Seating himself on the settee beside Zoë, Jerrold said, watching the guests file out of the drawing room, "No need to hurry. We have a few moments. I saw you talking to Lady Jersey. Both of you appeared quite serious. Was she unkind?"

"No, not at all. Oh, at first I thought she seemed a trifle critical, but later she told me she wanted to be my friend. Jerrold, she promised to send me vouchers for Almack's. And she'll try to have me invited to the Queen's Drawing Room!"

Jerrold's eyes lighted up. "Capital. You know, I presume, that there are hundreds of people in London who would commit mayhem for one of those vouchers . . ." He broke off, and then, startling Zoë, he swept her into his arms and kissed her. In an instant the light, almost impersonal touch of his lips quickened and deepened.

His mouth devoured hers with a hard pressure that sent a flood of sensual delight coursing through her body.

"Well, well," said a gently mocking voice from behind them.

Zoë wrenched herself from Jerrold's embrace and jumped up from the settee to stare in an agony of embarrassment at Lady Jersey, who stood in the door of the drawing room, now empty of guests save for the three of them.

Lady Jersey strolled slowly into the room, saying, "I'm missing an earring. I must have dropped it in here. Would you mind searching for it, Lord Woodforde?"

As Jerrold obediently began walking about the drawing room, examining the carpet, Lady Jersey approached Zoë. Her eyes brimming with laughter, the patroness of Almack's tapped Zoë gently with her fan. "My dear, you mustn't look so mortified. I quite understand an impulsive kiss indulged in by a newly married couple. After all, it wasn't so long ago that I was a new bride myself!" She tapped Zoë with the fan again. "La, I'm growing forgetful. You and Lord Woodforde aren't a newly married couple, merely a newly united couple. But the principle is the same. I don't begrudge you a kiss in public!"

Zoë dismissed Meg as soon as the abigail had helped her out of the beaded gown and brushed out her hair. She knew Meg's feelings were a little hurt. The abigail had been so eager to hear about Zoë's triumph at the dinner party, only to have her innocent questions cut off short. But at the end of the long evening, Zoë's lacerated nerves were at the breaking point. She didn't want to talk to Meg. She didn't want to talk to anyone.

Actually, she mused, watching Meg scuttle out of the room, she had no idea how she had survived the interminable dinner, striving to speak intelligibly to the prime minister seated next to her. Or the session afterward in the drawing room, drinking coffee and making vapid small talk with female guests. Or the drive home from Bruton Street, during which she'd kept her face averted from Jerrold, refusing to allow him to make any explanation for his conduct in the drawing room before dinner.

"I don't wish to discuss personal matters in public," she'd said stonily, although she knew perfectly well there was virtually no possibility that the coachman on his box could overhear their conversation.

Because there couldn't be any rational explanation for what Jerrold had done. He had pledged his word that, if she agreed to pose as his wife, their marriage would be one in name only. And he'd broken his word. The memory of his kiss made Zoë writhe in humiliation as she recalled her instant abandoned response to the searing touch of his lips. Had he noticed that response? How could he not have noticed it? And was kissing, or God knew what beside, what he'd had in mind when he proposed that they should be "friends"?

"Zoë, I want to talk to you," said Jerrold from the other side of the door.

"Go away. I've nothing to say."

The door opened and Jerrold walked in. He, too, was wearing a dressing gown, and Turkish slippers with curved toes. "We're not in public now, Zoë. Will you listen to what I have to say?"

She rose, facing him. "Do I have any alternative?" she said bitterly.

"No. I insist on clearing the air between us. You're angry at me because I kissed you tonight. That kiss wasn't the result of a sudden carnal urge, as you seem to suspect. As we were talking, I saw Lady Jersey entering the drawing room out of the corner of my eye. Melicent's been assiduously spreading the romantic tale that you and I are lovers miraculously reconciled after many years, so I decided to give Lady Jersey a concrete example of our feelings for each other. That's all there was to it."

Zoë felt suddenly deflated. And very foolish. She bit her lip, saying, "I'm sorry. I've been behaving like a child. I should have realized there was some explanation for—for what you did."

"No need for apology," said Jerrold quickly. "I took you by surprise. And quite frankly, perhaps I was entirely too impulsive." He paused. After a moment he said, with a note of urgency in his voice, "We've cleared the air between us, then?"

"Oh, yes. Certainly. I understand perfectly." I'm babbling, thought Zoë despairingly. I sound like an idiot. She said, trying for aplomb, "I enjoyed the evening very much."

"I, too. There will be many others, I hope. Good night, Zoë."

After Jerrold left, Zoë tried to calm her tumultuous thoughts. That kiss in Rupert Layton's drawing room had been meaningless. Jerrold hadn't broken his promise to keep their marriage on a platonic basis. Why, then, couldn't she put out of her mind the exquisite, beguiling memory of the touch of his lips on hers?

Chapter Twelve

Zoë ate her breakfast and bathed and dressed the next morning in a subdued mood. She hadn't slept well. Periodically she had awakened to the memory of the passionate kiss she and Jerrold had shared in Rupert Layton's drawing room, and then she hadn't been able to get back to sleep again. She wondered with an acute sense of embarrassment how Jerrold would behave toward her the next time they saw each other. She soon found out, when she went to the nursery for her morning visit with Philip. Jerrold was already there, dressed for the street.

He flashed her a friendly smile, unclouded by any constraint. "Good morning, Zoë. I hope you aren't too fatigued after our late night at Uncle Rupert's."

"Oh, no. I slept very well, thank you."

"Mama!" interrupted Philip, barely able to contain his excitement. "I was just coming to tell you about our plans. This morning Papa is taking me to the Tower of London to see the Royal—the Royal . . ."

"The Royal Menagerie," said Jerrold, chuckling. "It's a very big word, isn't it? Why don't we just call it the Tower Zoo?" To Zoë he said, "The Zoo is considered a trifle *démodé* these days, I fear, but I believe it remains a very suitable attraction for children."

Quite obviously Philip didn't care a fig whether or not the Tower Zoo was any longer fashionable. His blue eyes, so much like his father's, sparkled as he said, "Papa says we'll see lions and tigers and wolves and hyenas and *two* kinds of bears, black and white."

"It sounds wonderful," Zoë replied, laughing. "You're making me feel quite envious. I visited the Zoo once, some years ago, but I don't believe they had a white bear at the time."

"Do you care to accompany us?" Jerrold asked.

Zoë said doubtfully, "I should get to my easel. Lady Bradford sent over a note yesterday, wondering when her portrait would be finished." She hesitated, but only briefly. "Oh, well, why not? I like bears, and the other animals, too."

"Splendid, eh, Philip? Oh, and Zoë, perhaps you could spare me a few minutes of your time, later this afternoon, to look over my mother's jewelry, so you can decide which pieces you wish to wear."

Although Zoë had paid a previous visit to the Tower of London, the excursion today was an entirely different experience for her. She was seeing the Royal Menagerie, the Armory, the Jewel Office through the eyes of a child. As the yeoman warder in his crimson, gold-laced Tudor uniform was pointing out to a fascinated Philip the spot on Tower Green where Anne Boleyn had been executed, Zoë murmured to Jerrold, "Philip doesn't seem horrified at all by accounts of the blood that has been spilled here. To him all these incidents are just exciting stories."

Jerrold smiled faintly. "Why are you surprised? The yeoman warder's stories are no more real to Philip than the fairy tales you read to him every night. And as I seem to recall, some of those fairy tales are *very* bloodthirsty!"

Zoë laughed, forced to agree with Jerrold's whimsical comment.

A little later, on their return to Bedford Square, after Philip had gone up to the nursery, Jerrold turned to Zoë as they stood in the foyer, saying, "I enjoyed our visit to the Tower very much. I hope you did." He added with a trace of self-consciousness, "I suddenly felt very much a family man!"

Feeling a touch of warmth in her cheeks, Zoë replied, "I enjoyed the excursion, too. Thank you for inviting me, Jerrold." She knew quite well that she and Jerrold would not have been having this pleasant, almost intimate, conversation with each other a few days ago, before they had agreed to a truce.

At the end of the afternoon, before Zoë changed for dinner, Jerrold came to her dressing room laden with a collection of boxes covered with brocade and velvet. Opening one of the boxes, he handed it to her, saying, "I think these would go well with the deep rose *soie de Londres* ball gown you described." Zoë stared rather numbly at a magnificent ruby and diamond necklace and a matching tiara. He reached for a second box. "You might wear these diamonds with the silver tissue gown, and"—flicking open still another case—"I rather fancy the amethysts with the blue satin."

Zoë was overwhelmed by the munificence of the gems once worn by Jerrold's mother. She couldn't believe that Queen Charlotte owned a larger or more magnificent collection. She accepted and admired piece after exquisite piece in a sort of daze. Finally, after the jewels had been returned to their boxes, she blurted,

"I'll take very great care of them, and afterwards I'll be sure to return them . . ."

She stopped in confusion as Jerrold raised an amused eyebrow. "Afterwards? My dear Zoë, there is no afterwards, just as there's no question of returning the jewelry. I told you, they belong to you now, as Countess of Woodforde. And you'll be Countess of Woodforde for the rest of your life, even if I die before you. Then you'll be the Dowager Countess, if Philip is married by then."

"Oh."

He laughed at her startled expression. "Cheer up. It will be many years, if I have anything to say to it, before you're a widow!"

He closed the boxes and placed them in a small wall safe behind a painting on the wall near the wardrobe, a safe that Zoë hadn't previously realized was there. "You'll soon be wearing the pieces, now that your new wardrobe is complete," he remarked. "Next week we'll plunge into the Season in earnest. Do I have our schedule of engagements correct? Next Monday, dinner at Mrs. Skinner's. Tuesday, Lady Bradford's rout. The following night, your first visit to Almack's. Thursday, Lady Meriden's ball. Friday—"

"We haven't decided on Friday yet, remember? That is, we'll be attending some function or other, but we haven't decided which invitation to accept. There are so many of them. More and more each day. Sometimes two or three invitations for the same night . . ."

Zoë's voice trailed away. A heavy weight seemed to be bearing down on her shoulders, as she contemplated the responsibility of owning a king's ransom in jewels and the prospect of soon being the object of attention of every noble name in London as she and Jerrold launched themselves into society.

As if reading her mind, he said, "You're apprehensive about these engagements, but you shouldn't be. I predict you'll take London by storm."

"But all those horrible rumors ... and I've always moved in such provincial circles ..."

"You'll do splendidly," he said firmly. "You're a beautiful woman, you're accomplished and interesting to talk to. And don't forget, you'll have plenty of support. Melicent and I will be beside you at all times. Mark my words, you'll be a *succès fou*, and everyone in the *ton* will wonder how I managed to hide away my fascinating countess for so many years!"

In spite of herself, Zoë had to laugh. "Such flummery," she accused him. Flattery or not, however, she felt her jittery nerves subside, if only a little.

As the evening of her first visit to Almack's approached, Zoë found herself facing it with less dread than she might have imagined. The past few days had gone smoothly, without any further outbreaks of rumor or gossip, or none, at least, that had come to her attention. She and Melicent had paid a myriad of calls, mostly by card, some in person, and though she had felt the weight of curiosity, she had survived the occasions well enough. At Lady Jersey's house in Berkeley Square, in fact, her hostess had greeted her so warmly that Zoë had scarcely been aware of inquisitive stares.

The previous night's rout at Lady Bradford's house had been such a squeeze, to quote Melicent, that Zoë suspected she and Jerrold had gone unnoticed in the crush. The masses of people seemed bent merely on making their way up the thronged staircase and through the packed rooms to greet their hostess and back down the staircase again in one piece. There had been one embarrassing moment when Lady Bradford, holding up a line of guests, had wagged her finger playfully at Jerrold, saying, "My, but aren't you a sly rogue, my lord. Allowing me to think I was such a capable matchmaker, inviting Mrs. Manning to dinner without telling her you would be present, so that I could bring the two of you together for a private rendezvous. And all the while you were already married!"

Jerrold had saved the situation by remarking coolly, "Fond as I am of you, Lady Bradford, I must tell you that I don't reveal to you quite all of my secrets."

"Oh, you . . ." Simpering, Lady Bradford tapped Jerrold lightly with her fan.

Tonight in Almack's assembly rooms she would undergo a much greater test, Zoë mused, as she stood quietly while Meg adjusted the folds of her gown of ethereal silvery gauze, worn over a white satin slip. The dress was trimmed simply with silver ribbons on the brief sleeves, and knots of silver ribbon on the hem.

"Now for the diamonds, my lady," said Meg in an awed voice, and then stood speechless as she gazed into the mirror at the shimmering fire of the stones encircling Zoë's neck.

Zoë smiled. "You're always saying I look like a queen. Well, do I look like a queen tonight?" she teased.

Finding her voice, Meg gasped, "Oh, no, my lady. More like a—an empress!"

Jerrold's reaction to Zoë's appearance was equally enthusiastic. When she walked down the stairs to meet him in the foyer, he examined the dress for a long moment and said, breaking into an admiring smile, "You look positively dazzling. The gown is even more exquisite than you described it to me. And I don't want to take any of the credit away from you, Zoë, but I must claim a tiny bit of distinction. I *knew* the diamonds would go well with it."

Faintly embarrassed, Zoë murmured, "Thank you, but the diamonds are so dazzling that they would make any wearer look beautiful, you know."

"Nonsense. Dazzling jewels demand a dazzling wearer. Which you most definitely are, Lady Woodforde."

Despite Jerrold's deft compliments, Zoë started to feel a renewal of her qualms as they drove in their carriage to King Street, nor did an unwitting remark by Jerrold do anything to quiet the butterflies that had begun to flutter in her stomach.

"Melicent was telling me the other day that the patronesses of Almack's have granted vouchers to only a handful of Guards officers, out of a total of about three hundred," he said casually. "So, by that standard, I daresay one could argue that it's more a feather in one's social cap to acquire vouchers for Almack's than it is to be presented at Court."

Zoë's first glimpse of the famed assembly rooms proved to be an anticlimax. After she and Jerrold had given up their cardboard vouchers to the liveried guardian at the door and had ascended the staircase to the ballroom, she looked down the length of the ninety-foot room and reflected that, although the ballroom was impressively large, she had expected something infinitely grander. More like the interior of a palace, perhaps, from the glowing descriptions she'd heard of the assembly rooms. In a few moments, however, as she gazed at the elaborate gowns and sparkling jewels worn by the ladies and the severe perfection of the gentlemen's coats and breeches and marvelous cravats, she realized that the reputation of Almack's rested, not on its physical premises, but on its aristocratic guests.

A country dance was just ending. Melicent came off the floor on the arm of Oliver Layton and hurried toward Zoë and Jerrold. "Zoë, I knew that silver gauze would make up into the loveliest gown imaginable," Melicent exclaimed in delight. "You look positively entrancing. Don't you agree, Jerry?"

"Most enthusiastically." Jerrold smiled at Zoë. "As your escort I look forward to being the envy of every man in this room tonight."

Oliver chimed in, "Melicent is quite right, Zoë. What a charming gown. I say, Jerry, I hope you realize that you and I have the pleasure of talking to the two most beautiful ladies in the ballroom." Despite the effusiveness of his remarks, Oliver sounded vaguely ill at ease.

Jerrold, on the other hand, appeared self-possessed to the point of curtness. He raised an eyebrow at Oliver, saying, "My dear fellow, you can hardly expect me to be unaware of the charms of my cousin and my wife."

"Ah—quite so." Oliver looked disconcerted. A moment later he excused himself. "Must have a word with old Mainwaring, y'know."

Zoë remembered Melicent's comment that Jerrold had always disliked his cousin, and wondered if the feeling was reciprocal.

Gazing at Oliver's retreating back, Jerrold said to Melicent, "I'm surprised at you. Surely you could have found a more suitable escort. Why didn't you ask me and Zoë to come by for you?"

Appearing nettled, Melicent retorted, "For your information, Coz, I came here tonight with my old friends, Lord and Lady Mayberry. I merely danced with Oliver. We're cousins, after all, and even though he's not one of my favorite people, I saw no graceful way of refusing to partner him. And I'll remind you that Oliver can be very charming when he chooses to be."

Jerrold bit his lip. "I'm sorry. Coming it rather too strong, was I?"

"Yes, you were." Her dimples showing, Melicent flicked him a smile. "But I forgive you. In any case, Oliver's not important." She turned to Zoë. "I'm sorry Sally Jersey isn't here tonight. As you probably know, the patronesses take turns acting as chaperons of the weekly balls. Tonight Countess Lieven is the patroness who's doing the honors. There she is, over there. Come along with me, I'll introduce you."

Jerrold chuckled. "I was about to ask you to dance, Zoë, but I'll forgo my request—only temporarily, of course—in favor of such an important introduction!"

As she and Zoë walked across the ballroom, Melicent murmured, "You and Jerry seem to be getting on together uncommonly well."

"As a matter of fact, we've declared a truce," said Zoë candidly. "It certainly makes life much more pleasant." Even as she spoke, however, she realized that the past few days had represented more than a truce. The bitter memories of Gretna Green had actually begun to fade. For the first time she was seeing Jerrold as a man who might have changed and matured from the irresponsible wastrel of seven years ago.

The Russian ambassador's wife was chatting with several gentlemen on the edge of the ballroom as Melicent and Zoë came up to her. She was a slender woman of about thirty, with dark hair and a long, rather pinched face.

"Good evening, Madame Lieven. Do you remember

me? We met last week at Lady Sefton's house," Melicent began.

The ambassadress responded with a vinegary smile. "But of course, Lady Rosedale, I remember you perfectly." She looked expectantly at Zoë.

"Madame, may I present to you Lady Woodforde, the wife of my cousin Jerrold?"

The smile faded from the countess's face. She gave Zoë a long, disapproving stare, examining her from head to toe, then said with a chilling venom, "I am sorry, Lady Rosedale. I do not care to know Lady Woodforde. I am amazed that she dared to show her face in this assembly." She turned away to resume her chat with the gentlemen.

Zoë felt her face go stiff with shock.

Melicent said urgently, "Pay Madame Lieven no mind. Obviously she's heard some of these dreadful rumors, and she's reputed to be narrow-minded, very high in the instep. Zoë! You must act as it it never happened. I'm sure nobody noticed the incident—or practically nobody." Melicent took Zoë's arm and, drawing her to a chair at the side of the ballroom, stood regarding her in concern. "You look a little pale, Zoë. Are you feeling faint? Shall I find Jerry?"

"No, please don't. I'm quite all right. It's just that—that . . ."

"It's just that no one ever gave you the cut direct before. I know. Wait here. I'll bring you a glass of ratafia. It will make you feel more the thing."

After Melicent left, Zoë leaned back in her chair, grateful that the shadow of a large potted palm partially shielded her face from view. In spite of her disclaimer to Melicent, she was still badly shaken. Countess Lieven's discourtesy had struck her almost like a physical blow.

No one had ever behaved to her in such a deliberately insulting way.

"Good evening, Lady Woodforde."

As Zoë glanced at the woman who had sat down in a chair beside her, she had to choke back a protest. She didn't want to speak to anyone just now, and especially not to someone she had never met.

"You don't know me, Lady Woodforde," the stranger continued. She was a strikingly beautiful woman, with abundant Titian hair and a voluptuous figure that threatened to overflow the extremely low-cut bodice of her satin gown. "Let me introduce myself. I'm Dorothea Harlow. Your husband and I are—were—great friends."

Zoë grew very still. Jerrold's mistress. His ex-mistress, he'd told her.

Lady Harlow smiled. It was an unpleasant, gloating smile. "I saw how Countess Lieven received you. Or rather, didn't receive you. Surely you couldn't have been surprised. The countess has heard all the stories about your secret marriage to Jerry, and she doesn't believe a word of the romantic falderal, no more than the rest of us. I'd advise you to leave London now, before your head is completely bloodied. You'll never be accepted by the *ton*."

"Pray excuse me," Zoë muttered, and started to rise. Lady Harlow seized her arm in an iron grip and prevented her from leaving her chair.

"I haven't finished, my dear," said Lady Harlow. The gloating smile was still in place. "You see, I'm rather sorry for you. You're more sinned against than sinning. You had the gumption to recover from your indiscretion with Jerry—I understand you invented a husband for yourself and a father for your by-blow—and make a respectable life of sorts. I hear you're a portrait painter. I can't even fault you for allowing Jerry to persuade you into agreeing to pass off your son as the heir to Woodforde. The temptation must have been enormous—well, you know, the Woodforde fortune, and the great position you fancied you'd have. And of course I know Jerry's wiles all too well. But I wonder . . ."

Lady Harlow pursed her lips. "Yes, I wonder. Has Jerry been quite open with you? Has he been fair? Did he tell you the real reason why he decided to foist off your son as his heir instead of marrying and producing a legitimate child?"

Startled, Zoë looked hard at Lady Harlow, setting aside momentarily her anger at the farrago of malicious lies the woman had uttered. "What do you mean, the real reason?"

"So he didn't tell you. He didn't explain that he must claim your son as legitimate because he's incapable of fathering another child. Jerry is sterile, my dear. He had an unfortunate case of the mumps a few years ago. Did you know that a childish ailment like that can cause sterility in grown men? Sad, but true."

Shaking her head, Lady Harlow heaved a sigh of mock sympathy. "So poor Jerry is sterile. Otherwise he would have planned to marry when the death of his brother Trevor made him the new Earl of Woodforde." Her eyes sparked with anger. "Actually, he probably would have offered for his cousin, Lady Rosedale, who returned to England, a widow, about the time of his brother's death."

"Melicent!" Zoë's tone conveyed her disbelief.

Lady Harlow gave her a pitying glance. "He's loved her for years, didn't you know that? No, how would you know? You've never moved in polite circles. He offered for her when she came out, but at the time he was a second son with no prospects. She chose the heir to an earldom. Now that she's free to remarry, Jerry can't take advantage of her changed situation. If he and Lady Rosedale married, he couldn't father a child on her, and he needs an heir."

The woman paused, looking thoughtful. "I confess, at first I was a bit puzzled by his haste in resurrecting a long-lost 'wife' and son. Jerry had never displayed any interest in children, and strictly speaking, he already had heirs, his uncle and his cousin. Then I saw the light. I knew he hated his cousin Oliver, probably with good reason. I hear Oliver had the gall to act as second to the ruffian who killed Jerry's brother Trevor in that duel. So, in order to cut out Oliver Layton from any chance at the succession, Jerry had to have a son of his own."

The gloating smile returned to Lady Harlow's lips. "Your son, my dear. *That's* why you're now the Countess of Woodforde, and I wish you joy of it. Even if Jerry succeeds in passing you and his bastard off on the *ton*—which I doubt—there will always be folk who will believe that you're nothing but a brassy bit of muslin who set her cap for Jerry when he was too young to know better."

While the Titian-haired woman continued to vent her anger and spite, Zoë shook off the near-paralysis of will that had kept her rooted to her chair. "I don't have to listen to this. I *won't* listen," she muttered, half to herself. She rose on shaky legs and marched away from Lady Harlow. Catching a glimpse of Jerrold in the distance as he stood talking to an acquaintance, she wheeled and walked swiftly to the entrance of the ballroom. Her heart felt so lacerated after her talk with Lady Harlow that she couldn't bear the thought of facing Jerrold. Not yet.

In the corridor she paused for a moment, glancing wildly around her. Spurred by a vague instinct to hide, she headed blindly for the staircase leading down to the main entrance of the assembly rooms on King Street. In her inattention she collided with a gentleman who put his hand on her arm to steady her. "Lady Woodforde!" he exclaimed. "Are you ill?"

She looked up into the face of a stranger, a tall man with waving sandy hair, a somewhat plain face, and speaking gray eyes. He said in a concerned voice, "You *are* ill. Let me take you to the cardroom."

Before Zoë quite knew what was happening, the strange man took her arm and led her into the cardroom, where he sat her down at a small table in a corner of the room. "You'll be quite private here," he said soothingly. "The cardroom is almost empty of players." He smiled. "High play is no longer the reason people come to Almack's! Now, then, do you have some hartshorn with you? Shall I bring you some water?"

Drawing a deep breath, Zoë said, "I thank you, sir, but I'm not ill. It was just . . . I—I heard some rather disturbing news, that was all. I must have panicked for a moment. Really, I'm quite all right now." She tried to smile. "You have the advantage of me. You know my name, but I don't recall that we ever met."

"Strictly speaking, we haven't met, although I'm acquainted with your husband. I'm Stephen Carrington. My sister is Clarissa Bradford. At her rout last night she pointed you out. She was very disappointed that there was such a crush that she had no opportunity to introduce me to you."

"I see. Well, Mr. Carrington . . ."

"Actually, it's Sir Stephen," he pointed out with a trace of apology in his tone.

Feeling a little foolish, Zoë said, "Well, Sir Stephen, I don't quite understand why . . . that is to say, why on earth would Lady Bradford point me out to you?"

Sir Stephen gave her a frankly admiring glance. "You're much too modest. I can think of a number of reasons why my sister would point you out." As Zoë colored faintly, he hastened to say, "Forgive me. My wretched tongue. I didn't mean to embarrass you. Actually, Clarissa wanted us to know each other because we're both painters. In my case, I'm a mere dabbler compared to you. Clarissa has seen a number of your portraits, and she tells me you're easily as talented as Madame Vigée-Lebrun. That's why she gave you a commission to paint her and her daughter. I'm only a dilettante. I sketch, and I paint watercolor landscapes, and I'm keenly interested in art in general. I fear that's the extent of my artistic endeavors."

Zoë smiled. "Perhaps you're the one who's being too modest. I'd like very much to see some of your sketches and watercolors."

The baronet's eyes lit up. "Would you? I say!" He shook his head, smiling ruefully. "I'll wait until you actually see my work before I congratulate myself." He narrowed his eyes. "You may not be ill, Lady Woodforde, but are you feeling quite the thing? Do you want to go back to the ballroom, or would you prefer to stay here? We could sit quietly, pretending to play two-handed whist. No one would notice us."

Zoë felt a sense of relief. Her heart was still so bruised by Countess Lieven's rudeness and Lady Harlow's gibes that she didn't relish the prospect of confronting a ballroom full of people who might stare at her as scornfully as the Russian ambassadress and Jerrold's ex-mistress had done. And she didn't want to think about what

Lady Harlow had said about Jerrold's possible sterility or his feelings for Melicent, not just yet, while her mind was in such a storm of agitation. Stephen Carrington's suggestion offered her a respite from her thoughts, and she seized upon it with gratitude.

"Thank you, Sir Stephen. I'd enjoy a game of two-handed whist," she told him. "I must warn you, though. I'm not a skilled player."

A few minutes later Carrington cocked his head at her as he dealt another hand. "You mustn't tell such whiskers, Lady Woodforde," he said, grinning. "Not a skilled player, indeed! Actually, you're a real dabster at the game."

The good-natured raillery made Zoë laugh, and the next hour was an agreeable revelation to her. During the years since Gretna Green, living in the provincial backwater of Cumberland as a presumed widow and young mother and busy professional artist, she had had scant opportunity to mingle socially with men of her own age. She hadn't had the pleasure of sharing in a friendly, relaxed interval with a personable man who shared her tastes and who had a gift for making inconsequential topics seem amusing and for putting her at ease.

"Did you mean it when you said you would be willing to look at my sketches and watercolors?" Carrington inquired at one point as they played a desultory game of whist.

"Yes, of course."

"And you'll tell me your real opinion of my work?"

Zoë put down her cards. "I don't think I could force myself to give a false opinion about a work of art," she said simply.

He grimaced. "You frighten me. And yet, you know,

that is precisely what I would have expected you to say. Have you visited the Royal Academy?"

"No, not yet. When I was in London earlier in the spring, I was much too busy with my portrait appointments to do any sightseeing."

"Then may I have the honor of taking you to Somerset House? There's a new Lawrence portrait—of Lord Ashton—and a quite marvelous landscape by Turner."

Zoë hesitated. She was vaguely familiar with the continental concept of the *cicisbeo*, a gentleman who served as an official lover and escort—highly sanitized in its English version!—and she could see nothing scandalous in the notion of a respectable married woman being escorted to a public function by a male family friend. Her present circumstances were different, however. Her respectability was being questioned by some in society, and Sir Stephen was only a chance acquaintance.

He seemed to read her mind. "Perhaps my sister would care to accompany us."

"Oh, of course. I'd be happy to go with you and Lady Bradford to the exhibition."

Carrington looked pleased. "We'll go soon, then? And at a later time we might visit Christie's Auction Rooms. They say Christie handles almost all the great paintings that come on the market."

As he was speaking, Zoë chanced to look up and saw Jerrold standing in the doorway. Their eyes met across the room. Taking a quick breath, she turned her attention back to Sir Stephen, and when she glanced up again a few moments later, Jerrold was gone.

Carrington put down his cards and consulted his watch. "I had no idea it was so late. I haven't danced a step tonight." He rose, extending his hand. "Will you dance with me, Lady Woodforde?"

As she walked into the ballroom on Sir Stephen's arm, some of Zoë's nervousness returned, only to fade as she concentrated on the lively patterns of the country dance. Going down the line, she gradually forgot to be on the alert for critical eyes. She had always loved to dance, although in recent years she had had few opportunities to do so. Now she was conscious only of the joy of movement and Sir Stephen's ready smile and the firm clasp of his hand.

When Zoë and Carrington came off the floor after the country dance, they lingered, chatting, at the side of the ballroom. "That was capital," Carrington said appreciatively. "May I have the next dance also?"

Before Zoë could reply, Melicent and Jerrold joined them. Zoë introduced Carrington to Melicent. He bowed to Jerrold. "Evening, Woodforde. The last time we met, you were outshooting me at Manton's. I can't tell you how much I resent people whose skills are superior to mine."

"I daresay you have other virtues," Jerrold replied with a casual nod.

Carrington laughed. "Oh, as to that I can't say."

The two men were almost of a height, tall and slender, but Jerrold had the greater width of shoulder and grace of carriage. Zoë admitted to herself, with an unwillingness that she refused to interpret, that Jerrold's dark good looks and superb tailoring tended to eclipse any other man in the ballroom, including Stephen Carrington.

Under cover of the men's conversation, Melicent murmured to Zoë, "I was a little worried about you when you disappeared after Countess Lieven was so rude to you. Jerry says you were in the cardroom with Sir Stephen."

"Sir Stephen was most kind." Zoë knew she sounded curt, but she seemed unable to restrain herself. When she looked at Melicent, all she could think of was Lady Harlow's assertion that Melicent had been Jerrold's first love and that the two would now be planning to marry if . . . Zoë shut off her thoughts.

The orchestra had started up again, playing a Scottish reel, and Jerrold turned to Zoë. "May I have the pleasure?"

He held himself a little stiffly, and there was a note in his voice that Zoë couldn't quite decipher. Could it be anger? Annoyance, perhaps. He certainly couldn't be jealous that she'd danced with Stephen Carrington. She said quickly, "Thank you, but I've promised this dance to Sir Stephen."

"Very well. The next one, then?"

She didn't want to dance with Jerrold. She didn't want to cope with his feelings, whatever they were. Lifting her chin, she said, "I'm sorry. I've promised Sir Stephen that dance also." Something made her add, "Actually, the next two dances."

A glimmer of some kind of emotion surfaced in the dark blue eyes. He merely nodded, however, saying carelessly, "That's all right. We'll dance at the next ball."

Sir Stephen was too well bred to display any curiosity when Zoë rather diffidently told him he was to have the honor of dancing two more sets with her. Instead he smiled. "I'm a fortunate man, Lady Woodforde."

Then the evening was over. After that last country dance, as Sir Stephen walked with Zoë across the floor to where Jerrold stood waiting with Melicent, he said in a low voice, "Thank you for the most delightful evening

I've spent in ages. May I call in Bedford Square tomorrow to arrange our visit to Somerset House?"

For a moment Zoë hesitated. The remark, coming from anyone else, almost smacked of intimacy. But there was nothing but friendliness in Sir Stephen's open gray eyes. "Please do," she replied, smiling. "I look forward to it." He brought her to Jerrold, bowing over her hand and murmuring, "Good night—and thank you again."

Melicent's normally vivacious manner seemed more subdued than usual. "Did you enjoy your evening, Zoë?" she asked. She flicked a faintly uneasy, almost furtive, glance at Jerrold and looked away again.

"Oh, yes, very much," Zoë replied with a determined brightness. "I vow, I haven't danced so much since I was a girl."

"I'm glad. I'll call tomorrow, shall I? Good night, Zoë, Jerrold."

It's not my imagination, Zoë reflected, watching Jerrold's cousin walk away quickly. Melicent is relieved to leave us.

Jerrold's face was like a polite mask, his eyes unreadable, as he silently offered Zoë his arm and escorted her down the steps and into the waiting carriage. During the drive to Bedford Square he made no comment on the evening they had just spent at Almack's. In fact, he said nothing at all, sitting back against the squabs in a silence that said as plainly as words, "Do not disturb."

A ripple of apprehension crossed Zoë's mind. He was angry, she was sure of it now. His unspoken emotion triggered the release of the feelings of rage that had been bottled up inside her since her talk with Lady Harlow earlier in the evening, feelings she had been suppressing because she didn't want to face the implications of what Jerrold's mistress had told her.

She was furious with Jerrold for not being open with her. He had harassed her and coerced her into agreeing to make their clandestine marriage public, using the argument that they must both sacrifice their personal inclinations for their son's sake. Very noble, indeed, Zoë sneered to herself. But he'd neglected to inform her that he was sterile, that Philip was the only child he would ever have.

Giving Jerrold a quick sideways glance as he sat in the darkness of the carriage in his impenetrable silence, Zoë wondered what his actions might have been when he belatedly discovered that he and Zoë were validly married *if* he hadn't known he was sterile.

His mistress—his ex-mistress—claimed that he had been in love with Melicent before her marriage. When she returned from the continent, a widow, according to Lady Harlow, his feelings for Melicent had revived. Unfortunately, at about the same time, Jerrold learned that his long-ago indiscretion with Zoë had resulted in a legal marriage and a child. Supposing, just supposing, he hadn't been sterile at this point, with his love for Melicent clashing with the unwelcome knowledge that he was already married. In that case, wouldn't he have attempted to nullify that Gretna Green marriage so that he could marry the woman he'd always loved and father on her the heir he needed to prevent the cousin he despised from succeeding to the estate?

Zoë swallowed hard against the acrid taste of bile that invaded her throat. She felt used, like a breeding ewe that existed solely to increase the size of the flock. She was of significance to Jerrold only because she had carried in her womb a male heir, the only heir he could ever have. And he hadn't bothered to explain his situation to her. She wasn't important enough for that. Suddenly all the old emotions of anger and blame and desire for revenge that she'd once felt for Jerrold revived in full force.

Still wrapped in his implacable silence, Jerrold lifted his hand to help Zoë from the carriage when they arrived in Bedford Square, and in silence also they walked into the foyer of Woodforde House past the attentive footman manning the door. As Zoë headed for the staircase, Jerrold broke the silence, saying quietly, "Come to the morning room, Zoë. I want to talk to you."

In the morning room she faced him, standing just inside the door and lifting her chin defiantly. "Yes?"

Removing his gloves, he held them in one hand and pulled them absently through the fingers of the other as he stared at her, his lips pressed firmly together as if he was holding himself rigidly under control. At last he said, "Zoë, I think you'll agree that we're living together publicly for one reason only, to convince society that we are legitimately married and that Philip is the rightful heir to the Woodforde estates. Isn't that so?"

"Yes." Zoë uttered the bare syllable and clamped her lips shut. She stared back at Jerrold, giving no quarter.

He seemed baffled. "Then why in the fiend's name did you make a spectacle of yourself by sitting in Stephen Carrington's pocket for the better part of the evening," he burst out. "Melicent told me that Countess Lieven had cut you. Didn't that make you realize that our reputations are very fragile? Melicent has been spreading the gospel that you and I are reunited lovers. What do you suppose the guests at Almack's thought tonight when you spent an hour in a cozy *tête-à-tête* with Stephen Carrington in the cardroom and then danced exclusively with him for the rest of the evening?"

"I'm not concerned with what the people at Almack's

thought," Zoë snapped. "I did nothing wrong. I chatted with the brother of one of my patrons—Sir Stephen's sister, Lady Bradford, has commissioned me to paint her portrait. I danced with him. All in plain view of your precious public. Perhaps you thought I should have spent the evening hanging on your arm like a bedazzled new bride. I thought otherwise."

Suddenly the memory of her talk with his mistress cut through Zoë like a knife, and she lashed out at Jerrold. "A few minutes ago you summarized our situation exactly," she exclaimed. "We made a bargain to cooperate in this farce of a marriage solely in order to safeguard Philip's heritage. I'll abide by that bargain, but its terms don't prevent me from having a life of my own, with friends of my own choosing."

His eyes kindled into a blue flame. "If, in living that life of your own, you make me a laughingstock, or give the impression that I'm a cuckold, if living that life of your own in any way endangers my son's patrimony, why then I assure you, my dear wife, that I will take steps to control your behavior. Do you understand me?"

"Perfectly," she managed to say between stiff lips, before sweeping out of the room.

Chapter Thirteen

The portrait of Lady Bradford and her daughter was coming along very well, Zoë decided, as she leaned back on her stool, brush in hand, to look appraisingly at the painting. The texture of the little girl's hair still didn't satisfy her, and the diamond necklace around her mother's throat needed touching up, but the portrait was very nearly complete.

The studio door opened behind her, and her abigail said apologetically, "I don't like to disturb ye, my lady, but Lady Rosedale is here, and seeing as how she's my lord's cousin and all . . ."

Rising, Zoë began to clean her brushes. "That's all right, Meg. I won't do any more work today. Tell Lady Rosedale I'll be with her shortly."

A little later, as she walked down the stairs to the drawing room, Zoë wondered at Melicent's call so early in the day. Normally Jerrold's cousin scrupulously refrained from interrupting Zoë's morning working hours in her studio. The slight mystery was explained by Melicent's first remark after Zoë entered the drawing room.

"Zoë, I'm sorry if I disrupted your schedule, but I felt I had to talk to you about last night."

Zoë sat down. She herself had been trying not to think about her evening at Almack's assembly rooms and the angry encounter afterward with Jerrold. "What about last night?"

Melicent said hesitantly, "I would never deliberately interfere in your affairs, I hope you know that. . . . But Zoë, I'm convinced I'd be remiss if I didn't speak to you about your behavior at Almack's. My dear, it was most unwise of you to sit secluded for an hour or more in the cardroom with an eligible bachelor, and then to dance with him three times in a row. It would have been unwise in any case, but now, considering the—the cloud that hangs over the circumstances of your marriage, you must be especially careful to avoid any harm to your reputation. I think Jerry was quite concerned that your—your association with Sir Stephen last night might have occasioned added gossip."

"Jerrold has already given me his views on the subject, thank you very much," Zoë snapped.

"Zoë," Melicent faltered. "You and Jerry haven't quarreled about this, have you?"

Zoë tossed her head. "As near as makes no difference. It's interesting to learn that you both think I've been sullying my reputation. Good God, Melicent, you surely don't think *I* want any more gossip, do you? I've had enough of it to last a lifetime."

From the expression on Melicent's face, Zoë knew her vehement reply had been distressing, but for the moment she didn't care. She was torn between her sense of gratitude for Melicent's unfailing kindness and affection and the newer feelings aroused by Lady Harlow's spiteful revelations.

Zoë's mind was alive with questions. Had Melicent been in love with Jerrold before her marriage? Had she chosen to marry the future Lord Rosedale because, as Lady Harlow had intimated, he could offer her a rank and fortune that Jerrold as a younger son couldn't give her? Was she in love with Jerrold now, and did she know about his sterility? And if so, had she magnanimously put her own feelings aside in order to help Jerrold by easing his newfound bride's entrance into society? In which case, of course, Melicent's kindness to Zoë had been impersonal, indifferent, prompted primarily by her love for Jerrold and not by any real regard for Zoë herself.

Zoë looked at Melicent, whose normally bright, friendly expression had become subdued, and was ashamed of her suspicions. It didn't matter *why* Melicent had been so helpful. It only mattered that she had wholeheartedly supported Zoë from the first moment they met. A thought stole into Zoë's head, and she reacted in alarm. No, of course she wasn't jealous. She despised Jerrold, she didn't care a fig what his relations with other women might be, and if Melicent had the misfortune to be in love with him, why then she was sorry for Melicent.

"Melicent, I apologize," Zoë said now. "I shouldn't have barked at you like that. I know you meant well. And you were right. I shouldn't have spent so much time in Sir Stephen's pocket. To tell the truth, my feelings were a little bruised by Countess Lieven's remarks."

Melicent looked relieved. "Oh, I understand perfectly, and I'm so glad you're not angry with me for poking my nose into your business. I want only the best for you and Jerry. Well, now," she said, getting up from her chair, "I really must go. Oliver is insisting that I go with him to Rundell and Bridge—the jewelers, you know, on

Ludgate Hill—to help him select a gift for Uncle Rupert's birthday."

Zoë inquired curiously, "You see a good deal of Oliver, don't you? You danced with him last night at Almack's."

Melicent grimaced. "I see a deal too much of him, frankly. Sometimes I suspect—oh, it's ridiculous, I daresay, but . . ." She shook her head, frowning. "Sometimes I suspect he's paying me all these attentions because he's planning to offer for me." Melicent laughed ruefully. "There, tell me I'm a sapskull. Can you really imagine Oliver wanting to marry me? What an idea!"

As Melicent was leaving, a footman brought Zoë a note on a tray. "The man who brought this is waiting for an answer, my lady."

The note was in an unfamiliar hand. "Dear Lady Woodforde: I spoke to my sister about the exhibition at Somerset House, and she is most enthusiastic. If you have no other plans for this afternoon, Clarissa and I would be delighted to escort you to Somerset House at two o'clock. Your most obedient servant, Stephen Carrington."

Her eye on the waiting footman, Zoë hesitated, tapping the note against her teeth. Melicent had just gently chided her for spending too much time in Sir Stephen's company the evening before. And Jerrold . . . Jerrold had said he would take steps to constrain her if she embarrassed him by risking even a semblance of impropriety with another man.

The anger that she had been holding at bay during a restless night and through a morning of painting now burst to the surface. How dare Jerrold insinuate that she was so lacking in good breeding that she might disgrace him? How dare he threaten her with unspecified penalties? After all, what could be more innocuous than a visit to a public art gallery with a respectable gentleman, chaperoned by his equally respectable sister?

Taking a quick decision, Zoë told the footman, "Come to the morning room. I'll write my answer there."

Sir Stephen was prompt to the minute of two o'clock. When she entered the drawing room, he greeted her with a warm smile and an appreciative look at her mint-green muslin pelisse and her gypsy bonnet trimmed with matching ribbons. For a moment she felt a warning qualm. Was his smile too warm, his glance too appreciative? But no, she decided. Surely she had no reason to fear unwanted gallantries from this pleasant, sympathetic man who had helped her through some difficult moments the evening before.

"I hope you don't object to riding in a landau," he said. "It's such a lovely day, I thought you might enjoy a drive in the open air."

"It sounds delightful. I'm a country girl, you know, addicted to long walks in the fresh air."

Lady Bradford waited for them in the landau, her parasol unfurled above her fashionable Leghorn bonnet under the warm sun of a late May day. She was her usual self, friendly and loquacious. As her brother handed Zoë into the seat beside her and took his place opposite them, she cocked her head, saying teasingly, "La, my dear, I fair welcomed this opportunity to have a comfortable coze with you. *Now* you must tell me all about your secret romance. You really owe it to me to tell me your story. I went to a deal of trouble to bring you and Lord Woodforde together, you know, and it was all for nothing!"

"Clarissa," said Sir Stephen repressively, glancing at the impassive-faced coachman.

His sister lowered her voice, giggling. "Oh, Stephen, Lady Woodforde already knows I'm a gabster, but a harmless one."

Indeed, Zoë found it difficult to be annoyed with Lady Bradford's good-natured curiosity, which obviously had no malice behind it. As the carriage moved out of Bedford Square, she said with a smile, "My 'story' isn't really very exciting or dramatic, Lady Bradford. Jerrold and I met and fell in love when we were both much too young, we had a misunderstanding and quarreled, we parted company. When we met years later we discovered we still cared for each other. That's all. A commonplace 'love story' with a happy ending."

"Yes, but your little boy—"

"Don't be tiresome, Clarissa," Sir Stephen cut in.

Her good nature undisturbed, Lady Bradford subsided. She grinned at Zoë. "Do you have an older brother, Lady Woodforde? You do? Then you know how they're always telling their sisters what to do. Quite unconscionable." She turned thoughtful. "My dear, I've come to believe that we're all much too stiff and formal in society these days. Consider our circumstances, for example. We've known each other for some months now, and I hope we've become friends. Don't you think we might dispense with our constant 'Lady This' and 'Lady That' when we speak to each other? May I call you Zoë? And I'm Clarissa."

Taken aback, Zoë hesitated. She herself had sometimes chafed under the strictures of the exactingly formal etiquette observed by the London *ton*, accustomed as she was to the more relaxed usages of Cumberland, where she had known all her neighbors since childhood. Still, the unspoken rules dictated that she should not be on a first-name basis with anyone other than a friend of long standing or a member of her family. But after all, what was the harm? She liked Lady Bradford, and the woman was an important customer. She smiled. "Why, of course, Clarissa. Please call me Zoë."

"Thank you, my dear. We'll be much more comfortable with each other now." Lady Bradford shot a teasing glance at her brother. "What about poor Stephen? Need you be quite so formal with him?"

"Clarissa!" Sir Stephen exclaimed before Zoë could speak. His face had turned red. "Lady Woodforde will think we're inexcusably forward. She and I met each other only last evening."

Zoë heard herself saying, "Oh, but it seems we've been acquainted much longer than that, Stephen." Perhaps it was the memory of Jerrold's wounding lecture about her behavior that prompted Zoë's reply. Perhaps it was the wistful expression lingering in Stephen's face. She wasn't sure.

His eyes lighted up, and immediately Zoë felt a twinge of apprehension. She had never been a flirt, but was she now giving Stephen a subtle encouragement by relaxing the rules of formality? She shrugged mentally. What was done was done, and at bottom she did think of Stephen as a friend.

The main entrance to Somerset House was on the Strand. Entering the building by one of the three lofty arches, Zoë and Stephen and his sister passed through the spacious pillared vestibule and into the rooms housing the Royal Academy exhibition, crowded today with a large number of well-dressed visitors.

Zoë's painter's soul reveled in this mass display of art,

but as on a previous visit to the gallery, she deplored the practice of placing paintings immediately next to each other on virtually every square inch of wall from floor to ceiling, confusing the eye and making it almost impossible to view properly the pictures on the lowest and highest levels.

After pointing out to Zoë the latest Lawrence portrait, Stephen deftly piloted her and his sister through the crowd to view the other paintings. However, Lady Bradford soon left them to themselves and retired to a bench to chat animatedly with one of her acquaintances. Zoë suspected that Clarissa had little interest in art and had come along today out of the goodness of her heart in order to provide her brother with a chaperon.

"And here, Zoë, is my favorite, the Turner I was telling you about," said Stephen, pausing in front of a small landscape featuring a fisherman on the bank of a little stream meandering through a deeply wooded countryside. Its luminous yet muted grays and blues and greens contrasted with the more garish colors of the paintings surrounding it.

Zoë examined the landscape closely, absorbing every small detail of composition. Looking up at Stephen, she smiled, saying. "I see why the picture is your favorite. It's the prize of the collection."

"I was sure you would agree with me," Stephen replied in a tone of quiet delight.

Suddenly, cutting through the babble of conversation around them, a woman's carrying voice said, "Oh, yes, she paints. In fact, I hear she's quite famous for her portraits. However, I daresay she would prefer to be known as an expert on travel to Scotland."

Instinctively Zoë wheeled to face the speaker. Standing close to her was a middle-aged, fashionably dressed woman who fixed her with a piercing, contemptuous stare before ostentatiously turning her back on Zoë to speak to her two companions. Zoë gasped and felt herself turning pale.

"Steady," Stephen said to her in a low voice, placing his hand on her arm and guiding her away to a corner of the room where there were fewer people.

Zoë swallowed hard. "That woman meant for me to hear what she said. She meant to hurt me. That reference to Scotland—she was talking about my elopement to Gretna Green. She obviously doesn't believe I was married in Scotland, or anywhere else, for that matter. To her, I'm a fallen woman, and a lying one, to boot.'

"Listen to me, Zoë. Don't allow yourself to be overset by a cruel, spiteful woman like that."

"How can I not be overset? Doubtless she's only repeating what everybody in London is saying."

Stephen's fingers firmed on her arm. "Not everybody. Not most people. You're a strong woman, Zoë. You needn't heed that dreadful woman or her ilk. Carry your head high. Face down people who spout such filth. You know the truth. Make them believe it."

Zoë drew a long breath. Jerrold, Melicent, her brother Edmund had all told her to ignore the gossip. The rumors couldn't hurt her, they said, and would eventually fade away for lack of facts to feed upon. They hadn't convinced her. She had been living in morbid dread of the vicious gossip that would assail her when London society learned about her secret marriage. And to date, her encounters with Countess Lieven, the patroness of Almack's, and Lady Harlow, Jerrold's mistress, had intensified her apprehensions. She'd become certain that nothing she could say or do would sway public opinion in her favor. Now, for the first time, with

Stephen's quiet declaration of faith in her, she could begin to believe that she could outface the demons of rumor and innuendo.

She looked at him, smiling tremulously. "Thank you, Stephen."

"For what?" he retorted, but with a warm glint in his eyes. "I've only stated the obvious. You've no need to kowtow to anyone, Zoë. Just be your own self."

Zoë rode back to Bedford Square from Somerset House in a more relaxed mood than she would have thought possible earlier in the day. During the drive Clarissa Bradford chattered endlessly about how uplifted she felt after viewing the art treasures of the Royal Academy, and Zoë didn't flutter an eyelash in disbelief. She did, however, exchange a gently malicious grin with Clarissa's brother.

After they arrived at Woodforde House, and Stephen had handed Zoë from the carriage, he reached back for the thin portfolio that Zoë had observed earlier on the seat of the landau and carried it with him when he escorted her to the house. In the foyer he held the portfolio out to her, saying hesitantly, "I'm holding you to your promise. Do you mind?"

Zoë took the portfolio. "Not at all. I'm eager to see your work."

"Afternoon, Carrington. We meet again, it seems."

At the sound of Jerrold's cool and definitely unwelcoming voice, Zoë and Stephen looked up to see him descending the stairs.

Looking faintly puzzled by Jerrold's tone, Stephen said, "Good afternoon, Woodforde. I've just had the great pleasure of escorting Zoë to the exhibition of the Royal Academy."

At Stephen's use of Zoë's given name Jerrold shot him

a hard glance. After a pause he said, "Did you enjoy the exhibition, *Zoë?*" He gave her name an unmistakable emphasis.

"Yes. Very much," Zoë said coolly. 'Stephen and I especially admired a Turner landscape."

A muscle twitched in his jaw. Zoë's use of Stephen's Christian name had not escaped him. He tapped his finger on the portfolio she held in her hand. "And what's this?"

Stephen answered for her. "Zoë has kindly offered to give me her opinion of some of my sketches and watercolors."

"I see. I hadn't realized that you, too, were an artist, Carrington. Well, I'm sure you'll find that Zoë is an excellent critic on matters of art." Again Jerrold emphasized Zoë's name.

To Zoë, the tension in the foyer had become almost palpable. She wondered if Stephen felt it as strongly as she did. He seemed unperturbed, however, as he said, "I must be going." He bowed politely. "Thank you, Zoë, for a most pleasant afternoon. Good day to you, Woodforde."

As soon as the footman had closed the door on Stephen Jerrold said quietly "Will you come to the morning room, Zoë? I should like to speak to you."

Zoë followed him down the corridor, bracing herself for an explosion. Jerrold closed the door of the morning room behind them with a savage finality that matched the expression on his face. Standing with his back braced against the door, he said in a voice trembling with fury, "Did you hear a word of what I said to you last night about behaving discreetly? Or did you decide to deliberately flout my authority by haring off with Carrington to that damned exhibition at Somerset

House? And then, not to mention your display of last night, you apparently became even more intimate with him today, to the extent of allowing him to use your Christian name!"

Zoë gasped. "Intimate? How dare you . . .?" She drew a steadying breath. "For your information, I 'hared off' to Somerset House in the company of Sir Stephen *and* his sister, Lady Bradford, who, I think you'll grant, was a perfectly adequate chaperon. And since I consider both of them my friends, how I address them is my own affair."

Jerrold's expression changed. He said stiffly, "I misunderstood the situation, then. Lady Bradford's presence made your visit to the exhibition unexceptional. I apologize. I spoke too hastily."

"Yes, you most certainly did," Zoë snapped.

He looked ill at ease, she was glad to see. But even as she enjoyed her small triumph over him, she felt a tinge of regret that this chasm of coldness and seeming dislike had replaced the brief camaraderie that had developed between them after their "truce." She realized now that Jerrold had proposed the truce solely to make his relations with her more comfortable for *his* sake. And yet . . . for that brief space of time there had been a feeling of warmth and closeness between them that had never existed before, even if it had been based on pure illusion. She missed it.

Despite his apology, Jerrold continued doggedly, "This exchange of Christian names, however, is another matter. Surely you must realize it will raise eyebrows. I suggest you refrain from the practice, in public at least. And another thing: I'll remind you that accepting Carrington's escort more than occasionally, even in the company of his sister, might not be wise, considering our present circumstances."

Zoë knew that Jerrold had a point. Very probably it would be unwise to pursue her friendship with a man she had just met. But she couldn't prevent herself from saying defiantly, "As I told you last night, I see no reason why I shouldn't have friends of my own."

Jerrold's lips tightened ominously at her remark, but he apparently decided against pursuing the issue. After a slight pause he said, "I've promised Philip a boat ride up the Thames tomorrow. Would you care to accompany us?" He added quickly, "He made a point of asking me to invite you to join us."

Zoë's first impulse was to refuse. She had no wish to spend a day in close quarters with Jerrold, especially after this most recent confrontation. Nor, she was sure, did Jerrold have any desire for her company. Then she reminded herself that the only object of this pretense marriage was to safeguard her son's happiness and heritage. And Zoë knew Philip would be unhappy if he sensed any strain between her and the father he'd come to adore.

"Thank you," she forced herself to say. "I accept the invitation. I've never sailed on the Thames. I daresay I'll enjoy the excursion as much as Philip."

Jerrold nodded. "Philip will be glad."

With a certain sense of relief, Zoë reflected that tacitly she and Jerrold had agreed to put their fragile truce back in place. Only this time, of course, there would be no pretense of "friendship" between them.

On the following morning, during the drive to the landing stairs at Westminster Bridge, Philip was so beside himself with excitement that Jerrold chided him.

"Stop that wriggling and calm yourself. If you behave that way on the boat, you could easily fall overboard."

Philip's eyes widened in fear. "Papa! I can't swim."

His stern expression changing to an indulgent smile, Jerrold gave the boy a hug. "Not to worry. I can swim, and I'll make sure you don't drown. And later this summer, at Malvern Hall, I'll teach you to swim."

Philip looked at Jerrold with such loving trust that Zoë's heart caught. Her brother Edmund had given Philip a great deal of care and affection, but she knew that something vital had been missing in her son's life before Jerrold's arrival on the scene—the presence of a father. She knew, too, that she couldn't allow any grievance or quarrel with her unwanted husband to disturb the bond he'd fashioned with his son.

Jerrold had spared no pains in arranging his excursion up the Thames. When they embarked at the landing stairs, he conducted Zoë and Philip onto the deck of a large barge, luxuriantly carpeted and shaded by bright red awnings. On the forward deck there were chairs and tables for the passengers, and on the aft deck seats for a full contingent of rowers.

As soon as Jerrold and his family took their seats, the rowers unshipped their oars and the barge began moving smoothly beneath the high balustraded arches of Westminster Bridge. As Jerrold observed Philip's expression of delight, he said, "Someday, before we leave London, we'll go downstream to the Pool of London to see the docks and warehouses and more ships of every description than you've ever seen in your life before."

"Oh, Papa, nothing could be better than this," Philip breathed, taking in the sights and sounds of the river. It was a perfect day, the sun shining brightly from an intensely blue sky, a light breeze gently ruffling the water.

As the barge glided upstream, past the tree-lined terraces of Westminster Hall, Jerrold began to point out the points of interest to a rapt Philip. "Over there, son," he said, indicating a low willowed shore beyond which loomed a vast gaunt building. "That's Milbank Penitentiary."

"Are there lots of bad men in that place, Papa?" asked Philip with some misgiving.

"Quite a few, unfortunately." Jerrold patted Philip's shoulder. "But they're all locked up securely, you know. There's no way they can harm you."

Zoë sat back in her chair, relaxing, rather to her surprise, in the warmth of the lovely day and the soothing motion of the barge through the waves, content to let Jerrold entertain Philip. Jerrold was wearing his usual elegant town clothes, and as Zoë gazed at Philip, looking quite adult in his short-tailed coat, pantaloons, and boots, she thought again, as she had on other occasions, that the boy was such an exact miniature of Jerrold in his black-haired, blue-eyed good looks that no one could possibly mistake them for other than father and son.

Soon the grounds of the Chelsea Royal Hospital came into view, and then the Bishop's Palace at Fulham, followed, a little later, by the sight of the extensive market gardens and the stately villas lining a stretch of the river at Chiswick.

All too soon for Philip's taste the barge landed its passengers at Richmond. "Later this afternoon we'll go farther up the river to Kingston," Jerrold promised Philip when the boy expressed his disappointment that the upstream voyage had ended, "and perhaps there might even be time to fish for a spell from the banks. I ordered poles put in the barge. But for now, I'm hungry, aren't you? We'll have lunch at the Star and Garter Inn. It's quite a famous place hereabouts, and they serve very good food."

Jerrold offered Zoë his arm, and they began strolling away from the river, Philip trotting along beside them. A charming family group they must appear, Zoë thought with faint derision, young and well-dressed parents with a handsome child in tow. They walked past elegant villas and across the Green, with its impressive Theatre Royal and the gateway that was the only remnant of the old palace, and trudged up a steep hill behind the town.

"I didn't realize the hill was quite so far from the river," Jerrold remarked to Zoë at one point. "I usually come by road. I should have arranged for a carriage at the landing."

"Oh, Mama likes to walk, Papa," Philip assured his father. "So do I. We're not a bit tired, are we, Mama?"

"No, not at all." Zoë looked at Jerrold. "I told you I was a country girl."

At the top of the hill Jerrold pointed out to Philip the entrance to Richmond Park, across from the Star and Garter, saying, "We'll explore the park another day. You'll want to see the deer. I understand there are several herds of them, including both fallow and red deer." To Zoë he indicated the comfortable house sitting next to the hotel. "As a painter yourself, you might be interested to know that Sir Joshua Reynolds lived in that house for many years."

The proprietor of the hotel himself greeted them in the entrance hall. "Lady Woodforde, Lord Woodforde, Lord Silverbridge, I'm honored to see you. Your private dining parlor is ready. Please follow me."

As he walked along beside her, Philip tugged at the

skirt of Zoë's pelisse, muttering, "Who's this Lord Silverbridge, Mama?"

Zoë paused, bending down to him. "Sh-h-h, Philip." she murmured. "Don't you remember what I told you? *You're* Lord Silverbridge. You're Papa's heir."

"Oh, yes. Now I remember," Philip said, sounding unconvinced. Zoë had to suppress a smile. It was hard enough for a six-year-old to accept a change of surname from Manning to Layton, let alone take on the responsibility of still another identity as Lord Silverbridge.

Zoë soon realized that the lavish lunch, served by a bevy of attentive waiters in the private dining parlor, reflected the same careful attention to detail that had marked the boat ride up the Thames. Jerrold had ordered dishes that would appeal to a small child, especially to a country-bred child. Philip ate so heartily that Zoë gazed at him with disquiet, saying, "Nurse will blame your papa and me if you have no appetite for your supper."

"Come now, one excess won't hurt him," Jerrold observed. He leaned across the table, examining the enormous strawberry tart, piled high with clotted cream, into which Philip was making inroads. Jerrold said solemnly, "Actually, I'm wondering if you're really getting enough to eat, Philip. Is there anything else you might fancy?"

Philip glanced at the sideboard, laden with desserts. "The chocolate *gâteau* looks delicious," he said with a straight face. When Zoë began to object, father and son burst into laughter.

After the luncheon Jerrold ushered Zoë and Philip into the gardens of the hotel, saying, "We can't leave the Star and Garter without seeing the view from the top of the hill."

Awed and silent, Zoë stood on the garden terrace for

long minutes, looking down on the view far below her. Her painter's eyes absorbed every detail of the lovely vista of the Thames, undulating gracefully through its wooded valley as it wound its way toward the beech-covered hills of Buckinghamshire and the heaths and downs of Surrey.

At length Jerrold broke into Zoë's appreciative silence. "There's Ham House down there on the left, surrounded by elm groves," he said. "A little farther along to the right, across the river, you can see Hampton Court and Bushey Park. And Philip, look upstream to those hills in the distance. If you have sharp eyes you can just glimpse Windsor Castle. The old king lives at Windsor, you know, in the Queen's Lodge."

When Philip didn't answer, Jerrold turned his head, saying, "Philip?" A second later he exclaimed in surprise, "He's gone. He was here beside me just a minute ago. . . . Now, where do you suppose he went?"

Turning away from the view, Zoë glanced around the garden, looking for Philip among the walks and flower beds. At the moment she and Jerrold were quite alone in the garden. "Philip probably wandered back into the inn," she told Jerrold. "You know how curious he is about new places."

But Philip was nowhere within the Star and Garter, and none of the inn servants remembered seeing the boy during the past few minutes. Unconcerned as yet, Zoë shrugged, saying, "Then we'll find him outside, poking his head into anything that looks interesting." She added severely, "I intend to speak sharply to him, Jerrold. He shouldn't have gone off by himself."

"I expect he became bored with looking at the view," Jerrold observed. "Appreciating the beauties of the landscape is an adult taste, I fear."

There was no sign of Philip on the roadway in front of the inn or in the area nearby bordering a terrace of fashionable houses. Glancing across the road at the entrance to the park, Jerrold said with a trace of uneasiness, "I daresay he might have decided to go into the park to search for those deer I mentioned to him."

Her face shadowed with the beginnings of apprehension, Zoë exclaimed, "Let's go look."

However, though they walked a considerable distance into the wooded reaches of the park, Zoë and Jerrold found not a trace of Philip, or for that matter, any deer. At length Zoë slowed her steps, looking around her into the shadowy areas beneath the thick foliage, and said, a note of strain obvious in her voice, "Jerrold, I really don't think Philip would have come this far. It's mysterious and lonely here in the forest. He'd have been frightened."

Jerrold nodded. "I agree. Let's go back."

He paused outside the wall enclosing an unassuming house to the right of the entrance gates of the park. "The Countess of Pembroke lives here, I understand. Do you suppose . . .?"

"You think Philip might have gone inside the grounds?" Zoë said with a surge of hope. She sighed, shaking her head. "It's a private house. We can't—"

"Yes, we can," declared Jerrold, advancing purposefully on the gate in the wall.

Minutes later, standing in the gardens attached to Pembroke Lodge, Zoë and Jerrold looked at each other in dejection.

"I'm sorry, Zoë. I thought there was a good possibility he might have come in here—"

An excited voice interrupted him. "Mama, Papa, look!"

Philip's parents whirled around to see their son running toward them from around the corner of the house, holding aloft an object in his hand, his face split by a wide grin. As he came up to them he said, "The gardener is the nicest man. He let me help him prune the roses, and then he showed me his woodcarvings, and when I admired them he gave me this. Isn't it beautiful?"

Zoë stared numbly at the object Philip had thrust into her hand. It was the finely detailed carving of a deer. She sank down on her knees and threw her arms around Philip. Holding him convulsively close, she exclaimed, "My darling, I've been so worried about you. I was so afraid you were lost, or hurt, or—or worse."

Pulling himself away from her, Philip said defensively, "Of course I wasn't lost, Mama. I'm six years old! While you and Papa were looking down at the river I decided to explore a bit. I walked into the park, thinking I might see one of those deer Papa told me about, but it was so dark and quiet there under the trees that I didn't quite like it, so when I came to this house I heard somebody whistling the cheeriest tune, and I slipped inside the gate, and there was this very nice man, working in the garden, and he let me help him. . . . Mama, I'm sorry you were worried . . ."

Philip's suddenly contrite voice trailed away as Zoë smiled at him through a film of tears. "Philip, darling, I'm willing to forgive you anything, just so I know you're safe." She put her arms around him again and kissed him.

Looking both relieved and chastened, Philip returned his mother's kiss. "I'm glad you're not angry with me, Mama. I know I should have told you where I was going."

She rose, brushing her fingers across his cheek. "Mind you remember the next time." She bent down to kiss him again.

Philip cocked his eye at Jerrold. "Were you worried about me, too, Papa?"

'Well, I was, just a bit, you know. After all, you're the only little boy I have."

"Then p'raps Mama should kiss you, too. Kissing makes everything better when a person is feeling bad."

"I'm sure it does." A flicker of sardonic amusement crossed Jerrold's face. Zoë wondered if he was thinking of the kisses of Lady Harlow, or of any of the other women who had enjoyed his attentions over the years.

"Well . . .?" Philip looked expectantly at his mother.

Taken aback, she expostulated, "Your papa isn't a child, Philip. He doesn't need comforting in the same way a child does."

Clamping his lips together, Jerrold stared at Philip's wistful face. Then he smiled. "All the same, Zoë, Philip is right. Kisses are very nice to receive at any age." He reached out to take her arm, pulling her toward him. "Well?" he said, echoing Philip.

Zoë knew why Jerrold was doing this. He would go to any lengths to make Philip happy. Her feelings, or his own, for that matter, didn't count. Fuming inwardly, she raised her face to Jerrold and kissed him on the cheek. Before she quite knew what was happening, Jerrold shifted his head slightly and his mouth found hers. The cool, impersonal touch of his lips deepened almost immediately into a clinging kiss that set Zoë's heart pounding. She drew back abruptly, averting her eyes.

"There, Papa, don't you feel better now?" Philip exclaimed.

"Much better," Jerrold agreed gravely. He took out

his watch. "If we're to continue on to Kingston this afternoon, we'd best be returning to the boat."

A little later, as he was helping Zoë into the barge from the landing stage, he said in a low voice, "I'm sorry about the—the incident at Pembroke Lodge. I didn't mean to offend you, but I think Philip wants to believe that we're a loving family, so I . . ." His voice trailed off.

Zoë gave him a direct look. "No need to apologize. I understand perfectly."

As the barge moved away from the landing, she sat back in her seat, hoping she appeared calm, hoping Jerrold didn't realize how his kiss had affected her. She had told him she understood his actions perfectly, but she didn't understand herself. She didn't understand how she could feel such a powerful sexual attraction for Jerrold when they were so at odds in every other aspect of their lives.

Chapter Fourteen

It was after the excursion to Richmond that Zoë began to notice that her life in some respects was becoming smoother. Not that her relations with Jerrold improved, but neither did they worsen. As the days went by, they managed to keep intact the tenuous truce between them by treating each other with a formal courtesy in private and avoiding being alone together as much as possible.

In her relations with the world outside Woodforde House Zoë's self-consciousness gradually disappeared. Soon she found that she could enter a drawing room full of strangers, or walk down a street, or ride in the Park, without fearing that she was the object of intensely curious or hostile eyes.

The change in her mental attitude was no doing of her own. She knew the credit belonged to Stephen Carrington. She remembered every word he had drummed into her ears after her encounter with the spiteful woman at Somerset House: "You're a strong woman, Zoë. Carry your head high. Face down people who spout such filth. You know the truth. Make them believe it."

Stephen continued to offer to escort Zoë to artistic exhibits and cultural landmarks, always in the company of his sister. Clarissa Bradford gamely persisted in expressing her delight at being exposed to artistic stimulation, but her reaction to the Parthenon marbles, exhibited in a temporary building erected next to Lord Elgin's house in Park Lane, more accurately reflected her real feelings. She gazed fixedly at the priceless marble sculptures that Lord Elgin had appropriated from the Acropolis in Athens, and then exclaimed in disappointment, "Why do they bother with these things? They're all broken." At a session in Christie's auction rooms she ignored both the artwork and the bidding while she chatted audibly with a crony, to the annoyance of the auctioneer.

In the privacy of her studio, Zoë had carefully examined the sketches and watercolors in Stephen's portfolio. Soon afterward, during a visit to Westminster Abbey, when Clarissa was preoccupied with still another convivial crony, Zoë drew Stephen aside to say, "I enjoyed seeing your work."

Stephen's clear gray eyes bored into hers. "But? I know there's a but. Otherwise you'd have told me I was a rival to Reynolds, or to Lawrence."

"No, you're no threat to Reynolds or Lawrence," admitted Zoë. "However, I think you have real talent. I'd call you—"

"A rank amateur."

"No," she smiled. "A talented amateur." She hesitated. "Another thing . . . you recall we agreed to use each other's Christian names?"

"Yes." Stephen frowned. "I've been thinking. Perhaps we shouldn't . . ." He broke off as Zoë began to laugh.

"I see we've been thinking the same thoughts," she said. "People might talk if we were so informal with each other on such short acquaintance. In the future we can still be Zoë and Stephen in private, but in public . . ."

"In public I'll address you as Lady Woodforde." Stephen grinned. "That should keep the gabblemongers at bay."

Yes, and it will probably also prevent another unpleasant altercation with Jerrold, Zoë thought wryly.

In the first week of June, the Tsar Alexander and the King of Prussia arrived in England on a state visit to celebrate the victory over Napoleon, and the London populace went mad with enthusiasm over the Russian emperor. The crowds lined the streets, cheering wildly, when, as happened on most days during his stay, the emperor rode through London accompanied by an exotic entourage of colorfully uniformed Cossacks, with heralds and tossing banners and blaring bands complete with cymbals and trumpets.

Zoë had her first sight of the emperor one afternoon when she and Melicent were driving in Hyde Park at the fashionable hour of promenade. Melicent had ordered her coachman to halt the landau at the side of the roadway so that she and Zoë could chat with Oliver Layton, who had come by on horseback.

"You never appeared at Mrs. Osmond's soiree last night as you promised," Oliver was saying reproachfully to Melicent, when a swelling crowd noise caused him to lift his head and stare down the drive at a party of uniformed horsemen approaching them. The object of attention by all the pedestrians, riders and occupants of carriages in the vicinity, the group of horsemen cantered slowly past the landau. A tall, slender, blond man in an ornate uniform and cocked hat rode at the head of the party.

Oliver whistled after the horsemen had ridden past. "By Jove, it's certainly true that the Tsar has a taste for the ladies," he declared, rolling his eyes. "Melicent, did you observe the way His Imperial Majesty feasted his eyes on Zoë's charms? Zoë, I must drop a hint to Jerry that he has a most distinguished rival!"

"Oh, stow your whid, Oliver," Melicent said crossly.

"Melicent! Such vulgarity," protested Oliver, half shocked, half amused.

"Well, I mean it. You shouldn't say such things. You were putting Zoë to the blush."

Looking abashed, Oliver mumbled, "Beg your pardon, Zoë. I was out of line." But Zoë suspected that this young man, who looked so much like Jerrold, but who so often appeared gauche in comparison with the perfection of Jerrold's polished social address, had a liking for vulgarity. She wondered at Melicent's patience in allowing Oliver to trail constantly at her skirts.

Zoë's next encounter with the Tsar came several nights later, at the weekly Wednesday ball at Almack's assembly rooms. As she stood talking with Jerrold and Melicent at the side of the ballroom, she glanced around her at the crowd of guests, a little bemused by the fact that Almack's no longer represented an ordeal for her. She no longer imagined that every person in the room was busily engaged in searching for chinks in her reputation.

Lady Jersey bustled up to them, her good-natured face alive with excitement. "My dear, what a triumph," she said to Zoë. "But I'm not surprised, no, not a bit surprised."

Zoë smiled. She liked the vivacious patroness, who had been true to her promise, scotching rumors about Zoë and putting in a good word for her with the *ton*.

"What triumph is that, Lady Jersey? I wasn't aware of any."

Sally Jersey's bosom swelled. "My dear, His Majesty wishes to dance with you. Behold, I come as his emissary."

Out of the corner of her eye Zoë caught a glimpse, as the crowd parted, of a tall, impressive figure making his way toward her. Her stomach suddenly felt as if butterflies were playing hide-and-seek inside it.

"You do waltz, don't you?" Lady Jersey inquired on a sudden note of worry. "His Majesty wants to waltz. I'm told he *loves* to waltz. Oh, I know, here at Almack's we've frowned on the waltz up until now, but on the Continent it's long since been admitted to polite ballrooms."

"I—yes. I do know how to waltz." Lady Jersey's question had conjured up in Zoë's mind memories of stolen late-night sessions at Miss Drayton's Academy, in which Zoë and her fellow pupils had practiced the forbidden measures of the waltz.

The tall man stopped in front of Zoë. In person the Tsar was even handsomer than she remembered. "Lady Woodforde," he said, bowing. "May I have the pleasure of this dance?"

Zoë gulped as she dropped a low curtsy. "I'm honored, Your Majesty," she murmured. Alexander waited a moment until the orchestra struck up a waltz and then, with the other dancers clearing a space about them, he slipped his arm around Zoë's waist and swept her into the rhythm of the dance. Initially she felt so nervous that she feared her hollow legs wouldn't support her, but her nervousness started to disappear almost immediately. The Tsar's arm supported her firmly, and her feet seemed to remember the steps of the waltz without any help from her conscious brain. The Tsar was a superb dancer.

When the dance ended, Alexander brought her back to Jerrold and Melicent. Clicking his heels, he bowed gracefully. He smiled, saying, "Before I came to this country, Lady Woodforde, I refused to believe what I considered exaggerated accounts of the beauty and grace of English ladies. Now I'm a convert. Thank you for a most enjoyable dance."

After the Tsar had moved away, Zoë realized to her embarrassment that on this occasion she wasn't imagining a barrage of stares. Curious, envious, titillated, all eyes were on the woman who had been the recipient of royal favor.

Oliver Layton sauntered up to Zoë. "There, what did I tell you, Cousin? You've made a conquest. And *what* a conquest!"

His cheerful grin was almost a leer, and Zoë, pressing her lips together, didn't reply to his comment. However, Jerrold said curtly, "I daresay conquest isn't the word Zoë would use to describe her experience. She was pleased to dance with an emperor. Period." As Oliver's face reddened, Jerrold turned to Zoë. "The orchestra is playing what I predict will be the first of a spate of waltzes, now that the Tsar has put his stamp of approval on the dance. Shall we join in?" Without waiting for a reply, he drew her onto the floor.

Zoë was uncomfortably aware of the light pressure of Jerrold's arm around her waist and the firm grasp of his fingers holding her hand. Accustomed to a fleeting, impersonal contact with other dancers in country dances and reels, she had never been in such close physical contact with a man on a ballroom floor, save for her one waltz with the Tsar Alexander. And during her waltz with the Tsar, of course, she had been so excited that she had scarcely noticed that the Emperor was also a man.

She was acutely, excruciatingly conscious that her present partner was a man. She sensed Jerrold's strong bone structure and smooth, powerful muscle beneath the exquisitely tailored black broadcloth, and she breathed in the faint, enticing scent of immaculately laundered linen and shaving soap. Unbidden, unwelcome, there flashed into her mind the memory of being caressed by knowing, roving hands in that long-ago encounter in Gretna Green. She inhaled sharply, missing a beat.

"Sorry," said Jerrold as he steadied her. "I do know how to waltz, but I haven't had much practice lately."

"It wasn't your fault. I stepped off on the wrong foot."

A moment later, as they glided gracefully across the floor, Jerrold murmured, "I don't think we have any further need to worry about our acceptance by society. The Tsar has taken care of that."

Zoë lifted her head, giving him a startled look.

Jerrold nodded. "You've arrived, Zoë. Who in the future can question your position? The Emperor of all the Russias doesn't choose as his dancing partner in a polite assembly a nobody, someone labeled a bird of paradise." He flashed her a sardonic smile. "We're fortunate that you have a beautiful face and a graceful figure, my dear wife. His Imperial Majesty is reputed to be a man of discriminating taste when it comes to feminine charms. He wouldn't have condescended to dance with an ill-favored frump."

Zoë felt her cheeks growing warm. Jerrold had never before commented on her appearance—except, of course, on the infamous night when he had seduced a sixteen-year-old girl by plying her with champagne and compliments. Now he had casually described her face as beautiful, quite as if he was stating a fact and not merely an opinion. Not that there was any reason to feel flattered, she thought wryly. It was clear, from the cynicism in his voice, that there was nothing personal in his remark. He regarded her looks, which had prompted the Emperor of Russia to ask her to dance, as just another asset in his single-minded pursuit of social acceptance for his heir.

She said coolly, "Perhaps we should give thanks to Napoleon. If he hadn't gone down to defeat, the Emperor of Russia wouldn't be visiting England today, and he'd have had no occasion to ask me to dance."

Jerrold gave her a look of mild surprise. Then he laughed. "Thank you for the suggestion, Zoë. Would you believe it? For the first time in my life I have kindly thoughts for Napoleon Bonaparte." He swept her into an exuberant turn.

For a few fleeting moments, as she surrendered to the swaying rhythms of the waltz, Zoë fancied that the wall of chilly reserve between her and Jerrold no longer existed. But by the end of the dance she knew that the wall was still very much in place. As they walked off the floor, Jerrold remarked with a cool satisfaction, "This has been a very good evening for us, don't you agree? The Tsar singled you out, and you and I romantically danced the waltz. Who could fail to believe that we're a respectable married couple?"

Zoë held her brush poised over the shimmering pearls in Clarissa Bradford's necklace. Then she stepped back from the portrait, shaking her head. "No, I won't touch the pearls again," she said aloud, talking to herself. "I'll leave well enough alone."

Overhearing Zoë, Meg put down her feather duster and walked over to the easel. She looked admiringly at the portrait. "It's quite lovely, my lady," the abigail said. "Lady Bradford will be very pleased."

"I hope so. Well, we'll soon know. Have the portrait delivered to her tomorrow, please." Zoë glanced at the watch pinned to her bodice. "Great heavens, I hadn't realized it was so late. It's past time to dress for Lady Rosedale's dinner. Come along, Meg. We'll have to hurry."

"Yes, my lady." Meg chuckled. "You have a smear of paint on the tip of your nose."

A little later, after a hasty toilet, Zoë snatched a last look in the glass at her gown of apricot-colored silk gauze and hurried down the stairs to the foyer, where Jerrold was waiting, tapping his foot impatiently on the floor. He was superbly dressed as usual in a black evening coat and white breeches. Men with badly shaped legs shouldn't wear tight breeches and silk hose, Zoë thought irrelevantly. Of course, Jerrold didn't have the problem.

"Am I late?" she asked breathlessly. "I'm sorry. I know we're the guests of honor. I lost track of the time, I was finishing a portrait."

Jerrold lifted an eyebrow. "I daresay Melicent will forgive us. She's very tolerant of the artistic temperament." From his noncommittal tone Zoë couldn't tell whether Jerrold's remark concealed either a hidden sarcasm or resentment about her painting career. He offered her his arm and the hovering footman opened the door.

Melicent's large house in Park Lane was brilliantly lit.

A red awning protected guests from the elements as they walked up the red-carpeted steps, lined on either side by a row of attentive footmen. Carriages were already driving up to the door.

In the drawing room Melicent received them warmly. "Your gown is beautiful, Zoë. I'm almost sorry I didn't yield to temptation and buy that lovely material from under your nose!"

"Oh, come now, Melicent, your gown is the top of the trees," exclaimed Oliver, gazing at Melicent's gown of pale blue crape. He stood next to her, almost, thought Zoë, as if he were acting as host. Didn't Melicent tire of his constant presence? Jerrold greeted Oliver as he usually did, with a chilly brevity that caused Oliver to redden faintly.

Lady Jersey was already present and drew Zoë aside. Her eyes twinkling, the patroness of Almack's said, "My dear, I thought you'd like to know how much you impressed the Tsar. Count and Countess Lieven recently entertained for His Majesty—well, naturally, the Count is the Russian Ambassador to England—and at one point the Tsar remarked to Dorothea Lieven how much he'd enjoyed his evening at Almack's, and *especially* his dance with the beautiful Lady Woodforde. Well! Can't you just imagine how discomfited poor Dorothea felt? She who, a short time ago, had royally snubbed the same Lady Woodforde? Poetic justice, *I* call it."

"Oh, and what might that be?" inquired Rupert Layton genially, coming to stand beside them.

Laughing, Lady Jersey shook her head, saying, "No, no, Mr. Layton. We females must have some secrets. And now pray excuse me. I want a word with Mrs. Gordon."

Gazing after Lady Jersey as she walked away,

Jerrold's uncle remarked, "My dear Zoë, I'm happy to see you've made a friend of Sally Jersey. She can be most valuable to you." Taking Zoë's arm, he said, "Come sit with me and catch me up on your doings. I vow, you and Jerry have been so busy socially since you came to London that I've scarcely seen you at all."

Seated beside Rupert on a settee, Zoë studied him, noting, as she had on previous occasions, how much he resembled both Jerrold and Olive. Although he was so much older than his nephew and his son, his hair was only faintly gray, and his strong, even features showed few lines. Dark-haired, blue-eyed good looks were apparently a Layton family trait, Zoë reflected. Philip was undeniably a Layton.

Smiling, Rupert said, "I've been glad to observe that you and Jerry seem to be laying those nasty rumors to rest. If I might give you a bit of advice, however . . ." He paused, clearing his throat. "The fact is, I'm told that you're frequently in the company of Sir Stephen Carrington, and I just wonder, my dear, if this, er, friendship is entirely wise, under the, er, circumstances."

Zoë stiffened. "Did your informants also tell you that, when I'm with Sir Stephen, his sister, Lady Bradford, is always with us?"

Rupert looked uncomfortable. "Please believe I don't mean to criticize you, Zoë, but even if Lady Bradford is always present, do you really think—"

"I think Sir Stephen and his sister have become my very good friends."

"Yes, well, of course . . ." Looking embarrassed, Rupert quickly changed the subject. "Speaking of friends, Zoë, have you noticed that Melicent and Oliver seem to have become quite close?"

"I've noticed that Oliver spends a good deal of time

in Melicent's company, yes." Zoë kept her tone carefully neutral.

Rupert cleared his throat again. "I suspect—no, I'll be frank, I *know*—that Oliver is very much in love with Melicent. He would like to marry her. Now, you and Melicent are good friends. Perhaps she's confided in you. Do you know if she has any feelings for Oliver? Do you think she might look kindly on his suit? As a matter of fact, would you and Jerry consider putting in a good word for him with Melicent?"

Zoë hoped her voice sounded as chilly as her feelings. "I can't speak for Jerrold, Uncle Rupert, but I would *not* care to 'put in a good word for Oliver' with Melicent. That would be interfering in her life, and I have no right to do that."

"But . . ." Rupert clamped his mouth shut. After a moment he said with a rather strained smile, "Well, well, my dear, you must do as you think best." He went on to chat easily about the visit of the Allied sovereigns to London. "They do say, you know, that old Marshal Blücher is even more popular with the crowds than either the Tsar or the King of Prussia!"

Melicent's dinner was an elaborate affair, with more than thirty guests ranged around the long table in her spacious dining room. For Zoë, who was beginning to be satiated by the endless succession of dinners, balls, routs, and *soirées* that marked the London seasons, the dinner was also somewhat boring. She was glad when Melicent collected the female guests with a practiced sweep of her eyes and led them into the drawing room for coffee. After that, Zoë had only to make small talk until the gentlemen arrived after drinking their port, sit through more conversation or a game of cards until the servants brought in the tea cart, and then, finally, it would be time to go home.

At one point in the evening, as she checked her appearance in the cheval glass in a small dressing room set aside for the female guests, Zoë reflected that the London social scene was far less fascinating than she would have imagined a few short weeks ago from a vantage point in the wilds of Cumberland. She admitted ruefully to herself that she would welcome an idle evening at home to read a book!

Returning to the drawing room, she paused outside the door of the library when she heard from inside the room the sound of some object crashing to the floor, followed by a quickly stifled scream.

"What is it?" Jerrold startled her by coming up to her silently from behind.

"I—I don't know. I thought I heard a crash of some kind, and a scream. Perhaps it was only a servant tidying the room."

"At this hour?" scoffed Jerrold. He paused. "Melicent left the drawing room with Oliver a while ago," he muttered. "I wonder . . ." He jerked the library door open and strode into the room. Melicent was struggling desperately to release herself from Oliver's embrace. With a smothered snarl, Jerrold leapt across the room, dragged Oliver away from Melicent, and smashed his fist into his cousin's face. Oliver dropped to the floor.

White-faced and disheveled, Melicent looked dazedly at Zoë, standing in the doorway. "Close the door, Zoë," she gasped. "Jerrold, see to Oliver. Oh, God, I hope he isn't hurt."

"Would you rather I hadn't interfered?" Jerrold said grimly.

"No—no, of course not. But Jerrold, we can't have a family scandal . . ."

Oliver was already stirring. He scrambled to his feet, holding his jaw. A trickle of blood ran from the corner of his mouth. His eyes clearing, he lunged at Jerrold, who seized his arms and twisted them behind his back.

"Listen to me, you miserable loose screw," Jerrold growled. "You're leaving this house immediately. I'll come with you, to make sure you do leave. And if you ever say one word of what happened in this room tonight, I'll do more than plant you a facer. I'll squeeze my hands around your neck until you can't breathe— permanently. Do you understand?"

Oliver, his face averted, nodded his head.

"Zoë, stay with Melicent," Jerrold ordered. Retaining a hold on one of Oliver's arms, Jerrold marched him to the door and out of the room.

After the door had closed, Melicent sank limply into a chair. Her eyes filled with tears.

Zoë took a handkerchief from her reticule and pressed it into Melicent's hand. "What happened? Do you want to talk about it?"

Melicent seemed dazed. Dabbing at her eyelids with the handkerchief, she muttered, "I can't imagine why he—it's not *like* Oliver."

Zoë thought cynically that Oliver's behavior was probably very typical, but she remained silent, waiting for Melicent to unburden herself, if she cared to do so.

"Oliver asked me to come into the library. He said he had something to show me," Melicent went on in the same dazed tone. "He gave me these . . ." She thrust at Zoë a velvet-covered box she had been clutching in her hand.

Zoë opened the box and gasped. The diamond earrings were magnificent, both in the quality of the stones and their size. Nothing in the jewelry collection belonging to Jerrold's mother could compare with them.

"I told Oliver I couldn't possibly accept such an expensive gift," Melicent continued, "and then he said the earrings were a betrothal gift, and when I told him I couldn't marry him either, he grabbed at me. I tried to get away—I collided with that little table over there and knocked it down—but he caught me and began kissing me ..." Melicent scrubbed at her mouth with Zoë's handkerchief. Her eyes filling with tears again, she said, "I'm sure I never gave Oliver any reason to think I cared for him."

"Of course you didn't. Don't blame yourself."

Melicent went on unheedingly. "Poor Uncle Rupert, poor Aunt Beryl. Oh, I hope they never find out how badly Oliver has acted. If there's a scandal, it will be so humiliating for them, for all of us."

"There won't be a scandal," said Zoë firmly. "I won't tell anyone what happened here tonight, Jerrold won't tell, *you* won't tell, and I doubt very much that Oliver will say a word, not if he values his hide. You heard Jerrold threaten him. Wipe your eyes, Melicent, stand up and straighten your gown, and go back to your guests. They'll be wondering why you've been gone for so long."

If her guests had noted Melicent's absence, none of them was impolitely curious enough to say so. At one point Beryl Layton did wonder plaintively where Oliver had gotten to.

"I'm sorry, Aunt," said Jerrold. "I forgot to give you Oliver's message. He had a pressing engagement elsewhere."

"No doubt at White's or Boodle's," Rupert Layton

said with an indulgent smile. "The boy has so many friends."

"Just so," Jerrold replied with a straight face.

During their carriage ride home that evening, Zoë and Jerrold didn't speak of the subject that was uppermost on their minds, or at least on Zoë's mind. Had Jerrold knocked Oliver down out of jealousy, because he couldn't bear to have another man lay a finger on the woman he secretly loved? Or had he merely reacted chivalrously, to save Melicent from the unwanted attentions of a man he despised?

Whatever Jerrold's motives had been, he obviously wasn't prepared to discuss them. He remained silent during most of the drive to Bedford Square, rousing himself finally to remark, "I have news for you that I daresay will please you. Do you recall meeting Colonel Albright tonight? He's an officer in the Regent's household. He informed me that the Lord Mayor of London has invited the Regent and the Allied sovereigns to a gala dinner at the Guildhall next week. The affair will be one of the social events of the Season, and the colonel tells me that you and I will also receive an invitation, at the personal request of the Tsar Alexander. Quite a triumph for you, Zoë. The invitation is due to you. I have no illusions about my popularity with the Tsar."

Once again, it was impossible to tell, from Jerrold's dry, noncommittal tone, whether he was pleased by the invitation to the Guildhall. He should have been pleased, of course. Attendance at such a prestigious event would surely be still another indication that he and Zoë had achieved acceptance of their marriage. A startling thought struck Zoë. Jerrold couldn't be—no, the idea was ludicrous. He couldn't be jealous of her relationship with the Russian Emperor. Jerrold had no interest in her personally. She was important to him only as Philip's mother, the mother of his heir.

"I'm glad you suggested an early start," Zoë remarked to Stephen Carrington as he handed her into the landau to a seat beside his sister Clarissa. "Otherwise I'd have been inclined to cancel the excursion to Hampton Court. Tonight Jerrold and I are invited to the Lord Mayor's dinner for the sovereigns at the Guildhall. It wouldn't do to be late, and Hampton Court is quite a distance from here."

"Great Heavens, no, you mustn't be late to *the* event of the Season," said Clarissa, a note of envy in her voice. "And certainly we have a very long drive ahead of us to Hampton Court. It must be all of fourteen or fifteen miles." She added pensively, "I did think, you know, that we might have to postpone our trip today because of the weather. It rained such torrents yesterday." She looked up into the cloudless blue sky with a faint air of disappointment.

Zoë suppressed a smile. Clarissa was so transparent. She obviously was less than enthusiastic about this excursion. Good-natured and obliging though she was, she had doubtless grown weary of chaperoning her brother and Zoë on their numerous sightseeing forays.

The landau proceeded at a smart clip west on Oxford Street and into the Bayswater Road. Clarissa soon recovered her usual sunny spirits. "My dear, I simply adored my portrait," she told Zoë. "Of course, my husband swears that I haven't looked *that* beautiful since the early days of our marriage, but he was only funning, you know. My friend, Lady John Mainwaring—her husband is the duke's second son—saw the portrait, and now nothing will do but she must have her portrait done, too."

"Tell her to write to me. I'll arrange a sitting."

"I marvel you still find the time to paint, Zoë," Stephen observed. "You have such a busy social schedule."

"I make time to paint, no matter what." Zoë reflected on her remark with a slight feeling of surprise. It was true. She spent precious time with Philip, she carried out her social duties, but her mornings in her studio were sacrosanct. Today's excursion to Hampton Court was an exception to her daily routine.

Zoë had never before probed her feelings on the subject of her work. Now she realized with a sudden insight that her painting not only allowed her to express herself artistically, but also preserved her sense of personal identity. She was Zoë Manning, portrait painter, as well as the wife of the Earl of Woodforde.

The long drive took them through Chiswick, south along Kew Road, through Richmond and Kingston, and across the Kingston Bridge to Hampton Court Palace. Scarcely had they passed under the astronomical clock in the great gateway than Clarissa inevitably encountered a crony in the throng touring the building. Busily talking, Clarissa and her friend trailed along behind Stephen and Zoë as they examined the heraldic windows in the Great Hall and the tapestries in the Presence Chamber. As they were about to enter the chapel, however, Clarissa drew Zoë aside, saying apologetically, "My dear, I have *such* a headache. I think I should go home to bed."

"I'm so sorry. I'll tell Stephen. We'll leave immediately."

"No, no, that's not necessary. My friend, Lady Field,

wishes to return to London also, and she'll be happy to give me a seat in her carriage." Clarissa paused, looking vaguely guilty. "The only thing ... I know you and Stephen are so particular about observing the *conventions*. ..."

Although Zoë believed the sudden acute headache was largely imaginary, an excuse to avoid touring the vast palace and its grounds, she took pity on Clarissa's embarrassment. "Oh, I hardly think Stephen and I will raise too many eyebrows if we drive back to London without a chaperon, just this once," she said cheerfully. "Go along with your friend, Clarissa. I hope your headache is better soon."

Stephen was less charitable. "I'll tell you what, Zoë," he said, gazing with a jaundiced eye at his sister's retreating form, "I don't think Clarissa has a headache at all. She just doesn't like to walk."

Zoë laughed. "Give her the benefit of the doubt. It's a very big palace."

Stephen looked anxious. "You don't really mind that Clarissa wont' be accompanying us?"

"No. For one thing, who will know? We haven't met a single acquaintance here. Don't worry, Stephen. Let's enjoy our visit."

He smiled, the quick flashing smile that transformed his plain, rather sober face. "Let's."

They spent several more absorbed hours in the palace, admiring the marvelous mural decorations on the King's Staircase and the hundreds of paintings in the State Apartments, and then took a leisurely stroll through the extensive gardens. Leaving Hampton Court shortly after noon, they stopped briefly at the Griffin Inn in Kingston for tea and a light luncheon.

"It's been a lovely day, Stephen, and we're starting

back to London in good time," said Zoë a little later, as the coachman headed the landau out of the courtyard of the Griffin.

Stephen consulted his watch. "Yes, it's only half-past one. You'll not be late for the banquet."

Then disaster struck. Shortly after they had passed through Petersham, as the carriage rounded a blind curve in the road, they encountered a heavily laden wain. Trying to prevent a collision, Stephen's coachman jerked his team sharply to the left. The horses cleared the wain with inches to spare, but the landau itself grazed the wain, causing the rear left wheel of the carriage to sink into the ditch that ran beside the road.

"Oh, God. Are you all right, Zoë?"

Grasping the side of the landau, which was leaning at a perilous angle, Zoë said breathlessly, "Yes, I'm fine, Stephen."

"Here, let me help you out."

Once he and Zoë were standing on level ground, Stephen assessed the damage. The coachman had scrambled down from the box and stood at the head of his lead horse, trying to calm his skittish team. The groom, who had been thrown from his seat beside the coachman, was attempting to crawl out of the ditch. His face contorted with pain, the groom gasped, "I'm sorry, Sir Stephen, kin ye give me a hand? I think I've broke something. I cain't move me leg."

Stephen called to the coachman, "Jack, I need help."

Slowly, carefully, the two men pulled the groom from the ditch and deposited him on the verge. After running his hand lightly over the injured man's leg, Stephen rose, shaking his head. "It's a bad break, Zeke. We must get you to a doctor immediately."

"Might not be that easy ter do, sir," ventured the

coachman. "I jist looked at the left rear wheel. The rim's come off, and more'n a few o' the spokes is splintered. We need a wheelwright."

"Damnation." Stephen walked over to the wain, looking up at the driver, who was trying without success to edge his vehicle around the carriage.

The man said sourly, "Ye're blocking me way, yer honor."

"Yes, and you'll stay blocked until we can get help," Stephen retorted. "Where's the nearest doctor? And the nearest wheelwright?"

The wain driver replied sullenly, "Mayhap ye'll find both o' 'em in Appleby, that's down the road a piece."

Turning away impatiently, Stephen told his coachman, "Take one of the horses and ride to this Appleby. If there's an inn, ask the landlord to send a carriage so we can transport Zeke to the doctor. Fetch the wheelwright, together with some extra men to move the landau off the road. We can't be blocking traffic indefinitely. And hurry."

After the coachman had ridden off, Stephen went to Zoë, who was kneeling beside the injured groom. "I'm so sorry, Zoë. I never meant to land you in a ditch."

"It was an accident, Stephen, and I'm quite all right." The groom stifled a groan, and Zoë leaned over to wipe the perspiration from the man's brow with her handkerchief. She studied his pain-racked face for a moment, biting her lip in concern. Standing erect, she took Stephen aside. "The poor man is in so much pain. I'm afraid he's badly hurt."

Stephen nodded. "Yes, I fancy he has a nasty fracture. Don't worry, Zoë. He'll soon be under a doctor's care. And don't worry about returning to London in time for the Lord Mayor's dinner, either. As soon as I'm satisfied that Zeke is in good hands, we'll be on our way, in the landau if the wheelwright is able to make the repair to the wheel in time, in a hired carriage if not."

Stephen was wrong in every count. A doctor did, indeed, practice in the hamlet of Appleby, but he was out on his rounds when Zeke arrived at the surgery on the rough cart that was all the landlord of the local inn could supply by way of transportation. Stephen and Zoë waited with Zeke until the doctor returned from his rounds, and waited again during the agonizingly lengthy process of setting and splinting the groom's multiple fracture. They left Zeke resting comfortably in a spare bedchamber of the doctor's house.

Stephen's coachman now reported that the wheelwright would be unable to repair the wheel of the landau until late that evening or the following day. Moreover, there was not an available carriage of any kind for hire in Appleby.

"Ride to Petersham and find me a carriage, any kind of a carriage. I don't care if it's a gig," Stephen savagely instructed his coachman.

It wasn't a gig. It was a curricle that had seen better days. Stephen pronounced it capable of being driven. Unfortunately, by the time he and Zoë set off in the vehicle for London, it was already six o'clock in the evening.

"Zoë, I'm sorry," said Stephen miserably. "You'll miss the Lord Mayor's dinner."

"It can't be helped," replied Zoë with a calm she didn't feel.

When they arrived in Bedford Square, the footman who opened the door, averting his eyes from Zoë's windblown hair and the traces of mud on her pelisse, the result of kneeling down beside the injured Zeke, reported that, indeed, his lordship had left the house some hours previously to attend the Lord Mayor's banquet.

"Goodbye, Stephen," Zoë said quietly. "I enjoyed the day. Please don't feel guilty. The accident wasn't your fault."

She went up to her bedchamber. Meg jumped up from a chair when her mistress entered the room. "My lady!" the abigail gasped. "Are you hurt? Your pelisse is soiled, and there's a tear near the hem. And you're so late—the great banquet at the Guildhall . . ."

"No, I'm not hurt. I was delayed by an accident. Please order a bath, Meg, and I'd like something to eat. Something light. Tea and toast would be fine."

A little later, refreshed from her bath, dressed in a loosely comfortable peignoir, Zoë sat sipping a cup of tea in a chair by the window, watching the lights come on in the windows of the houses in the square as the sky darkened in the deepening twilight.

She sat, willing her nerves to be quiescent, waiting for the axe to fall.

She rose when Jerrold strode into the bedchamber from the dressing room without bothering to knock. His blue eyes were black with rage. "My God, Zoë," he exclaimed, "are you deliberately trying to ruin our son's life?"

Chapter Fifteen

Balling her hands into fists in an attempt to calm herself, Zoë said, "You're angry, Jerrold, and I can't blame you. I missed the Lord Mayor's banquet."

"Oh, you did that," flared Jerrold. "You also missed what everyone is calling the most magnificent spectacle ever seen on the streets of London. The Regent rode in procession from Carlton House in his state carriage with the King of Prussia and the Prince of Orange, escorted by Light Dragoons, a troop of Horse guards, the band of the Gentlemen Pensioners, and the Yeomen of the Guard, preceded by carriages bearing members of his Household, all of the Royal Dukes, the Speaker, and the members of the cabinet. At Temple Bar the Mayor, the Sheriffs and Aldermen, all mounted and wearing their robes, officially welcomed the Regent and his guests."

"The procession does sound magnificent," Zoë said in a subdued voice. "I wish I had seen it."

Ignoring Zoë's interjection, Jerrold continued in a tone of controlled fury, "The Tsar came in a separate procession, equally impressive. His Imperial Majesty asked for you, Zoë. He told me he'd been looking forward to seeing you again. I, of course, informed him, with suitable regret, that you'd been afflicted with a sudden mysterious illness that prevented you from attending the banquet."

Gritting her teeth, Zoë exclaimed, "Jerrold, will you please allow me to explain? I didn't deliberately avoid attending the Lord Mayor's banquet. There was an accident. Stephen's carriage collided with a farm cart as we were returning to London. The carriage was damaged and Stephen's groom was badly injured. We had to find a doctor for the groom, and after we'd assured ourselves that the poor man was being cared for adequately, we tried to hire a carriage to take us to London, and there were no available carriages. We finally had to hire a curricle."

Jerrold glared at her. "Aren't you omitting several pertinent details? The footman has already informed me that you arrived here in a curricle. He also said that you appeared quite disheveled and that your pelisse was torn and soiled, as if, indeed, you had been in an accident. He seemed quite concerned about you. Doubtless you and Carrington presented quite a spectacle as you drove along Oxford Street. But what I want to know, Zoë, is what happened to your redoubtable chaperon, Lady Bradford? You've assured me repeatedly that Clarissa Bradford *always* accompanies you and Carrington when you go gallivanting about the town."

"Clarissa developed an excruciating headache at Hampton Court," Zoë said levelly. "A friend who was also visiting the palace offered to drive her home, and she accepted. She refused to allow Stephen and me to cut short our excursion for her sake."

"If you had exercised a degree of common sense, you would have insisted on accompanying Lady Bradford. In that case you would probably have avoided the accident to Carrington's carriage, and you'd then have been able to arrive in London in time to fulfill your social responsibilities."

Zoë stared resentfully at Jerrold, her sense of guilt dissolving rapidly. "May I suggest that *you* exercise your common sense? You use the words 'would have' and 'probably.' That's pure guesswork. Even if Stephen and I had returned with Clarissa, we could still have had an accident, delaying our return to London. In any case, I used my best judgment at the time. Now, I've no wish to quarrel with you. I heartily regret missing the Mayor's banquet, and I've apologized to you. However, I don't intend to grovel in front of you in an orgy of remorse and contrition, and if that's what you expect from me, I'd like you to leave. I've had a trying day."

Jerrold flushed a dull red. "I keep forgetting your provincial background," he snapped. "Doubtless you don't fully understand the rules that govern the conduct of a lady of quality. We'll consider the matter closed, then." He turned on his heel. At the door of the dressing room he paused. "One last word. As the master of this house, I do not wish to receive Stephen Carrington in my home in future."

Angrier than she could ever remember being, Zoë lashed out. "Despite my 'provincial background,' I'm the *mistress* of this house, and I intend to receive whomever I like! Good night, Jerrold."

Zoë cleared her throat, breaking the silence that had prevailed between her and Jerrold during their drive to Lady Jersey's house in Berkeley Square. Silence, in fact, had been the norm between them for the past two days, since the night of the Mayor's banquet at the

Guildhall. Except for brief, formal exchanges at the evening functions they were obliged to attend together, they had avoided each other's company. When they did meet, the memory of their quarrel seemed to hang over them like a malignant London fog.

"I received a letter from my brother Edmund today," Zoë told Jerrold. "Before we left Heathfield, I'd invited him and my old friend Mrs. Randolph to visit us in London during the Season. Edmund wrote to say he and Mrs. Randolph would be with us on Friday. Do you have any objections? If so, they can always stay at a hotel."

"That will be quite unnecessary," Jerrold replied. The indifference in his voice was marked. "You're the mistress of Woodforde House, as you made perfectly clear the other night. Naturally, you're free to invite anyone you like to stay in your home. Your brother and your friends from Cumberland are welcome."

There was a slight emphasis on the words "your brother and your friends from Cumberland." The unspoken name of Stephen Carrington hovered between them. Stephen was not among the people Jerrold was willing to welcome to Woodforde House.

Lady Jersey's large mansion in Berkeley Square was festively alight for her ball. When Zoë and Jerrold mounted the stairs to the door of the ballroom, the vivacious patroness of Almack's greeted Zoë with a laugh and a playful tap on the shoulder with her fan. "Well, my dear, I hear you've been having some interesting adventures."

Jerrold smiled. "Surely that shouldn't surprise you, Lady Jersey. My wife is an interesting woman," he said suavely. But there was no amusement in his eyes.

Invitations to a ball given by one of the most prominent

hostesses in London were eagerly sought after, and the ballroom filled early. At first Zoë wasn't conscious of being in any way the center of attention. Then Lady Jersey joined her and Jerrold as they stood on the side of the ballroom. The patroness's face was flushed with annoyance. Glancing over her shoulder at the Russian Ambassador's wife, who was standing a short distance away, Lady Jersey exclaimed, "I always thought Dorothea Lieven was narrow-minded," she said to Zoë, "but now I must tell you that she's simply impossible. I wish I'd never asked her here tonight. Don't you pay any mind to her, my dear." With this cryptic pronouncement she flounced off with her characteristic febrile energy, leaving Zoë gaping after her, open-mouthed.

In a moment Melicent came up to Zoë and Jerrold, looking unwontedly serious. "Zoë, did Lady Jersey tell you about her quarrel with Countess Lieven?" she asked in a low voice.

"Quarrel?"

"I don't know all the details, but as I understand it, the Countess told Lady Jersey, with that vinegary smile of hers, that you had finally showed your true colors and had destroyed your reputation for good and all with your escapade at Hampton Court the other day. I gather someone spotted you and Stephen Carrington driving along Oxford Street in a curricle at the very time you and Jerrold were supposed to be honoring the Tsar at the Lord Mayor's banquet. Sally Jersey, of course, defended you. She likes you, Zoë."

Melicent paused, looking at Zoë with troubled eyes. "I know it's all a great to-do about nothing, but Clarissa Bradford has been making the situation much worse. You know she has a tongue that rattles on and on, and she's been wailing to all her friends how guilty she feels about causing such a scandal for you and Stephen Carrington. If only, she says, she hadn't had the headache, leaving you and Stephen to return from Hampton Court alone, and on and on she goes. Well, naturally, the more Clarissa talks, the more people speculate."

Jerrold shot Zoë a murderous glance. At the same time, with a sinking heart, she watched Stephen Carrington making his way across the ballroom toward them.

Stephen's normally sunny, open expression seemed faintly strained as he greeted Zoë and Jerrold. "May I have this waltz, Lady Woodforde?"

Zoë hesitated for a split second, and then, before she could reply, Jerrold clapped Stephen on the shoulder, saying with a pleasant smile, "Certainly you can have this waltz, Carrington, but don't think you can monopolize all my wife's dances. She's saving at least one for me." His smile broadened. "I'm thinking of calling you out, you know."

Stephen said feebly, "Er—really?"

Jerrold laughed. "Yes. My pride is suffering. Zoë tells me you're a far better waltzer than I am. Even better than the Tsar of all the Russias!"

Stephen's face was a polite mask as he led Zoë onto the dance floor, but his muttered remark echoed his confusion. "What's this about my great dancing expertise? I've never waltzed with you, much as I would have liked to."

"I know. Jerrold made all that up out of thin air."

Stephen slipped his arm around her waist and expertly guided her into the first turn. "Well, but—why?"

"I think—I suspect—that Jerrold wants to give the impression that he bears you no ill will."

Momentarily Stephen lost the beat of the music.

"Sorry. Zoë, have there been difficulties about that infernal excursion to Hampton Court?"

Zoë sighed. "Jerrold wasn't pleased that I missed the gala at the Guildhall, and he's worried about gossip. Well, you know our circumstances. We seem to be forever skirting the boundaries of respectability. Unfortunately a goodly number of people seem to have observed you and me as we drove through London in that infamous curricle! Then tonight Countess Lieven made a spiteful remark about the incident, and Lady Rosedale tells me that your sister has been talking too much, so . . ."

Stephen groaned. "Zoë, I'm so sorry."

"Don't be. None of this is your fault—or anybody's fault. And it may—I hope—turn out to be a tempest in a teapot. But Stephen, I think it might be better if we didn't indulge in any more of these delightful excursions for the time being."

"Yes, of course. I'll do anything you say." Stephen's voice deepened. "I'll miss those excursions. I'll miss you, Zoë."

Probably it was just as well that she and Stephen wouldn't be as much in each other's company in the future, Zoë thought uneasily as the waltz ended and they walked off the floor. Tonight Stephen was beginning to sound less like a kindly friend and more like an admiring suitor.

Stephen escorted Zoë back to Jerrold and was about to retire with a murmured word of thanks and a polite bow when Jerrold said, "By Jove, Carrington, it occurs to me that we haven't compared out marksmanship for some time. I believe I bested you at our last encounter. Supposing we meet at Manton's tomorrow morning and have a rematch?"

"Er, certainly. I look forward to competing. Eleven o'clock suit you?"

Jerrold beamed. "Splendid. Oh, and something else." He turned to Zoë. "When did you say your brother was arriving?"

"On Friday." Zoë gave Jerrold a puzzled look, which he ignored.

He turned back to Stephen. "Zoë and I would be pleased to make you acquainted with her brother, the Reverent Edmund Bennett, and with her dear friend, Mrs. Randolph, a neighbor from Heathfield, who will be arriving for a visit on Friday. Pray call at Woodforde House during their stay."

Manfully stifling a look of surprise, Stephen said, "A pleasure, I assure you."

Smiling, Jerrold extended his hand to Zoë. "Shall we have our waltz now, before Carrington claims them all?"

At the end of the evening, during the return drive to Bedford Square, Zoë broke another developing silence, saying to Jerrold, "I'm glad you went out of your way to be friendly to Stephen tonight. Your attitude should certainly help to quiet any rumors that there was something havey-cavey about my excursion to Hampton Court."

In the gloom of the carriage Zoë couldn't see Jerrold's face, but she could distinctly hear the coldness in his voice. "I'm willing to do anything necessary to secure my son's succession to my estates. That includes being friends with Stephen Carrington and allowing him to frequent my home, thereby asserting my belief in my lady wife's virtue. Admittedly, I also run the risk that people with nasty minds may suspect I'm allowing Carrington to plant horns on my head."

Zoë exclaimed, "Jerrold! You can't think that Stephen and I—"

He cut in with a chilly finality. "What I think doesn't matter. I don't care what your feelings for Carrington might be, only that you conduct yourself discreetly. My only interest is in Philip and in safeguarding the Woodforde family inheritance."

Edmund and Mrs. Randolph duly arrived at Woodforde House on the Friday.

"Oh, it's so good to see you, both of you," Zoë exclaimed as she threw her arms around her brother.

Holding her at arms' length, Edmund looked at her closely. "And how are you? You don't say much in your letters."

Zoë glanced away from her brother's searching eyes. Edmund could always read her mind. "I'm in prime twig, as you can see for yourself," she said lightly. "I've been far too busy to write long letters. Taking part in the London Season is a great deal of work! Now, then. Was your journey very tiring?"

Edmund accepted the change of subject. He replied ruefully, "I thought traveling by the mail might be too much for Mrs. Randolph, but as you can see, she looks far less fatigued than I do."

Mrs. Randolph laughed. "That's because you took such good care of me, dear Mr. Bennett." She took a deep breath. "I can't believe I'm actually here," she exclaimed in a marveling tone to Zoë. "I feel as if I'm in a dream. I can't wait to revisit all the wonderful sights I saw the last time I was here so many years ago." Her expressive plump face grew troubled. "But perhaps I shouldn't have left Mr. Randolph home alone in

Heathfield," she fretted. "I begged him to come along when the Reverend Bennett kindly offered to escort me here, but John doesn't *like* London, so I—"

"I'm sure Mr. Randolph won't suffer from your absence," said Zoë firmly. "Meanwhile, I'm very happy to have you here. We'll have a splendid time sightseeing." Zoë was perfectly sincere. She welcomed the presence of Edmund and Mrs. Randolph. They would enliven the chilly atmosphere of Woodforde House and take Zoë's mind off her virtual state of war with Jerrold.

"I've been reading about the state visit of the sovereigns to London," said Mrs. Randolph eagerly. "Have you seen the Tsar of Russia or the King of Prussia? You've *danced* with the Tsar? Oh, Zoë . . . how I should love to see a real emperor!"

Zoë laughed. "That won't be difficult. His Imperial Majesty progresses through the streets of London most days. I suspect you'll catch a glimpse of him. And Jerrold and I are invited to a dinner at Carlton House in honor of the sovereigns next week. Jerrold thinks he can obtain invitations for you and Edmund, too, through his friendship with the Regent's equerry."

"Oh, Zoë . . ." Mrs. Randolph's eyes gleamed with bliss. But, though a few days later she was suitably overwhelmed by the magnificence of Carlton House and her presentation to the Allied sovereigns, she seemed to enjoy equally her visits to the familiar London landmarks in the company of Zoë and Stephen Carrington.

Stephen had dutifully called at Woodforde House to meet Zoë's guests. During his visit, to Zoë's astonishment, Jerrold had suggested, seemingly with the greatest cordiality, "You're such a dabster in the sightseeing line, Carrington, why don't you escort Zoë and Mrs. Randolph about town?"

Oblivious to any undercurrents, Mrs. Randolph thoroughly appreciated Stephen's efforts to entertain her. "Such a nice young man, my dear," she commented to Zoë. "So devoted to you and Lord Woodforde. Is he a special friend of the family?"

"Why—yes," Zoë replied, crossing her fingers mentally at the bald-faced lie. "I suppose you could say that."

"Well, Zoë, I confess I was a bit concerned about you when I first learned about your secret marriage to Lord Woodforde. Forgive me for mentioning it, but there was a certain amount of gossip, and I did worry that you might not be happy in your new life. But now I see I shouldn't have worried. Here you are in this splendid house with a distinguished husband, a social life filled to the brim, and a wonderful family friend. What more could any woman want?"

"Nothing at all," said Zoë, and hoped that her old friend didn't detect the hollow note in her voice.

Her brother, however, was not so easily gulled. Edmund sought Zoë out on the very day after he arrived at Woodforde House. "Now, Zoë, I want the truth," he demanded when he unceremoniously invaded the sacred precincts of her studio. "In your letters you tell about your social engagements, and you describe Philip's activities, but you never say a word about your marriage. Are you happy? Or at least content? Has this strange compact you've made with your husband for Philip's sake worked out as you hoped it would?"

Zoë avoided his eyes. Lifting her brush to add highlights to the coiffure of her latest subject, she said, "La, Edmund, what a worrier you are. Yes, I'm happy. Or perhaps it would be more accurate to say I'm satisfied with my lot. My bargain with Jerrold has worked out very well. We understand each other. We have no problems."

"It sounds rather too pat," said Edmund dryly.

Zoë gazed at her brother's skeptical face and said reluctantly, "Jerrold and I were the subject of unpleasant gossip when we first arrived in London, and yes, it caused me some distress, but that's all behind us now. Except for . . ." She paused, biting her lip.

"Except for . . . ?"

Zoë surrendered, and gave Edmund a brief account of her excursion to Hampton Court and its disastrous aftermath.

Edmund lifted an eyebrow. "This gentleman—Carrington, is that his name?—is he an old friend of Jerrold, or possibly a relative?"

"No. Stephen is my friend. We met quite recently. He's an artist, too."

"Then I quite understand why Jerrold is concerned about the episode at Hampton Court. Frankly, I'm shocked myself," said Edmund severely. "Even in the wilds of Cumberland we have certain standards of conduct. A lady doesn't extend her friendship to a gentleman she has just met." He looked at Zoë's flushed, embarrassed face and relented. "Well, well, my dear, I daresay there were extenuating circumstances. And I've no doubt you've informed this Carrington that he's no longer welcome at Woodforde House. So that should end the matter."

Zoë took a certain malicious pleasure in saying, "Actually, Edmund, Jerrold has invited Sir Stephen to call at Woodforde House to make your acquaintance."

For a moment Edmund looked utterly taken aback. Then an expression of perfect comprehension settled over his face, and he nodded. "You have a very intelligent husband, Zoë. He's probably cut off this dreadful gossip at its roots, before it has a chance to grow."

During the course of his visit Edmund proved well able to entertain himself. He had an amateur's enthusiasm for classical archeology and made repeated visits to view the collections at the British Museum. He was also interested in the latest scientific discoveries, and attended several lectures by Humphry Davy at the Royal Institution in Albemarle Street.

Edmund's abiding passion, however, was stained glass windows. He spent many a happy hour during his stay with Zoë in a search for the choicest specimens in the great London churches. What was more, Edmund soon discovered a fellow admirer of stained glass. It developed that Melicent's interest in rose windows in particular and church architecture in general nearly matched Edmund's own.

Edmund had, of course, called on Melicent, as his most prominent parish member, when he first arrived in London, and Melicent had dutifully invited him to tea and to dinner. But soon, rather to Zoë's bemusement, Melicent and Edmund were making almost daily excursions in each other's company, seeking out treasures in the metropolitan churches. Indeed, their mutual interest was a least partially responsible for embroiling Edmund, that most peaceable of men, in an episode of physical violence.

It happened one day when Zoë, having finished her morning painting stint, sat in the morning room with Mrs. Randolph, enjoying a glass of wine before lunch. Mrs. Randolph was twittering happily about their engagement that evening at Sadler's Wells—"Oh, I know Shakespeare is uplifting, my dear, and I did enjoy watching that new actor, Mr. Keane, play Shylock the

other night, but I'm so looking forward to seeing a famous clown like Joseph Grimaldi"——when Oliver
Layton burst into the room.

"Where is Melicent?" he demanded unceremoniously.
"One of the servants at Rosedale House told me that
she'd be here." His clothes were disheveled, and there
was a distinct odor of spirits about his person. Zoë
hadn't seen him since the night of the dinner at
Melicent's house, when Jerrold had planted him a facer
for pressing his unwelcome attentions on Melicent. Zoë
knew that Melicent had been avoiding all contact with
Oliver since the dinner party.

Zoë rose, frowning at Oliver and making no attempt
to introduce him to Mrs. Randolph. "I'm expecting
Melicent for lunch," she informed Oliver curtly, "but
I'm quite sure she won't care to see you. I think you
should leave."

At that point Edmund swept into the room with
Melicent. "Zoë, we found the most unusual rose window
at St. Katherine Cree in Leadenhall Street," Edmund
was saying enthusiastically when he stopped short, staring at Oliver with a questioning look.

Oliver ignored him, going straight to Melicent. Seiz-
ing her by the shoulders, he exclaimed reproachfully,
"You're driving me to Bedlam, you know that, don't
you? You won't receive me, you return my letters. Why
are you so cruel to me, Melicent, when you know how
much I love you?"

Looking acutely embarrassed, Melicent tried to release herself. "You're foxed, Oliver. You don't know
what you're saying. Please go away."

"Of course I know what I'm saying. I've just told you.
I love you, Melicent. I adore you."

Clearing his throat, Edmund tapped Oliver on the

shoulder. "See here, my man, you're distressing Lady Rosedale. Please do as she asked you, and leave."

Releasing Melicent, Oliver swung around, glaring at Edmund. "I'll thank you to keep your nose out of my affairs, sir," he growled. "I'll leave when I've settled my business with Lady Rosedale, and not before."

Whereupon Edmund, who Zoë could have sworn had never raised his hand to a fellow creature, struck Oliver an awkward, sweeping blow to the jaw and managed to knock him down. However, after a brief moment of shock, Oliver scrambled to his feet and charged at Edmund, swinging his arms wildly. Before he could reach Edmund, Jerrold appeared in the doorway, grasped his cousin's shoulder and delivered a crisp jab to Oliver's chin that put him in a senseless heap on the floor. To the footman who entered the morning room to announce lunch, Jerrold said calmly, "I daresay Mr. Layton's carriage is waiting at the door. At the moment he's unwell. Pray help him into his carriage."

"Yes, my lord." Not a flicker of emotion crossed the footman's face. He hoisted Oliver over a broad shoulder and carried him from the room.

Jerrold remarked to Edmund, "I had no idea you were so handy with your fives."

Edmund looked shaken. "I don't know what came over me. I've never used violence to anyone in my life. It was most unchristian."

"I don't think you were unchristian at all, Mr. Bennett. You were merely trying to help me, and I thank you," Melicent assured him with a warm smile. Her expression sobered as she added to Jerrold, "Oh, how I wish this hadn't happened. I hope there won't be any problems with Uncle Rupert."

Jerrold shrugged. "I doubt Oliver will inform his father of this latest idiocy. If he does, Uncle Rupert will simply have to face the fact that he has a worthless loose screw for a son."

On the following afternoon Jerrold came into the morning room of Woodforde House, where Zoë and Philip sat waiting for Edmund and Mrs. Randolph to join them.

"There you are, son," Jerrold said to Philip with an affectionate smile. "I went up to the nursery with the idea of inviting you to Gunther's for an ice, but Sarah told me you were off on an excursion with your mother."

Philip grinned at his father. "I'm quite free tomorrow, Papa."

Laughing, Jerrold replied, "What an opportunist you are, Philip. You know very well I'd never force you to subsist for too long without a black currant ice!"

He turned to Zoë, and she felt chilled at the change of expression in his face. All trace of affection and amusement had faded. "And where are you off to this afternoon?" he inquired, with the cool formality that had characterized their relations since the disastrous excursion to Hampton Court that had caused her to miss the Lord Mayor's banquet.

Hoping that Philip hadn't noticed the deteriorating cordiality in his parents' behavior, Zoë replied, "Sir Stephen has invited Edmund and Mrs. Randolph and Philip and me to go see the preparations for the Regent's Grand Jubilee peace celebrations that are to be held in the public parks at the beginning of August. Sir Stephen says that some of the arrangements sound very elaborate. Did you know there will be a mock naval battle on the Serpentine in Hyde Park?"

"No." Jerrold made a face. "And I won't hold my breath in expectation." He looked up as Stephen was announced. "Afternoon, Carrington. Your clientele has been anxiously awaiting the arrival of London's premier sightseeing guide."

Jerrold's tone was pleasant, his smile was friendly, and Stephen apparently didn't notice the faintly satirical barb in Jerrold's comment, but Zoë did notice. She knew that Jerrold still resented the necessity of pretending to a friendship with Stephen that he didn't feel, out of the need to ward off gossip.

"You make too much of my gifts, Woodforde," Stephen said good-naturedly. "I warrant you know the London sights as well as I do. Well, shall we be off? I've brought the landau." He grinned at Philip. "Room enough for all of us, including you, Lord Silverbridge, even though you're growing very large."

Philip returned the grin. During the past several weeks, he had accompanied his mother and Mrs. Randolph on several excursions with Stephen, and Philip had warmed to the baronet. Out of the corner of her eye Zoë observed Jerrold's sudden sharp glance, and her own eyes narrowed. Surely Jerrold couldn't be jealous of Philip's association with Stephen?

It was warm and sunny, a perfect day to visit the public parks. In Hyde Park there was little of real interest to be seen, although workmen were already erecting booths and stalls, arcades, and kiosks of all kind, and swings and roundabouts for the children, in preparation for the hordes of people who would be streaming into the park to view the mimic naval battle.

In the Green Park a sort of Gothic castle or fort,

about a hundred feet square, with a round tower and ramparts, was beginning to go up. "They say the structure will revolve, so spectators can see the structure from any angle," Stephen reported with an air of doubt. "The main fireworks display will take place here, too."

It was St. James's Park, however, that occasioned Stephen's greatest interest. Here a "Chinese" bridge with a bright blue roof, reflecting the Regent's well-known taste for Oriental art, was going up over the Canal. "I'm told they plan to erect a seven-storied Chinese pagoda in the middle of the bridge, complete with temples and columns, and that they'll illuminate the building with the new gas lighting," Stephen remarked, shaking his head. "It will cost a fortune, I've no doubt."

Philip had little interest in Chinese buildings and soon wandered away from his elders to investigate the ducks and other wild fowl in the Canal. He was particularly fascinated by the pelicans, which, Stephen informed him, had inhabited St. James's Park since the days of Charles II.

"Philip, don't go too far," Zoë called.

Edmund smiled. "You're such a mother hen, my dear. You forget Philip isn't a baby anymore. Let the boy explore. What harm can he come to here?"

Feeling a little foolishly maternal, Zoë nevertheless kept watch on Philip out of the corner of her eye while she chatted with her companions about the Regent and his passion for Chinoiserie. It seemed to her that she hadn't lost sight of her son for more than a few seconds, when, checking on the whereabouts of his small form, she failed to locate him.

"Edmund, do you see Philip?" she asked with a sudden anxiety.

The rector gazed around him. "The last time I saw Philip, he was watching the ducks."

Mrs. Randolph asked suddenly, "Is the Canal very deep, do you know?"

The question galvanized the adults. As if with one mind, they started for the Canal. As soon as they reached it, Edmund, with a strangled cry, dived into the water. In a few moments he crawled out, carrying Philip, who was gasping and coughing. "The boy is all right," Edmund assured an ashen-faced Zoë. "I don't think he was under water for too long, but I'm afraid he swallowed far too much stagnant water."

"Thank the good Lord, oh, thank the good Lord," Mrs. Randolph said fervently. "But lawkes, Zoë, the child is shivering. He's perishing from the cold. We must get him home to a warm bed immediately."

Stephen whipped off his coat and wrapped it around Philip's drenched form. Then he took the child from Edmund and led the way to the waiting carriage near Birdcage Walk.

The landau drew up in front of Woodforde House after a hurried dash from St. James's Park. Stephen bounded to the pavement and reached up to take Philip from Zoë's sheltering arms. Clasping the child closely to him, he walked up the entrance steps, and Zoë hurried along beside him to ring the bell. Edmund and Mrs. Randolph trailed behind them.

As the group entered the foyer, Jerrold walked down the staircase. He froze when he caught sight of his son. Philip was still shivering, he was very pale, and he was making gagging noises.

"What happened?" Jerrold inquired sharply.

"Philip fell into the Canal at St. James's Park," Zoë explained with a worried frown. "Edmund thinks he swallowed a good deal of that filthy water, and he's feeling quite nauseated."

"Look, Woodforde, I think the boy should be put to bed as soon as possible," Stephen interjected. "I'll just carry him upstairs—"

Jerrold snatched Philip away from Stephen. "*I'll* carry my son. As for you, Carrington, I'm sick of the sight of you. I want you to leave my house and never come back."

Zoë gasped. "Jerrold! How can you speak to Stephen that way?"

"In my house I'll speak and do as I like," Jerrold snapped. As he headed up the stairs, he threw back over his shoulder, "Send for Dr. Ashby, Zoë."

"I don't understand," Stephen stammered. "What could I have done to offend Woodforde?"

Her face tight, Zoë replied, "I'm sure Jerrold didn't mean what he said—he's overset about Philip. And now please excuse me, Stephen. I must go up to my son. Edmund, you'll tell the butler to send for this Dr. Ashby?"

When Zoë arrived in Philip's bedchamber, Jerrold was helping the nursemaid to remove the child's sodden clothes. Quickly they slipped a long nightdress over Philip's head and piled him high with blankets. But still he continued to shiver, and in a few moments he was wretchedly ill in a basin held by his father.

Jerrold motioned Zoë to follow him outside into the corridor. "Did you send for Dr. Ashby?"

"Edmund is doing that. But Jerrold, I honestly don't believe there's anything really wrong with Philip. I think he's simply in a temporary state of shock. After all, he did come close to drowning, and then he swallowed that nasty water. There was a green scum on the surface of the Canal!"

Jerrold interrupted her. His eyes blazing, he said, "We'll let the doctor decide about his condition. In the meantime, I trust you'll reflect on your conduct. It's one thing to take Philip with you and Carrington on one of your infernal sightseeing excursions. It's quite another to become so engrossed by your admirer's attentions that you totally neglect your son. Your carelessness this afternoon very nearly resulted in Philip's death!"

Zoë stepped back abruptly, feeling almost as if she had been struck a physical blow. Fighting for control, she managed to say, "You're quite wrong, Jerrold, but I won't waste time trying to convince you otherwise." Turning her back on him, she walked back into Philip's bedchamber, where she sat down beside the bed to wait for the doctor's arrival.

Zoë waited to speak until Jerrold and Edmund had joined her and Mrs. Randolph in the drawing room after dinner that evening. She poured coffee for her husband and her brother and a second cup for Mrs. Randolph, who said with a beaming smile, "What an unexpectedly cozy ending for our day. I was so afraid that little Philip . . . but there, I shouldn't dwell on the accident. The dear child is doing famously, thank the good Lord."

"Yes, we're all grateful that Philip suffered no lasting effects from his fall into the Canal," Zoë said. She paused, clearing her throat. "I have something to tell all of you," she said quietly. "I've decided to leave London with Philip and return to Cumberland."

A strained silence settled over the room. Edmund

stared at her in consternation. Mrs. Randolph's plump, kindly face looked shaken. Jerrold put down his cup and stared at her intently. A muscle twitched in his cheek, but his voice was calm as he asked, "May I ask the reason for your decision? And may I also ask why you saw fit to make this announcement in public, rather than to me personally?"

Zoë bit her lip. "I don't consider this a 'public announcement.' Except for Philip, Edmund is my only relative. Mrs. Randolph is my oldest friend. I think they both deserve to know that I'm putting an end to this farce of a marriage."

Mrs. Randolph choked. "My dear—a farce?"

Zoë nodded. "Edmund knows all the details of my marriage to Jerrold, and I think you've had your suspicions from the beginning." She looked directly at Jerrold. "After what happened today, I realized that you and I can't live in the same house with even an approximation of civility. It's better that we don't try." Zoë rose. "Edmund, Mrs. Randolph, I hope one of you will extend me a temporary hospitality until I find a suitable place for me and Philip to live. If you don't feel you can do so . . ." She shrugged. "I'll understand. Good night. I'm going to my bedchamber to begin packing for the journey to Cumberland."

As Zoë walked out of the drawing room, Edmund charged after her, saying, "Zoë, don't go. We must talk. You haven't considered the consequences of what you're doing."

Zoë continued up the staircase. "I've made up my mind, Edmund."

He followed her into her bedchamber. "Zoë, think of the possible scandal. You've told me about the malicious rumors that have already been dogging you. What will people say if you now leave Jerrold?"

Jerrold entered the room. "Edmund, I want to speak to Zoë. Will you leave us?"

Zoë said coldly, "I don't wish to speak to you, Jerrold. I've said all I intend to say . . ."

Going to the door, Edmund gave Zoë an apologetic look, saying, "I'm sorry, my dear. You should talk to Jerrold."

After the door had closed on his brother-in-law, Jerrold said, "I think you owe me the courtesy of hearing me out, Zoë."

"Do I have any choice?"

Jerrold ignored the rejoinder. "You're overset, Zoë, and I know I'm responsible. I want to apologize for what I said to you this afternoon. Of course you weren't at fault for Philip's accident. I know how much you love the boy. You've never neglected him. I came unstrung when I thought he might be seriously hurt, and I lashed out at you and Carrington. Please forgive me."

The accumulated strain, not only of the day, but of all the past weeks, caught up with Zoë. She had intended to leave Woodforde House with dignity, without an acrimonious scene, but now the floodgates burst, and she couldn't contain herself.

She exclaimed bitterly, "How like you, Jerrold. You think you can make a pretty apology and I'll change my mind about leaving you. You haven't changed at all. You still believe you can use your charm and your position to get anything you want out of life, and hang the consequences. I shouldn't have expected anything else from you. After all, seven years ago you seduced a naive sixteen-year-old and left her without a single qualm or a concern about her possible future. You woke up in bed with a confused young girl and immediately assumed she was a strumpet for whom you had not the slightest responsibility."

Jerrold said quickly, "I've already told you I regret what happened at Gretna Green. I think you forget that I was very young myself . . ."

"Youth wasn't responsible for your behavior. It was your monstrous selfishness. It wasn't until you discovered that Philip was your legitimate son that you gave a thought to what might have happened to me during those seven years."

"Zoë, I've said I'm sorry. What more can I do? We've agreed that the only thing that matters is Philip's inheritance."

Zoë's breast heaved. "Truth matters, Jerrold. You've never been truthful with me. You never told me you were sterile, that Philip was the only child you could ever have."

Jerrold turned white. "How . . .?"

"Your ex-mistress told me all about your interesting physical problems. Or *is* she your ex-mistress? Yes, I believe she is, because she certainly displayed considerable jealousy when she revealed a bit more of the truth you never saw fit to tell me. She told me that you've always loved Melicent, that you would have asked her to marry you after your brother died, if only your embarrassing wife and son hadn't emerged from the shadows."

"That's not true," Jerrold said quickly. "Yes, I had a case of calf's love for Melicent when I was nineteen, twenty years old. She was never interested in me. She always loved Tom. And after she was married, I quickly recovered from my infatuation. I assure you, it never entered my head to ask her to marry me when she returned to England after her husband died."

Ignoring what Jerrold had said, scarcely hearing him, Zoë rushed on. "You probably would have attempted to nullify that Gretna Green ceremony if you hadn't been sterile. But you *are* sterile, Jerrold, and Philip is your only legitimate child. So you turned my life, and Philip's, upside down, in order to ensure that the sacred Woodforde line would continue. Today was the last straw, when you virtually accused me of cuckolding you with Stephen Carrington and neglecting Philip to the point of death!"

Jerrold's color had returned to normal, although his face still looked strained. "You hate me, don't you?" he asked quietly.

Zoë was past all prudence. "Yes. Though it would be more correct to say I loathe you."

His face hardening, Jerrold said, "I'm sorry about that, but it doesn't really matter how you feel, or what happened in the past. All that matters is the present and the future. I can't let you take Philip to Cumberland, Zoë. If you insist on doing so, I'll take immediate legal steps to obtain exclusive custody of my son. You must know as well as I do that I'll win my case. A father's right over his children is paramount."

Zoë's throat constricted. "You—you can't mean that. Think of the scandal a court case would cause. You've always gone to such lengths to prevent scandal."

"There will also be a scandal if you leave the protection of my roof and take Philip with you," Jerrold pointed out. "In the end, if I must, I'll risk scandal for the right to rear my son."

As Zoë stared at him, temporarily shocked into silence, Jerrold went on, coldly, calmly, "Think carefully before you leave me. Neither of us would have chosen this marriage, but if we abandon it, we will only harm our son. If you'll stay, I promise to do everything in my power to make your life as easy as possible. I won't criticize you, I won't prevent you have having your own friends, I'll behave to you at all times with the respect due to you as my wife and the mother of my son. All I ask is that you perform your duties as mistress of my household both here in London and at Malvern Hall, and that you observe a reasonable discretion. And oh, yes, I must insist that, in public and in private, we treat each other with—how did you put it in the drawing room a few minutes ago—with at least an approximation of civility."

It was checkmate. No, it was more than that, Zoë thought with a sudden bitter insight. It was defeat. Brief weeks ago, when Jerrold had persuaded her to live with him as his wife in order to safeguard Philip's future, she'd believed she could preserve at least a modicum of her own identity and independence. She'd believed that she and Jerrold could live together as rational, courteous human beings. At times she'd even thought that Jerrold's character had mellowed, that he'd come to regard her and Philip as persons, not as mere means to an end. Now she knew she'd been wrong. From the first moment that they met, Jerrold had acted purely according to his own selfish whims. He hadn't changed. Even his love for Philip she now believed was an affectation. Philip was simply a pawn in his father's dynastic aims.

Zoë drew a deep breath. She had no choice. She had to continue in this arid relationship, living her life on Jerrold's terms, or lose her son.

She gave her husband a level look. "Very well. I won't return to Cumberland."

Chapter Sixteen

Jerrold handed Zoë into the traveling carriage, hoisted Philip in after her, and took his place beside them. The footman put up the steps and closed the door, and the carriage moved out of Bedford Square, followed by the fourgon carrying their personal servants and the family's luggage.

Wriggling excitedly, Philip whooped, "We're off at last! Papa, how long will it take to get to Malvern Hall?"

"Almost three days."

Philip's face fell. "That long?"

"Malvern Hall is better than a hundred and fifty miles from London. If we were to drive continuously, stopping only for meals, as the mails do, we could make the journey in less than twenty-four hours, but we wouldn't wish to subject your mother to such discomfort, now, would we, Philip?"

"N-no, I s'pose not."

Jerrold smiled at Zoë, as if inviting her to share in his amusement at Philip's lack of enthusiasm for a leisurely journey to Herefordshire.

Zoë returned the smile dutifully, as she did most things nowadays. The savor and the sparkle had largely gone from her existence, as she'd faced the realization that henceforth, if she wished to keep her son, everything she said and did had to conform to the iron beneath Jerrold's infinitely civilized velvet glove. Occasionally she'd wondered why it had taken her so long to understand how one reckless, impulsive night seven years ago had taken away her freedom of action for the rest of her life. The fact that Jerrold, now that he had won his point, was apparently making an effort to be unusually pleasant and accommodating, did little to lighten her frame of mind.

Today was the second of August, Zoë reflected, and her first London Season was officially over. As the carriage passed the toll gate at Hyde Park Corner, Zoë's mind wandered back over the occurrences of the past few weeks.

Edmund and Mrs. Randolph had left London the week before. Both of them, hugely relieved that Zoë had decided against the scandal-making step of leaving her husband, had enjoyed the remainder of their visit, especially their participation with Jerrold and Zoë and Melicent in the magnificent *fête* given by the Prince Regent for the Duke of Wellington at Carlton House.

Mrs. Randolph had been very nearly overwhelmed by the experience. As she entered the huge octagon-shaped brick structure in the gardens of Carlton House, she murmured in awe, "My dear, I understand the Prince actually erected this building just for the *fête.*" The octagon room had an umbrella-shaped roof and was draped in white muslin and decorated with mirrors, and in the center of it a mass of artificial flowers in the shape of a temple concealed not one but two orchestras.

Covered walks led from two sides of the room to supper tents adorned with regimental colors. One of the walks was lined with allegorical transparencies, some of which celebrated Wellington's exploits.

Mrs. Randolph's awe had increased when the Regent and the Queen and most of the rest of the royal family entered the great octagon room and promenaded slowly around it. Later the Princess Mary opened the ball which, Zoë learned, did not end until six the following morning, although she and Jerrold and their guests left much earlier.

Even the usually austere Edmund had been impressed by the *fête*, though he couldn't refrain from muttering under his breath to Melicent, "I'm appalled, quite appalled, at what this affair must have cost. Could not some of the money have been better spent on the poor?"

Melicent smiled at him. "Don't you think, this one time, that we might excuse the Regent for his extravagance? We're celebrating a once-in-a-lifetime experience, the defeat of Napoleon."

Disarmed by Melicent's cheerfulness, Edmund smiled back at her. "Well, in the interest of patriotism, perhaps I should be a little less critical."

Overhearing the exchange, Zoë had a sudden flash of insight. Ostensibly because of her shared interest in church architecture and stained glass, Melicent had been almost constantly in Edmund's company during his visit to London. Could it be that they were developing a *tendre* for each other? In the next moment Zoë shook her head. It was a fanciful thought. Melicent's rank was so much higher than Edmund's. What would people say if she married the obscure rector of her home parish? And what about any feelings Melicent might still have for Jerrold?

Zoë herself would have enjoyed the *fête* at Carlton House, as her artist's eye sought out the details of the Regent's decorating scheme, which in its ebullient magnificence stopped just short of the bounds of good taste, had it not been for her encounters with Rupert Layton and Lady Harlow, the first embarrassing, the second unsettling.

Jerrold's uncle sought her out as she stood gazing at the front of a Corinthian temple in the gardens, on the wall of which was a large mirror with a "W" for Lord Wellington etched in the glass; a column in front of the mirror held a marble bust of the man who had conquered Napoleon.

"You're looking quite splendid tonight, my dear," Rupert said genially, gazing at her silver tissue gown and the blaze of the Layton diamonds at her throat. "The Prince commented very favorably on your appearance." He lowered his voice. "Zoë, is it true that Jerrold and Oliver had a set-to?"

Zoë looked at Rupert in surprise. "How . . .?"

"Oh, you've all been most discreet, but these things get about," Rupert said in the same low tone. "I finally forced an account of the matter out of Oliver. I'm convinced that both Melicent and Jerrold have treated the boy inconsiderately. He truly loves Melicent, and if he's been guilty of foolish or ill-judged behavior—and very probably he has, I won't deny it—it's because of the intensity of his feelings. He's abjectly sorry for anything he may have done to offend either Melicent or Jerrold, but they won't allow him to make amends, or even to speak to them. Zoë, you're not related to the Laytons by blood, so perhaps you can view the situation with more objectivity. Won't you put in a good word for Oliver? Surely you can't wish for an embarrassing family rift, and it's perfectly possible, you know, that Oliver would make Melicent a very suitable husband."

Zoë had never really warmed to Rupert Layton's faintly pompous personality, but now she felt a spark of sympathy for him in his blind inability to see his son's feet of clay. Would she be equally blind to any of Philip's faults as she grew older? she wondered. She said non-committally, "I'll tell Jerrold and Melicent what you've said, Uncle Rupert."

She knew her report of the conversation wouldn't mollify Jerrold and Melicent, nor would she have wanted it to—the less contact she had with Oliver Layton in the future, the better—but she observed a smile of real gratitude cross Rupert's face.

Lady Harlow caught up with Zoë as she was making her way to the supper room, where Zoë had arranged to meet Jerrold and their guests. The beautiful redhead blocked Zoë's path. "Well, well, my dear, I'm beginning to think you must be like those cats with nine lives," Lady Harlow drawled. "You go from one scandal to another and you survive them all. And here you are today the honored guest of the Prince Regent at one of the most prestigious events of the Season. What is the secret of your social success?"

"I have no secrets," Zoë said curtly, and tried to brush past Lady Harlow, who grasped her arm.

"Not so fast, Lady Woodforde. I'm convinced you must have a secret, a magic formula. Something, at any rate. How else could a nobody from the provinces with a questionable past rise to the very top of London society?"

The sound of Jerrold's voice caused Lady Harlow to spin around, releasing Zoë's arm. He said curtly, "I'll remind you, Dorothea, that you're speaking of my wife, and I find your reference to her as a 'nobody from the provinces with a questionable past' extremely offensive. However, I daresay Zoë is prepared to accept your apology."

Lady Harlow's expression was a mixture of conflicting emotions, mainly defensiveness laced with anger and resentment. After a long moment's hesitation she said to Zoë, with an obvious lack of sincerity, "If I offended you, I apologize." She turned to Jerrold, and now a slow, gloating smile curved her lips. "I'm so happy I chanced to meet you tonight, Lord Woodforde. The announcement will appear in the newspapers tomorrow morning, but you might like to know beforehand that I've decided to marry Lord Windermere."

A look of surprise crossed Jerrold's face. "Windermere? But he's . . ."

Lady Harlow quickly erased the frown of vexation that appeared between her perfect brows. "Oh, I know what you're thinking. Lord Windermere isn't a young man. But do you know, Jer—Lord Woodforde—I've come to appreciate maturity in a man, and considerateness. Lord Windermere is very considerate."

"And very wealthy." Jerrold bowed. "My best wishes for your happiness, Lady Harlow. And pray convey my congratulations to Lord Windermere."

"I shall. And please accept my hopes for your own happiness with Lady Woodforde." Her head held high, Dorothea Harlow swept away.

Jerrold looked at Zoë. "I'm sorry. I hope you aren't too distressed by what Doro—Lady Harlow—said. She can be very spiteful."

"I didn't regard her, Jerrold," Zoë replied coolly. Which wasn't true. The encounter with that woman had raised Zoë's hackles. And she wondered if Dorothea's announcement about her coming marriage had caused

Jerrold any regrets. True, tonight he had treated the woman with outward dislike and had castigated her for her behavior toward Zoë, but did such behavior indicate his true feelings? He and Dorothca Harlow, after all, had been lovers for many years. It would be only natural if he felt some lingering emotion for her.

The *fête* for the Duke of Wellington at Carlton House had been the last great social event of the London Season of 1814, which had officially ended the day before, with the public celebration in the royal parks for the populace which had been excluded from the more glamorous festivities given for the visiting Allied sovereigns and the aristocracy.

Despite the drizzling rain that fell during the morning of the public *fête* and the crush of the thousands of people who thronged the parks, Jerrold had taken his family to all the events of the celebration, much to Philip's delight, beginning with the balloon ascent of a certain Mr. Sadler, which occurred in the Green Park in the afternoon.

In the early evening a reenactment of the Battle of Trafalgar took place on the Serpentine in Hyde Park, and Philip cheered until his throat was hoarse when a fire ship routed the French fleet.

A little later that night Philip's eyes bulged at the magnificent fireworks display erupting from the battlements of the mysterious Gothic castle in the Green Park. For a fleeting moment Zoë had felt a sense of almost unbearable tenderness when she observed the nearly identical expressions of absorbed delight on the faces of father and son as they watched the fireworks. "Oh, Papa, look," Philip murmured rapturously after the smoke had cleared, when the castle, which had been constructed merely of canvas, disappeared, and in its place stood a Temple of Concord, marvelously illuminated.

The climax of the Regent's great victory celebration for the London populace—or perhaps, in retrospect, it was an anticlimax—had taken place in St. James's Park, when the Chinese Pagoda on the bridge over the Canal, the scene of Philip's nearly disastrous accident, burst into fire and disappeared into the water. In their excited appreciation, Philip and the other spectators didn't realize—and Zoë didn't tell her son when she discovered later what had happened—that the pagoda had burned by accident with the loss of several lives.

At the end of the evening, as he entered the foyer of Woodforde House with his parents, Philip failed to object, as he usually did, to his mother's request that he go up to bed.

Jerrold watched Philip trudge up the stairs and then turned to Zoë, his eyes twinkling with amusement. "I think the boy is thoroughly exhausted. I almost offered to carry him up the stairs! But I'm glad we took him to the celebration, aren't you? He seemed to enjoy it immensely. Well, so did I, if truth be told. Mind, I suspect many of our acquaintances would consider our attendance at such an affair to be quite common!"

Zoë didn't allow herself to respond to the friendliness in Jerrold's remark, which she took to be just another of his calculated offerings of an olive branch. She said merely, "Yes, I'm very pleased that we attended the celebration with Philip. As I thought I'd made clear by this time, I'm always willing to engage in any activity that will make him happy."

Jerrold's smile faded. "Oh, indeed, Zoë, I'm under no illusions about your motives. You've made yourself unmistakably clear."

* * *

As the Woodforde carriage rattled along the turnpike toward Acton and crossed the River Brent on the way to the first change of horses at Southall, Zoë leaned back against the squabs, feeling weary already at the thought of the long journey ahead to Malvern Hall. Weary and faintly apprehensive also. Living with Jerrold on his Herefordshire estate would begin an entirely new phase in their marriage, and she wasn't at all sure what to expect, except that at Malvern Hall she would not only be in much closer proximity to Jerrold but she would also be more isolated from friends and family than she had ever been before.

Their first overnight stop was at Oxford, where Jerrold had booked rooms at the Golden Cross Hotel. As they stepped down from the carriage in the courtyard of the inn, Jerrold glanced at his watch, saying, "We arrived here earlier than I'd expected. Philip, we have time for a stroll before supper. I attended Oxford, you know, and I'd like to show you my old college, where I hope you'll be a student one day, too." To Zoë he said, "You have no objection, I trust."

"No, not at all. But please don't be too long. It's been a long, tiring day for Philip."

"Mama! I'm not a baby. Of course I'm not tired," Philip exclaimed indignantly.

Zoë watched father and son leave the courtyard and then walked to the entrance of the inn. If Philip wasn't tired, *she* certainly was, after more than eight hours on the road. When she reached the large comfortable bedchamber to which the inn servant escorted her, she found Meg already at work unpacking the luggage. Jerrold's large valise was on the floor next to the door, and Zoë's lips tightened. Apparently Jerrold had decided that for the next two nights they would again share sleeping quarters.

"Ye look weary, my lady," said the abigail, a faint, involuntary expression of sympathy crossing her face as she gazed briefly at Jerrold's bag. "I've rung fer a pot of tea. It will revive ye."

Zoë was gratefully sipping her second cup of tea when Philip and Jerrold returned from their stroll. Philip rushed into the bedchamber to make his report. "Mama, did you know that Papa's school, Christ Church, is the largest college at Oxford? It was founded by a Cardinal Wol—Wolsey, a *very* important man, Papa says. The church has a bell called 'Great Tom' that weights seventeen thousand pounds, fancy that. I can't wait to go there!"

"Now, wait, Philip," Jerrold said teasingly. "There are many colleges at Oxford that are much older than Christ Church, you know. What's more, Merton has the oldest library, and New College has the most beautiful chapel. Are you sure you wouldn't do better to attend one of those other foundations?"

"Well, of course not, Papa. Didn't you tell me that Christ Church was the very best college in Oxford?"

Jerrold burst out laughing. "So I did. And I meant what I said, too. However, I do hope, Philip, that you're not developing an inconveniently retentive memory. In the future I don't want incautious remarks I may have made coming back to haunt me." At Philip's puzzled look, Jerrold smiled and patted the boy's shoulder. "Run along, now. I'm sure Sarah is waiting with your supper."

After Philip had scampered out of the room, Jerrold turned to Zoë, the amusement fading from his face as he glanced at his bag in the corner. "I'm sorry to cause you any discomfort, Zoë, but I thought it best that we share this bedchamber, as we did during our journey from Cumberland. My reason is the same. I see no need to make public the fact that the Earl and Countess of Woodforde have separate sleeping arrangements. As before, I'll try to disturb your privacy as little as I possibly can."

"Thank you." What else could she say, Zoë thought with a mental shrug. Jerrold's tone had been pleasant but firm, with no suggestion that the matter was open for discussion.

"Please join me downstairs for dinner whenever you care to do so," Jerrold went on. "No need to hurry, naturally."

Zoë watched him leave the bedchamber with mingled feelings, in which resignation overcame resentment. True, she had lost the latest battle of wills with Jerrold. In effect, giving in to Jerrold's threat to seek custody of their son, she'd relinquished any claim to personal independence of action in this sterile, artificial marriage. At the same time, however, there was some comfort in knowing precisely the rules of her subtly changed relationship with her husband. As long as she conformed outwardly to the standard of behavior that Jerrold considered would preserve the illusion that they had a loving marriage, she could say, or do, or think privately whatever moved her. It was, in some odd fashion, a liberating concept.

Zoë's thoughts wandered. Only a few days ago, in her anger with Jerrold at what she regarded as his unscrupulous manipulation of her love for Philip as a weapon against her, she'd characterized him as completely selfish, interested only in what would make his life more pleasurable or protect his family heritage. She had allowed her anger to cloud her judgment. Looking back on the very beginnings of his relationship with Philip, Zoë couldn't deny that Jerrold cared for his son, purely aside from the child's value as the next heir to the Woodforde title. Today, for instance, Jerrold could have had no suspect motives in taking Philip on a tour of Christ Church College. He didn't need to curry the boy's favor. Philip already adored him. And there were no critics present to applaud Jerrold's fatherly behavior.

The next overnight stop on the way to Malvern Hall was Gloucester. Late the following morning, before they reached the town of Ledbury, Jerrold announced to Philip, "We're almost home. We've just crossed into Herefordshire."

Almost despite herself, Zoë gazed with interest out the carriage windows at the countryside where she would probably be spending much of her life in the future. Herefordshire was a greenly beautiful region of thickly wooded undulating chalk hills, secluded valleys, gentle streams, prosperous farms, and picturesque "black and white" villages.

"Mama, look. The cows are red, just like the earth," Philip exclaimed at one point.

"Our Herefords produce the finest beef in England," Jerrold commented. Zoë gave him a look of faint surprise. It was the first time she had ever heard Jerrold express enthusiasm about anything agricultural.

A little later she said, "I see so many fruit trees. Apple, and yes, pear trees."

Once again Jerrold surprised her. "Herefordshire produces the best apple cider in all of England. Wait until you taste the cider from our home farm."

In late afternoon, after passing through Hereford and Leominster, the carriage crossed a rustic bridge over a sinuously curving river to enter a small village of half-timbered houses grouped around a spacious green.

"Stonebridge," said Jerrold. "It's mentioned in the Domesday Book. And the Laytons have been a part of it for nearly as long, since before they were created Earls of Woodforde." He lifted his hand to acknowledge the bows of several people in the one short street of the village, and then, as the carriage drove past the weathered stone church, Jerrold suddenly struck his cane against the roof to signal the driver. When the vehicle stopped, Jerrold opened the door and jumped down.

"I'll only be a moment," he called over his shoulder as he unlatched the church gate and went inside. A few minutes later he climbed back into the carriage. Looking mildly self-conscious, he said, "I wanted to check on my brother's grave, make sure it was being cared for properly."

Zoë's eyes widened. This must be the first show of real emotion—other than anger, of course, or his affection for Philip—that she had ever observed in Jerrold, because, surely, he couldn't actually suspect the church sexton of neglecting his brother's grave.

At a distance of several miles from the village a high stone wall loomed beside the road, and shortly afterward the carriage passed through imposing wrought iron gates hastily thrown open by a smiling gatekeeper who had clearly been on the alert for their arrival. From the gates a curving drive led into a large wooded parkland.

"Papa, look. Deer. A whole herd of deer!" exclaimed Philip, pointing.

Jerrold nodded. "Actually, there are several herds in the park."

The carriage, proceeding along a road which had

been gradually climbing, emerged from the wooded park into a drive circling a large forecourt, embellished with formal plantings and a fountain. The forecourt provided a sweeping perspective for the huge stone building standing on an eminence above it.

The carriage stopped in front of the portico, and for a moment after Jerrold handed Zoë down the steps, she stood staring in near disbelief at the hulking central facade, which resembled a Roman temple, with classical statues decorating the entablature.

"A little overpowering, do you think?" Jerrold asked, smiling faintly. "Malvern Hall is my grandfather's Grand Tour house, and looks it. As an artist, you may prefer the interior. Robert Adam had a free hand."

Zoë followed Jerrold up a flight of broad steps into an enormous entrance hall, which, to her incredulous eyes, looked rather like a temple itself. It was floored in black and white marble and lined with lofty pillars, with statuary adorning the recessed niches between the pillars.

What appeared to be an army of servants crowded the hall, to whom Jerrold gravely introduced Zoë and Philip. "Your new mistress, the Countess of Woodforde. My son, Lord Silverbridge. I trust you'll give them as faithful service as you've always given to me."

An immensely dignified butler and housekeeper extended greetings on behalf of the staff, which Zoë estimated hastily must be at least twice the size of the staff at the house in Bedford Square.

After the servants had been dismissed, Jerrold remarked to Zoë, "I think you'll find the ground floor plan is arranged very conveniently. There are two overlapping circuits: a suite of private family apartments to the left of the hall, and a series of state rooms to the right, which can be isolated from the rest of the house for purposes of public entertaining. Shall we take a brief tour, just so you can become acclimated, so to speak? I've been told Malvern Hall is so large that some visitors become confused."

Half an hour later, after walking through the state suite and the family quarters off the entrance hall, Zoë would not have described her feelings as confused. Rather, she was simply overwhelmed by the sheer magnificence of the rooms, with their riot of Rococo plasterwork moldings, exquisite painted furniture with inlays of exotic woods, lavish use of marble and gilt, and carpets that miraculously duplicated the intricate designs of plaster ceilings.

It was almost an anticlimax when she entered her own apartment, consisting of a large bedchamber and adjoining dressing room, to find Meg staring about her in helpless awe. "My lady, I never saw the like," the abigail murmured.

In her turn Zoë gazed, stunned, at the luminous hand-painted Chinese wallpapers, the green and gold lacquered furniture, a pair of ivory pagodas and Oriental mirror paintings in gilt frames, and a carpet writhing with golden dragons and brilliant peacocks. "I believe this style of decorating is called Chinoiserie, Meg. It's all the crack in London. The Prince Regent is said to dote on it."

Meg shook her head, repeating, "I never saw the like. I jist don't know as how I can get used to dragons on the carpet."

A knock sounded on the door. Meg admitted a footman, who bowed, saying, "Please, my lady, the housekeeper sent me. Mrs. Denys wants ter know if yer studio is satisfactory. Will ye follow me, please?"

On the next floor the footman threw open the door of

a room with a northern exposure. Zoë gaped. The room was hexagonal shaped, with a window on each wall flanked on either side by elegant painted panels of classical scenes. The coved ceiling blazed with gold leaf. It was as unlikely a studio as she had ever seen. More than likely, it had originally been a bedroom reserved for important guests. Probably royalty, Zoë thought wryly.

"Mrs. Denys is most anxious ter know if yer ladyship approves of the room as yer studio," prodded the footman.

Zoë found her voice. "Tell Mrs. Denys that the room will serve admirably." The quantity of light pouring in through all those windows was a painter's delight. She could just ignore the painted panels and the gold leaf.

Returning to her bedchamber, Zoë sat down in front of a dressing table to allow Meg to arrange her hair for dinner. Her mind was so distracted by the languid golden lilies festooning the edges of the dressing table mirror that at first she couldn't focus her thoughts. Gradually her accumulated first impressions of Malvern Hall sorted themselves out, and her shoulders slumped as if a physical weight had settled on them.

She, with her modest provincial background, was now the mistress of this huge pile, constructed and furnished with a Continental taste and utter disregard for expense, and of a vast retinue of servants who would probably spot her lack of social expertise immediately. What was more, the neighboring families among the aristocracy and the gentry would undoubtedly expect her to assume the social leadership of the vicinity, as befitted the wife of the Lord Lieutenant of the county. Could she possibly live up to these responsibilities?

Suddenly a thought struck her, and she laughed aloud, causing Meg to look at her in bewilderment. If she failed in these new duties that Jerrold had heaped upon her, what could he do about it? He certainly couldn't banish her from her position as Countess of Woodforde!

Her spirits were considerably lighter as she started down the staircase for dinner, especially since she knew she looked well in a favorite gown of embroidered green silk that matched her eyes. A hovering footman in the marble entrance hall directed her to an oval saloon in the state suite, immediately to the rear of the hall, where Jerrold awaited her, glass of wine in hand.

"As you can see, it's an easy matter to convert a part or all of the state rooms to family use," he commented. As Zoë cast an involuntary glance around the cavernous room, his lips curled in a slight smile. "Well, perhaps the saloon is a bit large for two people. We also use it as a ballroom, you know. In future we might have a before-dinner glass of wine in the library in the private wing." Handing her a glass, he inquired, "Your rooms are comfortable?"

"Oh, yes. More than comfortable. Quite munificent. When I inspected the 'studio,' as a matter of fact, I wondered if the room might not be more suitable for a king than a mere painter."

Jerrold raised an eyebrow at the ironic edge in Zoë's voice. "Was that a shot in the dark? My grandfather had that room decorated especially as a dressing room for Queen Charlotte when she visited Malvern Hall shortly after she was married."

Jerrold poured himself another glass of wine. Taking a sip, he said coolly, "I gather you think the house is somewhat grandiose. Actually, you'll find that we'll use every inch of space when we entertain. Take next month, for example. For many years the family has hosted a large house party in September, primarily for the cubbing and the stag hunting. This year we will, of course, continue the custom. You'll see. Every bedchamber, every attic, in Malvern will be occupied."

Zoë studied his confident face. "Whom do you plan to invite to this house party?"

"Why, friends from all over the country. Relatives. Melicent will come, I'm sure, and Uncle Rupert."

"I presume I may invite my own guests?"

He flashed her a faintly surprised look. "Certainly. You'll want to invite your brother, naturally. Possibly Mrs. Randolph and her husband, or other old friends from Cumberland."

"I've a mind to ask Stephen Carrington and Lord and Lady Bradford to stay with us."

He stared at her, his expression gradually hardening. "I think that would be ill-advised."

"Why?" Zoë put up her chin. "A few weeks ago—on the day Philip fell into the Canal at St. James's Park, remember?—you made a statement. You said—let me think, now—that if I would stay on in the marriage, you would make my life as easy as possible, you would make an effort not to criticize me, you wouldn't prevent me from having my own friends. Provided only that I was discreet. I presumed you had offered me a compact, Jerrold. I have no intention of being indiscreet. Stephen and Clarissa Bradford are my friends, and I would like to ask them to visit me at Malvern Hall."

Jerrold drew a long hard breath. "Thank you for your reminder, Zoë. I withdraw my objection."

Chapter Seventeen

Zoë put down her brush and looked closely at the painting on the easel. The August sun streamed in through all the eight windows in her hexagonal studio, and the brilliant light revealed not a flaw to her critical eye. Mrs. Marston's portrait was finished to the best of her ability.

"It's lovely, my lady," Meg said as she stopped by the easel.

"Lovely? I don't know about that, Meg. Mrs. Marston isn't a beautiful woman. But certainly I think the portrait is an honest one."

"It is that. Looks just like her, as I recall." Meg wrinkled her brow thoughtfully. "Do you know what I think, my lady? You've been painting much faster since you came to Malvern Hall."

Blinking, Zoë thought back over the past several weeks. "I think you may be right, Meg," she said.

It must the more relaxed atmosphere of the countryside that was responsible for her greater painting productivity, Zoë decided, as she began cleaning her brushes. During the London Season she had had to struggle to keep her working hours sacrosanct from the incessant social demands. Here in Herefordshire, although the local gentry had all called, and had extended invitations to dinners and small dances, her daily existence had been much more leisurely. Her apprehensions about her ability to cope with her responsibilities as mistress of Malvern Hall had also proved groundless. The housekeeper and the butler between them managed the house effortlessly, calling on Zoë merely as a polite gesture, she was sure, to approve their activities.

Her thoughts wandered farther afield. These few weeks at Malvern Hall had also given her fresh insights into Jerrold. Self-centered he might be, but his devotion to his ancestral estates was genuine. Every day, early and late, he was out, conferring with his tenants, the manager of his home farm, and his bailiff. Nothing about the estate seemed to escape his attention, or fail to interest him.

Zoë remembered especially one occasion when the bailiff, Harold Matthews, had asked to see Jerrold as he and Zoë were drinking a glass of wine in the library before dinner.

Jerrold put down his glass when the bailiff entered. "Yes? Is there a problem, Matthews?"

"I'm right sorry to disturb you at this time, my lord," the bailiff had begun apologetically, "but I considered I ought to call your attention to some alarming news I've just this minute heard."

"What is it?"

"There's been a spot of trouble with poachers up Presteign way. Last night, or rather, early this morning, Lord Colston's keepers were in a battle with what appeared to be a gang of poachers. His lordship lost a goodly number of deer, and a keeper was wounded. One of the poachers was shot, too. Not expected to live.

"Better for the fellow if he dies. If he lives, he faces the gallows."

"But why?" Zoë asked in surprise. "The keeper was wounded, not killed."

"It's the law, Zoë. Poaching with violence is a capital crime. If you're even caught carrying a gun while poaching, the penalty is fourteen years transportation."

"And a good thing, too, my lady, if I may say so," put in the bailiff, "else landowners would soon cease to have any game in their preserves." To Jerrold he added, "I've heard tell of poaching gangs before this, to the south of us, but not in our area."

Jerrold nodded. "It will get worse, I fear, now that the war is over. There won't be enough jobs for all the discharged soldiers and sailors, and many of them will join the poaching gangs."

"Just so, my lord. Will you authorize me to set out traps and spring guns?"

Frowning, Jerrold snapped, "No, I will not. These poachers may be felons, but they're still human beings. I won't condemn them to an agonizing death or to mutilation like animals. No, for now we'll assign additional keepers to patrol the property by night. Hire more men, if necessary. And Matthews, one other thing. Tell the head gamekeeper that if he or any of his men catch a local laborer in the act of poaching a hare or a pigeon, they are to look the other way."

"But my lord—"

Jerrold interrupted the bailiff. "No buts about it. I won't have any of the people sent before the magistrates for taking an occasional specimen of small game that I will never miss. A hare isn't worth imprisonment or transportation. Let's concentrate on the real criminals, the poaching gangs."

"Yes, my lord."

The incident had caused Zoë to wonder if she was witnessing still another softer aspect to Jerrold's nature. For some years her brother Edmund, who was inclined to a liberal cast of mind, had been convinced that the punishment meted out to offenders who had committed petty crimes was much too severe, but she doubted that even Edmund would look kindly on a farm laborer who poached his master's rabbits.

She was still thinking of the incident when she went down to luncheon that day. "Has there been any further news of the poaching gangs?" she asked Jerrold.

"No, not as the problem affects us in Herefordshire, at any rate. I believe most of the poaching gangs operate out of London. We may be a little too far away to suit the poachers' convenience. The London clubs and hotels are the prime markets for game." He shook his head, saying dryly, "The situation doesn't cast a very favorable light on English law enforcement, does it? It's very much against the law to sell game on the open market."

After luncheon, as Zoë was leaving the dining room, Jerrold inquired, "And what are your plans for the afternoon?"

Before Zoë could reply, Philip bounded into the room. "Papa, I've had my lunch, and I'm all ready to go."

Zoë said hesitantly, "But Philip, I thought we'd arranged to drive to Ludlow today to see the castle."

Philip's face fell. "I'm sorry, Mama. I'd forgotten. Papa's asked me to go with him this afternoon to ride around the farm and to visit the kennels to see the new puppies. And afterwards he was going to ask the kennel master to show me how the hounds are exercised. Did you know that the trainers must make the hounds lose all their extra fat by the end of this mouth if the dogs are to be ready for the November hunt?"

Gazing at the expression of lively anticipation on her son's face, Zoë forced a smile. "No, I didn't know that. And certainly I wouldn't wish to deprive you of the pleasure of your father's company today. We'll go to Ludlow another day."

Jerrold said quickly, "Go to the stables, Philip. I'll be with you in a few minutes." After Philip had left, Jerrold put out his hand to detain Zoë, who had started to leave the room. "Wait, Zoë."

She paused, turning her head. "Yes?"

"I'm sorry if I've disrupted your plans to spend the afternoon with Philip."

"Not at all. As I told Philip, there's always another day." Zoë prided herself on the calmness of her reply, but inwardly she was finding if difficult to control her hurt feelings.

Since their arrival at Malvern Hall, Jerrold had set aside time from his estate duties every day to be with his son. He had resumed Philip's riding lessons, which he had begun in Heathfield, occasioning Zoë many an anxious moment, because Philip was an impetuous rider and had taken numerous tumbles. Jerrold had also taken Philip along with him on visits to his tenants, and he had initiated the boy into the working schedule of the home farm. By now Philip had acquired quite a menagerie: a pony and a hound puppy, plus his own calf and a coal-black ram which remained at the home farm.

Zoë couldn't begrudge Philip his close association with his father. She had never seen the boy as happy and healthy as he was today. But more than once of late her heart had ached at the thought that she was no longer the center of Philip's life. And she had very little time left with him. Next year, or the year after, he would be off to school.

"If you like. Philip and I can postpone our outing so that you can go to Ludlow today," Jerrold offered. "After all, the kennels will still be there tomorrow."

Something in Jerrold's tone offended Zoë. He sounded so reasonable, so—so condescending. "That won't be necessary," she said, trying to sound composed. "Ludlow Castle will still be there tomorrow, also."

Giving her a straight look, Jerrold asked, "Are you being a little jealous, Zoë?"

Zoë gasped. "Jealous? Jealous of what?"

"Jealous of the time that I'm spending with Philip."

Making a great effort of will, Zoë replied coolly, "Hardly. Philip and I had six years together, years when you didn't know, or didn't care to know, that he even existed. It's really only fair that you should have the opportunity to know each other."

Jerrold's lips tightened at the phrase, "didn't care to know," but he said mearly, "I'm happy you feel that way."

Zoë spent the next hour at her desk in her bedchamber, approving the menus that Mrs. Denys the housekeeper had sent up, writing letters to Mrs. Randolph and Lady Bradford, trying to forget the latest encounter with Jerrold. Jealous? Was she jealous of the time Philip spent with Jerrold? Painfully, she had to admit that she was. From the time he was born, she had had all of Philip's love. Now she had to share it with someone else, and it hurt.

A soft knock sounded at the door. "Come."

The footman who opened the door offered her a tray containing a card. "The gentleman wished to call on his lordship, my lady, but I told him his lordship wasn't to home, so then he said as how he would like to see you."

Examining the card, Zoë said, "Tell Mr. Layton I'll be with him in a moment."

"Yes, my lady. The gentleman is in the library."

Walking down the stairs, Zoë could barely control her curiosity. Oliver Layton was the last person she would have expected to call at Malvern Hall.

He turned away from the window as she entered. "Hallo, Zoë. Lord, I'm in luck that you're here, and old Jerry isn't."

Zoë raised an eyebrow. "Oh? Why is that, Oliver?"

Flushing, he replied, "Well, as you'll recall, the last time we met, old Jerry gave me a nasty wisty-castor. He wasn't best pleased with me."

"No, he wasn't. So why are you here, may I ask?"

"Because I haven't any other place to go, that's why. I'm done up, Zoë, fast aground. I owe a fortune to the cents-per-cent, and I can't pay up. They're threatening me with debtors' prison. I need help, desperately."

"Your father . . .?"

"I didn't even apply to Papa. He doesn't have that kind of rhino."

"I see. So you want Jerrold to give you the money to clear your debts."

"Yes. That's it."

Zoë shook her head. "As you've pointed out yourself, Jerrold isn't very kindly disposed toward you. Why . . .?"

"Why should he help me? I'll tell you why. He can't want to see a member of his family in debtors' prison. He's fond of m'father. He won't wish to see Papa disgraced. Zoë, won't you talk to Jerrold for me? You can make him see reason. I'll promise him whatever he likes. I'll swear off gambling. I'll engage to stay away from my clubs. I'll pay him back if it takes the rest of my life. Please, Zoë."

Zoë looked at Oliver's sulky, aggrieved face, and felt very little sympathy for him. However, he *was* a Layton, just as Philip was now a Layton. She said, "I'll see what I can do. First, tell me how much you actually owe."

Oliver told her. She gasped at the amount, but made no comment. "Where are you staying?"

"In the village, of course, at the Layton Arms."

"Go back there and wait. I'll send you a message, or Jerrold will."

"Bless you, Zoë. You've saved my life."

"Don't be too sure of that. I haven't spoken to Jerrold yet."

As she waited in the library for Jerrold to join her for their customary glass of wine before dinner, Zoë wondered what his reaction to Oliver's request would be. She suspected it wouldn't be favorable. She was right.

"He owes how much?" Jerrold exclaimed. "Fifteen thousand pounds? I can't believe it. You'd think even a ninnyhammer like Oliver would be hard put to lose that much at the faro table unless he was deliberately trying to do so." His mouth hardened. "Well, so be it. How he had the gall to think I'd be willing to tow him out of the River Tick after what he did to Melicent . . ."

"He *is* your cousin, Jerrold."

He glared at her. "Good God, don't tell me you sympathize with that worthless excuse for a human being."

"I don't. But as I said, he *is* your cousin. He's also Philip's cousin. Do you really want a member of your family shut up in Newgate?"

Jerrold's expression changed. "No. I'd also dislike seeing Uncle Rupert shamed. Very well. I'll go around to the village tomorrow and put Oliver out of his misery.

Though it goes against the grain, let me tell you. If any man deserve to be in Newgate, it's Oliver."

Zoë was inclined to agree, although she was glad the matter had been resolved so easily, thanks to Jerrold's sense of family loyalty. Consequently she was somewhat surprised, on the following day, as she was cleaning her brushes after completing her painting stint, to receive a message that Mr. Layton was waiting in the library to see her.

"Well, Oliver?" she said as she entered the room, trying to suppress a tinge of annoyance in her voice.

His face clearly showing signs of strain, Oliver apologized. "Sorry to inflict myself on you again so soon, but as you can imagine, I'm anxious to know what Jerry's decided. You *did* speak to him?"

"Why, yes. He was planning to visit you today."

"He was? What—did he tell you what he was going to say?"

Before Zoë could reply, Jerrold, his face taut with anger, strode into the library. "Don't ask Zoë my intentions, Oliver. Ask me."

Oliver eyed his cousin with misgiving. "Jerry . . .?"

"I'm not going to raise the wind for you, Oliver. Unless you can find someone else to give you the blunt, it's debtors' prison for you." Jerrold added savagely, "Frankly, I wouldn't contribute a farthing to save you from the gallows."

"But Jerry—"

Jerrold cut Oliver off. "I was on my way to Stonebridge village half an hour ago to tell you I was prepared to give you the money for your debts. But then I spotted a familiar figure emerging from the inn. I couldn't mistake those peculiar whitish eyes and that shifty face, even though, thank God, I've only met the man twice. It was Percival Davenant, the Captain Sharp who killed my brother. I'd thought Davenant had left England, avoiding arrest on a capital charge for murdering Trevor. Evidently he's returned, hoping the situation has simmered down. Just as evidently, he's taken up with you again, Oliver. He came with you to Stonebridge, didn't he?"

Oliver's mouth twitched. "Well, yes, and I understand why you wouldn't approve, but let me explain. Davenant's under the hatches, too. Got no friends except me after that unfortunate duel. You wouldn't expect me to abandon a friend now, would you?"

"I would, yes, if that friend had murdered my cousin. Wasn't it enough for you that you assisted Davenant in that murder? Must you remain friends with the vicious hoodlum who killed Trevor?" Suddenly looking weary, Jerrold waved his hand. "Just go away, Oliver. Leave Malvern Hall. Leave Stonebridge. I'm sick of the look of you."

Clearing her throat, Zoë intervened. "I don't condone Oliver's conduct, Jerrold, but I think you should reconsider. We've discussed this before, remember? If you abandon Oliver, you also punish your uncle Rupert, and damage the family reputation."

Jerrold remained silent, clearly struggling with his emotions. Oliver watched him, his expression strained. Finally Jerrold said curtly, "I've changed my mind. I'll instruct my banker to pay you the fifteen thousand pounds, Oliver, but that's the end of it. Never ask me for another shilling. For that matter, I want nothing more to do with you. In future, don't approach me, don't greet me if we meet on the street or in the clubs, don't come to my home. As far as I'm concerned, you're as good as dead."

Oliver winced at the contempt in Jerrold's voice. His

face reddened with anger, and he opened his mouth as if to expostulate. Then, evidently thinking better of it, he drew a deep breath, muttering, "Thank you, Jerry. I knew I could count on you."

Jerrold nodded without replying, and after another look at his cousin's bleak, unresponsive face, Oliver walked slowly out of the room.

"I think you did the right thing, Jerrold," Zoë said quietly.

"Do you?" Jerrold smashed his fist into the open palm of his other hand. "I'm not sure. Oliver probably overstated his indebtedness. I suspect he'll come out of this with a little extra cash on hand, and I don't doubt that some of that money will go to Davenant. How do you think I'll feel, knowing that I'm helping to support my brother's murderer?"

Zoë could think of nothing to say. She gazed at Jerrold's tortured face, and for the first time in their acquaintance, she actually felt sorry for him.

Relations at Malvern hall were quite tranquil during the next few days. Zoë started a new portrait, which was going well. Jerrold was rather subdued, his manner retaining a certain grimness, although he didn't speak of Oliver. Apparently he'd decided to put the matter out of his mind. Zoë took Philip on the delayed excursion to Ludlow, which Philip enjoyed hugely. He regaled his father with the tales of sieges and knightly warfare that the caretakers had related to him. Edmund wrote to accept the invitation to the Malvern Hall house party scheduled for September.

On an afternoon toward the end of August Zoë looked up from her accounts as an ashen-faced Meg burst into the room. "My lady, come quick to the nursery. It's Master Philip. He's been hurt."

Springing to her feet, Zoë dashed out of the bedchamber and up the staircase serving the family apartments to the first floor. A cluster of servants around the door of Philip's room parted in order to allow her to enter. She found her son stretched unconscious on the bed, his shirt splotched with blood, with Jerrold kneeling beside him, pressing a thick wad of cloth against a wound in the boy's right shoulder. Philip's nursemaid, Sarah, stood by, controlling herself with difficulty.

"Jerrold, what happened?" Zoë asked in a strangled voice. "Is Philip seriously hurt?"

Without looking up, Jerrold replied, "Yes, it's a bad gunshot wound. I don't know yet if the bullet struck a bone. Right now I'm more worried about the bleeding. I can't seem to stop it."

"The doctor . . .?"

"I've sent for him. Dr. Gates should be here soon." Jerrold removed the blood-soaked bandage from Philip's shoulder and put out his hand to the nursemaid, who gave him another wad of cloth.

In tense silence Zoë stood beside Jerrold, watching as he repeatedly renewed the bandages on Philip's wound. Finally Jerrold muttered in relief, "I think the bleeding is stopping."

"Thank God, Jerrold," Zoë breathed. "Oh, thank God."

The doctor bustled into the bedchamber just then, exclaiming, "Lord Silverbridge has been shot, I hear. What a terrible thing. Let me see to the boy."

Jerrold rose, allowing the physician to make an examination. "You've done well, my lord," said the doctor after a few moments. "You've stopped the bleeding. Now, if you'll order some hot water sent up, and more clean bandaging, I'll take out the bullet and see what I can do to make young Lord Silverbridge more comfortable."

Jerrold ordered the nursemaid Sarah to bring up the hot water and bandaging, and then took Zoë's arm and drew her out of the room. He quietly dismissed the crowd of anxious-faced servants who had been lingering outside the door.

Zoë turned to Jerrold. "Now, tell me. You say Philip was shot? Who did it? Why . . .?"

"I don't know. Philip and I were riding in the woods behind the home farm, and someone fired a single shot. I made no effort to find the marksman, naturally, I was too concerned with Philip. However, I heard yesterday that poachers had struck the night before on Lord Wolverton's estate, not far from here."

"Another poaching gang? But they don't normally operate in the daytime, do they?"

"No. That's what troubles me. You'd think the poachers on Lord Wolverton's land would have made a quick getaway by now to London, or wherever they came from. I suppose it's possible that this gang might have been locally organized, out of Leominster, say, and in that case one of the members may have lingered behind to do a little private poaching of his own in the daytime." Jerrold shook his head. "The only other possibility is that one of our own people was out poaching and fired a stray shot that hit Philip."

Zoë's brows drew together. "I'd hate to believe that, especially since you've instructed your keepers to be lenient toward the poaching of small game by your tenants."

Jerrold shrugged again. "Perhaps we'll never know. What's important, in any event, is Philip's condition."

Zoë nodded. They waited without speaking, staring at

the closed door of Philip's bedchamber. After what seemed an eternity, the doctor emerged from the room. He looked grave.

"My lord, you know me. I've tended to you since you were a boy. You know I've always believed in being honest with my patients. So I must tell you and your lady that I'm not altogether happy with your son's condition. The wound is not a clean one. The bullet nicked the collarbone, and though I think I found any stray splinters of bone, I can't be sure. Again, I'm not a great believer in routine bleeding of patients in any event, and I find with bullet wounds that the problem is usually that the patient has lost too much blood. That's the case with your son. He's lost a great deal of blood, and he's very weak. Also I'm concerned that he hasn't yet regained consciousness."

Zoë said in a trembling voice, "Doctor, are you saying that Philip may die?"

"No, no, my lady, not at all. I won't deny, however, that I consider his condition serious. He requires very careful nursing. Keep him warm, keep him quiet. I'll return tomorrow to change the dressing. However, don't hesitate to call me if there's any change."

After the doctor had left, Zoë went into Philip's room and sat down beside the bed, holding back her tears as she looked at his still face, white as paper except for the dark smudges under his eyes. Jerrold pulled up a chair next to her. Together they sat there, silent and unmoving, through a succession of interminable hours, as the summer twilight lengthened into darkness and the clock moved toward midnight.

At last Philip stirred, moaning faintly, and opened his eyes. "Mama, Papa, I hurt."

Her eyes filling with tears, Zoë murmured, "I know,

darling." She put a glass, containing wine mixed with water and a few drops of laudanum, to his lips. "Try to drink this. It will make you feel better."

"It tastes bad, Mama," Philip complained, but she gently coaxed him to swallow the medicine. The moments passed, and gradually Philip's pain-racked features relaxed. He closed his eyes and settled into what looked like a natural sleep.

Jerrold whispered, "You look exhausted, Zoë. Have something to eat and then go to bed. I'll stay with Philip, at least for a few hours. But I think he's passed the crisis. He's going to be all right."

Instinctively Zoë shook her head in refusal. However, as she straightened her shoulders, she suddenly realized how stiff and tired she was. She was of no use to her son in this condition. Reluctantly she rose, and with one last look at Philip's sleeping face, she left the room and went downstairs to her bedchamber.

Meg was waiting for her. "I have some milk warming on the hearth, and some sandwiches, my lady. They told me you wouldn't go down to dinner. Is Master Philip better?"

"Yes, thank God. And thank you, Meg." Almost too tired to eat, Zoë sipped her milk and swallowed one of the sandwiches, and then collapsed on her bed without bothering to remove her clothes.

She slept only a few hours. The first faint streaks of dawn were already stealing into the room when Jerrold's hand on her shoulder shook her awake.

"Zoë, you'd best come. There's been a change. Philip is worse. I've sent for Dr. Gates."

Zoë shot out of the bed and ran from the bedchamber and up the stairs. Philip's condition had indeed changed. She had left him pale from loss of blood but peacefully sleeping. Now he was deeply flushed and moving restlessly. His eyes were open, although it was clear he didn't recognize either of his parents.

Dr. Gates, when he arrived, only confirmed the obvious. "The boy has a fever. A common occurrence with gunshot wounds. I'd been hoping it wouldn't happen in this case . . ." He shook his head.

"Doctor, what can we do?"

The doctor eyed Zoë compassionately. "Nothing very much, I fear, except to apply cooling compresses and try to get as much liquid into the child as he will take."

Zoë's heart began to pound. "Does that mean . . . ?"

"No, no, my lady. You mustn't give up hope. Chances are Lord Silverbridge will shake off this fever handily." Turning to Jerrold, the doctor said, "You'll remember, my lord, that you had a similar experience when you were a lad. Scratched your hand on a rusty nail, you did, and developed a raging fever. When I saw that ugly red line marching up your arm, I told you you'd die unless I took the arm off, and you wouldn't let me. And here you are, hale and hearty all these years later."

"Dr. Gates is right, Zoë," Jerrold said quietly. "A fever isn't necessarily fatal. Philip will throw this off, you'll see."

Gazing at her son's brilliantly red cheeks, listening to the disjointed mutterings from his lips, Zoë failed to take much comfort from Jerrold's reassurance, or that of the doctor. Nor did her spirits rise during the long hours that followed. She and Jerrold remained by Philip's bedside during the rest of that day and through the night, into the next day and the late evening hours, taking a hurried bite of food or snatching a few minutes of sleep when their exhausted bodies refused to go on any longer.

Toward midnight of that second day Zoë suddenly clutched at Jerrold's arm as he sat beside her. "Jerrold, look! Do you think . . . ?"

He stared at the faint film of moisture gathering on Philip's forehead. At that moment the boy's eyes opened, and for the first time in many hours they appeared lucid. "Mama. Papa," Philip whispered.

"The fever's broken," Jerrold exclaimed exultantly. "Zoë, the fever's broken, we've won . . ." He broke off as Zoë slumped back against her chair. "What is it? Are you ill?"

Lifting her head, she said, "No, I'm fine. For a moment I felt a little dizzy, that's all." She leaned forward to take Philip's hand. "Darling, I'm so happy. You're going to get well."

Philip responded with a weak attempt at a smile and a slight pressure of his fingers.

"Zoë, I want you to go to bed now," said Jerrold in a low voice.

"Oh, no, I can't leave Philip, not when he's just beginning to recover."

"You're done up, at the end of your tether. You can scarcely hold your head up."

"You're in no better case," muttered Zoë, gazing at Jerrold's haggard face.

"That's as may be. Look, I'll make a bargain. You go to bed, and I'll sit with Philip awhile longer, until I'm sure he won't relapse again, and then I'll put Sarah in charge, with instructions to notify both of us immediately if there's any change in Philip's condition."

Zoë lacked the strength to argue. "If you insist. I'll sleep, just for a few hours." She rose, holding on to the back of her chair, because her legs suddenly seemed too weak to support her. After a moment she made her way slowly out of the room, feeling curiously lightheaded, and down the stairs.

"My lady?" Her abigail jumped up from a chair as Zoë tottered into the bedchamber. "Master Philip?"

"Philip's fever has broken, Meg, he's going to recover," said Zoë, and collapsed. When she regained consciousness a few moments later, she was lying on the bed, already half divested of her clothes by the capable abigail.

"There now, my lady," said Meg, helping Zoë into a nightdress and covering her with blankets. "You must get some rest. What is it?" she asked in alarm as Zoë began to shiver uncontrollably. "Shall I bring more blankets?"

"Yes, please."

But the added blankets were of no use. Zoë continued to shiver from a bone-deep cold. For a time Meg stood helplessly by, watching her mistress, and then, taking a sudden resolve, she left the room. Zoë scarcely noticed her absence. In a few minutes, however, when Jerrold strode into the bedchamber, followed by Meg, Zoë aroused, starting up wildly from her pillow. "Philip? Is he—"

"He's all right. He drank some milk, and he's sleeping naturally." He walked to the bed. "Meg says you're ill."

"As you can see, my lord, her ladyship is so cold," Meg murmured. "She can't seem to stop shivering."

Sitting on the edge of the bed, Jerrold grasped Zoë's hands, massaging them between his own. "I don't think you're really suffering from the cold, Zoë. I think it's a delayed reaction from the shock of Philip's injury. You must try to relax."

"I—I can't. I'm freezing to death, Jerrold."

Rising, Jerrold told the abigail, "You can go, Meg. I'll

take care of Lady Woodforde." He started to take off his coat.

"But—"

"That will be all, Meg."

Zoë was vaguely conscious of a thumping sound, followed by another, and then experienced a moment of acute shock when Jerrold, having divested himself of his boots, slid into the bed beside her. She began to struggle as his arms went around her. "Don't . . . you can't . . ."

"Hush. You must get warm, Zoë," he muttered, and enveloped her more closely in his arms.

For several moments she continued to struggle, and then she felt a blessed warmth beginning to spread through her body. Involuntarily she relaxed against him.

Jerrold lifted his head to look down at her. "You're not shivering as much. Are you feeling better?"

"Yes. The dreadful cold is going away."

"Good. Perhaps you can sleep now. Do—do you want me to stay with you?"

Zoe started to say "no," and the word caught in her throat. Suddenly she was acutely aware of the solid masculine hardness of his body, and as she gazed up at him, her eyes widening, she felt through the flimsy material of her nightdress an instant, insistent swelling against her inner thigh. Her heart began to pound, and a sharp fiery sensation, almost like pain, knifed through her loins. As if mesmerized, she put up her hand, her clinging fingers tracing his eyes and his cheeks and slowly descending to brush the triangle of throat beneath his loosened neckcloth.

A shudder ran through his body. "Zoë?" he whispered uncertainly. If it was a question, he answered it himself. His mouth swept down on her lips with a hard urgency, to which Zoë, after a fleeting moment of resistance, ached to respond with a hunger that matched his own.

She had never before experienced such a feeling of wanton abandon as his hand skimmed over her breasts, glided lower to brush her thighs, returned to untie the ribbons of her nightdress so that his eager mouth could explore her exquisitely sensitive bare breasts. She surrendered completely to the seeking lips and caressing hands that seemed to claim every inch of her body. When at the end he entered her, her entire being disintegrated in an ecstasy that erased past and future and left only this one incandescent moment in the present.

Keeping his weight on his shoulders, he lay over her with his face buried in her shoulder, his breath coming in short gasps. "Zoë—God, Zoë . . ."

Writhing under him, she pushed frantically at his chest. He rolled away from her, his face registering his confusion. "What—"

Zoë snatched at a blanket to hide her nakedness and slid to the far side of the bed, turning her back to Jerrold. "Go away," she said in a strangled voice. "Oh, please, just go away."

Chapter Eighteen

Zoë came slowly awake. Her eyelids felt granular, and her head ached. Her glance fell on the empty pillow next to her head, and her face flamed. For a fleeting moment she'd half expected to see a darkly handsome face beside her, just as, all those years ago in the inn at Gretna Green, she had awakened to find a stranger in her bed.

She'd finally fallen asleep after several hours of intense, shamed self-searching. Now that she was awake, the agonizing questions surged through her mind again. How could she have allowed herself a second time to fall prey to Jerrold Layton's sensuality? She shook her head. No, she was being unfair. What had happened last night wasn't entirely, or even mostly, Jerrold's fault. She was as much to blame as he was. She hadn't resisted him. Drowning in physical desire, she had responded to his lovemaking with a wild abandon that caused the hot blood to rush to her face at the very memory of it.

She sat on the edge of the bed, burying her face in her hands. She felt betrayed, not by Jerrold, but by herself. She'd surrendered the self-esteem she'd laboriously crafted during those hard years since Gretna Green to a few moments of sexual passion with the man who was responsible for those hard years, and she wasn't sure she could repair the damage.

"Oh, ye're awake, my lady. I brought yer tea, jist in case. And I expect ye'll want ter get dressed right away, so's ye can go up to Master Philip."

The sound of the abigail's voice brought Zoë out of her fog of self-reproach, only to plunge her back into it immediately. Philip! How could she have forgotten about her son, even for a moment?

Pausing only long enough to throw on a gown and allow Meg to run a brush through her hair, Zoë hurried up the stairs to Philip's bedchamber. Dr. Gates was just emerging into the corridor.

"Well, well, my lady, our patient is doing famously. Famously!" the doctor said, beaming. "Seldom have I seen such rapid recovery from an acute fever. Why, Lord Silverbridge is demanding to sit up! Can't have that, of course, not for a day or so. The child's hungry, too, a good sign. I've ordered him some gruel. Lord Woodforde is feeding it to him now."

"That's wonderful news, Doctor. Thank you." Zoë went into the bedchamber. Jerrold sat beside the bed, supporting Philip's shoulders with one arm while with the other hand he spooned gruel into the child's mouth.

"Papa, must I eat this stuff?" Philip was complaining. His color had returned to normal, and his voice was strong.

"Yes, you must. I know it tastes foul, but the doctor says you it's good for you. You want to regain your strength quickly, don't you?"

"Yes, Papa." Philip sounded resigned, if dissatisfied.

He looked up to see his mother and smiled at her affectionately.

Zoë moved to the other side of the bed and leaned down to kiss Philip's forehead. "Good morning, darling. I can't tell you how happy I am to see you looking so well."

"Oh, I'm practically well, Mama. I'd like to get up and ride my pony, but the doctor won't let me."

"Nor will your papa," said Jerrold dryly. His eyes met Zoë's as he spoke. She looked away, feeling the color rising to her cheeks.

By the end of the day, Zoë had recovered from the effects of her long vigil by Philip's sickbed, but she decided against going down to dinner. She was being cowardly, she admitted. After all, she was living in the same house with Jerrold. She couldn't avoid him for long by keeping to her room. Tonight, however, the thought of being alone with him was more than she could face.

He came to the bedchamber as Meg was removing Zoë's supper tray. He was dressed in the evening clothes he had worn to his solitary dinner, and he, too, seemed well rested from the ordeal of Philip's illness. As soon as the abigail had left, he said, "We must talk, Zoë. I know you were overset by our lovemaking, and I'd like to explain . . ."

Zoë rose to face him. "You're not using the right word," she corrected him. "What we did last night had nothing to do with love."

He looked startled. Before he could reply, she went on: "Circumstances—actually a kindly impulse on your part, and I thank you . . ." Zoë reddened at the thought of that "kindly impulse," which had impelled Jerrold to warm her shivering body by clasping her in his arms. "Circumstances," she continued doggedly, "created an atmosphere of intimacy between us at a time when we were both exhausted, incapable of thinking coherently. We gave in to a purely physical impulse. It meant nothing. It won't happen again. I suggest we put it out of our minds."

Zoë felt rather proud of herself. She'd expressed her views logically, lucidly, calmly. She hadn't give Jerrold a hint of her emotional turmoil. She'd salvaged a potentially disastrous situation in a civilized manner.

His expression impassive, Jerrold heard her out. When she finished he said quietly, "There's one thing you haven't taken into account." His eyes bored into hers. "I thought you enjoyed our lovemaking—or physical impulse, whatever you care to call the experience. I certainly enjoyed it. Why can't we do it again?"

Zoë gasped. "How can you propose such a thing? You promised—you swore—that our arrangement would be—would be ..."

"Purely platonic. I well remember. Don't worry, Zoë. I have no intention of forcing myself on you. However, I made that promise primarily because I understood I was physically repugnant to you. Last night proved otherwise." Jerrold hesitated, as if searching for words. "I'll be frank with you," he said at last. "Under our present circumstances I'd as lief not go elsewhere to relieve my needs. Casual relationships are inconvenient and, er, carry certain hazards. More permanent arrangements are time-consuming, often boring, and can cause scandal. We're legally married, Zoë. If the pleasure is mutual, why shouldn't we sleep together?"

Something was squeezing at Zoë's heart, making it almost impossible for her to breathe. "Because we don't care for each other," she managed to say in a choked voice.

"Many married couples in our walk of life find themselves in that position," Jerrold pointed out. "After a London Season you can't be unaware that couples marry for many reasons, not always for love. And yet these people manage to enjoy themselves sexually, judging by the number of large families I see among my acquaintances."

Zoë was regaining her poise after the shock of Jerrold's seemingly cold-blooded proposal. "What other people do is of no consequence to me," she said curtly. "I can't conceive of a real marriage without at least some kind of affection."

Jerrold's expression remained calm. "I gather you're rejecting my suggestion. It's up to you, naturally. If you should change your mind . . ."

"That won't happen."

"As you say." Jerrold turned to go. Pausing with his hand on the door latch, he said, "May I assume, at any rate, that you bear me no ill will because of what happened last night?"

Zoë looked at him steadily. "The situation between us is what it's always been."

"Ah, yes. The status quo." Jerrold smiled faintly. "Good night, Zoë."

She couldn't sleep that night. She couldn't prevent the memories of those feverish, enchanted moments in Jerrold's arms from invading her mind. She found herself reliving every moment of that impassioned interval, longing for the hard pressure of his flesh against hers, and for the touch of his roving hands on the most intimate parts of her body. She even dared to ask herself if there was any real reason why she shouldn't allow Jerrold to make love to her even though they shared nothing of the spirit. The answer came quickly. If she slept with Jerrold, she would lose whatever integrity she had left. She would be no better than the succession of Fashionable Impures who had shared his bed.

Finally she fell into a fitful sleep. In the morning she tried to put the problem of her sensual relations with Jerrold out of her mind by concentrating on Philip's recovery. She spent much of her time with him, reading to him and otherwise keeping him amused during his convalescence.

The late August days went by quietly, except for one incident that made Zoë's blood run cold. Jerrold came to her one morning as she was about to enter Philip's room. "I don't want to worry you unduly," he began, "but something has happened I think you should know about."

She looked at him apprehensively.

"I saw no reason to trouble you with the details unless, or until, I had any real information, but the fact is that I instructed my head keeper to make quiet inquiries around the estate, in the hope of proving or disproving my suspicion that one of our own people might have shot Philip by accident. The keeper found no evidence one way or the other, but he did hear rumors that a laborer on one of our tenant farms seemed unusually prosperous for his state in life."

Jerrold paused, his face growing grim. "Well, so the keeper and I confronted the laborer about the source of his newly acquired income, and soon forced him to admit that he had been bribed by a gang of toughs from Leominster into giving them information about the choice hunting preserves in the area. I turned the laborer over to the authorities, of course, and he's now awaiting trial. In consideration of a lighter sentence he agreed to identify the members of the gang, who have all been rounded up."

Zoë frowned. "Why are you telling me this, unless . . ." She drew a quick breath. "Do you think that one of these people, the laborer or the members of the Leominster gang, shot Philip?"

Shrugging, Jerrold said, "It seems more than likely, although none of them has admitted to it under interrogation."

"Well, they *would* deny any guilt, I daresay," said Zoë, appalled. "Didn't you tell me that poaching with violence was a capital crime?"

"I did. Unfortunately, though it seems more than coincidental that a poaching gang was operating in our area at the very time Philip was shot, we have no proof of anyone's guilt. But it really makes no difference. The whole gang is in custody, and they'll be punished for their other crimes, if not for injuring Philip. The important thing is that they can never harm our son again."

"You're sure?"

"I'm sure," Jerrold replied firmly. "Before long the whole kit of them will be transported to the Antipodes."

Her fears allayed, for the time being at least, Zoë went into Philip's bedchamber to read to him.

All too soon for her taste, Dr. Gates pronounced his patient ready to leave his bed. Philip at once demanded to resume all his activities. Zoë felt reluctant to allow him out of her sight.

"It's too soon to begin riding your pony again," she protested to Philip one morning when he was about to join his father on a long-postponed excursion to visit the cave where Jerrold had played as a boy.

"I'm perfectly fit, Mama," Philip protested. "Dr. Gates says I'm in prime twig."

However, though she chided herself for being morbid, the memory of Philip's injury during his last ride remained vivid in Zoë's mind. She couldn't restrain an instinctive fear that another disaster would befall Philip if he again went out on horseback. She went to Jerrold in an effort to dissuade him from the excursion. "The cave is so far away," she told him. "Philip will get too tired."

"It's only a five-mile ride," he replied. I don't think it will be too much for him."

"Oh, I daresay it won't. He's made such a splendid recovery. It's just that . . ."

"It's just that you can't forget what happened to Philip the last time he rode out with me. I understand. But Zoë, try to keep in mind that the person who shot Philip is in jail. He—whichever of the poaching gang he is—can't harm our son again. Philip will be perfectly safe during his ride."

Jerrold had reverted to the cool courtesy that had marked his behavior to her since their arrival at Malvern Hall. In the intervening days he had never referred to their lovemaking on the night of Philip's recovery from the fever. The interlude might never have taken place.

Zoë had to accept Jerrold's assurance that Philip would be in no danger during his ride, but irrationally or not, she remained on pins and needles until the boy came home safely from the cave.

"Mama, you should have come with us," he told Zoë eagerly. "It was such a lark. We had to climb way up a steep hill to reach the cave. I felt almost like an explorer! The cave is huge. We needed a lantern to find our way about in it. There are tunnels reaching deep into the hill. Papa says he and Uncle Trevor got lost in one of the tunnels and almost didn't find their way back again. And there's one tunnel that seems to end in a blank wall, but if you look up to the roof you see a—a fissure, Papa called it, and if you crawl into the fissure, you're in a secret cave within a cave. Papa says he and Uncle

Trevor used to hide there from Cousin Oliver, when they didn't want to play with him."

"Cousin Oliver?" Zoë asked in surprise.

"Oliver used to visit Malvern Hall quite often when he was growing up," Jerrold said briefly. Obviously he had no fond memories of those visits. Zoë suspected that Oliver's name had come up inadvertently today while Jerrold was describing his boyhood adventures to Philip.

"Papa was telling me how he and Uncle Trevor pretended they were Robin Hood's men, hiding in the cave from the Sheriff of Nottingham," Philip continued, his eyes shining. "Papa showed me the bow and arrows he made all by himself to hunt the deer. And we found the very knife that he used to carve the arrows. He gave it to me. Look." Philip proudly displayed a rather battered-looking pocket knife with a cracked ivory handle. "I've always wanted a knife. This one will be so useful."

"It looks very sharp," said Zoë, with an apprehensive look at the blade.

"Philip understands he must use the knife responsibly," Jerrold assured her. "I can tell you one thing, he won't be carving arrows with it." His lips curled in a deprecatory grimace. "My arrow making was a real exercise in futility. My homemade arrows never went true, and even if they had, they wouldn't have hurt anything. I did once hit a sheep. Didn't hurt him, either."

Philip looked crestfallen. "Papa, you're funning, aren't you? The bow and arrows weren't just toys? You did go after game with them?"

Jerrold laughed. "Well, perhaps I exaggerated a bit. Trevor and I did manage to bag an occasional rabbit, and once we even shot a sitting partridge."

Gradually Zoë's uneasiness about Philip's safety abated, and as September approached, she plunged into preparations for the house party. At first she was apprehensive about her ability to make arrangements for housing and entertaining forty people, many of whom, friends of Jerrold, were strangers to her. Soon, however, she discovered that the housekeeper, Mrs. Denys, and the butler were unobtrusively relieving her of most of her labors, and she allowed herself to relax.

Edmund was the first of the guests to arrive. "I very nearly wrote to tell you I wasn't coming," he told Zoë sheepishly. "Well, I'm not a great one for socializing, you know. And I started to feel guilty about leaving the parish in the midst of preparations for the Harvest Festival next month. But then the Reverend Jenkins, who's conducting services while I'm gone—a very nice young man, newly ordained; you'd like him, Zoë—Mr. Jenkins assured me he would do everything possible to help with the Festival."

Zoë smiled. "You know very well, Edmund, that Mrs. Randolph always runs the Harvest Festival singlehandedly. I suspect that's really why she didn't accept my invitation to the house party, though she *claimed* she couldn't persuade Mr. Randolph to accompany her so far from home."

"I expect you're right," Edmund replied good-naturedly. He glanced around at the delicate wall paintings of the octagon studio, where he and Zoë were talking. "What a lovely room. Most impressive, but then, all of Malvern Hall is impressive. My word, Zoë you're practically living in a palace!" He gave her one of his familiar searching looks. "And how are you, sister-mine?"

"I've come to terms with this marriage, if that's what you mean."

"That's all?"

"It's a great deal, when you consider that a few weeks

ago I was set to leave Jerrold," Zoë retorted. "Don't worry about me, Edmund. Philip is happy. That's the important thing."

"I'd hoped ..." Edmund sighed, and changed the subject. "Lady Rosedale will be a member of your party, I believe. When do you expect her?"

"Melicent will arrive tomorrow. As you perhaps know, she's been visiting her parents with little Dickie."

"Yes, she told me her plans." Edmund shook his head. "My word, it seems a very long time since we met. Actually, I believe it's been only six weeks or so. It will be very pleasant to see her again. She and I have become quite good friends."

Zoë looked at him sharply. More than once during his recent visit to London, she'd suspected that her studious, ascetic brother had a *tendre* for Melicent. Could it be that he'd disguised his feelings, even to himself, as mere friendship? Better if he had, Zoë thought. The world would view a match between him and Melicent with pained disapproval.

Yet, when Melicent arrived the next day, Zoë observed her closely for any sign of partiality toward Edmund. But Melicent simply appeared her usual self, cheerful and gracious, seemingly no more eager to greet Edmund than anyone else. Perhaps she was even a little warmer in her greeting to her favorite cousin Jerrold.

With Melicent a flood of guests began descending on Malvern Hall. Rupert Layton came with his wife. Though he was affable and urbane as always, Rupert made it clear to Zoë he was disappointed by his son's absence. "Oliver has been attending these house parties since he was a lad," Rupert told her. "I don't mean to reproach you, Zoë, but you'll recall I asked you to smooth over relations between Oliver and Jerrold. And yet Oliver received no invitation."

Zoë's reply was noncommittal. "I did speak to Jerrold, Uncle Rupert.'

Smiling thinly, Rupert said, "Ah, well, my dear, I'm sure you did your best."

Stephen Carrington arrived with his sister. Stephen was unaffectedly glad to see Zoë and apparently failed to notice that his reception by Jerrold was lukewarm. Clarissa rattled along merrily in her usual fashion. "My dear Zoë, Bradford has the gout and positively refused to budge from home, but I was determined not to miss the opportunity to see Malvern Hall, so I came without him. And I have the most famous idea: you must paint Stephen's portrait while he's staying here. Since he succeeded Papa I've been after him to have his likeness taken, and he pays me no mind."

"Clarissa!" exclaimed an outraged Stephen. "You know full well that Zoë paints only women and children."

"Well, but perhaps Zoë would like to try her hand at a different kind of portrait," said Clarissa. She cocked her head at Jerrold, standing next to her. "What's your opinion, Lord Woodforde?"

Impassive-faced, Jerrold replied, "I wouldn't venture to have an opinion. My wife always makes her own decisions, professional or otherwise."

There was the faintest edge of mockery in his voice. Was he thinking of Zoë's decision not to sleep with him? Nettled, she smiled at Stephen. "It might be interesting to see if I have the ability to do a male portrait. We'll arrange a sitting."

However, with the arrival of the full complement of guests, Zoë had to curtail her work at the easel. She discovered that hostessing a large country house party was a complex and time-consuming activity.

In the mornings the gentlemen were out early with Jerrold, hunting, fishing, racing. After the ladies had come down to a lavish ten o'clock breakfast, Zoë sat with them while they gossiped, read, sketched, played the pianoforte, embroidered screens, and did shellwork, and accompanied them on restorative walks in the gardens and visits to the extensive Malvern Hall greenhouses. In the afternoons the gentlemen piled into carriages with the ladies for long drives through the Herefordshire countryside. Evenings, after a lavish dinner and the obligatory drinking of port, male and female guests gathered in the sumptuous Adam drawing room for more gossip, games, cards, and usually, dancing.

Sitting beside Melicent one evening, Zoë gazed around her drawing room, her eye flitting from the whist players at the table near her to the accomplished young woman playing the pianoforte to the billiard table set up for the gentlemen at the rear of the room, and murmured, "Do you ever get bored at these house parties, Melicent? You must have attended so many of them."

Melicent smiled. "Oh, perhaps a little. After a while, one house party seems much like the last. Sometimes I'd much prefer to stay in my room reading a good book, or playing with little Dickie."

Sighing, Zoë said, "Well, I must admit that having house guests is a great deal of work. I scarcely have a moment to myself, and I hardly see Philip."

Melicent patted her hand. "You hide your feelings very well. So many people have told me what an accomplished hostess you are. Jerry said the same thing only yesterday."

For a moment Zoë indulged herself in a wistful yearning to hear Jerrold tell her how splendidly she was managing. But, of course, the fact was that there had scarcely been a moment since the house party began when Jerrold could have spoken to her personally. They were, both of them, continually surrounded by hordes of people.

At length, feeling smothered by so much socializing, Zoë took refuge from the daily pressure by beginning work on a portrait of Stephen Carrington, though she had to schedule sittings for an early hour before the formal breakfast.

"What an exquisite room," Stephen observed, gazing about him at the rococo octagonal studio when he arrived for his first sitting. "It suits you, Zoë."

"Thank you." Zoë made a face. "The room is really far too grand for a working painter, though, don't you think? Now, then, Stephen, if you'll just take that chair—yes, the blue one, next to the pedestal—we can get started."

For half an hour Zoë worked absorbedly with a charcoal pencil, making a preliminary sketch. Then, laying down the charcoal, she said, "You can relax for a bit, Stephen."

He rose, walking to the easel to look at the sketch. "I'm jealous," he confessed. "I slave for hours at my water colors, and then you, with a few strokes and a shadow or two, create a perfect likeness." He looked down at her, his eyes kindling. "I'm so glad to have this opportunity to be alone with you," he blurted. "You've been surrounded by your guests since I arrived here. I've had scarcely a private word with you. And I've missed you so much. London was a dead bore after you left for Herefordshire."

"Oh, come now, London was stale because *everyone*

had left town for the country," said Zoë lightly, to defuse the unmistakable emotion she heard in Stephen's voice.

"No, it was because you left." Stephen paused, biting his lip. A slow color rose in his face. "I know I shouldn't talk to you like this . . ."

"Then don't. Please, Stephen."

"I can't help it. If I thought you were really happy . . . But you aren't, are you? Oh, everyone talks about your great romance with Woodforde, and how it came to life again when you met all those years later. I don't believe it. I've watched you when you're with him. You don't have the look of a woman in love. In fact, sometimes I've seen a shadow on your face that makes me want to weep. *I* love you, Zoë. I love you so much."

Suddenly he reached for her, folding her in his arms. Holding her close, he pressed his eager lips to her mouth. For a moment, caught utterly by surprise, she relaxed against him, responding instinctively to the passion in his kiss. But only for a moment. Thrusting her hands against his chest, she broke the embrace and ran blindly to the door. Behind her she heard Stephen's voice crying, "Zoë, I'm sorry. Zoë, don't go . . ."

Ignoring the pain she could hear in his voice, she raced down the corridor to the staircase, passing a chambermaid who stared at her in confusion. Reaching her bedchamber, she slammed the door shut behind her and sank into a chair, covering her face with her hands, while she fought the demons that were overwhelming her.

In a flash of insight she realized that in the years since the elopement to Gretna Green she had ignored her sensual urges, probably as a form of self-protection, to prevent her fragile ego from being shattered again by a surrender to the flesh. Now, after the night she had spent in Jerrold's arms, she was alive again physically.

She had responded to Stephen's kiss, not because she returned his affections, but simply because he was a man who, for a fleeting moment, had stirred the impulses that Jerrold's practiced lovemaking had reanimated after all the dead years.

Dropping her hands from her face, Zoë sank back against the chair, closing her eyes. She knew now that, having tasted the enticing joy of physical passion, she didn't want to live the rest of her life without it. She knew also that she couldn't satisfy her newly aroused sensual desires at the expense of her hard-won sense of self-worth, either by sleeping with the husband who had always used her for his own needs, or by an illicit affair with Stephen Carrington that could only hurt them both.

Wearily Zoë rose from the chair, removed her painting smock, and sat down at the dressing table to smooth her hair. Whatever her lacerated feelings, she had to ignore them. She had work to do as the mistress of Malvern Hall.

On her way to breakfast, she remembered that she had promised to search for a book that one of her female guests had expressed a desire to read. Retracing her steps, she went to the library, pausing on the threshold as she realized she had inadvertently interrupted an emotional scene.

Melicent and Edmund faced each other. Edmund, his face drawn with anguish, was saying, "Melicent, you must know I would gladly die rather than hurt you . . ." He stopped short as he caught sight of Zoë over Melicent's shoulder.

Turning, Melicent said, "Do come in, Zoë. Perhaps you can make your stubborn brother see reason."

Zoë closed the door behind her. Raising an eyebrow, she asked, "How is Edmund being unreasonable?"

Flushed, but appearing more angry than embarrassed, Melicent said, "Edmund has just informed me that, although he loves me, he will not ask me to marry him."

Looking desperate, Edmund exclaimed, "Melicent, be fair. What would society say if the Countess of Rosedale, the daughter of the Earl of Farrington, elected to marry the undistinguished rector of her own parish church?"

Melicent raised her chin. "I've told you I don't care what society says."

"You must care! My rank, if you can call it that, is far inferior to yours, I have no fortune, I don't know how to conduct myself with your aristocratic friends . . ."

"Oh, it's true you have no good qualities to commend yourself to me," Melicent retorted, "save one. You love me, and I think you can make me happy." She looked at Zoë, saying, "You asked me the other night if I wasn't bored with country house parties. Frankly, I'm a little bored with the whole social scene. I don't much care if I never take part in another London Season. I've done my duty to the Rosedales. I've given the family an heir, and of course I intend to rear Dickie to live up to his responsibilities. Now I love Edmund, and I don't think I'm selfish to want a little personal happiness, do you?"

"No, I don't," Zoë heard herself saying, even though Edmund's arguments against marrying Melicent were the same ones that had already occurred to her. Actually, she was in a state of mild shock. Despite the close friendship she had observed developing between Melicent and Edmund during his visit to London in the summer, she had always assumed that any romantic feelings were largely one-sided on Edmund's part. She had never been able to shake her conviction that

Melicent still had a lingering regard for Jerrold that would prevent her from falling in love with anyone else.

Groping for words, she said, "Edmund, there are many reasons why people are unhappy, but gossip shouldn't be one of them. If fear of what society will say about you is the only obstacle keeping you from asking Melicent to marry you, then perhaps you don't deserve to be happy."

He looked at her intently. He was reading her mind, as he so often did. He knew what had prompted her remark. It was the thought of her own sterile future with Jerrold.

He hesitated for a long moment. Then, taking a deep breath, he said, "Melicent, I would be honored if you would accept my proposal of marriage."

Smiling radiantly, Melicent said, "I accept with pleasure. And I call on you to witness, Zoë, that your brother actually made me an offer, in case he should change his mind later!"

Jerrold was late for lunch that day. He apologized to his guests, explaining that his bailiff had requested an interview. Zoë thought he appeared unusually preoccupied. She took him aside after lunch. "Jerrold, Melicent wants us to join her in the library." At his questioning look, she added, "It's a kind of family conference. I've already spoken to your Uncle Rupert and Beryl."

Melicent was waiting in the library with Edmund. Jerrold gave Edmund a faintly surprised look, as did Rupert when he entered the room with his wife a few moments later.

"Well, now, Melicent, what's this about a family conference?" Rupert inquired genially after they had all seated themselves around the fireplace. He flicked another look at Edmund.

Melicent smiled. "You're wondering why Edmund is here, Uncle Rupert, since this is a 'family' conference. He's here because he'll soon be a member of the family. We're to be married, probably in the spring. I wanted to tell all of you privately before I made a formal announcement."

After a blank moment, Jerrold said, "I wish you happy, Melicent. Congratulations, Edmund."

His face flushing, Rupert exploded. "In the fiend's name, Jerry, what can you be thinking of? Melicent marry a nobody, a country rector from a hamlet in Cumberland? A man of no family, of inferior background? You can't mean to approve such a match. Or rather, such a gross mesalliance."

"Melicent is of age, and in full possession of her senses, Uncle Rupert. I wouldn't presume to tell her whom to marry. She's free to marry anyone she likes. And I might remind you, in case you'd forgotten, that my wife shares Edmund's lineage."

Rupert shot Zoë a venomous look. "I see it all now. You've been scheming for this from the first, haven't you? It wasn't enough that you inveigled my nephew into legitimizing a disastrous marriage into which you trapped him in the first place. No, you determined to raise your brother to the same social position you had achieved, and by the same means, an advantageous marriage. You didn't hesitate to get rid of any other respectable suitor for Melicent's hand, including my own son—"

His face a frozen mask, Jerrold interrupted. "That's enough, Uncle Rupert. Your accusations against Zoë are vicious and untrue. You'll either apologize to her for this unwarranted attack, or you'll leave Malvern Hall immediately."

"Jerry! I'm your uncle. You can't speak to me like that . . ." His angry color fading, Rupert choked off his words, obviously struggling for calm. After a long pause he said to Zoë, "Please accept my apology. I spoke intemperately."

Before Zoë could reply, a knock sounded at the door, followed immediately by the entrance of a harassed-looking footman. "Begging yer pardon fer intruding, my lord, but Sarah insists on speaking ter ye, and seeing as how she's the little lord's nursemaid an' all . . ."

Sarah burst past the footman into the room. "My lord, my lady, I'm that sorry ter bother ye, but I had ter talk ter ye. Y'see, I'm so afeared something terrible has happened ter Master Philip."

As one, Zoë and Jerrold jumped to their feet and hurried to the nursemaid's side. "Tell us, Sarah," said Jerrold tensely.

"Master Philip went out riding in the park early this morning wi' one o' the grooms. When he didn't come up ter the nursery at his usual time fer his lunch, I went down ter the stables ter inquire, and they said he wasn't back yet. That was over two hours ago. Master Philip still hasn't come back."

"You did right to come to us, Sarah. Thank you." Jerrold nodded his dismissal to the harried nursemaid. To Zoë he said, "I'll ride into the park to look for Philip."

"I'll go with you," said Edmund. Rupert chimed in immediately. "So will I."

As the men went out the door, Melicent came to Zoë, putting an arm around her shoulders. "Don't think the worst. There could be—there probably is—some perfectly simply reason why Philip is late coming back."

"I wish I could think of one," said Zoë bleakly. She and Melicent waited in the library, speaking little, frequently glancing at the clock on the mantelpiece, while the minutes ticked on past the half hour to the hour. They rose when Jerrold strode into the room. Zoë caught her breath as she looked at his somber face. "Jerrold?" she faltered.

He shook his head. "I didn't find Philip. I did find his groom, Jed Hawkins, lying unconscious on the path that leads to that little folly on the western side of the park. I've sent the stable hands with a wagon to bring Hawkins in. I don't think he'll live. Somebody dealt him a fearful blow to the skull. Whoever did it undoubtedly left him for dead. There was no sign of Philip."

Zoë cried out in anguish, "Jerrold, what are we to do? What do you think has happened to Philip?"

"My God, I don't know, I don't know." The anguish in Jerrold's voice echoed hers. He swallowed hard. "I'm ordering a massive search immediately. Thank God, with all the male guests in the house, we'll have enough riders to man the search. Our neighbors will help, too, I know." He hesitated. "Zoë, I can't keep this from you any longer. Remember I was late for lunch, because my bailiff wanted to see me? He told me that three members of the Leominster poaching gang had broken out of jail in the course of a riot, during which they'd murdered the laborer from my estate who'd informed on them."

Zoë clenched her hands together so fiercely that her nails bit into her skin. "And you think . . . ?"

"I think these escaped prisoners have decided to revenge themselves on me by striking at Philip. I was the one who forced the confession out of the laborer. They'd never have been apprehended but for that confession."

Chapter Nineteen

Jerrold was the last of the riders to straggle in. Since early afternoon horsemen from Malvern Hall and gentlemen from neighboring estates had fanned out across the countryside, searching every field, every copse, every hedgerow, every outbuilding, for some trace of Philip. The search had continued through the long twilight and into the evening, aided by the light from a brilliant full moon. Philip was still missing.

Jerrold walked into the drawing room, where the entire house party was keeping vigil, including his fellow horsemen who had already returned from their fruitless efforts. A low murmur of disappointment arose when those in the room observed that Jerrold, too, had returned without Philip.

Jerrold was gray with fatigue. He had been in the saddle continuously for more than eight hours. He went straight to Zoë, handing her a grimy piece of paper. "The landlord of the Layton Arms in Stonebridge found this note in his taproom, addressed to me," he said. "The landlord doesn't know how it got there."

Zoë slowly deciphered the note, written in a scrawling and almost illegible hand: "Lord Woodferd—we hav yer boy. If ye wants him back, it will cost ye 5000 yeller boys. Ye hav 3 days to find the rhino. We will let ye know how to git it to us."

The color draining from her face, Zoë looked up from the note. "This message is from those escaped prisoners, isn't it, Jerrold? They've kidnapped our son." Intent on her own misery, she was only vaguely aware of the collective gasp of horror that went up from the roomful of people.

Jerrold said heavily, "I think we have to assume that the escaped poachers have taken Philip, yes. Well, at least they've given me time to obtain the ransom. I don't have five thousand in gold in the house."

Rupert hurried up, saying, "Good God, Jerry, what a dreadful thing. My heart bleeds for you and Zoë. A pretty pass we've come to in this country if our children aren't safe from felons. You must call out the militia at once. An outrage like this demands instant and drastic punishment."

"I intend to call on the militia in the morning for help in finding Philip. At the moment, however, I'm not too concerned about punishing these criminals. Time enough to think about that after we get Philip back, Uncle Rupert."

"Yes. Yes, of course. The child's safety is our first concern."

Taking Zoë's arm, Melicent said, "Dearest, you must go to bed. You, too, Jerry. Neither of you can do anything tonight for Philip. Tomorrow you'll need your strength."

Numbly Zöe allowed Melicent to lead her out of the drawing room to her bedchamber, where the abigail, Meg, rose at their entrance, her face puckered with anxiety.

"My dear, do you want me to stay with you?" Melicent asked. The question was an implicit admission that she was quite aware that Zoë and Jerrold didn't sleep together, but Zoë scarcely noticed.

"No, you needn't stay, Melicent. Meg will take care of me."

"Well, then, if you're sure ... Zoë, don't give up hope. Philip will come back to you safely, I'm sure of it. Good night."

"Her ladyship is quite right, my lady. Master Philip will soon be home, you'll see," murmured the abigail comfortingly as she deftly helped Zoë out of her clothes and into a nightdress and dressing gown. Coaxing her mistress to swallow the milk she had kept warming on the hob, Meg said, "It will help you to sleep, my lady. You must get some rest."

But after Meg had reluctantly left, Zoë couldn't sleep, though she felt mentally and physically drained. She couldn't erase from her mind the image of Philip, bewildered and terrified, in the hands of rough men who had nothing to gain from treating him kindly, who, in fact, had nothing to gain from ...

A wave of nausea swept over Zoë. These escaped poachers already faced the gallows for the killing of the Malvern Hall laborer who had informed on them. The law could inflict no further punishment on them if they murdered a small boy after collecting his ransom. Perhaps they had already killed Philip. Why would they bother to keep him alive?

Scarcely thinking, reacting instinctively, Zoë bolted out of the room and raced down the corridor to Jerrold's suite. She knocked once, briefly, impatiently, and then, not waiting for an answer, she tore open the door and plunged into the bedchamber.

"Jerrold?" she said uncertainly, gazing around the large room, dimly lit by a single small lamp on the bedside table. He wasn't in the bed. For a moment she thought he wasn't there. Then she saw him. He was sitting at a desk on the far side of the bedchamber, his head resting on his crossed arms. His shoulders were heaving.

Without thinking, she rushed to the desk and put her hand on his shoulder. Obviously startled, he jerked his head upright. His cheeks were wet with tears. "Zoë, what are you . . ." He broke off, awkwardly rubbing his eyes dry with his fingers as he rose to his feet. Concealing any embarrassment he may have felt, he appeared quite calm as he asked, "What is it? Is something wrong?"

Her voice trembling, she said, "I had to talk to you. I couldn't bear to be alone with my thoughts. You see, I suddenly understood that those dreadful men who kidnapped Philip had no reason to treat him kindly, or even to return him to us after the ransom is paid. They can't be punished for what they've done to him, can they, Jerrold? They already face the death penalty."

His precarious calm dissolved. He threw up his hands. "Oh, God, Zoë, I've been thinking of nothing else since the ransom note arrived. I hoped, for your peace of mind, that the danger wouldn't occur to you . . ."

Jerrold paused, his face twisted with pain. "It's all my fault," he said suddenly. "God is punishing me through the innocent, as He always does. Zoë, you told me once I was completely selfish. It's true. I never cared much about anybody or anything, except my brother Trevor or the Malvern Hall estate. At Gretna Green that morning, after I emerged from my alcohol fog, I realized you were no strumpet, but I didn't bother to find out who you really were, or if I'd wronged you in any way. I just never thought about you again. And Philip. You were right. I didn't care about Philip either, except as the heir to Malvern Hall. But that was only at the very beginning. Soon he was my whole life. Now God is taking him away."

Seeing Jerrold's anguished expression, hearing the hopelessness in his voice, Zoë responded without thinking. She put her hand on his arm, saying, "You're not to blame for Philip's kidnapping. And God won't punish you for loving your own son. God won't punish you for being the best father in the world."

For a moment Jerrold stood frozen, staring down at her. Then he reached out gropingly to fold her in his arms and bent his head to her mouth. At first there was no passion in the kiss. It was almost as if Jerrold was simply seeking warmth and comfort from physical contact with another human being. Zoë made no attempt to draw away, even when Jerrold's breathing quickened and the pressure of his lips on hers became harder and more demanding. She felt a stab of a familiar fiery, enticing sensation in her loins.

Releasing her mouth, Jerrold buried his face in her hair, murmuring huskily, "Zoë, darling, on this terrible night I need you so much. For just a few hours, can't we put the past behind us? For those few hours let me imagine you don't hate me, that you love me as much as I love you. For those few hours let me love you. Please, Zoë . . ."

Hesitating for only a moment, Zoë slowly slipped her arms around Jerrold's neck and relaxed against him.

"My love—my beautiful love," Jerrold whispered between fluttering lips as he traced gentle, clinging kisses on her eyes and cheeks and throat, while his hands glided caressingly down her back and cupped her bottom, pressing her against the hardening swelling of his arousal. He groaned, pulling her roughly into a closer embrace as he sought her mouth again with an insatiable hunger.

Nestling his head in the hollow of Zoë's throat, Jerrold murmured in a voice drugged with passion, "I don't want to leave you, not just yet. . . . Am I too heavy for you?"

"No . . . no . . ." Zoë lay dreamily, relaxed in the aftermath of the exquisite pleasure she and Jerrold had shared. She felt safe, complete, fulfilled, for the first time in her life. She wanted to remain joined to him for as long as possible.

"I *am* too heavy." Reluctantly Jerrold withdrew and settled beside her. Propping himself on an elbow, he looked down at her, putting out a finger to gently caress the curve of a bare breast. He caught his breath. "You have the most perfect body, Zoë." As she flushed a deep red and made an instinctive move to pull the coverlet over her, he said heavily, "Are you sorry we made love? I hoped—"

"No, I'm not sorry."

The blue eyes kindled. "Zoë?"

The words escaped her before she knew what she was about to say. She blurted, "Why didn't you tell me before that you loved me? Or didn't you mean what you said?"

"Of course I meant what I said. I began falling in love with you on that journey from Heathfield to London, when I'd wake up in one of those cursed uncomfortable chairs you'd banished me to, and I'd watch my beautiful wife in name only sleeping comfortably in a bed. I fell more deeply in love with each passing day, as I saw how tenderly you loved Philip, as I watched you conquer London society. I suffered hellish torments of jealousy when you seemed to be favoring Stephen Carrington." He paused, looking a little sheepish. After a moment he said, shrugging, "I wanted to tell you how I felt, I started to tell you, so many times. But how could I tell you I loved you, Zoë, when you'd made it so plain that you hated me?"

"I did hate you. I was sure I could never forgive you for what happened at Gretna Green. But somehow . . ." Zoë frowned as she tried to sort out her thoughts. She said slowly, "I think my feelings started to change when I realized how much you loved Philip, and how much he needed you. No man who was such a tender, caring father could also be a complete blackguard. Of course, I couldn't admit to myself that you might have any good points. Otherwise I'd have no grounds for despising you, and I'd been nursing my grievances against you for so many years that they'd become a part of me. I'm so ashamed of myself. I can see now that you tried in every way you could, short of words, to tell me that you cared, and I shut my heart against you. Now . . ."

"Now?" Jerrold's voice was strained, questioning.

Zoë snuggled close to him, sliding her arm around his neck. "Now I can let the dead years go," she whispered against his eager lips. "Now I can love you."

Zoë drifted awake, dimly aware of a chill caused by the absence of a warm vital male body next to her in the bed. The first faint light of morning was filtering into the room. She stirred, muttering, "Jerrold?"

Fully dressed, he settled on the edge of the bed, leaning down to brush her lips lightly in a kiss. His face was tender as he said, "Darling, I'm sorry if I woke you. I hoped you could get a little more rest. I'm off to Leominster to arrange with my banker about the gold ransom."

Fully awake now, she sat up abruptly, overwhelmed with guilt. "Oh, God, Jerrold, how could I have forgotten, even for an instant? Philip is still out there in the clutches of those dreadful men."

"Shush," he soothed her. He kissed her again. "Philip wouldn't have begrudged us a few hours or love. We'll both be the stronger for it. And Zoë, we're going to need every bit of our strength."

She stared at him with a strained intensity. "Jerrold, what we talked about last night—Philip's safety. Tell me the truth. Is there any real chance that we'll get our son back, alive and uninjured?"

"I don't know," Jerrold said somberly. "That's the best answer I can give you. I don't know." His expression hardened. "I'll tell you this: we'll do everything in our power to bring Philip back safely. Last night I arranged with Edmund and Uncle Rupert to take charge of renewing the search this morning at dawn. Today in Leominster I'll put out a call for the militia. If Philip is still in the area, we'll find him." He put his arms around her in a sudden fierce embrace. "Thank you for loving me," he murmured against her hair. "Without your love I don't think I could get through this horror." He gave her one last hard kiss and stood up, saying, "Goodbye. I'll come back to you as soon as I can."

After Jerrold had gone, Zoë retrieved her robe from

the floor, where it fallen last night when Jerrold had slipped it from her shoulders, and went down the corridor to her own bedchamber. Meg greeted her with a wooden-faced lack of surprise that told Zoë the abigail knew exactly where her mistress had spent the night.

"The gentlemen were all out at first light, my lady," Meg reported. "They'll find Master Philip, you'll see. He'll be home safe in a trice."

"I hope so, Meg." Zoë dressed hurriedly, drank an equally hurried cup of tea, and gulped down a few bites of toast before she realized that her haste served no purpose. She was of no earthly use in the search for Philip. She could only wait.

Wait she did, into the morning, sitting in the drawing room with all the female guests of the house party. Melicent sat beside her, occasionally reaching out to grasp her hand tightly. Rupert's wife, Beryl, stiffly mannered as always, offered her a few limp words of reassurance. Clarissa Bradford, her normal ebullience a mere ghost of itself, said to Zoë in a low voice, "Stephen is out with the search party, so he asked me to give you a message. He sends you his apologies for causing you any distress, and hopes you will forgive him."

Zoë looked at Clarissa blankly. It was only yesterday that Stephen had thrown her into confusion by declaring his love for her, but already it seemed so long ago, and so unimportant, in comparison with the trauma of Philip's disappearance.

"Tell Stephen I understand," she told Clarissa. "There's no need for him to apologize."

In late morning Jerrold entered the drawing room, and Zoë rushed to meet him. "I have the gold," he said in response to her questioning look. "The militia are out in force. If the search parties don't find Philip, all we can do is wait to hear from the kidnappers about the ransom demand."

"Wait?" Zoë repeated in a trembling voice. "I don't know how much longer I can wait . . ."

Jerrold folded her in his arms, holding her close, not speaking. Instantly Zoë felt a wave of reassurance pouring over her, making her fears bearable.

"My lord?"

Jerrold released Zoë, turning to the footman who had addressed him. "Yes, Sutton, what is it?"

The footman gulped, looking hideously embarrassed at the sight of his master and mistress locked in a public embrace. No doubt most of the people in the drawing room, also, disapproved of the embrace as a breach of good taste, Zoë thought, but she didn't care. At this terrible time she needed the comfort that only Jerrold's physical closeness could give her.

The footman said, "My lord, the doctor says as how ye should come right away. That Jed Hawkins, he's come ter his senses."

Jerrold became suddenly alert. "Hawkins is the groom who was with Philip when he was kidnapped," he told Zoë. "The man was so seriously injured that the doctor thought he would die, that he would never even recover consciousness." His hands clenched. "If only Hawkins is able to talk, if only he can remember anything that might help us to find Philip . . ."

Zoë felt a surge of hope. "Let's go to him, Jerrold."

The injured groom lay in bed in a tiny cubicle in the servants' quarters. Dr. Gates turned away from the bed as Jerrold and Zoë entered. "I'm flabbergasted, I can tell you. Against all the odds, I think Hawkins is going to survive," the doctor said in a low voice. "He's been in and out of consciousness since early yesterday evening, but he was speaking so wildly that I considered there was little point in calling you, my lord. Now, however, he seems to be somewhat more coherent. You can talk to him, but I must tell you he's still very weak. Sometimes, too, patients with head wounds who have been unconscious for more than a few hours experience a form of retrograde amnesia. I don't know how much Hawkins will be able to tell you. In any case, to preserve what little strength he has, try not to talk to him for too long."

As she stood with Jerrold beside the bed, Zoë's heart sank. The injured man looked so pale and fragile. His eyes beneath the heavy bandaging seemed to recede into his face, and they had a vacant expression.

"Hawkins," said Jerrold softly. The man responded, stirring slightly. He blinked his eyes. "I'm happy to hear that you're feeling better," Jerrold continued. "Can you tell me what happened when you and my son were attacked? Can you describe the attackers?"

The groom's eyes slowly cleared. In a thread of a voice he faltered, "I dunno, yer lordship. It happened so fast . . ." His voice grew a little stronger. "It were two men, I think, who came at us, out o' the blue. Didn't see one o' 'em clearly, the one who had hold o' Master Philip. T'other 'un, he knocked me down an' knelt on my chest and raised his hand ter hit me again, an' I seen *him* clear enough. I'll never fergit what he looked like, never. Dressed like a gent, he was, wi' a polka dot kerchief around his neck. An' he had funny eyes. White, they were."

Jerrold inhaled sharply. "Hawkins, did he say anything you can remember?"

"Not him, yer lordship, but t'other one, he called out

somefing like, "Hurry up, Percy, we've got ter git out o' here."

"Percy? Are you sure that's the name the fellow used?" Jerrold's voice was urgent.

"Yes, yer lordship, as near's I can remember, anyways."

Jerrold had turned pale. He placed his hand lightly on the groom's shoulder, saying, "Thank you, Hawkins. You've been a great help. We'll see that you continue to get the best of care. Goodbye. I'll be back to visit you soon."

Zoë followed Jerrold into the corridor. Her eyes fixed on his haggard face, she said tensely, "What is it? Did Hawkins give you a clue that might hep us find the poachers?"

"Oh, my God, Zoë," Jerrold burst out. "Philip wasn't kidnapped by escaped poachers. He was taken by Percival Davenham and some thug he hired to assist him. Davenham, the man who killed my brother. Davenham, who has walleyes, the white eyes that Hawkins described."

Zoë gasped in horror. "But Jerrold, why . . ."

"For money, that's why. Davenham's been a fugitive on the Continent for the past year for the murder of my brother in that duel. He's destitute, according to Oliver." Jerrold's mouth straightened in an ugly line. "And I'll stake my life that Oliver put him up to it, for a share of the ransom money." Jerrold drew a long, hard breath. "No wonder we haven't found a trace of Philip. We haven't been looking in the right place. I think I know where our son is, Zoë. Remember the cave where my brother Trevor and I played when we were boys? Oliver played there, too, when he came to stay at

Malvern Hall. Oliver told Davenham where to hide Philip until the ransom was paid."

The stable yard was a purposeful swarm of activity. Hostlers were saddling fresh horses for the riders who had returned from the early morning search for Philip. The estate gamekeepers were mounting, too, each with a musket poised across the pommel of his saddle.

Edmund came up to Zoë as she stood holding the reins of a placid mare. "Jerrold asked me to talk to you, Zoë. He says you won't listen to him. He begs you not to accompany us. It may be dangerous. You could be hurt."

Zoë shook her head. "I'm going, Edmund. I *must* go. Philip may need me."

Edmund opened his mouth to remonstrate, but before he could speak, Rupert Layton stormed over to Zoë. "Will you please tell me what is going on?" he said angrily. "All Jerry will say to me, to anyone, is that he believes he knows where little Philip is being held, and that he needs help to rescue the child. And then, in the same breath, he refuses to allow me to accompany him."

Zoë bit her lip. Jerrold had decided, and she had agreed, not to reveal that he suspected Oliver Layton had a part in Philip's kidnapping. If Jerrold's suspicions proved to be wrong, he would have blasted Oliver's reputation unnecessarily, not to speak of devastating his parents. On the other hand, if Davenham were to be unmasked as the villain on this expedition today, Oliver's connection with the plot would inevitably come out. Jerrold wanted to spare his uncle the humiliation and grief of coming face to face with such a discovery.

She said quietly, "I think you should do as Jerrold says, Uncle Rupert."

"But this is monstrous," Rupert exclaimed. "I'm to be excluded from helping to rescue my own great-nephew?"

Jerrold strode up to them. His face was set in cold, grim lines. "I can't physically prevent you from going with us, Uncle Rupert. I can only warn you that it's in your own best interests not to go."

Rupert's expression was equally cold. "What do you take me for, Jerry? I ride with you."

Jerrold shrugged. "As you wish." He drew Zoë aside. "Has Edmund talked some sense into you?"

"I'm sorry, Jerrold. I can't stay behind."

Throwing up his hands, he said, "Stay close to me, then. And if I tell you to leave, you go. Understood?"

"Yes."

With Jerrold and Zoë in the lead, the long cavalcade filed out of the stableyard. Jerrold rode in silence, lost in his brooding thoughts, which Zoë hesitated to break into. She was conscious of possible danger, but it weighed lightly on her. She still found it almost impossible to believe that Oliver Layton had played any part in Philip's kidnapping. She was virtually sure in her own mind that a search of the cave where the three cousins had played as children would reveal no trace of Philip.

Through the park they went, across stubble-filled fields and into the woodlands of the hunting preserve, toward a range of hills rising gently to the east. At length Jerrold reined in his mount at the edge of a clearing below the steep flank of a hill and raised his hand to halt the riders behind him. He dismounted and reached up to help Zoë from her sidesaddle. Taking a pistol from the pocket of his riding habit, he said curtly, "Go to the rear, Zoë."

The iron in his voice permitted no dissent. She turned the mare around and led the animal slowly away. The other riders had dismounted, tethering their horses to convenient bushes and trees. A cold chill crept over Zoë as she observed the pistols in the hands of the gentlemen and the muskets held firmly by the gamekeepers.

From her position at the extreme edge of the clearing, she watched the men gather around Jerrold, who spoke to them briefly in a low voice that was inaudible to her. Then he struck out alone across the clearing, halting at the foot of the incline. Zoë remembered Philip's description of his visit to the cave: "We had to climb way up a steep hill to reach the cave." Hard as she looked, however, she couldn't make out an entrance to a cave in the tangle of brush and vines that clothed the hillside.

"Davenham," Jerrold called, cupping his hands around his mouth to make his voice carry. "We know you're in there. We know you have Philip. Come out. We have this cave surrounded by more than forty armed men."

Jerrold's voice echoed in the clearing, but the seconds ticked by and there was no reply. Jerrold was wrong, thought Zoë, hardly knowing whether to be glad or sorry. Then she heard a dull, muffled sound, and another. The sounds seemed to come from the direction of the hillside. A clutter of vines parted, making an opening some fifteen feet up the hill. A familiar figure appeared, clutching a hand to his bloody shoulder.

"Oliver!" It was Rupert Layton's voice, compounded of agony and disbelief. He started across the clearing, and Zoë, reacting instinctively, stumbled after him. She was in a daze, hardly able to grasp the terrible truth that

Oliver had not only masterminded Philip's abduction but had actually taken part in the kidnapping.

As Rupert and Zoë came up to Jerrold, he shouted, "Come down here, Oliver, or I shoot."

Slowly Oliver descended the slope, still clutching at his shoulder, losing his footing and stumbling several times before he reached level ground.

His face a mask of barely controlled rage mixed with an awful anxiety, Jerrold exclaimed, "Philip? Davenham? Where are they?"

Oliver said dully, "Davenham's dead. He didn't want to surrender. He wanted to shoot it out. When I refused, he shot me. I killed him."

"What about Philip? Did you shoot him too, so that he couldn't identify you as his kidnapper? If you've harmed my son, Oliver, I'll tear you apart limb from limb with my bare hands."

Obviously aware that nothing he could say or do could lighten the punishment that was coming to him, Oliver exploded in bitter bravado. "I wish to God I had killed him. Certainly I meant to kill him. And of course I couldn't have let him live to identify me."

A smile of pure evil distorted Oliver's lips. "I tried once before to kill him, you know. Remember that time I came to Malvern Hall to beg you for money to save me from rotting in debtors' prison? You promised me the money, right enough, for Papa's sake, but you treated me like vermin beneath your feet. So Percy and I went prowling in your woods, biding our time, until we spotted you and that by-blow of yours out for a ride. Percy was the 'poacher' who shot your son, not an escaped prisoner from the Leominster jail. A pity the little bastard survived. You'd have had no heir, then, Jerry. I knew from a remark that Papa once dropped that you'd never have another child. My father and I would have inherited Malvern Hall."

Oliver's voice deepened into self-pitying resentment. "I thought the thing was done when we snatched the boy away from his groom, but once we had him in the cave, he got away before Davenham and I could put him out of his misery. He managed to cut the ropes we'd tied him with—he must have had a knife on him somewhere—and ran off into one of those infernal tunnels that branch out from the cave. Percy and I had been searching for him for hours when we heard your voice down in the clearing. Perhaps he slipped and fell on the rocks in the darkness and broke his neck and we just didn't find him. It would serve him right."

While his son was talking, Rupert had seemed to shrink within himself. He looked like a much smaller man. "Oliver," he exclaimed now in a broken voice, "you don't mean that. You can't mean anything you've said. There must be some mistake . . ."

Oliver sneered at his father. "Oh, I meant every word, Papa. Did you think I'd let Jerrold foist his by-blow on the family, cutting you and me out of our share of Malvern Hall?"

Uttering an inarticulate growl deep in his throat, Jerrold lunged at Oliver. Frantically Zoë clung to Jerrold's arm, holding him back, until Edmund came to her aid, grasping Jerrold's other arm. Two burly game-keepers ran up to seize Oliver.

In a moment the wild light died out of Jerrold's eyes. "Philip," he muttered. "We've got to find Philip." He started up the hill, with Zoë on his heels. In the cave he walked past Percival Davenham's still body without a glance, stooping only to pick up a lighted lantern that had evidently been overturned during Oliver's struggle with Davenham.

Holding the lantern high, Jerrold plunged into a tunnel at the rear of the cave, calling, "Philip—Philip. Where are you?" Zoë and Edmund and several gentlemen crowded after him. When Jerrold arrived at a point where the tunnel divided into several branches, he unhesitatingly took the left-hand branch, still calling Philip's name. Soon they reached the blank stone face at the end of the tunnel. Jerrold raised his lantern to illuminate a narrow fissure high on the tunnel wall. "Philip? Are you there? It's Papa."

Instantly there was a scrambling sound deep inside the fissure. A small face, dirty, exhausted-looking, terrified, appeared in the opening. "Papa? Is it really you?"

Handing the lantern to Edmund, Jerrold reached up to extricate his son from the fissure. Seconds later, safe in his father's arms, Philip said pridefully, "I remembered the hiding place, Papa. You said Cousin Oliver could never find you and Uncle Trevor here. And he didn't find me either."

Zoë and Jerrold rose, cramped and stiff, from their chairs beside Philip's bed. They had sat with their son from midafternoon, after they had brought him home to Malvern Hall from the cave, until late evening. He had lain wide-eyed and wakeful for hours, too deep in delayed nervous shock to relax into a healing sleep, refusing to allow his parents out of his sight. Finally Dr. Gates had insisted on administering a heavy dose of laudanum. "The child hasn't slept for over twenty-four hours. He must rest, or he'll be ill."

Now Philip lay in a deep slumber, the marks of strain

and fear smoothed from his face. "He'll sleep for many hours" the doctor assured Zoë and Jerrold. "We can safely leave him to the care of his nursemaid. And you, Lady Woodforde, must get some rest yourself. You look exhausted."

"No, I'm fine . . ."

Zoë opened her eyes to find herself lying in her own bed, with Jerrold seated beside her, chafing her hands, and Dr. Gates hovering in the background. "What happened?" she asked, bewildered.

"You fainted dead away," Jerrold said.

"Allow me," said the doctor. He put his hand briefly on Zoë's forehead and felt her pulse. He stepped back, saying, "You don't need me any longer, my lady. I misdoubt there's anything seriously wrong with you. It's as I said. You've had a very trying day, and you simply need rest."

After the doctor had taken his leave, Jerrold sat down again on the edge of the bed, eyeing Zoë anxiously. "How do you feel? It's all very well for Dr. Gates to say there's nothing wrong with you, but you did faint, after all."

Zoë smiled up at him. "I'm not ill, but there may be a good reason why I fainted. I think I'm increasing."

"Good God," said Jerrold blankly.

"Yes, isn't He? You're not sterile after all, my love. Philip will soon have a little brother or a sister. I wonder which it will be?"